FROM
DUST to
STARDUST

ALSO BY
KATHLEEN ROONEY

FICTION

Cher Ami and Major Whittlesey
The Listening Room
Lillian Boxfish Takes a Walk
O, Democracy!

POETRY

Where Are the Snows
Robinson Alone
Oneiromance (an epithalamion)
That Tiny Insane Voluptuousness

NONFICTION

René Magritte: Selected Writings
For You, for You I Am Trilling These Songs
Live Nude Girl: My Life as an Object
Reading with Oprah: The Book Club That Changed America

FROM DUST to STARDUST

A NOVEL

KATHLEEN ROONEY

LAKE UNION
PUBLISHING

Published by Lake Union Publishing, Seattle

www.apub.com

Amazon, the Amazon logo, and Lake Union Publishing are trademarks of Amazon.com, Inc., or its affiliates.

ISBN-13: 9781662510588 (hardcover)
ISBN-13: 9781662510595 (paperback)
ISBN-13: 9781662510571 (digital)

Front cover design by Olga Grlic
Back cover design by Ray Lundgren
Cover image: © Kerry Norgard / ArcAngel; © Peratek / Shutterstock
Interior image: © Museum of Science and Industry, Chicago / Contributor / Getty

Printed in the United States of America
First edition

For Beth Rooney,
brilliant taker of pictures
and maker of worlds both large and small

Let us go forth, the tellers of tales, and seize whatever prey the heart long for, and have no fear. Everything exists, everything is true, and the earth is only a little dust under our feet.

—W. B. Yeats, *The Celtic Twilight,* 1902

I do not think anyone could estimate what value such films have. It is incalculable because it makes the stay-at-home citizen a man of the world.

—Iris Barry, *Let's Go to the Movies,* 1926

Contents

PROLOGUE: THE DOLLHOUSE

Once upon a time, an unprepossessing child with mismatched eyes—
one brown, one blue—arrived to poor parents at precisely the right
moment.

Eileen Sullivan, the girl I once was, was born on August 19, 1902,
in Port Huron, Michigan. Doreen O'Dare, the girl I became, was born
the summer of 1916 in Chicago, Illinois, not long before she hopped
a California-bound train.

Movies of those early days appealed to my imagination because they
required the spirit of the viewer to supply so many elements—the voices
of the actors foremost among them. The silence of the stars rendered
them intimate yet godlike. A peculiar art form.

And it was cheap! You could hand over a dime and purchase a
dream. For the movies were a dream that you dreamed with a thousand
others, a bewildering hypnosis that told you all to do the same thing:
be astonished.

Moving pictures drew me in the way the moon pulls your eyes on
gossamer chains. Pleasure and sadness, pleasure in sadness.

"Bitten by the movie bug," my mother had lightly put it, trying to
hide her alarm.

I went west at fourteen in an old-fashioned hat and long Mary
Pickford curls. I knew I had to get out there; it was all happening, and
I had to be a part of it, not a minute to waste. I was righter than I knew,
it turned out, because the whole whangdoodle would be over by 1930.

But that was all before I built the Fairy Castle.

My castle is the reason why today—December 2, 1968—I'm on my way to the Museum of Science and Industry on Chicago's South Side. The museum has had custody of my creation since I donated it nearly twenty years ago, and now they've asked me to record a message for the visitors who come to see it.

My first dollhouse was a scrounged alley find made of cigar boxes, dragged home by my six-year-old self and crummily furnished. I no longer have it. We moved so many times, often under such hasty circumstances, that there was no chance of it surviving. During the Depression, reporters fishing for some sentimental folderol about my early days of financial precariousness would ask me if I missed it. Not on your life, I told them. The half-a-million-dollar castle was better than the boxes. There's no romance in living with want.

Granny Shaughnessy always used to differentiate our striving from her own childhood poverty back in Ireland by saying we were not so much *desperately* as *inconveniently* poor.

Like any art, the castle is a fossil of a feeling I'd had. The structure has remained the same even as everything else has changed. Everyone has grown older than I ever expected.

I am going to tell very little of this to Gladys and her recorder.

Chapter 1

THE MAGIC GARDEN

Chicago in winter: wands of ice and a silver river. I could have had my driver take me, but instead I walk south from my apartment on North State Parkway to the bus, which I ride like any other retiree to the Museum of Science and Industry. Except I'm not retired, per se, and the exhibit I'm visiting is one that I made.

The Beaux-Arts structure of the MSI rises like a temple from the flats alongside Lake Michigan. Passing through the Ionic columns beneath laurel wreaths and caryatids makes me think of a movie set. Something grandiose by Griffith or DeMille.

In the basement, where they've stashed my Fairy Castle—like buried treasure? or like the restrooms?—I hesitate before a sign hung at the entry:

CLOSED FOR MAINTENANCE
PLEASE FORGIVE THE INCONVENIENCE

I've only spoken to Gladys by telephone. Her voice through the receiver was one that should belong to the singer of a torch song. That's why I'm surprised when a woman in her early thirties in thick tweed trousers, bottle-bottom glasses, and a mouse-brown pixie cut appears at my elbow looking serious as a nun.

"Ms. O'Dare," she says. "If you're ready, we'll step inside."

"Please," I say, "call me Doreen. Your voice is gorgeous. They should have you record this thing."

"I'm more comfortable behind the scenes," she replies, tugging her burnt-sienna sweater around narrow shoulders as if to emphasize her desire to hide. Gladys has not been chosen for this job because of any special affinity; this is obviously another day at the office for her. Maybe that's for the best. Her indifference may offset the emotions that have beset me.

A folding table and two chairs await. Gladys explains that I'll be delivering my commentary to the microphone but that she'll be working the tape recorder.

There, behind Plexiglas, stands my most enduring creation. The museum keeps the room dim, the better to show off the enigmatic interior lighting, and the battlements and turrets appear in just the right amount of shadow. I have every centimeter memorized, but I haven't been to visit it in quite a little bit.

We built the castle in Los Angeles, on a scale of one inch to one foot. Nine feet square, and seven feet high at the tallest tower, it's made of aluminum to be light but still tips the scales at two thousand pounds.

On top of that, the Dollhouse piles hefty recollections.

"Do you need some general facts?" I ask, keeping my voice steady. "Like 'Designed to pack and ship, the castle consists of two hundred interconnecting pieces, each with its own wiring and plumbing.' That kind of thing?"

"We'll get to that later. For now, we want the more personal gloss on each room and its contents," says Gladys, fidgeting with the knobs. "Where do you want to start? The courtyard, since we're facing it?"

"Well, it's not a courtyard, it's the Magic Garden," I say, regretting what must sound like pedantry. "But yes, let's begin there."

Gladys clicks record, and I proceed.

"Solid gold, the cornerstone rests under the porch. Inscribed with the year 1935, it was installed by Sara Delano Roosevelt, mother of Franklin, who was president at the time, during the gala opening in New York City. The arches depict *Aesop's Fables*, including my favorite, 'The Fox and the Grapes.' The moral of that one is 'there are many who pretend to despise and belittle that which is beyond their reach.' I reminded myself of that one whenever I got a bad review. Oh, Gladys, some of this might not be pertinent. Should we erase that?"

"No, Ms. O'Dare—"

"Doreen."

"All right," she says, pressing stop. "Doreen. You'll have final approval over the recording, including erasures and additions. You were doing fine."

I'm not sure I was. Strange as it may seem, talking about myself is not my forte.

Abruptly, intrusively, I hear the words of my old friend Adela, on the line last week from Los Angeles: *You love telling stories. Why not tell your own?* That's not quite true. Adela loves telling stories; I love playing roles. I've been putting off my response.

"Don't worry," I tell Gladys, "I'll hit a groove," reassuring her as I once did directors. Gladys stares expectantly with that look people get—lips pressed into a half smile, eyes strained and waiting—when dealing with a confused old person or a distracted child.

I have arrived on set unprepared. While I knew my reunion with the Fairy Castle would bring back flashes of early years that I've grown more accustomed to viewing through nostalgic gauze, I'd also figured that by working through the Dollhouse methodically—room by room, treasure by treasure—I could keep my feelings in check. That, I now see, was dumb. The closer I look at the Magic Garden, the more signs I find of the girl I was then. Stones and stucco of painted aluminum. Climbing vines laden with ripe fruit. The Weeping Willow Tree, dripping with real tears, where lovelorn maidens hung their broken hearts. Just as I hung mine.

I clear my throat and nod to Gladys, and she starts the recorder again. "The cradle of Rockabye Baby hangs in the willow's treetop," I say, "but the fairies see to it that the bough never breaks. Made of gold, it's set with pearls my Irish grandmother gave to me."

~

Everyone knows that when an old woman appears in a fairy tale, you should treat her with kindness and do as she says.

Though she didn't appear to me, exactly—rather, she had always been there, a watchful guardian of my childhood—this is how I thought of Granny Shaughnessy. She was old from the moment I met her. Her green eyes beckoned from between her wrinkles, like towns on a map that the wrinkle-roads led to.

She'd grown up crushingly poor in County Galway, in the flat, drizzly basin of the River Shannon. At fourteen she left for Dublin to go into service, then saved up enough money to immigrate to New York, where she met and married my grandfather; they settled in Michigan. She gave birth to seven daughters, my mother among them, in Port Huron, a town of shipbuilding, dry docks, and the railroads for which my grandfather, dead before I knew him, labored.

My mother, Agnes, worked as a schoolteacher before my father, Charles Sullivan, washed into town, sweeping her up like driftwood from the shore of Lake Huron. An engineer by training, he spent my childhood working as a businessman of some indeterminate sort, a collector for banks, and the manager of a plumbing company, along with more odd jobs than I can recollect. Short of temper, he had so many so-called fallings-out with bosses that it came to feel as if we were always falling. Perhaps that's why I became such a committer, picking one endeavor and sticking like a burr, for better or worse.

None of my mother's six sisters had children, something I paid little mind but that seemed significant later, when I wanted kids desperately and discovered that I couldn't bear them myself.

My parents were also desperate for kids, very specifically for boys, and a boy they had: Cal, born in 1895, by their accounts as blessed and golden a son as anyone could have dreamed of. To lend a hand with his care, Granny Shaughnessy came to live with them, and she never left, even after Cal fell to typhoid, dead at the age of five.

By then my parents were aging. I was their last-ditch attempt, and when I arrived, I was no proper replacement: a letdown before I could even speak, aggravating by existing in the form of a girl. Under those circumstances my childhood might have been sad indeed but for Granny and her unwavering conviction that being a girl was an excellent thing.

If anyone had a right to a gloomy temperament it was Granny, yet her eye was as bright as a rose in spring, her step as crisp as an apple in autumn. Most and best of all, her memory for stories—fairy and folk tales in particular—was limitless. In her tiny home village at the edge of a dreaming bogland, she learned every story anybody knew, and in Dublin she told and retold these stories, trading them with her fellow maids as they washed other people's dishes, scrubbed other people's floors, and cared for other people's children.

My mother, aspirational, disliked the stories for their often bizarre contents, offensive to middle-class taste. "What can you expect from a daughter of the old sod," Granny would reply, "save that she'd be earthy?"

But so too was she curious, and alert to beauty. She was always whistling odd airs from her childhood, tunes that seemed somehow older than any human tongue, shaped by their own odd logic. Whenever I tried to mimic her, my mother would tell me that any girl whistling made the Virgin Mary cry.

Like my mother, like my father, and by extension like me, Granny Shaughnessy was a devout Catholic, never plagued by any apparent doubt in our lord and savior Jesus Christ. But even her belief was peculiar, indifferent to airy abstractions, rooted less in the church than in the stones beneath it. The Son of God, she swore, was manly and perfect in all his proportions, for holiness and harmony are known to go together;

thus, he alone of all mortal men stood exactly six feet tall, all others being at least a hair more or less.

She was equally devoted to her folk-faith in fairies and seemed to recognize no distinction between the two. Each spring she scattered mayflowers—or whatever similar plant was in bloom wherever we happened to be living—on our windowsills and thresholds to gain the passing favor of the secretive beings she called the Good People. She would lay new milk on our back doorstep for them, much to the exasperation of my mother, who condemned the waste. It always disappeared. "The neighborhood toms," my mother scoffed. But she had no proof, so how could she say?

Granny believed in entreating both God and the Good People for what they could give. *Ask little, receive little* was one of her mottos. The fairies were kind to those for whom they contracted a liking. Handsome in their tiny forms, they were said by some to be a portion of the fallen angels: less guilty than the ones who were driven to Hell, these were suffered to dwell among mortals and might undertake beneficent projects to tip the Final Judgment in their favor, whenever it came.

Granny's devotion to the Good People was braided with her devotion to storytelling, and she'd move seamlessly between anecdotes from her youth and ancient accounts of fairy escapades. Twilight was the time of day about which she felt most passionately, when she'd gather me into her lap. "Away back in the days when I had sky-black hair," she'd start. A more vivid narrator you never heard.

I often asked for "The Twelve Wild Geese"—the tale of a brave princess who rescues her brothers, lost to a curse before she was born—because I liked to imagine saving my own dead brother, though there had been only one of him, not a dozen. My favorite story was "The White Trout," about a lovesick lady who turned into a fish and later converted a villain from his villainous ways, which encouraged my belief, not always correct, that a bad man can change.

Granny's stories were dear, said my mother, because they were impossible. I pretended to agree, but I knew they were true. There were such beings as fairies.

I knew because I'd seen them.

They appeared to me many times, though not regularly or often, and usually in forms I didn't recognize at first: a black squirrel approaching on its hind legs, a bouquet of wood violets falling from an open sky to land at my feet, a dancing man in a beaver hat whom no one but me could seem to see. When I was very young my parents would tolerate my descriptions of these encounters, but they soon took to scolding me for mentioning them, deriding them as silly, and possibly blasphemous. Granny, of course, was far more accepting, so much so that she seemed to regard these experiences as rather ordinary.

Improvisational and unlucky with money, my father often changed his work—his phrase for getting fired—which required relocating. For the first few years of my life, a certainty animated him that our best opportunity lay just around the bend, in one more fresh town. "Only dead fish follow the stream!" my father would say to anyone who remarked on our unsettled existence, including my mother. His tenor voice had a tendency toward cheer. He gave an earful of charm to each prospective employer. And what a singer! But at home, as likely as he was to sing, he as often revealed his misdirected anger—at me for failing to be a boy, at my mother for desiring things we had no money to buy, at the world for not granting him the life he deserved.

He gave me the belt at the slightest misbehavior, real or perceived: a dropped dish, a muddy shoe. Other times it was a single ringing slap across the face. Or the worst one, the Thump. He'd position his hand—tense as a spring, bigger than my head—perpendicular to my temple and snap his index finger out from his thumb, thwacking my skull as if testing a rotten melon. My mother blamed me: I should stop provoking him.

Just as my parents' frustration with me, and mine with them, helped spur my headlong plunge into the realm of the fairies, so too did it fuel my bent for magical thinking. *If I do* X, I'd convince myself, *then Dad won't compare me to Cal. If I can make* Y *happen, then my mother will love me.* My parents got it in their heads that my stubbornness and curiosity were signs of innate vanity.

"You think you're so interesting, but you've another think coming," my father would say.

"You're determined to become a harlot, and you're not even much to look at," my mother, herself a real beauty, would declare.

I knew that every belittling thing my parents said about me was said in error. I was not going to be a strumpet; I could succeed without my mother's beauty. They'd see. Granny would add her own dissent to mine: a harmonious duet protesting my innocence. We can't control what other people think of us, but we can learn to choose whom to believe.

Though Granny loved me all her life with a changeless love, she was never indulgent. When our wanderings kept displacing me from new school to new school, leading me to become diffident and aloof, she insisted that I be brave and introduce myself to the strangers in each schoolyard. "Only conceited children are shy," she would say.

Granny helped us financially, too, as best she could with her widow's railroad pension. Any of my aunts—well married now, flung lavishly from Boston to Milwaukee—would also have happily assisted us. But my parents were proud. Once, when we were living in Atlanta, I stood before Granny in my secondhand dress and pinching shoes and confessed that I was embarrassed to be seen by my peers. "You can't always dress as nicely as you'd like," she said, "but you can always walk with your shoulders back."

She was right—though my preferred means of locomotion were hops, skips, jumps, and not uncommonly a full-tilt run. High-spirited, my mother called me. Not meant as a compliment.

Each summer she sent me away to Chicago to stay with her eldest sister, my Aunt Elizabeth, whom nobody called that, for in high school she had changed her name to Liberty. "So men could say, 'Give me Liberty or give me death!'" she joked.

That, combined with her Gibson Girl looks, had worked. Her first marriage failed, but somehow the stigma didn't stick. "We all make mistakes!" she would say lightly whenever anyone brought up her divorce, which most people did not.

Aunt Lib owned more dresses than anyone I'd ever known. Pin-check ginghams and chocolate-brown taffetas. Tailored blue serge and summery straw hats. Velvets and furs stowed in mothballs for the winter months. An aura of perfume surrounded her—but never too much; she was a lady, an intangible fact that hung above her like a halo in a painting of a saint.

In her younger days, a flock of would-be swains sighed for the chance to be by her side, and this was no less the case when she became a comely divorcée. From these latter droves of beaux, she chose my Uncle Walter, her second and lifelong-from-then-on husband.

Aunt Lib liked to call me "the child of my soul." Uncle Walter called me "the child of my imagination." A hard-bitten newspaperman, he had a glass eye, and he'd never tell anyone how he got it; I'm not sure that even Aunt Lib knew the truth. Legend attributed the orb to the circulation wars of his early days in the Windy City—a time when gangs employed by rival papers waged battles in the streets—or, less romantically, to Walter's passing out drunk and impaling himself on a copy spike. The quip among his underlings was that you could identify the glass eye because it was the warmer one.

Mum as he always remained on that topic, he loved to regale me with tales of his biggest scoops. The one that launched his career came in the final days of 1903, when he was strolling through the snowy Chicago Loop and happened upon a knight and three clowns climbing from a manhole. They were actors fleeing the Iroquois Theatre, which had gone up in flames during a matinee performance of the musical *Mr. Blue Beard*, based on the fairy tale. The inferno killed six hundred people, most of them children and their mothers: the deadliest theater blaze in United States history. Uncle Walter filed his copy as people were still escaping into the sewers via the theater cellar, breaking the story nationwide in the next day's early editions, establishing his reputation for aggressiveness and steady nerve.

I loved Uncle Walter more than I did my own father. I admitted this to no one but the fairies, as I set out small treasures for them on the guest room windowsill. From Granny's stories I knew the Good People to be fond of child swapping, and I begged them to make me Walter and Lib's changeling.

Wings veined with silver luminous as the moonlight, the Fairy Princess appeared to me in the night and explained, *It doesn't work that way. But we're interested in you. So we'll see what we can do.* Her companions formed a circle bright as a chandelier and echoed her words in unison before vanishing. Feeling as if I'd slept a dozen years, I woke the next morning to find the windowsill bare.

I'll never know exactly what role the fairies played, but while Lib and Walter never adopted me, each did take an early hand in steering the remarkable course of my life, by means I can't imagine that either ever intended. In a funny way, the tragedy at the Iroquois Theatre played a part, too. Though Walter always told the story of his first big scoop in a tone that framed it as an adventure, it had in fact shaken him—just a callow lad then, fresh from Des Moines—deeply. For the rest of his life he could no longer sit comfortably in a theater without his eyes being drawn toward likely hiding spots for pyrotechnics, potential obstacles to exit routes. His aversion didn't rub off on Lib, who'd take in a show anytime the chance arose. When entertaining a visiting niece, for instance.

So you see, I was never *pushed* to be an actress. I was *pulled*—from the instant I saw my first play.

One muzzy summer afternoon when I was five, Aunt Lib and I rode the El from their apartment in Uptown to the Loop, where the Maude Adams production of *Peter Pan* was playing at the Illinois Theatre. Aunt Lib was as eager to see the illustrious actress as I was to see the tale of the boy who refused to grow up. I sat on the edge of a red velvet seat as plush as a muffled heartbeat and grabbed Aunt Lib's hand at the curtain going up, the theater tense and waiting.

As much as Wendy and Tiger Lily and all the Lost Boys, what made an impression was my comprehension of the spell cast in captivating an audience. Equally enrapt by watching the performance and the other children's reactions, I realized that people's emotions are delicious to me.

Tears streamed down my face as Tinker Bell lay dying, but I didn't notice until Aunt Lib dabbed my cheeks with a handkerchief. She whispered through the dark, "Are you all right, Eileen?"

Peter came to the footlights and spoke to us directly. "All the children who believe in fairies, please clap your hands. If you truly believe, then you can save Tinker Bell!"

I scrambled to stand on my chair, damp-faced and screaming, clapping like a trained seal. "I believe in fairies!" I piped, my tiny voice amplified by some magic of architecture. "I really do!"

Every eye turned from the stage to me. Maude Adams herself laughed, in her feathered cap and floppy collar, and the audience followed suit.

Many people, I know, find notoriety mortifying. In that instant, I learned that I am not one of those.

"Thank you, little miss," Maude said, becoming Peter again. "All you lot, join her and clap! Help us save Tink!" and by a river of applause, the show flowed on.

Aunt Lib's gentle hands pulled me into her lilac-scented lap, but those fingers may as well have been the steady force of my dream taking permanent hold. An actress? No, I thought even then. I did not intend to become only an actress.

I meant to become a star.

Chapter 2

THE COACH

Gladys stops the tape recorder, then takes off her glasses to rub the lenses with a cloth.

"Would you believe I've been commissioned to write a memoir?" I blurt, because I am a blabbermouth who never learns her lesson. "My friend Adela—Adela Rogers St. Johns, the writer?—got me a contract with a publishing company. She didn't tell me beforehand that she was doing it. She wants me to put in a lot of dishy gossip."

"Why not?" Gladys says. "You can't grow a garden without some dirt."

Acting and gossip are practically twins born hand in hand, Adela always says, so she would agree. She's a good egg, fundamentally, and a dear pal, but even after all this time we still have the same debates: the actress who wants to charm people with fantasies, no matter how silly, versus the journalist who wants to scandalize them with facts, no matter how sordid.

"That's probably plenty about this garden. Shall we head inside?"

"First, can you tell me about that little carriage?" She points at the coach-and-four that stands by the gate, then starts the recorder again.

"The Fisher brothers of Detroit—whose company originally built horse-drawn carriages—made it and donated it to the castle. By that time, they'd become major manufacturers of automobile bodies, though they kept an old-fashioned carriage in their corporate emblem. An exact replica, by the way, of the rig which carried Napoleon and Marie Louise to their wedding at the Tuileries."

I take a closer look at the coach, gleaming in the museum's artful half-light. I think of what it signified to me when I first placed it inside the gate: arrivals, but also departures. And travel: a young girl's journey across a freshly modern country, into another world.

~

After the cataclysm of seeing my first play with Aunt Lib, I began to practice my craft. Granny believed that children needed to study the art of self-amusement, and I amused myself by putting on plays in the car barn of our rented house in Warren, Pennsylvania—yet another town my father bounced us through—audaciously charging my friends a penny apiece.

Hubris of youth! I deemed myself the only capable actor I knew. As soon as I was old enough to read aloud, I borrowed my father's ancient book of Shakespeare, decided which plays to put on based on what character names seemed the most fun to shout histrionically, and fed the rest of my cast all their lines. Uncomprehending but game, they uttered them.

When a neighbor down the street bought an upright piano, I persuaded the deliveryman to deliver the empty crate to our own backyard, where it served as a proscenium stage. We began to attract more notice—not all of it well intentioned, but all of it welcome as far as I was concerned. No matter whether someone stepped through our gate out of curiosity, or pity, or even with the aim of making fun, it was a chance to win them over, or at least to hold their attention a little while, and give them something to remember.

Once, as I was maneuvering two female schoolmates through the haunted midnight rendezvous that opens *Hamlet*, the neighborhood bully hollered at us through the fence: "Hey, dummies! Don't you know girls can't be a thing except housewives?"

I felt confused more than attacked. Of the many reasons he might have for dismissing the performance—the fact that my Danish sentries were armed with brooms instead of halberds, for instance, and wearing potato sacks for armor, and all under four feet tall—I couldn't understand why he focused on their sex as the big implausibility. (I know now, of course.)

But I *did* understand, even then, that the important thing for me to do was maintain the illusion, to envelop his taunt in the imaginary world of the play. Seizing on the first vaguely Shakespearean phrase that came into my head, I called back, "Life means experience—and I intend to have some!"

Sometimes your tongue knows something before your brain and your heart do. I thought of that improvised phrase often in the ensuing years. I couldn't have articulated it then, but my ambition came partly from a desire to prove myself to my parents and partly from a desire not to be like them.

That winter, after the cold closed down the car-barn theater, I happened upon another cataclysm. I saw my first motion picture—the answer to a prayer I didn't know I'd been praying.

Going to plays took preparation, and considerable money; I could only attend with Aunt Lib, when I was visiting Chicago. But a person could waltz off the street and right into a movie in any metropolis or backwater. My first encounter occurred not in a grand palace but in a modest nickelodeon. If you wanted a snack, you had to bring in your own licorice or what have you. Regarded as a rather rowdy entertainment, less than respectable for women and kids, they'd be set up wherever the community could support them—old storefronts, buildings about to be torn down—often with chairs rented from funeral parlors. From outside you could hear the tinkling piano and practically hear the hearts all aflutter within. The entrepreneurs drew attention to them with glaring arc lamps and ballyhoo phonographs and hung the vestibules with signs: No Smoking, and Hats Off, and best of all, Stay As Long As You Like.

I'd sneak out to catch them whenever I could get away with it, and sometimes when I couldn't. The first one I remember was a Hale's Tours film, shown in a theater designed to look like a railway coach: bench seats on either side, footage sponsored by the railroad companies. A man in a conductor's uniform took your ticket. The reel spun, and they clanged a bell, and the car began to move, swaying on its rockers.

Awestruck, I stayed inside that show all day: a tour of the Andes Mountains. When I came out it was night, and when I came home I got the Thump. My father had been looking all over for me.

In 1911 my father rooted us at last in Tampa. It was a prosperous city—the closest port in the continental US to the soon-to-be-open Panama Canal—and there we too finally came to prosper, achieving the respectability that my mother had sought.

It's hard to remember now, even for me, how different Florida was back then, years before the land boom, decades before any rockets lifted off from Cape Canaveral: still a wilderness once you got off the main roads. I loved Tampa, with its palm trees and strange birds and fresh fruit in every season. From our house on Magnolia Avenue at the corner of Platt, if I ran south past the fire station, I could hop into Tampa Bay.

But I never thought of it as home. By then I'd grown so used to rootlessness that it never occurred to me to stay once it was within my power to leave. While Tampa was no longer just a cluster of weather-beaten houses afloat in an ocean of sand, the suffocating heat and humidity made it feel smaller than it was. I used to linger at Tampa Union Station to watch the trains depart on glistening rails or to listen to the click of the electric telegraph and imagine messages coming from afar: Detroit, New York, Los Angeles. To help heat our home during the brief winters, I'd stroll the tracks with pail in hand, collecting lumps of coal that had fallen from the hopper cars, taking each as evidence of the vastness of the outside world, somewhat akin to a meteorite. I didn't want to stay in town. I didn't want to go to school.

The movie that first made me shift my ambitions from the stage to the screen was *Cinderella*, which my father took me to see as a Christmas treat. The fan magazines I obsessively pored over had informed me that its star, Florence La Badie, was known in the trade as "Fearless Flo" for her readiness to do her own stunts. I often daydreamed of befriending her once we were both successful actresses—sheepishly confessing, perhaps, how much she had inspired me—but I never got the chance. She died young, in a car accident, in 1917.

The boys in my neighborhood all wanted to become firemen or prizefighters, policemen or railroad engineers, and the girls all wanted to marry a fireman or a prizefighter, a policeman or an engineer. The Cinderella ethos was not merely manifest in so-called fairy tales; the real-life consensus held that the best a girl could do was to be lovely, thus to attract a well-off man.

I didn't buy it. At Mass each Sunday, I clutched the coin my father gave me for the offertory and dropped it into the proffered basket like a tourist tossing a token into a fountain. *Dearest Blessed Virgin Mary, please permit me to be in pictures!*

I nibbled stories in the fan mags like a mouse stealing crumbs at a banquet. I took notes.

Sometimes I'd court the disapproval of my prim Southern friends, not to mention my parents' wrath, by seeking out more risqué entertainment. Did you ever love someone you never met? That's the essence of fandom, I guess. The first object of my obsession was Theda Bara, the notorious Vamp, invariably cast in temptress roles and wardrobed in bizarre, indecent costumes. I razored her picture out of magazines, unmooring her from columns of print that detailed her Egyptian origins, her penchant for the occult. (In reality she was a nice Jewish girl from Cincinnati.) Peacock feathers and crystal balls, soulful stares and tiger-skin rugs. Inveigling maneuvers and preying upon men. You just knew the air around her smelled of tuberoses and incense. When I snuck out and saw her in the scandalous *A Fool There Was*, I got so excited I swallowed my gum.

But I knew I could never carry vamphood off myself. Bara's whole appeal lay in giving the sense that she possessed esoteric knowledge of every carnal and mystical sort, while I was just a convent-school kid with mosquito bites at my ankles and a saltwater coiffure; I didn't know anything about that stuff. As for other established routes for breaking into pictures—like the beauty contests that were then sweeping the nation, offering screen tests as grand prizes—they seemed closed to me as well. Gangly and freckled, straight-haired and flat-chested, I didn't have to look to the screen to see that I didn't stack up, only to my popular schoolmates—or to my own mother, for that matter—far prettier than I according to the taste of the day: voluptuous and bosomy, naturally curly haired.

So I practiced harder.

Although I'd long since stopped crying when my father hit me—*If you don't cry*, the Fairy Princess told me once, on a warm spring night when the sandy lawns of the neighborhood blazed with fireflies, *then he'll get no satisfaction from it*—I taught myself the crucial on-screen skill of crying at will while riding the streetcar to and from my lessons at the Convent of the Holy Name. I felt no shame, even when strangers approached to ask what was wrong.

I even found potential silver-screen applications for the hobby that my family came to refer to as Eileen's Miscellany.

When I was five, my Uncle Walter gave me a locket containing a tiny book, a minuscule dictionary with entries A to Z. As I grew up, he said, I would find inside all the words I'd need to describe the adventures of whatever life I decided on.

Uncle Walter's gift of the tiny locket dictionary had sparked in me an insatiable affection for miniature objects, which in turn had sparked a fascination with dollhouses, starting with the ones that my father fashioned from cigar boxes, then graduating to hardier constructions. My standards for furnishing them were strict. While I couldn't be choosy about their contents—I didn't then have the means—I did hew to the rule that every object had to have a purpose for being in the house.

These explanations became stories, which in turn became original plays that I'd stage for and about the fairies.

My fairy audience remained invisible during these performances, but I felt sure that they were watching me: a nice rehearsal for a film career, acting for unseen onlookers.

I very rarely saw my mother and Aunt Lib's five other sisters, but Granny Shaughnessy and I both wrote them often. They often traveled abroad with their rich husbands, and it's to them I owe my expertise in fine and tiny antiques of the sort they'd send me: infinitesimal gifts with hard-to-pronounce names, here a piece of Sèvres porcelain, there a bergère—the latter a chair, accompanied by a note explaining that Louis XV had a penchant for sitting in them, though I knew from my schoolgirl French that *bergère* also meant *shepherdess*. They sent a semainier—a tall chest with seven drawers, "big enough to hold the Fairy Princess's clothes for a week," Granny said—along with diminutive enamel snuffboxes and delicate demitasses: in my plays the fairy men partook and sneezed, while the fairy women sipped the darkest of coffees, their fingers reaching for fruits from a silver-plated bowl. Thirsty fairy throats quaffed from dainty crystal goblets; fairy children pecked itty-bitty profiteroles off bone china plates. I had ashtrays should they wish to smoke, minute soap dishes for when they washed their hands. I made little place cards, menus with lists of fairy wines. Granny told me that fairy banquets included fanciful treats: honeycomb, seaweed, the teeth of a snail. A single pansy petal might feed a party of twelve.

A realm of such extravagant plenty was itself a dreamland to me. I vowed I'd live in it one day. I'd bring my parents with me, to show them what my hard-to-define talents could earn. To show that I wasn't just some substitute, some non-son.

In ancient Greece, we learned at the convent school, male actors played every role, even those of female characters. Ditto Shakespeare's England. I was grateful not to have been born in the past, and said so. The nuns maintained that motion pictures were too new to be included in the pantheon of great arts; I believed them to be the domain of the tenth, youngest, most energetic Muse, as yet unnamed.

On this point, as with most others, my mother held firmly with the nuns. "Cheap pleasures for cheap people," she called them whenever I raised the topic, which was always.

She trotted out the phrase in the summer of my fourteenth year, as she was about to place me on the train for my annual visit to Chicago. At my insistence we'd stopped at a kiosk in the station, where I'd spied a new issue of *Motion Picture Classic*. "Something to read on the journey," I said, paying with box office receipts from my backyard plays.

She sighed so hard the flowers on her hat bobbed as if in agreement. "Why don't you read something improving, Eileen?"

"Mother dear," I said, striking an attitude, "it *is* improving. Improving my chances at making it to Hollywood!"

"The Sodom of the twentieth century," she spat, and I knew she was picturing orgies on par with the ancient perverts; I didn't imagine the place to be all cake and honey, but surely it couldn't be as bad as that.

"The Paris of America!" I retorted, pointing to the epithet I preferred, emblazoned on the cover. I hugged her tightly and boarded the train. "We'll talk more about it when I get back!" I said, dashing down the aisle to deny her the last word.

Riding the rails north to Illinois, slipping past scenery I'd never get to explore, it occurred to me that men had always been permitted to gamble: gold rushes and oil booms and westward expansions. Now women and children, too, could go west and take their chances on a new adventure. Why not me? Why stay in Tampa and be like my mother, the barely acknowledged daily performer of one hundred and one little thankless tasks?

Uncle Walter and Aunt Lib were sympathetic to my dream, perhaps because they tended toward drama themselves. Throughout each visit, I watched them fight: screaming rows in which no blows were thrown, only cutting insults and wild complaints. They were passionate people. As a rule, Uncle Walter avoided cursing around me, making himself say "go to blazes" and the like, but all bets were off during these verbal drag-outs.

I also watched them make up, returning every time to what seemed like a greater state of affection. After one especially boisterous brou-haha, when each had been giving the other their coldest shoulder, Uncle Walter came home with a hat that must have cost a minor fortune, with a life-size fake white bird on top. "The dove of peace," he said, "for my dearest dove," and placed it on Aunt Lib's forgiving head.

That summer, I spent a few afternoons each week loitering around Essanay Studios, which was cranking out the Broncho Billy westerns and Charlie Chaplin's comedies. Walter and Lib's fashionable place in Uptown was a ten-minute walk from Essanay's redbrick edifice on Argyle Street. Filmmaking was a loose business in those days, and any-one could stroll in and watch the proceedings—especially since it didn't matter whether you made noise or not.

Essanay had made *The Tramp* right there. Now I hovered among the other lookie-loos, hoping to catch a glimpse of my idol beneath his bowler. I fantasized about a director turning his gaze from the action to my figure amid the throng, then hollering, *That face! That face is what this scene is missing!* Suffice to say, my dream went unrealized.

Until, until. One night in early September, two days before I had to head south again for the start of school, Aunt Lib teased me over dinner. "Your hours of pining after the pictures," she said, "have put me in a real pickle, you know. Whenever Agnes writes to ask how her only daughter has been spending her summer, I have to fib. We'd better get our stories straight before we put you on the train."

I zigzagged past her practical concerns to my preferred topic. "Aunt Lib, if I could only catch a break, I *know* I'd get in."

"Hollywood's harder to crack than a Brazil nut, cuteness," Uncle Walter said. I felt stunned—normally so encouraging, now he sounded like my naysaying mother—but he was still coming to his point. "Are you ready to stop mooning and do something about it?"

I responded with the same fervor that had made Maude Adams laugh nine years earlier.

"All right, then," he said, his good eye staring into mine, "today's the day. I got you a six-month contract with D. W. Griffith."

Their cherry-paneled dining room looked the same as ever. The open windows still let in the cool lake breeze, but I struggled to breathe. "That's not funny," I said.

"You're godda—gosh-darn right it's not," he said. "It's deadly serious. I helped Griffith get one of his pictures past the Chicago censors last year. He owes me a favor, and I'm cashing it in in the form of little old you. You should have heard the old boy groan when I called him up. *Lord, not another niece!* he said. But I insisted."

I realized I was clutching the walnut frame of my chair as if in fear that I'd fall off. "But he's never seen me act! Did you explain how hard I've been practicing?"

"Griffith doesn't care a whit for your talent, Eileen. This is purely a payoff." He shifted his concentration to his pork chop, a trick that I'd seen him use before to keep his voice steady when he was being uncharacteristically sincere. "But Lib and I care," he said. "We know you've got the stuff. You just need a chance to squeak through the door."

The blood whooshed in my ears, and I shrieked in a manner that might well have resulted in the arrival of the police. Then I pulled myself together and buried Walter in barely coherent thanks. "When do I leave for Hollywood?" I eventually gasped.

From his and Lib's stricken looks I knew at once I had been hasty. "Well," Walter said, "there's the rub, as you thespians put it. You might not."

"What? You mean I'm to work here at Essanay? But Griffith doesn't—"

"I mean you might not work at all, depending," Walter said. "Your contract's contingent on passing a screen test. It's about your eyes. He's not sure how they'll look on celluloid."

He meant my heterochromia, which I'd always prized, which Granny Shaughnessy claimed meant the fairies had blessed me: one eye brown, the other blue.

"But I've been in scads of photographs! They always look matched!" This was mostly true, though sometimes you could tell.

"He needs proof that they register the same. Otherwise it's no go."

"Are you deliberately trying to torture me?" I wailed.

Lib put a reassuring hand on my back. "Be patient with Walter, dear. He thinks in inverted pyramids, which is a fine way to write newspaper copy but not always appropriate for conversations among normal people."

"It's probably nothing to fret about," Walter said. "The test is set for tomorrow morning, at Essanay. We've got to get it done before you head back to Dixie. Which, by the way, is a feature of your brief biography that Mr. Griffith, being a pompous Southern gentleman, did cotton to, so to speak. So that's a grain on your side of the scale."

Though my head was spinning, I was glad that Walter had surprised me with this news. Less time to be nervous. "Okay," I said. "I'm going to give it my all."

"That's our little scrapper," said Aunt Lib. "We'll make double sure Griffith sees that you're some pumpkins. Now finish your peas."

I choked them down, no longer at all hungry.

That night, Aunt Lib helped me wash my hair and put it up in rag curlers to achieve the style then in vogue: long ribbony ringlets suggestive of innocence. My straight red hair never held curlicues for long, but we figured we'd better try, given Griffith's fixation on girlish modesty. The bumpy hillocks would be hard to sleep on, but how was I to sleep anyway?

The film that Uncle Walter had helped Griffith get past the Chicago censors was *The Birth of a Nation*. Aunt Lib mentioned this with a forced, clench-toothed offhandedness as she was working on my curls, and I wondered in passing—as fourteen-year-olds are apt to wonder in passing about topics they think have little to do with them—why

Walter hadn't said so, given what a wild success the movie had been. Quite some time later, I learned that it was one of several topics that Walter and Lib had agreed never to raise in one another's presence.

I suppose I might have guessed, since it had prompted shouts among my own household, too. *The Birth of a Nation* was one of very few movies that all four of us—including my cinema-shunning mother—had gone to see together, impelled by the endorsements of many of our neighbors, particularly those of old Southern stock. And it was remarkable, all right. About a million miles removed from gimmicks like the Hale's Tours, *The Birth of a Nation* was the first film I ever saw that told its story the way a novel by Dickens or Trollope might, following the paths of many characters, using their travails to advance sweeping ideas about American life in the half century since the end of the Civil War.

It was also—to borrow a metaphor that my father used as we were exiting the theater, if not quite his same phrasing—a load of horse manure.

Over the years I've met a lot of film historians, and among them I've noticed a tendency to talk about the technical achievements of *The Birth of a Nation* while brushing aside its racism, suggesting that its attitudes were typical of its era. That's not correct. First, the film is not *casually* racist, as were, quite regrettably, a lot of other early pictures, now impossible to recall without a wince. Rather, it's about a crooked Reconstruction government that allows "brutish" freed slaves to terrorize decent white Southerners until order is restored by the film's heroes, the Ku Klux Klan: racism is its entire purpose and point. Second, plenty of people recognized it as repugnant, libelous balderdash even at the time and protested against it—hence the trouble with the censors that Uncle Walter helped fix.

I'm not sure Walter ever saw the movie; he opposed censorship on principle. Aunt Lib was furious, insisting that the simple statement of a stupid opinion was a very different kettle of fish than deliberate mendacity cloaked in spectacle and melodrama, and suggesting that

Griffith's film amounted to a shout of *Fire!* in a crowded theater, a rhetorical metaphor that Walter also took as a below-the-belt reference to the blaze at the Iroquois that still gave him nightmares. They barely spoke for a week.

I wish I could say that I, too, was instantly horrified by Griffith's wicked film, but I can't. I wasn't flattered by it, like so many of my neighbors were. Little affinity existed between me and the South, roving as my life had been; if anything, I considered my true home to be Chicago, or anywhere Granny Shaughnessy happened to be. *The Birth of a Nation* had overwhelmed me as a work of art, thrilling me with the vast imaginative possibilities of what film could do. I didn't connect it to the real world at all, didn't recognize it for what it was: a full-throated endorsement of mob rule, and a suggestion that any perceived offense against a white person was justification for the murder of black people, black people like the kids in my neighborhood who sometimes gave me pennies to see my productions, who had to enter Tampa's movie palaces through separate entrances and sit in the worst balcony seats.

I didn't recognize it, that is, until my father's outburst on the sidewalk. Needless to say, my parents were hardly freethinking radicals—they would have been upset to learn, for instance, that I declined to segregate my backyard odeon—but during my father's knockabout years he had often noted the dignity and accepted the generosity of black fellow laborers. He was also worldly enough to see past Griffith's high-toned humbug and identify what lay beneath. "If you like the way they treat the blacks," he said, ostensibly to us but at a volume clearly meant to reach the other families filing from the theater, "wait till they start in on the Jews and the Catholics." (*Blacks*, too, as I recall, was not the word that he used.)

He wasn't mistaken just as Aunt Lib wasn't mistaken. The Ku Klux Klan was revitalized overnight, terrorizing and corrupting and killing again, now with a new theatricality supposedly drawn from secret traditions but in fact lifted straight from Griffith's film. Like most people who didn't directly suffer from it, I was barely aware of this at the time. Otherwise I might have been forced to concede that movies were a dangerously powerful medium, all the more so because of their unregulated novelty: able to persuade in ways that statesmen's speeches and stirring anthems couldn't, equally able to deflect blame with the assurance that it was all meant as entertainment.

Young people tend to be optimistic, and I tended to be more optimistic than most, so the lesson I chose to take from *The Birth of a Nation* was that the groundbreaking techniques that Griffith had deployed in the service of bigotry could and should and *must* be used in other films to promote fairness and kindness. Surely someone possessed of Griffith's artistry, I reasoned, couldn't be *all* bad and would probably mend his ways once educated out of his ignorant assumptions. Now came the possibility that Mr. Griffith might be the figurative door to Hollywood that would admit my figurative foot, along with the literal rest of me, mismatched irises and all. Courting power leads to shameful compromises.

The next morning Lib and I settled on my second-best dress, a white French lawn. My best was blue, and though the film would only capture me in black and white, somehow we didn't think it wise to risk the frock's color bringing out one eye more than the other.

When she walked me to the big green double doorway at Essanay, she bid me break a leg and left discreetly. Were she to come inside as my chaperone, it would make me seem even younger than I was.

I looked up at the studio's terra-cotta logos, as I'd done on at least a dozen occasions that summer, feeling as though I was encountering them for the first time. The place looked so holy I felt I should genuflect. Then I told myself not to be a sentimental ass and marched in.

A middle-aged man in plaid shirtsleeves and trousers leaning against an exposed brick wall looked up as I entered.

"Eileen Sullivan," I announced, "here for my screen test. To be sent to Mr. D. W. Griffith."

Dropping the name, I felt suddenly that hidden empires were all around us, filaments of connection and power. Uncle Walter had snuck me into the spider's web, and I was determined to climb that strand as high as I could.

"That's right," he said, "the would-be Harp actress."

Harp was a term—not strictly friendly—for Irish people, after the golden harp on the Irish flag. Granny often said of such sentiments that ignorance was more to be pitied than protested, so I merely nodded.

"Come on in, we'll have a nice chin-wag," the man said, not taking off his cap. "Dick the cameraman at your service."

"Pleased to meet you," I lied. "Will I be meeting the director as well?"

"Director?" He brayed like a donkey. "Hell no, this here's a nothing little thing."

"I see," I said, struggling to keep my disappointment hidden. "Well. Shall we get this nothing underway, then?"

He laughed again, somewhat less obnoxiously. "Ah, the irresistible charm of the Irish!"

We stopped before an empty set done up to look like a poor family's kitchen: rickety furniture, washtub, sparse possessions—an awful lot like places where my family had lived before Tampa. He followed my gaze to the faux windows. "Lace-curtain Irish, see? A gal like you should feel right at home."

Everyone has their reasons for who they've come to be. Growing up, I saw how my dad could be terribly bitter about the discrimination that he encountered. Even after he managed to stabilize our finances, he'd bristle over the tiers he remained unable to ascend. "They'll never ask a Catholic with a name like mine to join the country club, no matter how I break my back." I hadn't appreciated his humiliation until this audition. But I was there to act, not to react, and I vowed not to give Dick the satisfaction of riling me.

"Stand there, in the light," he said, ignoring my nonresponse.

The clanging of workmen and the cries of directors from other sets rang throughout that warehouse of a space, something I'd noticed on prior visits but that struck me forcefully now: the only thing quiet and polished about moviemaking was the finished product. The process was alive with raw energy and sound.

"All right, now," he said, sounding bored, "the note says here I'm supposed to ask you to look jealous. Can you handle that?"

"Don't I need to put on makeup or something?" I asked, recalling the tips I'd read in my magazines, fretting about my freckles.

"Listen, Irish, this is pretty much what you might call a mechanical assessment. Those peepers'll peep the same, or they won't."

"Okay. But should I cry, do you think? To show Mr. Griffith that I can?"

"If you want to," he said. "Now, I'm going to be over there behind the camera. You'll hear me start cranking. I'll call 'Action!' and you'll do whatever makes your little heart content."

I went into myself. A screen test! *The* screen test. It felt like showing up to a lab and demanding my own dissection. Cold instruments, colder eyes. A few hundred feet of film to determine my fate.

"Action!" he said. And out I came.

Since the focus was on my eyes, I decided I might as well cry. Dick made me angry, not sad, so I thought of something melancholy: the prospect of failing this screen test, my destiny decided not through effort but by anatomy. Piercing tears. For the jealousy, my deep green envy of all those walking around with identical irises.

Then something changed, and I drifted outside myself. I considered my situation as if I were already seeing it projected on a screen, and I realized how beautiful it is to want something enough to cry over it. An image flashed through my mind of a young trapeze artist in midair, of the months of practice that readied her for her surrender to the forces of momentum and gravity, much as I had now surrendered to the chemistry of silver and celluloid, to the way my weeping image was carried through Dick's lens by the light from the morning sun, the light in which I suddenly saw—or thought I saw—a bright set of small silvery wings, fluttering and hovering.

"Cut!" Dick called.

"That's it?" I asked, incredulous.

"How many times do I have to tell you? This ain't a Mary Pickford feature. At the end of the month, we'll send the reel out West with the others and see what happens."

The end of the month. My tears were too real, but I kept my composure. "Of course. I'll look forward to hearing the news."

I saw myself out. Utterly at loose ends, I rode the train into the Loop and made my way to Uncle Walter's office in the brawny seventeen-story skyscraper of the *Chicago Tribune*.

Closing his pebbled-glass-paneled door behind me, I told him how arbitrary the test had been, how rude Dick was. He listened brusquely, feet on his desk.

"You never hear about people *going* into pictures, do you?" he said. "They're always *breaking* in, like it's a bank vault. It takes grit and nerve. And the right amount of pride: not too little, not too much. If you're disgusted by this camera fellow now, you'll never survive the strain."

"No!" I said, drawing myself up in my chair, ashamed to have given the impression that I wanted coddling. "I'd never give up because of someone like him. It's the waiting that I don't know how I'll survive!"

"Everything you want takes longer than you'd like," he said, gesturing toward the chaos beyond the transom: telephones jangling, the snap of typewriters. "Even in a deadline business like this one."

"The only thing worse than waiting," I said, "is waiting in Tampa. Do I really have to leave tomorrow?"

"You do," he said, placing his white oxfords firmly on the floor. "That reminds me of one more thing to think about. Have you settled on a stage name?"

I had never imagined going on the screen as anyone other than myself. Whenever I vowed that stardust would settle on my shoulders, the shoulders I pictured were Eileen Sullivan's. "Why can't I go as me?"

"Agnes will never allow it, for one," he said. "Too much shame on the family name. For another, it's high time we had a bona fide green-blooded Irish star."

"I can't argue about Mother. But my name already sounds plenty Irish, at least to the Dicks of the world."

"Think bigger, Eileen," he said. "Think for the screen. You've got a name that says you're Irish, but what you need is one that hollers it. The name I propose is: *Doreen O'Dare.*"

The "O" gave me pause, so top-o'-the-mornin'.

"It's unmistakable," he said, as if reading my thoughts. "It's pretty, but approachable. A sweet colleen. Who could resist? And it's short enough to fit on a marquee easily."

I counted in my head. "It *is* three letters shorter."

"Two," Walter said. "Include the apostrophe."

"And one fewer syllable. And it does sound . . . daring."

"Trust me, Eileen. This is the name under which to be a star. It's airy. It soars."

In this area he knew what he was talking about, given his long career of seizing people's attention with artful arrangements of consonants and vowels. The more I thought about it, the more I liked it: it seemed like a comfortable resting spot—akin to a bus stop or a hotel lobby—between one's private life and the characters one played on-screen. Hadn't Theda Bara—an anagram for Arab Death concocted by the studio to titillate—first come into the world as Theodosia Goodman?

"Doreen O'Dare," I said, reaching my right hand to shake my left. "Pleased to meet me."

～

Back in Tampa, I told my family the news. Granny was happy, my dad was neutral, and my mother was adamant that no matter the verdict on my eyes, no daughter of hers would go parading any portion of her body in Hollywood. Agnes—that summer I'd resolved to start referring to her by her given name like Lib and Walter did, inwardly if not to her face—never felt more alive than when she was worrying, except maybe when she was trying to make other people worry.

The humid days grew shorter, the humid nights longer. I went to school. I waited.

Like Granny, I figured I might as well hedge my bets, backing up the fairies' promise with some help from God. At Sacred Heart I began the novena, lighting candles and praying for nine days straight, willing Griffith to say yes.

The ninth day drew upsettingly to a close with still no news. At dinner I pushed my food around my plate. Chicken, greens, pecan pie for dessert, but I could barely eat. What was the use of religion or magic?

The telephone rang. My father answered. It was Uncle Walter. I'd passed my screen test. I was to report to Hollywood the following month.

"Charles, tell him we're most obliged, but we'll have to talk it over," said Agnes. She'd turned to me before he'd even hung up. "You can't truly expect us to let you skip high school for that predatory Gomorrah. If you've passed the screen test now, then you'll pass it again in four more years. Maybe by then you'll have learned some common sense."

I'd had weeks to ready myself for this argument, and I kept calm. "Are those your only reasons for forbidding me from following my one and only dream?" I asked.

"Those are reasons enough."

"I'll go with the child, Agnes," Granny said from the head of the table. Her tone had a firmness I'd never heard from her before: a mother's voice, not a grandmother's. "For God's sake, it's only six months. I'll see that she keeps up with her lessons and keeps her virtue intact. If stardom doesn't work out, we'll come right back."

My mother looked buffaloed. The beat before her response stretched, a yawning void in which I dangled. Ever since I'd come back from Chicago, going to pictures had felt like listening to a party next door, one that would change my life if I could only attend.

My father broke his silence. "We can't afford to uproot the whole family," he said. "So Granny's plan would seem to present an ideal solution. Hell, I think we ought to let her try it, Aggie."

My mother pressed her lips together as tightly as a clamshell. She'd never challenge my father's word, at least not within anyone else's earshot. When she spoke, all she said was, "If that's what you think best, Charles."

On my feet, I didn't know who to hug first but decided on Dad, then Granny, and Agnes last. Into the top of my head, she said, "I expect we can do without you for half a year."

"It might be considerably longer," said Granny. "I knelt and kissed the strand goodbye before I left Ireland, and I'll never see that shore again. Eileen might do well to do the same to Tampa Bay."

She took a sip from her glass of buttermilk, and we fell back to our plates. I attacked every morsel, suddenly ravenous.

Once upon a time, a fourteen-year-old girl got exactly what she wanted . . .

Soon I'd be expected to fill in the rest.

Chapter 3

THE LIBRARY

Gladys's recorder clicks off with a dull snap, like an ember in a dying fire. The museum basement is chilly in December, warm breath of the heat vents notwithstanding.

"And did you miss it?" Gladys asks. "Tampa Bay, I mean?"

"The bay is a warm bathtub, and the Pacific is so mysterious and cold. I love them both. Maybe that's why I did the Library with an undersea motif."

"Instead of the Library, pretty as the undersea theme is, shouldn't the Great Hall come next?"

"Well, the Great Hall *is* the formal entrance. But the fairies prefer to go in through the Library. The hall is for guests, but the residents like to slip in among the books."

"All right," says Gladys. "Let's defer to the fairies."

I pause, imagining myself five inches tall, beginning a mental stroll that I haven't taken in years: along the portico from the garden, through the twisted-iron gates. Little shell chairs and a little snail bench for the Good People to sit and read. An anchor in the fireplace. Seahorses all around. The walls blend frothy waves into the clouds of the sky, and the rainbow hides a pot of gold at both ends.

"That's the very first book, there on the lectern: the dictionary my Uncle Walter gave me. The rest of the collection is on the verdigris copper shelves. Many are antiques, some quite old. Others I commissioned myself, each an inch square. Over the years I've asked a number of distinguished writers to sign tiny books and write messages to the fairies in them, and as you can see many have been good sports. F. Scott Fitzgerald. Willa Cather. Arthur Conan Doyle. To this day, I always keep a few blank books in my purse, just in case I run across a famous writer while I'm out and about."

I've always had such admiration for authors; the idea that I'm meant to join their ranks is mortifying. Adela, I'm sure, will be only too eager to help—but she's part of the tale and couldn't possibly be impartial. So that won't do. If I write it'll have to be honest, and not just aim to please, as is my wont. *It's time the world got to know the real Doreen,* Adela told me over the line from Malibu. *The spicier cake under the sugary frosting.*

Why do I recoil from the notion of telling my story? Partly it's the same old dispute with Adela—people's tawdry fixation on facts strikes me as sad and morbid, and I persist in believing that poems do more than newspapers to mend the world—but it isn't just that. I've also worked hard to create a public image that's unfailingly light and plucky, that offers encouragement and relief. A Hollywood memoir would require tattling and wallowing, two things that Doreen O'Dare simply does not do.

Beyond that, if I'm really being honest, is the plain fact that I don't want my mother to be proven right. To her dying day Agnes insisted that getting yourself put up on a screen so other people could gape at you was sinful: a hop down the block from prostitution. If I did it, then God would make me suffer. And suffer I did. But not, I think, because of God.

～

Once the matter had been decided, it took my engineer father no time to engineer a plan. Within a month I was off to Chicago again, now with Granny by my side, and with nary a backward glance at Tampa. In Chicago, my father reasoned, Lib could help with my wardrobe, I could thank Walter in person, and Granny could visit a daughter and a son-in-law whom she hadn't seen in years.

I suspect that another reason my father had for sending us to Chicago first was the hunch that Uncle Walter would insist on covering the cost of our trip, which he did. At Dearborn Station, beyond the ticket counters and the Fred Harvey restaurant, the sleeping car gleamed in the lamplight—signature Pullman green, with gold-leaf lettering set off smartly by a black roof—as Walter saw us off a few minutes before midnight.

"Enjoy your siestas, sweet peas," he said. "You especially, Doreen. Stock up on that beauty rest."

My new name still sounded strange to me, and maybe a bit silly.

"One more thing," Walter said, standing in the aisle, obstructing the work of the porters. "Blast it, there's so much we should have talked about. Listen, Doreen. Hollywood is plagued by a species of people called press agents. The studios salary them to spin out stories about the players under contract, the better to get editors like me to run those stories. The moral being: never believe one damn word you read about yourself."

I had no idea what he was talking about. "I won't," I said. "I promise."

Late though it was, I couldn't imagine sleeping, but our little stateroom on the rocking train felt so snug and safe that my eyes closed and seemed to open instantly on a blazing morning and the bare autumn fields of Missouri. At breakfast I studied the à la carte menu with perplexed glee: Ham Griddle Cakes, the Melon Mint Cocktail, the Apple Pan Dowdy. I'd hardly ever eaten away from home before—ice cream sodas, sure, and snacks in tearooms, but rarely full meals, not even with Walter and Lib. The dining cars of the Santa Fe line struck me as the epitome of sophistication: china plates and waiters in pure white coats.

I tried to figure out how to eat the entire menu over our three breakfasts aboard the train, but Granny accused me, correctly, of having eyes bigger than my stomach, so I ordered the California Peach and Rice Fritters, because they had California in the name.

By day I stayed as long as I could in the swiveling chairs of the parlor-observation car. I often found myself comparing the experience to a Hale's Tours film, and I wondered whether it was strange or wrong to compare something to a fake version of itself.

By night the train swayed and the landscape wobbled, the sunset into which we headed as ripe as a rose. This was before air-conditioning, so the porter stretched an extra sheet across the open window to keep out dust and cinders while we slept. I'd wait until Granny was snoring softly, then peek out at telegraph wires and corrugated shacks in the blue moonlight.

By the second morning we were in Colorado. The scenery reminded me of westerns I'd watched. It hadn't been so long ago that covered wagons snailed their way along a similar route, and now here we were, shooting through the same terrain faster than they could have imagined: smooth wheels on steel rails beneath a hot, dry sky of electric-blue silk.

By the next day that landscape had begun to seem positively lush by contrast. Arizona was mostly bare sand of striking yellow and orange, dotted with peevish-looking plants. Now and then a mountain emerged, black with pine trees, sometimes draped with snow. Often we'd pass clusters of tarpaper buildings at the edges of barren fields, and I'd wonder who lived there, and why, and how, but I never saw anyone. I thought my family had been poor—we *had* been poor—but I couldn't imagine living like that.

Then it was the fourth morning. The word *California*, with all its grandeur, didn't seem grand enough. Better, I thought, to call it the Land of the Sun-Down Sea, a poet's phrase often borrowed by chambers of commerce; that at least captured the precarious, upside-down, edge-of-the-world feeling of the place, where twilight blazed from behind the crashing Pacific to gild the misty clouds and craggy mountains.

Arriving in Los Angeles felt less like the end of a trip across the country than like the culmination of a journey through the heavens—as if we had entered a magical realm barely tethered to the rest of the continent. The broad dome of La Grande Station looked less like a depot and more like the buildings in library books—Moorish fortresses, Byzantine temples—and declared that the rules and customs that prevailed east of the Continental Divide did not apply.

The terminus of the railroad! Yet automobiles, rattletrap and careening, dominated the city streets more than anywhere I'd been.

Triangle, Griffith's film corporation, had assigned a dun-clad woman named Miss Frink to meet us. We found her bobbing around the platform like a grackle, looking for the morsels she'd been instructed to retrieve. She held a small sign that read DOREEN O'DARE.

"Doreen at your service," I said, thrusting my hand out to shake.

Extending her own, she made the appraising sweep of me—shoes, figure, face, hat—that I'd come to see everyone in Hollywood make. She looked less than impressed.

"Indeed," she said. "Follow me."

We followed her to a Maxwell touring car parked haphazardly at the curb, which she started with a clatter and launched into the maelstrom of pedestrians, streetcars, automobiles, and horses. "That was the river behind us," she said, jerking her head backward. Granny and I craned our necks but couldn't see anything through the station's bulk. "We're now in the North End of the business district. At the horizon, ahead and to our right, you'll see the Santa Monica Mountains. Go eighteen miles due west and you'll be at the Pacific Ocean."

Miss Frink continued this unbroken monologue as she drove. I heard almost none of it. My attention was split between the many imminently fatal obstructions that she was weaving us among and the grand facades of the redbrick buildings, the boasts and lures of their painted advertisements. Much of Miss Frink's narration sounded useful—*yellow streetcars run inside the city, red ones are interurban*—so I hoped that Granny was listening.

Looking back, what strikes me the most about that first drive through LA was what I *didn't* see. No palm trees. No Hollywood sign. Few movie theaters and apartment buildings. It still had the uncertain electric buzz of a frontier town, which it practically was. As Miss Frink propelled us northwest on Sunset Boulevard, the tall buildings were replaced by modest houses, then construction sites, then empty lots dotted with chaparral, stretching up into the hills.

She installed us in a bungalow court on Fountain Avenue, in one of six identical tiny houses with gabled roofs, redwood siding, and pleasant verandas. "A bit farther from downtown than I'd expected," Granny said.

"The studio likes to house its girls in this area so they can walk to work," Miss Frink said, handing her the key.

"Well, it's good exercise, and it's thrifty," said Granny. She was able to get along with almost anybody.

"Triangle's at 4500 Sunset," Miss Frink explained, her tone less that of a hotelier than a barracks chief. "Doreen is to report there at seven thirty Monday morning. Ring me up if there's anything you need, and I'll tell you how to get it. Good day."

It became a better day once she was gone. Granny and I made a quick survey of the house, which was so small and so sparsely furnished that a slower survey wasn't really possible. The austerity of our new home seemed of a piece with the aridity of the climate, so different from Florida's; the windows had no screens, we marveled, nor any need for them given the absence of the vicious mosquitoes that plagued the peninsular coast. The interior was joltingly different from the fussy and suffocating house in Tampa, a Victorian chaos that recapitulated the contents of my mother's mind: the parlor with its stereopticon and shell flowers under bell glass, the knickknacks on the credenza and the what-nots in the cabinet. I decided that I loved the bungalow just as it was. Fortunate, because I'd soon see that I'd have no time for decorating.

Granny announced that we ought to take a walk—for groceries, to find a church, and to get the lay of the neighborhood. We had arrived after the graceful rains that I would learn were routine for November, a time when everything became a disconcerting emerald with a freakish shimmer, and the flowers emerged like an unseasonable mirage. The poinsettia and oleander, calla lilies and heliotrope, privet and trumpet vine all might have seemed a trick of the light but for the fact that you could smell them, pick them, tuck them behind your ear. The profusion of blossoms encouraged me to think of California as a land of fresh starts, a place to break free from your past, as I had apparently broken free of Eileen Sullivan. Therefore I was both charmed and alarmed to learn that the cast-iron bells hanging from shepherd's crooks above some of Hollywood's street signs marked the route of El Camino Real, the old Spanish highway that missionaries and soldiers once traversed through tribal lands.

There was fake history, too. At the junction of Sunset and Hollywood Boulevards, Granny and I encountered the gates of Babylon: the vast, towering, inconceivably expensive set of *Intolerance*, the film that Griffith made after *The Birth of a Nation*. Having been quite justifiably accused of bigotry, he'd responded with a sentimental epic that took in the whole of human civilization in order to decry small-mindedness—specifically the alleged small-mindedness of Griffith's own critics.

A few months earlier, this Babylon had appeared in nearly every theater in America. Now here it was in wood and plaster, a few blocks from our bungalow: walls covered in bas-reliefs of lions and bulls and winged deities, all framed by colonnades topped with columns, themselves topped with elephant gods prancing grandly. To avoid the expense of demolishing it, Griffith was trying to promote the leftover set as a tourist attraction, but it was already collapsing, not built to endure. During our time there, we came to see that it functioned mainly as a perilous playground for neighborhood children.

This man was now my boss.

Griffith was hardly the only thing jangling my nerves. As I walked around with Granny that first day, I could not help but notice that when it came to attractive girls, Hollywood was a great big basket of peaches. We stopped for lunch in a coffee shop and our coffee was served by what I swear was the prettiest coffee server anywhere in the world. Quick and polite, graceful on her feet, her movements were automatic, like those of a factory girl. She only seemed fully present when a man or group of men entered the shop, and then only until she'd determined that no prominent actors or directors or studio executives were among them.

Granny, following my gaze as the girl walked away, put down her fork. "Quite a few comely lasses in this town, aren't there?" she said.

I sighed heavily into my food.

"Eileen," she said, for she still used my real name, "keep in mind that beauty alone is not enough."

"Oh, Granny, I know," I said, in no mood for a platitude.

"No, I'm afraid you don't, so put down that cheese sandwich and listen. Some of the girls we've seen this morning are more gorgeous than any star of the screen, I'll grant you that. You think that gives them a leg up on you. I don't agree. What do people want to see in the movies? Character. Animation. Without it, all the queenly qualities in the world seem barren. And you've got it. You're not the prettiest girl ever to come out of Florida, but you don't need to be."

"You're right," I said, embarrassed for needing a boost three hours after arriving.

"That's better," said Granny, sipping her coffee.

Having settled on the Immaculate Heart of Mary as our church, about a mile from our bungalow through East Hollywood, Granny and I set out our usual offerings for the fairies: a thin slice of bread, a saucer of milk and honey.

At fourteen I was old enough to suspect that these magic customs were childish, but I was not quite willing to give up their comforts, nor old enough yet to understand that they weren't childish at all. "Do you think the fairies can find us here?" I asked. I tried to imbue my question with the tone of playful mockery employed by generations of teenagers, but I couldn't bring it off: I was genuinely concerned.

Granny's answer came slowly, which only added to my worry. "Here in California, you mean?" She stoppered the honey jar, returned the milk to the icebox. "Oh, I think so, child. I can tell you that I wondered the same when I left Ireland. The Good People are tied to the land, tied so closely that it feels as if they could never be anywhere except the spots we've found them. But I think they're all around us, even in a desert like this. We'll just need time to learn their ways."

I couldn't think of a reply, so I glided over in my stocking feet to hug her, near tears from exhaustion.

"You'll recall," she said, "that in Ireland we speak of *thin places*, where the borders between our world and the next are narrow enough to leak a bit. Though I'm not yet sure what to make of it, so far this Los Angeles seems like a very thin place indeed."

In the magazines, the process was straightforward: a girl arrived in Los Angeles a starveling and ended up a star. A ragtag little bobtail bobbed into town, and voilà! Easy! Hollywood flung her upward to take her place in a marvelous galaxy.

For me, such was not the reality. Not on that first morning, at any rate.

Triangle cranked out several films a week, and its studio lot was a city within the city. Workmen in overalls wolf-whistled as I wended my way toward Griffith's office. In my head I heard my mother's voice, reciting one of her favorite sayings: *Better not to move at all than to make a false move.* If I'd listened to her, I'd still be in Tampa. I was here to be an actress, and what better way to practice than by acting as if the whistling men didn't exist?

Inside the complex of offices buzzed more pretty women. In most cases these weren't even actresses but PGs—publicity girls—sending out news of the studio's leading ladies and gentlemen. There were slim and graceful stand-ins, too, who'd pose in certain spots for hours at a time, doubling for the stars. If you had the same shape and size, the same hair and complexion, then you could get hired to be Blanche Sweet or Bessie Love, at a distance and a discount.

The woman who accompanied me to what turned out to be my one and only meeting with D. W. Griffith was the neither sweet nor lovely Miss Frink. "He hasn't much time," she said, ushering me ahead of her, "so curtsy, then listen."

There he sat, behind his great barge of a desk. I had expected him to be pompous, larger than life, and also a bit repugnant in spite of all his power and know-how, and he was. These days, scholars of film make much of the fact that Griffith was a self-taught director, but back then everyone was. Who would have taught them? An instinctive grasp was the best anyone could manage, because the medium was new; they made up its grammar as they went along. Same with film acting: someone like me with no training could make her own way. That's what I kept telling myself, anyhow.

Griffith was tall, tidy, and formal. He nearly always wore a wide-brimmed hat, even indoors, and dressed in tweed three-piece suits like the Southern gentry he imagined himself to be.

Miss Frink came into the office behind me, left the door open, and took a seat off to the side. Griffith raised his head from the papers he'd been riffling through, and I could feel him estimating, swiftly, my worth. He had dollar-sign eyes.

"Welcome to Triangle," he said, with twanging traces of Kentucky. "I suppose you think yourself something for having arrived, but remember: a girl has got to realize that a career on the screen demands everything but promises nothing."

"Yes, sir," I said, reminding myself that he was probably more afraid of me than I of him. Uncle Walter had told me that Griffith was a great admirer of women but would never see a girl without a third person present, in order to protect his reputation. He feared chippies who might fabricate funny business to blackmail him.

"What makes you think you're pretty enough to work for me?" he said.

"I don't," I said, "because I don't think pretty is the point. I think people want to see real human beings on-screen. I believe that I can be a real human being."

Miss Frink chortled. A fly buzzed by the window. A brass cuspidor stood near the door.

At last Griffith nodded. He dipped his fine-nibbed pen in a jar of blue ink and jotted a note at the bottom of a document. "Take this," he said. "It's a revised contract. I'm sending you to go work on a picture with Withey. You're no use to me personally."

I barely mustered a muttered "thank you," grasping the paper as Miss Frink shunted me out into the corridor.

"Don't stand there like your dog died," she said. "This happens all the time. Your contract is to work at Triangle, and that's what you'll do. Here, I'll take you to the bad boy."

My eyes must have grown three sizes. "Pardon me?"

"Don't be a ninny," she said. "I'm not referring to Mr. Withey. *The Bad Boy* is the title of the picture."

Although she was right—I did feel as if Griffith had cast me aside— the feeling didn't last. When Miss Frink delivered me to the set of *The Bad Boy*, I found the atmosphere refreshingly different. For starters, everyone in sight looked younger and more fun than her or Griffith.

"Mr. Withey," said Miss Frink, handing me off to a man not over thirty, with mellow brown eyes and short hair swept straight back, "here's the new arrival, Doreen O'Dare. She's to play Ruth. I trust you'll keep her in line."

"Technically, Frinky's an office manager," said a familiar-looking dark-haired girl who'd been standing beside Withey, yawning like a naughty kitten, "but she acts like a truant officer."

Miss Frink either didn't hear or chose not to, and into the chill of her departure Chester "Chet" Withey poured the warmth of his delight.

"You'll be a perfect Ruth," he said. "Mildred here'll fill you in on the scenario and help you get dressed."

Mildred. Mildred Harris! Pink cheeks, bright melancholy eyes, a prominent nose that could be regal or comical. She'd been acting since she was eleven, in *Intolerance* and dozens of other films, many of which I had seen.

"Come with me," said Mildred, and clasped my hand.

In those days it was often said—in tones of scandalized despair or snobbish amusement, depending on who was doing the saying—that scientists had calculated the mental age of the average American to be about fourteen. I don't know if this was true, or what *mental age* means exactly, but I can confirm that the age of the people the public most wanted to see on-screen hovered around that number. Partly that's because the camera's lens was as unsparing as any evil queen's magic mirror: that mechanical eye favored the youngest specimens, especially the women, who were often treated like withered hags by the age of eighteen.

But partly, too, it's because adolescence is when many people get their biggest helping of a certain kind of freedom. A great many of them, I fear, don't realize they had it until they've lost it. For them the movies can be a chance to get it back, vicariously, for an hour or two.

What I began to realize that morning on the set of *The Bad Boy* was that with a few prominent exceptions, Hollywood was being run by a pack of children, or at least by the childlike: those who had not yet lost the capacity for wonder, who could dream during the daytime, who refused to draw a line between what was real and what was possible.

I suppose it seems Peter Pan-ish, that insistence on never growing up. But my allegiance to Peter was longstanding. Anyway, who would you rather be? Peter, running wild and free, or Wendy, the little mother stuck at home with nary a checkbook of her own?

The dressing room was no more than a puny parlor with a rug and a few Windsor chairs. It was also an utter mess, thanks to the untidy Mildred, who always dropped a trail of shed garments after she finished a day's shooting. Whenever he passed, Withey would shout, "Clean up this ragbag!" but no one ever did.

Mildred sat me down and peered with concern at my naked face. "This is no place for a soap-and-water woman, honey," she said. "Around here they like the paint heavy on the canvas. Especially if you're going to play Ruth."

The Bad Boy, she explained, was a crime drama about a troubled small-town youth, Jimmie, who falls in with a gang of criminals and has his head turned away from his true love, Mary, played by Mildred, by a worldly city gal, Ruth, played by me. If anybody else saw irony in a worldly city gal being played by someone who'd been in Los Angeles for a touch over forty-eight hours, they didn't mention it. This was acting, after all.

I did my best to absorb Mildred's instructions, but it was a struggle, both because I was in disbelief to be sharing a dressing room with someone I'd watched for years and also because of her voice. I was astonished at her nasal tone. It was like hearing a beloved doll from up on the shelf suddenly begin to sing, then noticing that she had a cold.

Movie makeup, Mildred explained, was purely for the camera's benefit: it bore little resemblance to cosmetics applied for an appearance on the stage or the street. It was oddly to my advantage that my parents had never allowed me to wear any and that I had never acted in the theater. I had no habits to break.

I had, however, always been attentive to Aunt Lib's accoutrements of beauty, her jars of rosewater and pots of rouge, so I took eagerly to the task at hand. Mildred opened a large satchel of the sort that I imagined an impressionist might carry to paint outdoors, and she ran through the contents. I snatched a piece of scratch paper and a broken eyebrow pencil and made a list: cold cream, mascara, powder, lip rouge, Vaseline, sticks of greasepaint (Mildred favored Leichner's).

"For blue or gray eyes, a light gray makeup is best," she said. "For brown or black, a light brown." She looked at my mismatched irises, momentarily flummoxed. "I suppose in your case, we can do a kind of blend. Also, Doreen, you're going to have to memorize exactly what you do with your makeup so that you'll match in scenes shot on different days. You can use my kit today, but tomorrow you'd better bring your own."

She let me know about wardrobe, too, because when you were a beginner, the clothes were up to you. "You'll need an afternoon suit, and an outer coat to match. Two summer frocks, a sailor blouse with a dark skirt, a negligee, plus an evening gown and wraps. Hats you can't do without. And don't forget dancing slippers." My list of items to be purchased now stretched over both sides of my scratch paper, and I began to dread Granny's reaction when I told her.

Mildred also warned me never to say anything that wasn't in the scenario while the cameras were running, because there were lip-readers in every darkened theater. The slapstick comedians couldn't swear anymore; the serial heroines could no longer prate about the weather. "Time was when you could say, maybe during the final close-up when you were kissing your hero, 'How's about we get a malted round the corner when this is over?' But too many people wrote in to complain. So either you mustn't say anything, or it's got to be something appropriate to the moment."

She made some final adjustments, declared that I looked swell, and took me out to the set. Now I felt slightly more at ease, since this was an environment that I knew from my many watchful hours at Essanay: the cameras and the lights, the backdrops and the curtains, the sandbags and the ladders.

"I'll introduce you to Bobby," Mildred said, "our leading man."

Bobby turned out to be Robert Harron, one of Griffith's favorites, already famous at nineteen for playing naive and sensitive types. His brown eyes were limpid lakes of feeling.

Bobby in person, I was surprised to find, was a great deal like Bobby on-screen: soft spoken, quiet, gentle, and sympathetic—a devoutly Catholic virgin, I was sure of it. (Takes one to know one.) Back in Tampa I had been so single-minded in pursuing my Hollywood dream, and had failed so completely to connect with my peers, particularly my male peers, that I had avoided romantic encounters of even the puppy-love sort. Now it occurred to me that I'd have to convincingly perform in situations that I'd never experienced, which would be fine in a scene that required me to, say, escape from a rogue elephant but might be awkward in one that involved simply sharing a bag of popcorn with a handsome young man, as today's did.

Fortunately, acting opposite Bobby felt like waltzing with a professional dance instructor. "You're nervous, aren't you?" he said. "That's only natural. But if you have stage fright, hide it, or it'll show up on camera."

The elaborate task of getting the lighting right gave us plenty of time to talk, and I hung on his every word. It was important, Bobby said, to be sure the director liked me. But the really wise actors took extra pains to befriend the cameraman, for he held the power when it came to beauty. The director could help me act, but the cameraman could make me shine.

When the filming was underway, we ate the increasingly stale popcorn, which presented an occasion for our characters to brush hands and gaze into one another's eyes. Withey gave guidance but never took tyrannical control; he told us what to do in broad strokes, then let us spool it out. Unlike other directors I would come to know, he never yelled, because he knew the camera captured every last thought.

But neither did he overpraise. "You call that acting, Doreen?" he said after the first take of the popcorn scene.

"Yes, as a matter of fact, I do," I said. He burst out laughing, and I knew that I had won him. I didn't want to be a mouse at the feast; I wanted it all, and had to be bold.

"That's the spirit," he said. "That's swell, what you're doing with your feet. Keep that up, exactly that. But remember, I said *smile* at Jimmie; I didn't say simper." Stung, I stopped smiling, because he was right: I must not make myself look silly, batting my little eyes to get what I wanted. This Ruth was a tough customer; she wouldn't do that. "Otherwise that's good," Withey continued. "Sparks are flying, kindling is catching. We'll do that again." I'm sure it was calculated, but I was glad that he'd padded his criticism with encouragement on both sides.

"If it helps," said Bobby, his cheek next to mine, his breath minty and light, "remember that the audience will supply a great deal of what you need. At your suggestion, they'll imagine your character's thoughts and essence—your character's character. You can trust them to do some of the work, so you can do less."

The next take went better, though we still ended up doing it half a dozen times. Withey assured me that this was just how filming went: with a thousand variables at play, you had to be repetitive to be able to select the best of the bunch. A lot of it was purely technical. Sometimes he'd yell "Cut!" to us, then, "Boys, your attention just one minute, please!" to the crew, and they'd reposition a piece of furniture, an electrical cord, one of the cameras.

And the lights! Hot is an understatement. Henry Freulich, my favorite cameraman—who later became my personal cameraman, so much did I take Bobby's advice to heart—used to say he could light his cigar at a hundred yards with a spotlight beam.

Just as I began to fear my skin was blistering under the layers of Mildred's makeup, we were done for the day, and everyone scattered with cheery goodbyes. As I walked home to the bungalow, my mind racing, I felt unexpectedly grateful at having been moved around so often as a child: after starting over at so many schools, this had felt a lot like any other first day, in a way.

That evening, when I told Granny Shaughnessy all about it, tiptoeing around and finally arriving at the topic of my list of cosmetics and garments, I expected her to wince at the expense, but she didn't. She led me through an inventory of our haul from the shopping excursions in Chicago with Aunt Lib, most of which we'd packed into trunks straightaway; we found with relief that much of what I'd need I already had. In short order she helped me buy the rest, her only advice being that whatever I wore, I'd be smart to dress conservatively and to act well bred—which wouldn't even be acting, because look who raised me.

On each day of the two weeks that we worked on *The Bad Boy*, I soaked up the camaraderie of the cast and crew, as well as the jargon. *Save 'em*, for instance, was Withey's phrase to notify the electricians to shut off the lights.

Mildred favored joking with the publicity men who came by, and with the other actors to-ing and fro-ing, including—though this was supposed to be a secret—Charlie Chaplin.

While he could attain a small degree of anonymity by removing his Little Tramp makeup, it was ridiculous to think that Chaplin was able to do anything secretly in 1916.

In general I don't endorse the dictum *never meet your heroes*, but I was never more disappointed in an idol than I was in Chaplin. Despite her efforts to hide it, it was obvious that Mildred and he were having an affair. Given that she was practically my own age, and that for me intimate relations had progressed no further than the occasional chaste kiss beneath a sprig of mistletoe, this realization shook me greatly, and made me consider—just for a second—that I might have granted more credence to Agnes's assessment of Hollywood as a vale of corruption. The fact that Bobby seemed as shocked by it as I was helped matters; although he and I never discussed the subject, we'd exchange wide-eyed looks whenever Chaplin collected Mildred from the premises.

I felt certain that the affair would end badly. This made me sad, because Mildred was fun, and kind, and always heartening. When I got my first paycheck from Triangle—hardly Chaplin-sized, but still a king's ransom measured against the take from my Tampa backyard—she told me that I should rush out and buy something extravagant, so certain was she that I was ascending the funicular to stardom. I didn't do that; growing up poor had taught me caution when it came to financial matters, and I handed the check over to Granny, who deposited it.

But when I got my second check, I couldn't resist making an addition to Eileen's Miscellany. On Fountain Avenue between the studio and the bungalow I'd found a curiosity shop that mostly stocked unremarkable junk, with one notable exception. For weeks I'd had my eye on what the owner claimed was an Egyptian alabaster pot: a thimble-size jar that must (he claimed) have held some ancient lady's cosmetic. Even then I was skeptical, but I couldn't deny that it had a certain aura—a heft that testified to seriousness of purpose, a smoothness that indicated many decades of careful use. It was also precisely the right size for a fairy urn. I bought it on my second payday: the first miniature I purchased for myself and didn't get as a gift.

Whoever made that alabaster pot must have thought of all the love-liest cream-colored things under the sun as he did so: clouds clotting the curve of a blue desert sky, woolly sheep bleating in the sandy heat, the sail of a ship about to slip down the Nile. As if I were myself a miniature Alexander the Great perpetually pursuing conquests, I began to set aside part of my earnings for buying miniatures.

It was comforting to have someplace else to put my nervous energy, because the joyous thrill of my arrival in the movie business was about to run out. *The Bad Boy* had a happy ending—Jimmie on the straight and narrow, reunited with Mary—but it felt like a tragedy to me, because the job was over, and our little troupe went our separate ways. I figured we'd work together again—we were all under contract to Triangle—but we never did.

I was half-right about Mildred's affair with Chaplin ending badly: it was their marriage that ended badly. I don't think he'd really had any intention of tying the knot with her; there was scuttlebutt about a preg-nancy scare. The news that Chaplin had wed a sixteen-year-old seemed to shock the public, but I always had the sense that he had a yen for child-women—the better to boss them around. When I met him on the set he scarcely spoke to me, deciding quickly that he wasn't interested. I think he could tell that I'd be unwilling to play Little Red Riding Hood, dawdling along with her cake for Grandma. I had no time to trifle with wolves. Ambitious naïf that I was, it never occurred to me to seek out Chaplin's love; what I wanted was his fame.

Upon its release, Granny insisted that I take her to *The Bad Boy*. I was elated to oblige, but as I sat there next to her, anonymous in the audience,

I found myself cringing whenever my image appeared on-screen: I was obviously looking at either Bobby or Withey like a lost puppy at the start of each take, desperate for guidance on what to do. I tried to force myself to learn from this, then started averting my eyes once I was convinced that I had. I watched Bobby instead: how natural he seemed. Well, not natural, exactly. What I was doing on-screen—blanching self-consciously whenever the film rolled—seemed like natural human behavior. But Bobby, and Mildred too, somehow knew that it wasn't a camera watching them at all. It was people gathered in darkened theaters several weeks in the future; it was Granny and I, and Walter and Lib, and my parents, and thousands of others whom none of us would ever meet.

I would do better next time. First, I had to make a pest of myself at the Triangle office to make sure there *was* a next time. I said yes to everything they sent my way. I pushed and pushed. Even in my most tiny and terrible roles—ingenues, babes in the woods, more Irish maids than I care to admit—I did my best.

I loved the work; that was never an issue. But given the depth of the Hollywood labor pool, even under the contract it was always a scramble to get roles, not to mention to get paid for work I'd already done. I lost count of the impudent letters I sent to studio bigwigs and probably spent as much time demanding what I was owed as I did earning it in the first place. I promised myself that a day would come when no one, not even Griffith, would dare to mistreat me.

In the meantime, my work ethic was audacious.

When I wasn't at the studio, I forced myself to see the pictures I'd been in, taking notes on each performance until it stopped being a torment, until I could see what worked as clearly as what didn't. I started paying attention to how the camera treated me: which angles betrayed the incongruent color of my eyes, which gave me a double chin.

At Griffith's suggestion—by way of Miss Frink; he still had no time for me—I cultivated a versatility of skills: ballet and driving, swimming and social dancing.

And I thought seriously about the metaphorical dance that actors do with reality. I used all my sympathy whenever I played a character, feeling every emotion as I enacted it—yet I couldn't lose my head. Early on I saw that if I got too swept away, I'd be exhausted, struggling through additional takes. It became a complicated tightrope act: I couldn't faint, just look like I'd fainted. I could learn to evoke a pallor or a blush without actually being sick or embarrassed. My brain was like a stack of colored gels: layers I could manipulate, bringing some to the fore while shuffling others aside. Before a scene that called for exuberance, for instance, I could work myself up to the proper pitch by kicking up my heels and laughing with my head thrown back.

I'd come home exhausted, and Granny would buoy me, patiently listening to my plans and fears and frustrations, always with an encouraging word. After *The Bad Boy*, she told me to ask in no uncertain terms for more money on every subsequent picture so my rate would rise.

People began to notice me, to know my (fake) name. I became a teensy tree decked out in Hollywood tinsel, someone about whom the publicity department of Triangle released meaningless biographical information to titillate fans. I had fans!

But then: disaster. Griffith let my contract lapse. Though I'd made a dozen films—all of them fine, getting good notices—and though I'd never been difficult or unreliable, I was done. Payoff to Uncle Walter dispensed.

When I went to his office to protest, Miss Frink told me with visible pleasure that Griffith would not be able to see me. I'm proud to say that I didn't give her the satisfaction of watching me break down. I fixed her with my most withering smile, shook her hand for the second and last time, and thanked her for being the first person I met in Los Angeles.

Then I went home and wept in Granny's lap. For a few moments, she let me. But when I said, "It's because I bought the little alabaster pot, isn't it?" she'd had enough.

"Cry all you like," she said, "but stop that nonsense this instant, Eileen."

"That's what Agnes would say. I got overconfident, so God punished me."

"Your mother takes comfort in such thinking, sweet Jesus knows why," Granny said, green eyes flashing. "I don't believe a bit of it. What's life supposed to be about if you can't take delight in your own magic?"

She hoisted me upright and guided me to the kitchen table, where we conducted all our serious discussions. "I've seen how you've worked," she said. "Others have, too, or they will soon enough. These people can't all be fools. Triangle letting you go isn't a death blow. It's a chance to find someplace better."

However dire the straits might be, we can achieve a lot simply by knowing that one trusted person believes that we can.

"But that could take weeks, or months," I said. "What'll we do for money till then?" I pictured the glee with which Agnes would receive news of my prideful defeat, the litany of I-told-you-so's that she'd inflict, demanding we decamp to Tampa.

"We'll get by, dear," Granny said. "Just don't breathe a word of this to your parents."

Chapter 4

THE SMALL HALL

"Six months of hard work, then that," says Gladys, clicking the recorder off. "What did you do?"

"I still couldn't afford to pay an agent's cut of any deal, so I kept pounding the pavement with my own two feet. I heard a rumor that Selig Polyscope was looking for damsels willing to be in distress in their westerns, so I gussied myself up and knocked on their door. A door which was modeled to look like the Mission San Gabriel, no less."

"Much grander than the Small Hall we've got coming up next," says Gladys.

"Miraculously enough, they let me through," I say. "Colonel Selig told me that the king of all cowboys, Tom Mix himself, had seen a few of my ingenue roles and wanted to cast me as the love interest in *The Wilderness Trail*."

"Giddyap," says Gladys, and I laugh, recalling the relief I felt when I got that reprieve, like a drowning woman who'd been tossed a life ring ever so casually.

"This hall *is* small," I say, "and thus difficult to see if you're not a fairy. But there's a mural on the wall that I'm quite fond of. It shows Noah, on dry land at last after the forty days and nights of rain. I've always been rather impressed by Noah: a builder, a traveler, a caretaker, and a heeder of signs."

~

During the years that my mother would have had me attending high school, and maybe even college, I instead felt as though I was enrolled in a course on balancing: socially, financially, and artistically. Not to mention atop a horse.

Who wouldn't want to feel the wind in her hair? To be wrapped in the arms of a virile cowboy?

The Polyscope picture was set among the fur traders of Canada, but we shot it in Flagstaff in February, with the sometimes unpredictable assistance of twenty horses, half a dozen sled dogs, and a trained bear named Theda Bear-a. The ponderosa forest and high desert panorama had a rugged manly beauty: sun and cumulus giving way to gray and black, white covering the ground, the wind cresting and crashing.

When I finally met Mix—a sweep of black hair over a face as chiseled as a Rocky Mountain—I practically swooned. "Well, aren't you sweeter than a cherry soda and a bowl of jelly beans?" he said, his smile as big as a horseshoe.

He was a known womanizer. Wrong though it may have been, I longed to be womanized. I never knew what to say to him, so mostly I listened; everyone did.

Evenings after shooting, we'd gather by the hotel fire to be regaled. As a young man he rode in Teddy Roosevelt's inaugural parade, and he'd been acquainted with several honest-to-goodness gunfighters, like Seth Bullock and Wyatt Earp. He'd spent time in Oklahoma, working as a night marshal, a bartender, a rancher, and a stunt rider in a Wild West show. "The land out there is so flat," he said, "you can watch your dog run away for days." His silver buckles, his fringes, and his turns of phrase all made my crush grow.

Men who had ridden the range ought to be called *cowhands*, he explained, not *cowboys*: cowboys were actors, prettied up for the screen. Yet Mix was the prettiest thing in his pictures, flamboyant in rodeo clothes astride Tony the Wonder Horse.

By then he was a big enough star that he could have gotten away with lackadaisical performances—grinning through a few close-ups, then sitting in the hotel bar while stunt riders handled all the action at a distance—but that's not what he did. He racked up an impressive collection of minor injuries in an array of dangerous scenes, and he seemed just as committed to his acting: tireless through multiple takes, making thoughtful suggestions while respecting the director's authority. He inspired me never to shirk or quit, no matter how hard a scene was.

That's why I almost didn't survive the first day of outdoor shooting.

"Can you ride?" the director had asked when he cast me.

"Born in the saddle," I'd replied.

But I had lied. That's how badly I wanted the role: not only would a Tom Mix picture lift me several rungs higher up the Hollywood ladder, it was also a chance to learn—about acting, about filming action, and about, well, anything else Mr. Mix felt inclined to teach me.

In fact, I hadn't been on a pony since I was ten, when I'd alit briefly upon an arthritic, all-but-immobile mare at the Florida State Fairgrounds during the Gasparilla Carnival. I mostly remember that she smelled, and seemed to have some kind of skin ailment.

Fireball, a dark bay a bit larger than our Hollywood bungalow, was to be my horse on the *Wilderness Trail* shoot. On the first icy morning when Mix himself led me to him, I clambered atop without hesitation, worried less about being killed than being caught in my equestrian fib. The picture was supposed to be a stirring romance of the northern snows; I tried to appear romantic but ended up looking, I suspect, like a floppy centaur.

"You ain't ever ridden a horse before, have you, Jelly Bean?" he asked, lithe and squinting in the winter sun.

"Not exactly," I hedged.

Fireball's black flanks twitched like the gears of some extremely dangerous machine.

Mix looked impassively at me, at the horse, and at the horizon for what felt like several weeks. "All right," he said. "Here's what you do. You hold tight, real tight, to the horn of the saddle. When the camera starts to rolling, I'll whack Fireball on the behind, and he'll run to the peak of that there hill, like the director said. I'll meet you up top, help you dismount."

Fireball had other plans. He was meaner than Satan, a real ornery cuss, and bucked as if I were sticking him with hatpins. He did, however, take me to the top of the hill as Mix had said he would, by which time I'd lost track of the saddle horn and hung askew, half-entangled in his mane, clinging to his sweaty neck for dear life.

True to his word, Mix met me there, but helping me dismount was out of the question. He galloped up, grabbed me by the waist, and swept me off. Then he gave me a firm talking-to, which I thoroughly deserved.

"Listen, Jelly Bean," he said when he'd finished, "I believe you've got quite a bit of riding yet to do on this picture."

I didn't respond, but he must have noticed my eyes dampening.

"If you like," he said, "I reckon I could give you a tip or two."

Later that day he watched patiently as I cantered around the training ring atop a calmer beast. "The thing to know about horses," he said, "is how spooky they are. How they're liable to behave is up to you. A horse's natural instinct is to meet any strange situation with the strategy of bolting. You've gotta make 'em want to stay."

So a horse is like an audience, I thought to myself, mostly to keep my terror in check.

I was grateful for the riding lessons, which served me well throughout my career, but reserved most of my enthusiasm for our love scenes. During a couple of these I nearly fainted away, though I must say I never forgot to keep my best side toward the camera. The infatuation was entirely one-sided; he was thirty-nine, on his fourth wife, and clearly saw me as just a kid—although I don't suppose he could have done otherwise, given the circumstances.

My mother was there.

By then it was clear that I wouldn't be slinking back to Tampa. To get the family back in proximity, Agnes and my father were thinking of moving to Los Angeles—but first she wanted to come with me on location, to make sure that I was serious about the so-called career I'd chosen, and to see for herself that the movie business wasn't just a trick that degenerates used to circumvent the Mann Act. I was mortified, but what could I do?

There she was in Flagstaff, regal amid the pines, watching me while Tom Mix watched her. I couldn't blame him; she was lovely, the hourglass ideal of womanhood. During a scene in which his character was teaching mine how to shoot, as his arms were wrapped around my own, his cheek pressed against mine, he kept glancing at her sidelong.

Agnes, for her part, saw him—I can admit this now—as what he was. A terrific liar, she called him. Full of stunts and humor, yes. But not to be trusted. Especially if you were a woman.

I begrudged her dimming the light of my passion, but I've never forgotten him, or stopped thinking of him fondly. He died in 1940, on the road between Tucson and Phoenix, when he came upon a washed-out bridge, jammed on the brakes, and instantly had his neck broken by a heavy suitcase—filled with gold coins and jewelry, or so the story went—that slid loose and struck him in the back of the head. It was another killing blow for the myth of the West, but also a death that suited him, one that I think he'd be satisfied with, if dying in the saddle wasn't an option.

I was glad when Agnes returned to Florida, leaving me to Granny, and to my fantasies. My parents would join us in California soon enough, but I was able to put it out of my mind, because by the time they arrived I'd be an adult. It pleased me to know that Granny wouldn't be alone all day, and Agnes's control over my freedom would finally be limited.

Not that I'd be entirely free. Congress passed women's suffrage later that year, which excited me, though I wouldn't be old enough to vote till I turned twenty-one in 1923. Disenfranchised though I was, I studied how other women in Hollywood managed to accrue power.

One of the best places to do so was the Hollywood Hotel. Yellow and pristine as the lemon cake that it served at afternoon teas, the inn took up a whole block at the corner of Hollywood Boulevard and Highland Avenue.

The place had been a dismal summer guesthouse before Mira Hershey came to town. The maiden heiress to a lumber fortune—another branch of the family prospered in chocolates—she'd decided that Hollywood needed a hotel that befit a respectable community, whether or not the movie colony qualified as such. Each evening, elderly waitresses in starched aprons strode through the dining room serving five-course meals. Sundays after church, during concerts in the rotunda, Miss Hershey herself would settle at the piano, adjust her pince-nez, and tear into Bach. Movie mothers sat atop her veranda to knit or rocked in the chairs that lined the porch.

But once a week the bounds of propriety could be tested, if only because Miss Hershey couldn't be everywhere at once. "The Thursday dance," as Mary Pickford phrased her invitation, "is our night to howl."

I still had moments of disbelief that she—whose curls Aunt Lib and I had studiously duplicated before my screen test—was now one of my friends, or at least a friendly acquaintance. I'd met her during my earliest days on the Triangle lot, where she was the brightest of all Griffith's jewels. Never haughty or aloof, she was eager to meet new arrivals and to help however she could. She was particularly kind to other women, acting as sort of an informal talent agent; it had been she, for instance, who introduced Griffith to the Gish sisters.

In person Mary was down to earth, if not exactly earthy, with a mischievous streak—which came as a relief, since her curls had become something like a national symbol of chaste feminine virtue. The first woman ever to be called "America's Sweetheart," in her twenty-seventh year she was still playing girls.

Youth was hardly the public's only demand. Smallness, too, was then tiptoeing into vogue on dainty feet, and almost everyone I knew was on a reducing regimen. We all ate little and went out dancing often: fun and naturally slimming.

That's how I presented Mary's invitation to Granny when I asked her permission to go, but Granny required no such wholesome pretext. "Why, it sounds like a royal ball," she said. "You'll likely learn a lot from Miss Pickford."

So I rode the trolley to meet Mary at the Hollywood Hotel. The temperature was hot and hazy for May, the shine of the sunset glossy and pouting, the sky a smear of honey you could stick a dream to—though good luck getting it unstuck later.

Advertised as liquor-free, Thursday nights were lubricated by smuggled booze: gin, champagne, cases of Scotch stashed in automobiles. Carsful of revelers made concoctions with seltzer bottles and bergs of cracked ice. The ceiling was decorated with stars bearing the names of the famous players who dined there—Douglas Fairbanks, Rudolph Valentino—and on most Thursdays the players themselves sat cooperatively under their names.

Inside the ballroom I saw no one I knew. When this happened at parties, I usually busied myself by winding the phonograph until someone asked me to dance, but for that night's event Miss Hershey had hired an all-female quartet to play refined selections. I stood wishing desperately that I hadn't arrived alone when I saw, through the air going blue with smoke, an apparition at the punch bowl: Mary Pickford, Lillian Gish, and a golden waif with seaside eyes.

Gish, in the world but never of it, stood sweatless in the sultry ballroom. I knew her from Triangle, too; if anything, it had been even more of a struggle than it had been with Mary for me to overcome my paralyzing admiration and speak to Lillian like an ordinary person. From the first time I saw her on the screen, it was clear that she understood film acting better than anybody alive: how it differed from the stage, what old tricks it nullified, what new ones it made possible. Much tougher than her anemic appearance suggested, she worked as hard as a ditchdigger, doing whatever it took to connect with the audience. I often heard stories about jaded film crews applauding spontaneously when she finished a scene. She was only nine years older than I, but that was an eternity in an industry so young: to a great extent she'd created the job that I aspired to do. Mary and Lillian both became and remained my close friends, but Lillian has always been a bit of an enigma. Great actors tend to disappear before your very eyes, obscured by a cloud of whatever you already think about them.

Dormant for months, all my fears of being a cloddish pretender rushed back as I spotted them standing there with the unknown third, and I considered skulking away, back home to Granny. But Mary spotted me and waved me over. "Doreen!" she called. "You know Lillian already, don't you? Allow me to introduce you to Marion Davies."

"P-p-pleased to meet you," said the blonde, with a Brooklyn accent and a disarming stammer. "I've just moved from New York, and I don't know a soul except for Mary and W. R."

Keeping my mouth shut has never been my strong suit, but thankfully I managed to do so long enough to figure out what everyone else apparently knew: W. R. was William Randolph Hearst, the publishing magnate and sometime politician who, rumor had it, was then building an enormous estate up the coast, halfway to San Francisco.

What everyone else also apparently knew was that Marion was his mistress. Hollywood morality was forgiving on such points, and though I knew that being involved with a married man was a sin, I somehow couldn't fault Marion, who was funny and observant and seemed not to take herself too seriously. "My uncle's an editor for one of W. R.'s papers out of Chicago," I said, wanting her to like me.

"My apologies for how damn demanding that must be!" Her delicate laugh was like petals falling, and the eloquence of her expressive face outshone her stutter. She was one of those souls who made others feel good. "He barely agreed to let me come here tonight, but Mary persuaded him."

Mary was the only one in our party who had earned a ceiling star, so we sat at her designated table and took in the party over gossip that ran juicier than all the citrus in the hills.

My newcomer status was a gift to my tablemates, an occasion for them to dust off their favorite dirt. "Do most of these beautiful young people live at the hotel?" I asked, widening my eyes, embracing my role.

"Many do," Mary said. "I wouldn't in a million years. That's Miss Hershey over there." She nodded toward a bosomy matron patrolling the floor. "She polices her tenants for everything from unseemly behavior to snitching an extra dish of peas at dinner."

"I heard," said Marion, her Kewpie face cracked into a knowing smile, "that she taps nightly on starlets' doors to confirm they're in their own beds, alone. If not, she evicts them."

"But her Victorian powers have their limit, as you can see," said Lillian, demure as a stained-glass Madonna—except for her eyes, which she cut shrewdly.

Miss Hershey was in the process of prying a couple apart, having deemed their dancing lewd. She fanned her red face to dispel whiffs of sex, then noticed us onlookers. Her high-necked dress emitted a puff of camphor as she approached. "You ladies needn't sit waiting for a gentleman's invitation, you know," she said. "You could be like those two. See how they dance together so gracefully?"

As she resumed her patrol, Marion said in a stage whisper, "The dear old thing doesn't realize they're lesbians!"

That was the first time I'd heard the word spoken. Marion said it with no trace of malice; I'd learn that she accepted everyone without question, sprinkling her kindhearted spirit like powdered sugar over all proceedings, making everything sweet.

The quartet shifted from a waltz to a five-step schottische, and Marion took my hand and pulled me off to dance. Lillian joined us on the floor with D. W. Griffith, who was a tremendous hoofer. "Of all exercise, dancing is the finest," he opined as they whirled past, seeming to think we'd been suffering from the lack of his authoritative pronouncements, unable to resist directing even in leisure.

Triangle had somewhat recently gone belly-up—an event I noted with satisfaction after they jilted me, not to mention relief: they'd done so because they were broke, not because I was no good.

Chaplin was there that night, too, but he kept to his own party, as I'd learn was his wont. His own party invariably included whatever child-woman he was taking around town. I would have loved to have seen Mildred, but she was nowhere in sight.

We returned to our table for refreshment, where I elicited a warning from Lillian. "Careful, Doreen," she said, "the cocktails are ferocious." Lillian never drank.

I didn't either, much—the occasional gin fizz, certainly not to excess—and I might have taken offense at her admonishment. But there in that room lit with chandeliers, flocked with gay and improvident movie people tight-skinned with youth, gobbling up life in huge mouthfuls, I couldn't object: I felt three-quarters drunk already. Looking in fresh disbelief at those three indelible faces—Lillian, Mary, and Marion—I felt the shivery thrill of new worlds opening. It was a feeling I knew, but had only ever associated with the presence of the fairies. I thought of the three Graces, and the three Furies (God forbid), and especially the three Fates—not the Greek and Roman versions so much as the three Morrígna, powerful and ambiguous figures from Irish myth who featured in Granny Shaughnessy's tales. I felt certain that for good or ill, my adventures in Hollywood would be bound up with these three women.

And then I did something I'd increasingly been in the habit of doing—imagining what my current situation would look like on the silver screen—and it occurred to me that a camera would see not three magic, oracular figures gathered at our table, but four.

Mary broke me from my reverie by reaching for a champagne bottle. "Oh, yes, Lillian," she said with good-natured sarcasm, "please do tell us more about the benefits of abstinence."

"To sustain success on the screen," Lillian said, striking a beatific attitude that placed her both in on and slightly above the joke, "there's nothing more important than clean thoughts and clean living. They do register on camera."

"A reading from the book of Griffith," Mary said.

"Oh, Lil," Marion chimed in. "Surely a gal can drink her bubbles and still keep her bubbly persona." She refilled her own glass. "If you get hungover, just see all the Charles Ray pictures you can. They'll wash your liver clean."

I laughed, as did we all: though Ray's films are justly forgotten now, in 1919 this was a very funny quip. But I also set down my whiskey-and-whatever-it-was and reached for some water. "I can't stay out too late anyway," I said. "I have to catch the streetcar home, and to be on set tomorrow morning."

"Doreen, so d-d-do I," said Marion, floss-blonde hair curling around her porcelain face. "Let me give you a lift. W. R. has hired me a driver."

On the ride home she spoke of New York City and her stint as a chorus girl in the Ziegfeld Follies. "I want to do comic pictures, but W. R. has his heart set on seeing me in period dramas. Something to do with dignity. Appearances are terrifically important to him. You might not guess that from our unconventional arrangement."

I wanted to ask, not without envy, what it was like to have a powerful man yanking every string he could for you. Marion was twenty-two; I wasn't sure, but figured Hearst for well over fifty. This fast life of rich men and their mistresses: I couldn't see myself ever getting into it.

But neither did I want to follow Lillian's path. She was widely understood to be a mama's girl, disinterested in sex in some fundamental way. There were, of course, rumors about her and Mr. Griffith. (That's what she unfailingly called him.) I don't think they were true, though her devotion was oddly steadfast: decades later, after his reputation had declined and he was long dead, the way that she defended his genius always made me a little sick. I adored her but felt in her a certain void: not a hunger, just an absence. Maybe that's unfair. Maybe she simply understood that to be the most elusive was to be the most beguiling. Her virgin pose made her glow all the more, for who doesn't long for what's unattainable? If you ever tried to touch her, she'd dissolve into wisps.

My mind, weary and electrified, kept wandering from what Marion was saying, and the bungalow was drawing near. "Do you really think comedy's worth doing?" I asked.

I'd been toying with the idea because I'd been working constantly but advancing little. My résumé was written in a single color: melancholy blue, all drama. The more time I spent around my idol Lillian, the more I began to suspect that my own skills might lie elsewhere. Diversifying my repertoire beyond heartwarming ragamuffins and Irish goody-goodies was bound to expand my prospects.

"Oh, Doreen, yes!" said Marion. As we slowed to a stop on Fountain, the streetlights fell upon her eyes, blue as the sea at Santa Monica. "Don't tell Lillian, but I think the stage has still got the movies licked when it comes to drama—but they're perfect for comedy. If I were you, I'd march right up to Mack Sennett tomorrow and demand to learn the craft."

As it happened, Granny put an immediate halt to that scheme. I shouldn't work for Sennett, she said, because his brand of comedy was slapstick and tawdry: bathing beauties and banana cream pies.

That left Al Christie, a subtler comedy producer known for his slower paced, more urbane offerings.

As I made my way toward Christie's office, passing the hopefuls on the studio lot, I had the unfamiliar and unpleasant sensation of feeling old: more skillful than I'd been at fourteen, that's for sure, but not necessarily more promising. *Dress aggressively* seemed to be the rule that this year's crop of would-be starlets was following. Every casting call was a roomful of exclamation points: *I'm your girl!* Some of them were savvy, no doubt, but some were easy prey. *Never lie down on a casting couch,*

I wanted to tell them. *It might work for a moment or two, but you'll get cast off for the next sweet patootie.*

On the one movie I made with the great Japanese actor Sessue Hayakawa—a ridiculous mess in which he played Akbar Khan and I played his Persian lover—we had a lecherous director. He was flattering and attentive at first, persuasively conveying an interest in my thoughts. Then his cues became suggestive: "You enchantress, I could watch you descend a staircase all day," he'd say. "Now rise as though you slept nude on a bed of roses."

One evening, after everyone else had left, he grabbed my wrist and propositioned me. Chubby fingers, sweaty palms, a toad-like face, and slick hair smelling of Aqua Velva. I wrenched away and refused him.

"So that's the way you like to play it?" he said. "String 'em along but never relax in the slightest? You want to be the goosey dame who giggles a lot?"

"I'll do more than hiss and honk if you lay a hand on me again," I snapped. "I don't know how you think I'm playing it, but the game's over. I'll do you the favor of forgetting about this. I recommend you do the same."

He looked chastened, and for a moment I felt strong, but after I ran out the door I was shaking. He hadn't gotten what he'd wanted, but he'd still put the burden of papering over his boorishness on me. Even in my refusal he'd goaded a performance out of me, and he'd never face any consequences.

I wanted to work for a studio where I wasn't under threat.

Live, Love, Laugh, Labor and Be Happy was the motto on the wall of Christie's office: a checklist for my dreams, hanging above the shoulders of a man in a straw boater hat with a jaunty red band, which he tipped politely upon my entry. Christie had a Canadian accent and a lantern-jawed face not quite shaped to be in front of the camera.

When he asked what brought me his way, I blurted, "I need to get funny, and quick!"

He guffawed. A good sign?

We both knew that it was unusual for a dramatic actress to move toward comedy. Usually it went the other way—Gloria Swanson starting as a bathing beauty, then becoming a drama queen—but the more I thought about it the more sure I was that I had to do it.

"And I don't want to wear bathing suits and negligees, and to frolic on beaches and in boudoirs!" I went on. "I want real parts!"

"You're a good girl, Doreen," he said.

"And you really know your onions," I replied.

He hired me.

Al—and all of us called him Al—seemed young but still authoritative. Big and homely, he had gray eyes with black lashes and a marvelous laugh. He offered equal support to everyone, from the sauciest sugar babies to the most wizened grandmas, for he knew that anyone could steal a scene, especially in a comedy. His friendliness imbued the studio with a jolly atmosphere.

He used me for his transition from short films to features. The fact that neither of us knew exactly what we were doing made for a good collaboration: he could puzzle through how to make each sequence work, while I concentrated on keeping the audience attached to my character. As we figured out how to sustain a consistent level of humor over the course of a full-length picture, I discovered that the highest form of technique is to make people forget that there's any technique at all. Natural laughs—ones that arose from the story—were preferable to forced circumstances, so I pressed for gags that arose from situations, and for characterizations rather than caricatures. To this day I believe that it's harder to get a laugh than to draw a tear.

Electricians were always perched overhead, out of the frame, and if I could hold their interest, then I knew that a bit was probably decent.

For years Granny had coached me to reject studios' lowball rates, but with Al I never needed to. He kept my rate rising, something I attributed to the good work I was doing, and also to the tribalism typical of the industry. "We Irish have got to stick together," he'd say, blowing the ink dry on another munificent contract.

Though I'd never set foot in Ireland, my notices read as if I were fresh off the boat. One critic wrote that I was "still a wee wisp of a child—with hair soft as the moss in the glen, and eyes like the shadows of the Killarney lakes where the sunlight glints." Less poetic but more direct, a *Photoplay* editorial simply said: Doreen O'Dare is Irish. You can't help liking her.

Enthusiastic and *girlish* were my most frequent descriptors, which I began to imagine as pitted against their silent opposites: *talented* and *manly*. *Charming* was another word I often got, and this one I didn't mind. That little *-ing* put me into motion: you had to be *active* to arouse delight. Thanks to Granny and the fairies, I also felt connected with the noun to which that *-ing* was attached: a thing to ward off evil.

But my charmed existence at Christie Studios didn't last. One evening, after we'd wrapped my third feature, Al—without knocking—lumbered into my dressing room. I was sitting at my vanity, about to take off my makeup, wearing only a slip. He stood behind me in his tweed three-piece suit, staring at my body in the mirror, and put a warm arm around my bare shoulders.

"You know, my dear, you're a very nice girl," he began, scratchy fibers prickling.

"And you're the nicest director I've ever worked with," I replied, and stood to face him.

"I've been thinking that you and I—"

"You've been so good to me, Mr. Al," I said, hoping that a *mister*-ing would make my point and that he wouldn't get forceful. "If you were my own father, I couldn't like you more."

His ardor deflated at that. The respect I'd had for him had already done the same. As giving as he was, he still wanted to take.

"You're a real sweet little girl, Doreen," he said, running a hand over the strands of red hair on his balding head. "I hope you never change."

He backed out of the room with the sad mien of a trained bear. For some reason, even though the awkwardness was all his fault, I felt that *I* was to blame.

To a certain extent he agreed, for the next day he said he thought it best that our time working together came to an end. He was going to loan me out.

~

You'd never guess how noisy a set could get when five or six companies were at work on as many pictures. Someone might be doing a tense, dramatic scene—a reunion between an estranged brother and sister, say, or a man on his deathbed pleading forgiveness—while someone else was breaking a saloon mirror for a brawl, and someone else was filming the whirl of a dance hall.

But Marshall Neilan was a quiet director. I felt luckier than a rabbit's foot that he was the man to whom Al Christie had loaned me.

Given everything else about Neilan's personality, you'd never expect such serenity on set. He had originally been a chauffeur for Griffith, who sometimes had him fill out crowds as an extra, usually while still in his driver's uniform. The camera revealed his almost musical grace, as the camera somehow sometimes does, and that's how he became a Griffith player.

Neilan's repute as a great director was matched only by his reputation as a hell-for-leather profligate. Once after shooting a ballroom scene, he'd kept the orchestra on set, on the studio's dime, and gave an impromptu dinner-dance for the entire cast. He played the piano beautifully and had a way of telling a story that made a mere trifle seem twice as funny as it was. He worked all day and threw parties all night. When the band at the Cocoanut Grove finished at twelve, he'd invite them and everyone else over to his mansion, and they'd keep going until dawn.

When he cast me to play the long-suffering mother in his Irish immigrant story *Dinty*—not a comic part, obviously, but not an ingenue either, so thank heaven for small favors—I said, "Thank you, Mr. Neilan," as I was leaving.

"Hey, Irish!" he called. "The name's Mickey. Don't ever call me *mister* again."

He gave me a huge salary, typical of his open-handedness, but which also established a precedent that I could command such a price. *Dinty* was a hit, which further bolstered my case. Momentum was building. I couldn't wait to see what would happen next.

What happened next was that Mickey cast me as the leading lady in *The Lotus Eater*, starring John Barrymore.

John Barrymore! Of the distinguished acting family! The greatest actor alive! And there I was, a promising but still struggling and certainly unformed actress, set to play opposite him. I would have to do a love scene. Oh, I suffered sensuously! Tough and sexy, dashing and physical, he had the profile of an Olympian and the body of an Atlas. My appeal then, I knew well enough to admit, was still a little Sunday-school.

When I was all aflutter about meeting Barrymore, Mickey didn't tell me to calm down. "Go on and panic!" he said. "I'd panic like hell if I were you. A little panic means you care."

He was a born wiseacre, and he and I had a common accord. It was almost enough to persuade me to discount his wild behavior.

Almost. Not long after we'd wrapped the production of *Dinty*, he crashed his car into the traffic signal at Fourth and Pico; a mystery woman fled in a taxicab as he got arrested. She might or might not have been the actress Blanche Sweet: Mickey was then in the process of being divorced on the grounds of abandonment, and Sweet was named in the filings. The two of them would later marry; it didn't last long.

Worse, Mickey drank too much. Worse still, he insisted on viewing Hollywood through the lens of ethnicity. This made sense up to a point: the movie business was one of very few industries where smart and hard-working immigrant kids could make a lot of money fast, without the need for seed capital or degrees. For many of us, this was a basis for fellowship; for Mickey—and he was hardly alone in this—it meant that someone was always getting something that should have been his. Even for those of us who loved him, this got tiresome. Because he couldn't hold his liquor or his tongue, Mickey would be done as a director by the late twenties.

But in 1920 he was still a delight and hadn't an unkind word to say about anyone, not even the most temperamental of actors. Barrymore, for instance, had recently done amazing concurrent performances in *Dr. Jekyll and Mr. Hyde* on-screen and *Richard III* onstage, during which he'd suffered a complete mental breakdown; he refused to travel to California, so we went to him in New York. This trip marked a pivot in my career, for Granny let me travel unescorted: my first taste of honest-to-God freedom and the responsibilities of being an adult at age eighteen. Not that anyone around me was being remotely mature in their conduct.

At the Bronx studio where we filmed the interiors, Mickey had the set walls built tall; the whole place was hushed so that Barrymore could concentrate. Mickey would confer with us softly about the action, then go back to his chair next to the camera. Blunt honesty, never unkind, was his signature form of feedback.

The Lotus Eater was a tale of the sea, so we commissioned a yacht and set sail for Palm Beach. On the sun-kissed sands of Florida, attired for some reason in a toga, I played the innocent maiden of an island culture scarcely touched by man. The palms rustling in the salty sea breeze reminded me of Tampa.

Near the end of the first day of shooting, a young man I'd never met joined Mickey behind the camera. Hatless, he squinted in the late afternoon sun, his eyes the aqua blue of a tidal pool, smile lines stepping down his cheekbones toward a sturdy jawline. My infatuation with Barrymore vanished like sea spray.

"Hey, Irish," Mickey said, "meet Victor Marquis."

I couldn't believe that the warm hand into which I placed my own belonged to one of the industry's most esteemed directors. At only twenty-seven, he already had his own studio, Marquis Manse, where he was trying to achieve the sort of creative independence that Griffith and his cronies often talked about—and to do it without their wealth and established stardom. I often heard Marquis spoken of with admiration, but no one had told me that he was better looking than half the men in front of the camera. I realized that when it came to romance I had been goofing around with schoolgirl fancies, waiting to be struck by some great *aha!*

"Aha!" I said. "What brings you here?"

He laughed. "Pleased to meet you, too, Eileen," he said. His smile was like the light on the water. "Is it presumptuous of me to use your real name?"

"It is," I said. "But as it happens, I do prefer that my friends call me Eileen."

"I'd like us to be friends, so I'll keep doing it. But I have to level with you that this is a business visit. I told Mickey that I'm looking for an actress to play the lead in my next picture, *The Sky Pilot*. He said I had better get Doreen O'Dare or have a damn good excuse for why I didn't and that if I didn't want to take his word for it, then I could come and see for myself."

I hiked a skeptical brow. "All the way to Palm Beach from Los Angeles, huh?"

"I'd have traveled to Timbuktu," he said, "but I *do* appreciate that in Palm Beach it's easier to watch the moon rise over the ocean while sipping a cocktail."

"Easier by a hair," growled Mickey. Prohibition had been in effect since the start of the year, and he was still sore about it.

"Well," I said, "my favorite auditions are the ones I don't know I'm doing. So how did it go?" I tilted a hip in my toga.

"I refuse to do *The Sky Pilot* without you," he said, winking.

Normally I couldn't stand for a man to wink, but when Victor did it I wanted to beg him to do it again.

"I'm going to go swap this ridiculous outfit," I said.

All the way back to the beach shack dressing room, I struggled to catch my breath.

That evening, on the yacht, a few members of the cast and crew formed a rowdy contingent, Victor among them. I asked meekly whether Mickey minded if I had a glass of his champagne. "A glass?" he replied. "Say, if you don't drink a quart, I'll disown you!"

Mickey and Barrymore swiftly got stewed to the eyeballs, arguing the relative merits of the history plays that I always skipped in my father's Shakespeare omnibus, resolving their disputes with shouts of "down the hatch!" (It soon became clear that Mickey hadn't read any of those plays either.) Meanwhile, Victor and I lounged at the prow and talked.

"How do you like working with those two jesters?" he asked, eyeing them fondly.

"All I know is that I'll never know enough."

"Nobody does," he replied with surprising seriousness. "None of us. We're learning as we go. We're pioneers."

"I suppose. I just don't want to get crushed in the wagon ruts," I said, more candid than I'd planned to be. "I've been in the business for years, and I'm just holding steady. I can't be sure of anything."

"What I'm starting to learn," he said, "is that the kinds of attitudes you hear praised as self-assurance in this town—and by *this town* I mean *that* town—are mostly bluff. Admire the bold explorer, but join the expedition that packs an extra week's rations. I don't see any harm in admitting that it's a tough business. But if you believe you can do things, you'll do them."

One glass tumbler, then a second, smashed against the deck in a splatter of shards and whiskey, and two figures in skivvies leapt into the ocean. "Last one in's a rotten egg!" yelled Mickey from midair, and everyone else tore off their shoes and made to dive.

"How sure are you," I cried to Victor as I followed their lead, "that you can spot a bluff?"

Then I sailed over the rail.

The water was cool, but not cold, and I stayed under as long as I could, wondering if any of the drunk partygoers would notice or care, my hair fanning out in the currents like seaweed. A hand clasped my shoulder and pulled me up: the arms of a terrified Victor. I felt awful for scaring him, but all I could do was laugh.

I enjoyed when men paid me little courtesies, such as caring whether I was dead.

"My God, Eileen, you were down there for a week!" he said, not letting go of my hand, towing me back toward the boat.

"I'm sorry, Victor. That was a mean joke. I grew up here in Florida, on the Gulf side, anyhow. I'm practically half merrow."

"How's that?" he said, treading water. "Does marrow hold oxygen? I'm a director, not an anatomist." Behind him spread a backdrop of a preposterously colorful sunset. Behind me, the first rays of the moon that he'd predicted were adding silver to the gold.

"*Merrow*, with an *e*. It's Irish for mermaid."

He stayed by my side for the rest of the night before heading to shore; he had to catch a train the next morning. I mooned silently at the stars in his absence until Mickey stumbled up.

"This makes no never-mind to me, Irish," he said, "but it might to you. Our friend Marquis is a married man. Married to Florence, no less."

Of course. Not only was he married, it was to one of the most gorgeous and tempestuous actresses in Hollywood. Florence Marquis. "It does matter to me, Mickey," I said. "Very much. Thank you."

Smitten as I was—and it certainly seemed reciprocal—Mr. Al had been right. I was a good girl.

The next morning we were awakened by a pair of Palm Beach city constables, who politely explained that they'd had so many noise complaints that we were being ordered to leave. We headed south to Miami, then home to California, and each day that passed with no word from Victor convinced me that I'd never be cast in *The Sky Pilot*.

"You've got to fry fish on several fires, Eileen," said Granny when she caught me moping, not knowing the real reason for my dejection.

Chapter 5

The Drawing Room

"All that aye-and-begorrah Irish nonsense," says Gladys. "Why did you put up with it?"

The truth is that the fairyland that glowed in the eerie light of the screen was the only place I really wanted to be, and if I had to pass through a tall and trackless forest to get there, then that's what I'd do.

But what I say to Gladys is, "I sometimes wonder whether the movies I acted in did more to reflect stereotypes or to propagate them. It was always a strange double game, appealing to the pride of Irish Americans who wanted to see themselves on-screen while giving the wider audience the opportunity to think, 'Oh, that's exactly how those people are.'"

"Sounds like a project for one of the sociologists over at the U of C." She tilts her head in the direction of the Gothic campus, steps west of the museum we're tucked inside.

That would be interesting. The meaning of a work of art changes over time, put to different uses in different eras. I'd like someone to track the way that happens to mine—but I'm afraid they wouldn't have much to work with, and I don't want to think about that right now. The Fairy Castle, at least, is durable. "I suppose we ought to keep going," I say. "On to the Drawing Room."

Gladys starts the recorder.

"The chandelier incorporates precious stones from my jewelry; this seems like a far better use for them. The floor is rose quartz, with a green jade border. Those amber vases by the arch are from the Ming dynasty, over five hundred years old."

The furniture is sterling silver, and a chess table waits for the fairies to play. They wind the gold clock on the mantel every day; it never loses a minute.

"Then of course there are the instruments," Gladys prompts.

A rosewood piano. A perfect violin. The musicians often play so softly that you can only hear them in complete darkness.

Aside from what I occasionally hear from my granddaughters' transistor radio, I have little idea of what young people are listening to these days, but when I think of my own youth, it's the music that floats back, at least as much as the memories of the silent films. "My favorite thing in this room," I continue, "is the sheet music collection: manuscripts handwritten by the original composers. George M. Cohan transcribed 'Over There.' Irving Berlin did 'Alexander's Ragtime Band.' But closest to my heart is the song 'California, Here I Come,' by Buddy DeSylva. He jotted it for me not long before he died."

~

California, here they came, *they* in this case being my mother and father, as promised and as threatened. My prospects were still uncertain from picture to picture, and money was often tight, so Granny Shaughnessy and I left our beloved bungalow and moved in with them, to a house on Grand View Street.

By then I'd been in Hollywood long enough to recognize that some actors acted because they felt more comfortable being someone else. In my most introspective moments, I could see that to some extent this applied to me. The iron reign of Agnes had made me doubt my ability to ever be a proper lady; my dad's slow slide made me fear that

I, too, might wind up a person made sour by disappointment. Two thousand–odd miles away from them, I could pretend these anxieties into submission. Now, here they were again, with all their expectations.

They accepted that acting was my reality—otherwise they wouldn't have come—but they still weren't terribly impressed with me. I shouldn't have cared, but it pained me whenever Agnes would walk off to make dinner as I was describing the plot of a picture, or when my father would glaze over during a story about a castmate's blunder. Even though my paychecks paid for our room and board, my mother maintained her bias against harum-scarum film-colony types, declaring her preference for seeing her daughter's face unsullied by greasepaint.

But many of us were as wholesome as a sandwich and a glass of milk. In the wake of Olive Thomas's terrible death and Mary's little brother Jack Pickford's subsequent scandal—Olive had died after drinking a bottle of Jack's syphilis medication; it was probably an accident; they were a wild couple, so the papers hinted at suicide or foul play; all of this happened in Paris, I should note—reporters swept into Hollywood from all over the country hoping to find hell and all its devils. They ended up condemning our little burg for being dull. By 10 p.m. Hollywood Boulevard resembles the main aisle of the catacombs, wrote the *New York World*. If two people walk down Hollywood Boulevard together, the natives mistake them for a parade. *Life* called the town "the deadest hole."

Their opinions smacked of sour grapes. Though California was dry, money fell like rain. Boosters boosted relentlessly: abundance and prosperity. Buses went up and down Hollywood Boulevard, whisking potential buyers to new subdivisions as phantasmagorical as movie sets: castles and pagodas, haciendas and mock Tudors, emphasis on the mock.

What looked like a kitsch nightmare to eastern snobs, I found dreamy: shops and cafés in the shapes of windmills and bulldogs, brown derbies and frankfurters. Admittedly, the boom did have its casualties. They cut down still more of the pepper trees to let tourists gawp at the architecture. Bulldozers carved up the hills to build pseudo-Spanish everything, the scent of the orange groves stunk up by gasoline.

Still, Hollywood was beautiful, and there was plenty of fun if you knew where to find it, which those reporters clearly didn't. We movie people were hardly the only ones flooding in; so many midwesterners had settled in Long Beach that people started calling it Iowa by the Sea.

My mother—who insisted on maintaining an Edwardian silhouette, even though King Edward had been dead for over a decade—took umbrage at Los Angeles's crassness, especially in the style of women's dress: no gloves, hatlessness in cafés, open-toed shoes, diamonds before sunset. I'd never bought into decorum for its own sake, so the laxness felt like a reprieve. When I'd arrived, I couldn't walk in heels worth a cent; Triangle had to hire a double for my legs. They didn't mind; youth was what they wanted, hence the common practice of casting actors in parts well beyond their years. Once, while we were preparing to shoot a comedy, Al Christie rejected many a child—including a baby—for not looking young enough.

Cameramen wore their caps back-to-front because the peak prohibited them from peering through their viewfinders; directors did the same, then actors, and before long men were doing it everywhere, with no inkling of the original purpose.

We had powers that we were only beginning to learn to use. As much as I still had to bounce from director to director to land in a picture, everything had a happy-go-lucky air, from the attire to the climate.

I was happy, too, mostly. But not yet satisfied.

~

Then, months after I'd let go of all hope at the prospect, Mickey Neilan got a call from Victor Marquis. Victor wanted to borrow me for the female lead in *The Sky Pilot*.

Marquis Manse, Victor's own studio, was in Santa Monica, but for *The Sky Pilot* we were to go on location—and go we did, with a degree of ambition heretofore unseen. Victor was an *auteur* long before there was a term for it, and Fate's hand seemed there for the taking if we kept reaching out. So I thought, anyway, in the caravan trekking up to Truckee—sun and altitude, pine-scented air and clear mountain brooks.

We were, I see now, young and impudent. Some of the demands of the shoot would prove almost inhuman, but I hardly noticed. I was too busy noticing Victor Marquis.

At dinner that first night, as the cast and crew crowded into a log cabin–style mess hall custom-built for our purposes, he invited me to sit at his table. He complimented my eyes.

"They're both beguiling," he said, "but the blue one is a surprise. Like stumbling on a spoonful of the Pacific Ocean."

His own eyes turned up slightly at the corners, and his teeth were white as the snow on the Sierra Nevada peaks. Granny Shaughnessy would have called him a fine figure of a man. I didn't know what to say.

"And you look so young," I said. "Someone might mistake you for an assistant director."

"Thanks a lot, Eileen, for that vote of confidence. I'll have you know that I'm a full nine years older than you. Unless, like most actresses, you're already lying about your age."

"I'm not," I said. "What I meant, if you accept only compliments that are precisely worded, is that you seem like a match for the scenery up here. It has an almost vengeful beauty."

"Vengeful? It's only the mountains."

I shivered in the cold that crept through the ill-sealed logs. "It seems the kind of place where Mother Nature could get up to some tomfoolery."

"Whether she does or not," he said, smiling, "we'll have plenty to get up to in the scenario. If you're game, that is."

"I am," I said. With him I felt up for anything.

If you recite their plots, many of the films I made sound insufferably melodramatic. But when you put actors in them—all these supple, charismatic little bodies (and a lot of us were shrimps, well shaped but small)—well, then they became attractive, and borderline believable, or at least engaging enough to earn the benefit of the doubt.

The Sky Pilot—the title was slang for a man of God; back then we usually called people who flew airplanes *aviators*, not *pilots*—was a corking drama about a preacher who comes to a rowdy western town to minister to the heathen. I played Gwen, the dauntless heroine.

When I made my entrance, it was as a tomboy on a cart pulled by two fiery horses. I wore chaps—pants!—and a wide-brimmed hat. Boisterous! Unladylike! I got to make a horseback rescue of the preacher, who was played by the rugged John Bowers. It was gratifying to portray a powerful woman, not another shrinking ingenue wearing a lace gown and a docile look.

Our interior sets were built open to the sky to scoop all that fat California sunshine. Strokes of chalk marked where we should stand. Victor obsessed over the perfection of his takes.

Directors in those days affected an air of quasi-military authority. Cecil B. DeMille, a real autocrat, even carried a revolver; he also hired a violinist to follow him everywhere, providing background music.

Victor, thank God, was never pretentious. But he always looked the master of every situation and made you feel as though you could be, too.

Under a thoughtless director, a cast could collapse of heatstroke as their leader took forever to set up a shot. Victor kept note of every moment, saturating the set with an ambient encouragement. The cooperation he was able to orchestrate was unlike that of any other film I had worked on.

The weather in Truckee, as I had feared, did not cooperate. We arrived in late September and filmed chronologically in a faux frontier town erected across the railroad tracks from the actual village, complete with saloons and gambling dens. The film took place in both summer and winter, and we had shot all but two of the non-snow scenes when we went to bed one mid-October evening.

We woke to find ice crusting the pitchers in our bedrooms and looked through our frosted windows to find that the clouds had spilled snow all night. The blizzard kept up for two more days. The Truckee graybeards said the storm was the earliest in sixty-five years. The script called for bare earth in those remaining summer scenes. The weather had idled us.

By then, Victor and I had grown close—maybe too close, considering his marriage. We hadn't done anything untoward but had begun to spend every evening together, taking long walks on mountain paths, talking. I'd never experienced such instant and easy rapport with any man.

We discussed our philosophies for our chosen crafts. "Art *as* art never gets you anywhere with the masses; we've got to make them believe!" Victor said one evening as the mountain chickadees sang in the trees. "Every crank of the camera's got to wring their emotions." His goal of making morally upright pictures with an uplifting message might have seemed at odds with his behavior—he was clearly courting me—and yet.

To a greater extent than anyone else I'd known in the business—than anyone I'd known at all except Granny—he listened with full attention as I put my ideas about acting into words. "Detractors say that actors are narcissistic. And the bad ones are. Egotists are incurious, no matter what their profession. But you have to pay attention to everyone: on the street for inspiration, in the cast for cooperation. Or you'll stink."

Our talks made me remember why I loved the movies. Back in Tampa, I'd never thought of the screen as a flat white surface: it was a cosmos. Where else could stars come from but an infinite sky? Nowadays people arrange their furniture around their television sets and expect the world to come to them, but what I sought from the movies back then was to be transported, to be initiated into mysteries. *Tell me the secret of being in love,* I'd say.

In Truckee, there Victor was, telling me the secret.

The night after it finally stopped snowing, he invited me for a walk as usual, but for the first time he took my mittened hand.

"For warmth," he said. I didn't need a pretext. My hopes had piled high, and I fell for him like an avalanche.

"I was thinking," I said, wanting to be helpful, to be indispensable. "What if we shot the snow scenes now, then returned to the summer scenes after this melts?"

"Eileen," he said, "that is a brilliant idea, but it won't work. I haven't told anyone in the cast yet, because I want their reactions to be fresh, but in the film's final scenes, the preacher's church and some other buildings will be burned to the ground in the dead of winter."

"Oh," I said, startled, then impressed. It would be a fantastic ending. But. "We can't shoot out of sequence because we need the buildings for the last of the summer scenes. We can't un-burn them."

"Got it in one," he said, squeezing my hand. "It's far from ideal, but there's no point in panicking. Budgets aside, we'll have to ride it out."

"I hope Marquis Manse can afford the overrun," I said, knowing what a dry-eyed lot financial backers could be.

"You keep money on your mind, I see," he said teasingly. "What do you do with your salaries, Eileen?"

"Bank them, mostly," I said. "I'm no skinflint—remind me to show you my collection of miniatures someday—but it's never unwise to save for leaner times. A very clever fellow once told me something about joining the expedition that packs extra rations. Do you remember him?"

His laugh was too dry to fog the cold air. "I do," he said. "I believe the fellow specified an extra *week's* rations. So, provided all this snow makes it to the Pacific Ocean within another couple of days, I'd say we're in the clear."

I was increasingly able to see that he really *did* worry about such disasters, and thus the fact that he never burdened others with his worry seemed increasingly admirable.

"You're really committed to this lunatic business, Eileen?" he continued. "With your drive and acumen, I reckon you'd be a success in any endeavor you set your shoulder to. You could be a captain of industry, and you chose the movies!"

"I chose *your* movie. And US Steel isn't exactly placing want ads for female executives, if you know what I mean."

"Their loss. A pretty face and a cash-register brain. Not a common pairing. A hard worker, too."

"As Granny likes to say, diamonds come out of the earth cloudy. You have to work to make them gleam."

Then we came to the realization—unspoken, simultaneous—that we had passed through the clearing that marked the point where we usually turned back toward our cabins; the blankets of snow had muted our usual landmarks. That night was as bright as midday LA, a sugar bowl of crystalline white lit to radiance by the fullest moon. I gasped.

"Yes," said Victor, "I see it." We both turned in place to survey our enchanted surroundings and ended up facing each other. His stubble was faint around the bow of his lips. He took my hand again. Then he took the other one.

A situation can only accumulate so much tension before it breaks. The stars had awaited the right moment, then pounced.

We kissed until we could no longer feel our toes.

Reluctant, we walked hand in numbed hand back to town, only dropping our link when we got within sight.

No words were ever spoken to this effect, but we had to keep our relationship hush-hush: he was married to Florence, who worked for Paramount. I had never met her and couldn't decide whether that made being with Victor easier or harder. A much bigger star at the time than I, Florence was often compared by those who knew her to a swan: pretty, but mean. Based on my own experiences with him, I'm sure that Victor gave her reasons; many men make better romantic fantasies than husbands, and Victor was the epitome of a romantic fantasy. On the few instances when I asked him about Florence, he gently steered us away from the topic, and I was never sure whether it was because he was embarrassed by his infidelity or just because he didn't want to speak ill of her. For my part, I confess, I let myself be steered.

He had difficult years ahead, but he ultimately earned a spot—as I knew he would—in the pantheon of early directors broadly regarded as great. *The Sky Pilot* would be the only time he directed me. The blossom of our romance pushed through the snow like a flower. I had been a schoolgirl up to that point, a blushing virgin.

A couple of nights later, with the snow still as high as the lowest rooftops, it was there, in my cold little room in the mountains, to Victor, that I lost my virginity.

I hate that phrase. I didn't lose it. I gave it willingly.

How comfortable in love we became, finishing each other's sentences.

All the cast and crew had grown more familiar during those snowed-in days. We played baseball in the main street and built snowmen galore, baffling the townsfolk as to why we weren't working. When it was too frigid to be outside, we amused ourselves with card games and put on vaudeville shows by night.

Because my unease about the weather had proven prophetic, Victor suggested that he and I put together a psychic routine. "Doreen's a perfect name for a star," he said as we were practicing, "but not for a seer. Thus, I dub thee Madame Zaza."

"Very well," I said. "No one will believe that *you're* anything but a rank charlatan unless we declare your expert qualification. Thus, I dub thee LaTour, Professor of Parapsychology."

During our debut, Victor tied a silk blindfold on me, then wandered through the audience of actors and townspeople, scooping up personal effects: coins and jewelry, watches and photographs, cigarette cases and fountain pens.

I then identified each object without seeing it, but with a great deal of theatrics.

"Madame Zaza," Victor demanded. "What is it that I am holding in my right hand?"

We had rehearsed a code by which he signaled to me the object. No, I won't say what it was.

"An engagement ring!" I'd reply. Or "A powder compact!" Or, or, or. Correct every time.

When an item came up for which we had no specific signal, I would press my hand to my forehead. "Dark vibrations are swirling through my mind," I'd say, and Victor would run through some patter during which he delivered clues only I could receive, until I was able to pronounce, "A theater ticket!" or what have you. The act became so popular we reprised it nightly.

We passed three glorious weeks in this manner.

Victor had learned that violets were my favorite flower, and some mornings I'd wake to them tucked into the boots I'd left in the hall. To this day I've never figured out where he found them.

Having discovered a mutual passion for codes and ciphers, we came up with a system to keep our biggest secret safe. A circle on the dressing room door meant *Eternal Love*. Three vertical lines meant *I Love You*. LND meant *Love Never Dies*.

For years in the future, whenever I needed to bring a smile to my face during trying times—of which there would be many—this was the period to which my heart returned.

At the end of the third week, Victor received a telegram from the producers declaring that they would no longer fund our idyll. We had to finish or immediately decamp. Victor hired a snow brigade from Truckee and the surrounding towns to complete the Herculean task of shoveling the heaps completely away, enabling us to shoot the last two summer sequences.

The preacher's turn to rescue me—Gwen—came in a pivotal scene of a stampede. I was to fall among the thundering animals, forcing the preacher to leap from his horse to turn them aside. The producers offered to provide doubles, but Bowers declined. "I'm so dead tired of being an ice-cream hero," he said. "I'd take any risk."

There's something hypnotic in the click of the camera; it makes you do things you'd be scared to death to try in real life. "Me too," I said. "I'm not afraid."

The crew dug a hole for my body with a barrier atop it, so my face could be seen but the steers couldn't crush me. I fared fine, ducking my head in when the hooves got too close, but my character was paralyzed; I spent the rest of the film trying to languish as luminously as Lillian Gish.

When at last we needed snow, there was none to be had. Indian summer set in, golden and balmy. Further word came up from the producers that they could not subsidize our sojourn in the mountains indefinitely.

Victor went into debt to have salt hauled in—so much salt, like sand at a beach—for the scenes in which we burned the sets. The film's villain set the church aflame, and the preacher fell, overcome by the smoke, and then, restored through prayer and the love (naturally) of the preacher himself, my character regained the ability to walk and dragged her love to safety. Much rejoicing!

But not between Victor and me. We had discussed every angle, and the only answer I could see was that our affair had to end when the picture did, before we headed back to LA. He was married. I was Catholic. There could be no future in it. If I became his mistress, I knew it would become public—as Mickey Neilan's affair with Blanche Sweet had—and my reputation would tarnish more than Victor's.

"Victor, you know that people in pictures receive more scrutiny than those in any other industry," I said, shrugging my naked shoulders in bed next to him. "Can you imagine if publishing were covered with the same breathless judgment? *Prominent Editor Divorced?*"

He laughed. "You're right," he said. "But it's not just that, is it?"

It wasn't. It was also my religious faith. And the fact that I felt bad for Victor's wife.

"It seems you don't just play a good girl, Eileen," he said when I had fully explained myself. "You *are* a good girl."

He gave me a book of Sara Teasdale's poems, which would have been romantic enough on its own, but the inscription inside read: *To a Flame, from a Fool of a Moth who has no regrets for his folly, to remind the Flame of some exquisite weeks, which to both of them will remain unforgettable.*

The reviews of *The Sky Pilot* raved and rhapsodized. The critics pronounced it a delicious hit, and my Gwen the sweetest flavor in the whole confection.

On February 1, 1921, Victor and I went to the Manhattan premiere, and afterward swore never to see each other again, with possible exceptions granted for public encounters in Hollywood groups, glances across crowded rooms. We said goodbye once and for all at Columbus Circle, beneath the statue.

For almost half a century we've done our best to adhere to that vow. We've remained friends.

You can't send anything terribly ribald in a telegram—the eyes of Western Union are always upon you—but we had ways to communicate. These included missives within our movies: Victor would include violets in his set decorations. I'd mouth to my leading men that *Love Never Dies*.

~

I suppose that there is no moral to this story, other than that it's wonderful to be a free young person sometimes. And that the consequences of what you do in youth can ripple out over the pond that is the rest of your life.

After I got back to Hollywood following the premiere, I ended up in the hospital with tonsillitis. Lying in that lumpy bed, exhausted from overwork, I almost welcomed the illness, my burning throat in miserable competition with my fractured heart.

Unbeknownst to me, as I was recuperating, my photograph was fluttering from studio to studio thanks to *The Sky Pilot*, and one of these landed on the desk of an upstart publicist at First National Pictures named Jack Flanagan.

~

In the summer of 1921, the Los Angeles Chamber of Commerce began placing ads in national newspapers to discourage the hopefuls who were then flooding the city. Don't Try to Break into the Movies Until You Have Obtained Full, Frank, and Dependable Information, they warned, above a photograph of thousands of people responding to a call for a handful of extras. In smaller print below, they added, Out of 100,000 persons who started at the bottom of the screen's ladder of fame, only five reached the top.

Which five? I wondered and worried, clinging with all fingers to some middle rung.

I was a success; I was not a star. I was a reliable but interchangeable piece of equipment that moved from production to production. I needed a home, the backing of a studio, somewhere to attach so I could work what I imagined would be my ultimate metamorphosis.

That summer I was working on a film called *The Wall Flower*, a part for which I felt almost too well suited: it called for a heroine "who must be pathetic at first but must later blossom into a thing of charm." Many an actress had passed on the role because the script explicitly said she couldn't be gorgeous, and I understood their reluctance, but seeking as I was to transform my image, I told them to count me in.

Midway through the shooting schedule for *The Wall Flower*, one day before I turned nineteen, Mickey Neilan rang me up. "Hey, birthday gal," he said, "whaddya say we gargle a couple a whiskeys this evening?"

"Geez, I don't know," I said, my working days and my social calendar having respectively gotten long and packed.

"I've got a man you want to meet," he said. "He's had his cap set at you for months, ever since he was putting your headshot in press packets for *The Sky Pilot*."

"Oh, Mickey, Middle America thinks I'm meeting too many men already." The beaux I'd seen on and off since I broke things off with Victor had become back-fence gossip around town and in the papers, as was the custom.

"Listen, Irish, this fellow's not just any man. He's Jack Flanagan, western press representative for all of First National. Now, he's gonna tell you that he's a nobody who earns his nickels banging an Underwood, but that's false modesty. He's got a flair for attention and knows how to get it."

Mickey always knew what to say to tempt me. "That's sweet of you," I said, "but I don't want to see anybody just to use them."

"What's your favorite adverb?"

"Excuse me?"

"Mine is *quickly*, so make up your mind. You'd be a nut to say no. This guy's a looker, Irish. He's already crazy about you, and he can only help your career."

"Well," I said, "it *is* my birthday."

That evening I put on a dress in gracklehead silk to bring out my eyes: one blue, one not.

"Your gentleman's here," said Granny, with a knock at my bedroom door. "He's a charmer. What's taking so long?"

What was taking so long was that I'd been staring in the mirror, about to apply perfume, when I was struck by a feeling of momentousness. It came to me that tonight I wasn't just doing Mickey a favor by rounding out his foursome; I was about to make a move that would change my course. It had to do with the man who was waiting outside, but it wasn't the *aha!* of my first encounter with Victor. It was more like the point in a story when the magic potion is drunk, the magic lamp is rubbed: the decision, innocuous in the moment, from which all else proceeds.

I couldn't explain it, so I gave myself a couple of puffs from the atomizer and opened the door. "Just getting spangled for the evening," I said, kissing Granny goodbye.

And there was Jack Flanagan, standing on the porch, over six feet tall and slim, with jet-black hair and cornflower eyes, dressed impeccably. His attention settled on me like I was the only thought in his head.

"Doreen O'Dare," he said with an easy grin. "Celluloid does you no justice."

I cackled at his obvious line, but next to him in the back seat, I felt aglow with anticipation. Mickey sat behind the wheel, Blanche at his side, but all I could concentrate on was Jack. Even with his long legs folded he sat tall. When he stopped talking, his profile was aquiline, his brow permanently caught in thought.

Jack had gotten his start making press books to send to theaters in the hinterlands, then worked his way to a managerial position.

"Good publicity conceals itself," he said. "Like good acting. If we could land you an extended multipicture contract at First National, getting you attention would be a cinch. People ought to be falling all over themselves to cover you."

I woke up every morning with the thought that I ought to be famous, but it never occurred to me that there might be another person alive who also woke up with the thought. Speechless, I blushed like a tomato in the sun.

"Publicity is a commercial commodity," he went on. "Publicity changes luxuries into necessities. I can make people feel that they *need* to see Doreen O'Dare's pictures."

"Told you he was timid, didn't I, Irish?" said Mickey, laughing from the front seat. "You might need to come on a bit stronger, chum. You're disappearing into the upholstery."

"Really, Jack," I said. "You needn't be such a shrinking violet. You're among friends here. And please, call me Eileen, not Doreen. That's my real name. It's what I want people in my real life to call me."

"Eileen," he said. "Eileen, Eileen."

I'd be crazy not to come that night, Mickey had said. Within ten minutes' time, I was crazy for Jack. The smell of him attacked my animal brain, a combination of a cologne that I'd learn was called Hammam Bouquet (sandalwood and civet) and whatever aura was his and his alone. I wanted to sit in his lap like a cat. To lick him.

And he, it seemed, was crazy for me. Or maybe just crazy.

Glamorous lunatics: you met them in Hollywood more often, I swear, than anywhere else. It was like these people could fly. Like the rules that we mortals assumed applied to everyone didn't apply to them and therefore might not apply to us either, if we decided to ignore them. Inventive, capricious, he reminded me of the fairies, utterly unconcerned with laws, from Prohibition to gravity. Jack wanted to tie a pair of golden wings to my back. What if I let him?

The Sunset Inn was the perfect spot to challenge propriety and physics. I don't know why it was called that; I'd heard it was because the party there didn't get started until sunset, and then it tried to double for the sun all night, ablaze with orange lights and fanfare from the orchestra. How I adored it! Dancing there a week earlier with my leading man in *The Wall Flower*, I'd won a cup. The press wrote it up, making it sound like he and I were much more than friends.

I knew they'd write up my being there with Jack Flanagan, too. I figured, let them.

Down the road toward Santa Monica a few miles from Hollywood, the Sunset had a kitchen that specialized in liquids more than solids. During Prohibition, a number of speakeasies sprang up overnight to manufacture whoopee at affordable prices, but it seemed that movie people, at least the ones I went around with, flouted the rules at our usual haunts.

"You can sure talk," I said to Jack once we'd grabbed a table. "But can you dance?"

Without waiting for his answer, I pulled him onto the floor. The Charleston was my specialty. Eight years later I'd dance it on-screen in *Why Be Good?*—they sped up the clip, yes, but those double-time legs were mine, all mine. Medical authorities worried on the pages of *Life* that such a vigorous step might be too much for delicate young ladies. They might have been right; I didn't know any delicate young ladies.

That night I stomped and flailed and flipped my hair, and to my surprise Jack kept right up. Usually tall men are not the best dancers, but he was the exception that proved the rule.

When the orchestra slid into a lovey-dovey number, we fit together hand in glove and glided. Mickey thumbsed-up from where he sat getting soused with Blanche.

Before Jack and I had made our slow circuit of the parquet, he'd confessed his intentions. "I've known you were the one for me since I saw your photograph," he said. "I stare at beauties in black and white all day. You outshine all the rest. No contest."

"Goodness," I said. "You *are* a publicity man."

"Eileen, I know you think I'm just a sheik on the make." He had a knack for using the latest slang while mocking himself for doing it. "But I'm serious. I want you to marry me."

I burst into laughter. He took it in stride.

"Think of it," he said. "It's all in our timing. My birthday is August 16: yesterday. I'm freshly twenty-seven. Here we are today, meeting. Your birthday is tomorrow. That's three days in a row to celebrate. Lucky number three. We've got to get engaged. Marry me, Eileen. I'll make you a happy woman and I'll make you a star."

His conviction disarmed me. He believed so fully in what he was saying: to himself, to me. No trace of deceit, but also no hint of naivete. That tension was attractive: all the enthusiasm of a boy starting a remote chapter of a movie star's fan club in some clean-cut place like a clover-filled Ohio pasture, mixed—when needed—with the unblinking tenacity of a boxer determined to pummel his opponent no matter the personal cost.

By then it was late, and the air was a vapor of expensive cigarette smoke and mingled perfume. Disoriented, I couldn't tell the real fragrance of the gardenias and jasmine blowing in from the artful imitations on the shoulders of the women twirling with their men.

"Call me up in the cold gray dawn and tell me that," I said.

The song changed again, and we began dancing too fast for the conversation to continue.

Mickey tapped us on the shoulder when it was after midnight.

I'd gone into the evening still heartbroken over Victor, thinking that Jack could be a sweet distraction, but as we drove home—his hand hot on the back of my neck, mine on his thigh—I realized that he was captivating, and that I liked being captivated.

~

The next morning, the LA air damp, fog swirling, the light pearly, the telephone rang.

"Remember me?" Jack's voice asked softly across the line.

"How could I forget?" I said, dazed and flattered.

"It's the cold gray dawn, and I still love you, Eileen," he said.

"Jack—"

"Come to dinner with me this evening."

"I'm having my birthday dinner with Granny Shaughnessy."

"Bring her with us!" he said. "Think about it this morning. Ring me after lunch."

As soon as I'd hung up, the doorbell rang: a bouquet of hydrangeas. A half hour after that, the first of what would turn out to be nineteen telegrams arrived. Assembled in order, they spun a fairy tale about the two of us and our destiny to unite: "happily ever after."

Pulling out all the stops for my birthday, I thought. As I came to know him better, I learned that he never left in any stops. His notes were no mere *Thinking of you*s. More like, *My heart is a treasure ship sailing your way with its richest love.*

Looking back from liberated, cynical 1968, it might seem improbable that such effusiveness could win me. But as corny as it is to admit, expressive extravagance still does the trick on this old lady. How reticent most men are, how miserly in their affections, how emotionally constipated—perhaps you can see the appeal.

The fact that Jack and I were in the same field would circumvent the starstruck callowness that made it hard for me to connect with most ordinary men. And while most men who *were* in the movie industry shared the domineering expectation that any actress they'd marry would abandon her dreams of success on camera and become their little woman behind closed doors, Jack would never demand that. Quite the contrary.

On the afternoon of my nineteenth birthday, imagining that Jack's fanciful *happily ever after* really could come true, I rang him back and agreed to dine.

At dinner, he was a tremendous hit with Granny, too. He spoke of his plans for his career and mine, of all that we could achieve if we were to become a team. "Any fool can see that Eileen glows like radium next to baser minerals," he said, speaking in poetry, as he often did. "We just need to get her in front of more fools!"

"Only an Irishman could be so creative," Granny said approvingly after he dropped us at home. Agnes, finding another vase for still more of Jack's flowers, told me to slow down, which naturally made me want to go that much faster.

Chapter 6

THE DINING ROOM

Gladys has run out of tape. She disappears down the corridor in search of a replacement as I sit in silence beside my castle. A glint of motion draws my eye back to the Drawing Room, and I can tell that the Fairy Princess has flitted through by inhaling the trail of her amber perfume.

Had she permitted me to see her face, I know I wouldn't have glimpsed one more wrinkle there than when I'd first laid eyes upon her. The castle and its population of fairies remain ageless.

I, however, do not. Since Gordon, my third and most husbandly husband, died four years ago, anxieties have perched in my brain. Loneliness is once more a dirty bird I have to shoo away. I'll grant that it *is* better to have loved and lost, but I'd still rather just have loved and loved. Now I'm old. I look good for my age, but let's be frank: that's not good enough for most men, too insecure to take on a lady their own equal in years.

Gladys returns, threads the new spool onto the take-up reel. Noises from the cafeteria waft across the basement; it's nearly lunchtime, and the school groups must be filing in for their portions of meat loaf and mashed potatoes.

"Should we head into the Dining Room, too?" asks Gladys, motioning to the Fairy Castle. "That semicircular table makes it look Arthurian."

One of the things I love the most about the Camelot story is that it's suffused with melancholy: every moment of romance and adventure is sweetened by our knowledge that it cannot last.

"Each of those five tapestries on the walls," I say, "has twenty-five hundred stitches per square inch, all done in a single thread of silk. We commissioned them from the studio of a needlepoint artist who fled Vienna before World War II. Only two of her craftswomen could manage such fine embroidery, and it took months upon months. Anything worthwhile requires more patience than you'd like."

My enthusiasm for acting consisted of joy cut with impatience—a fizz of pleasure at doing some of what I knew myself capable, plus an eagerness for the chance to do even more. My ambition wasn't singular; in Hollywood, desire was the air we breathed. On set, half the property boys longed to be actors. "There's no place for sluggards in this house," my father used to say when he was trying to earn a buck. I'm not sure who he was talking to; himself, maybe. I was never a sluggard.

Neither was Jack Flanagan. A one-two punch of romance and finance, he kept me perpetually swept off my feet. I'll never forget dragging myself home after a grind of a Tuesday, nothing to look forward to, and finding Agnes waiting with an announcement. "Your gentleman's here, Eileen," she said, with that air of dyspepsia that never quite left her. "Unannounced."

Jack and I had made no date, but there he stood in the front parlor, his strapping back turned to me, fiddling with the hurricane lamp. I flung myself melodramatically upon the davenport, a hand to my forehead. "I cannot go on!" I lamented. "Five studio visits today, and all I have in hand is five insincere *we'll be in touch*-es."

"Come, now, darling," he said, laughing, gathering me into his arms. "It can't be as bad as all that."

"Why do I remain less known than my inferiors?" I said, not really meaning it, fishing for a buck-up. "Why am I Doreen the workhorse, not Doreen the star? Maybe I should throw in the towel!"

"Delayed success isn't failure," he said, and kissed me. "Even failing isn't failure. Only not trying is failure. You work harder than anyone I know—"

"Besides yourself, you mean."

He kissed me again. "Well," he said, "I *have* been working pretty hard on something. How'd you like a five-picture deal with First National?"

I sat up, horsehair upholstery tickling my elbows, the only thing reminding me that the moment was real. "You're kidding," I said.

"I'd never kid about something like this," he said, his hand on his chest. "And that's just to start. If you'll agree, they'd like you to come in at nine tomorrow to sign the paperwork."

"If?" I laughed. "If! I'd drive back out tonight if anybody would be there."

"I thought instead I could take you to dinner to celebrate."

"We'll toast to the gleam of dreams coming true!" I cried.

"What's all the commotion?" asked Agnes, peering around the doorframe.

Jack explained.

"That's nice," she said. "I wish you would have told me sooner, though, about not dining with us. I wouldn't have gone to the trouble of setting you a place."

I refused to allow Agnes to rain on the blaze in my heart. Granny, when I told her, would understand. For years I'd been passed around like a hot potato—hot because no one would keep me, potato because Irish—but in one swoop Jack had ended that game. No more transfers from hand to grubby hand.

The reason why we're told so often that money doesn't buy happiness is that it's a lot of bunk. When you've got a pile of cash in the bank, you worry less, plain and simple. You'll have other problems to solve, sure, but solving them's bound to be easier if you're not scrimping at the same time. When it comes to emotional health, money's like a vitamin. The money that Jack got out of First National was stunning. I continued to save: I wanted to put away enough to buy a house—two houses, actually, to get my family and myself under separate roofs—and enough to keep Granny comfortable until the end of her days.

No less stunning was the reassuring feeling of my name being attached to a string of projects. Even their titles—*Come on Over* was one, *Broken Chains* another—sounded like invitations to and declarations of freedom. No more hustling from door to studio door, no more fear of being out on my rear once a picture wrapped.

Perhaps most stunning of all was the fact that Jack's negotiation of my First National contract was something he did during breaks from his other projects, the most notable of which was his idea for the WAMPAS Baby Stars and their attendant Frolic.

Though their name sounds like the onomatopoetic rendering of comic book violence, the WAMPAS Frolics were the forerunner of the Academy Awards. The goofy acronym stood for the Western Association of Motion Picture Advertisers; Jack's scheme was to use their auspices to showcase actresses who were just shy of bursting across the threshold of fame. I, needless to say, was to be one of these.

The Frolic would present starlets like debutantes at the brand-new Ambassador Hotel on Wilshire. There were thirteen of us in that first class. "Like the Last Supper," I said to Jack.

I was nervous at putting myself on display that way. Acting was one thing—I always knew what to do—but banquet dances were quite another.

"Darling, you'll be marvelous," he said, unwrapping the gown he'd bought me for the event, making suggestions for how to do my hair.

Our preparation for the Frolic felt like *The Wall Flower* at a hundred frames per second: a flash, a flurry, and I was transformed.

As it turned out, Jack was right: the first Frolic was nothing to be afraid of, just a chance to stand up, say some grateful words, and be clapped at when my name was called. And the Frolic did become an enduring to-do, so my membership in that first class had a cachet that only grew, especially when various cohorts went on to prove that WAMPAS's faith in them had not been misplaced. Clara Bow, God bless her, was a Baby Star in 1924; Mary Astor and Joan Crawford in 1926.

The ceremony was held in the indiscriminately tropical Cocoanut Grove nightclub inside the Ambassador. After the official hubbub of the Frolic and the clearing away of dinner plates, we Baby Stars were expected to frolic—lowercase and literally—on the dance floor, the better to be appreciated by the press corps. I wanted to dance with Jack amid the fake palm trees—made of papier-mâché and fronds from some Oxnard beach, they'd previously imparted oriental atmosphere to the set of Valentino's *The Sheik*—but he was across the room hobnobbing. Drink in hand beside a real waterfall and beneath a trompe-l'oeil Hawaiian moon, he stood chatting with other executives.

The Mediterranean-blue ceiling twinkled. Stuffed monkeys blinked from tree trunks, their amber eyes electrified. I was staring up at one of the Moroccan chandeliers of pierced metal, trying to look dreamy, when a sharp voice behind me said, "Got time for a word with *Photoplay*, Doreen?"

I turned to face the appraising gaze of the Mother Confessor of Hollywood, a girl reporter well known for holding her own among the hard-boiled, hard-living newspapermen.

"Adela Rogers St. Johns, unless I'm mistaken?" I said. "I'm glad to meet you, but I'm afraid I haven't got a sob story for your tearstained pages."

"Familiar with my work, I see." She took out a gold cigarette case and lit up. "I'd offer you one, but something tells me you don't indulge."

"I don't," I said, feeling suddenly prudish.

Uncle Walter had heard of her all the way in Chicago, and he had warned me never to get on her bad side. "There are reporters who break the mold," he'd told me. "She's not one of those, because there was no mold. She made her own." I gorged on her celebrity profiles and admired from my insider's perspective how cleverly they were designed to throw tidbits to the rapacious public while withholding enough to keep their subjects grateful.

She exhaled a long, precise plume at the nearest stuffed monkey before speaking again. "Doreen O'Dare," she crowed. "The bonny Baby Star with the sweetness of an Irish rose, whose comic roles pack the punch of a shillelagh. Adornment of the arm of that other exponent of the old sod, Jack Flanagan, determined to make her the foremost star of First National."

"You seem to know a lot about me."

"I do," she said, lowering her voice to a normal register. "That's my job. But that was all kid stuff, what I just said. I could have got it just by walking into the room with my eyes open. Listen, I'm pals with Mickey Neilan, who thinks the moon and stars of you. Says you're on your way up, and I don't doubt it. I figured we ought to know each other. If our conversation gives your career a kick and me another byline, then so much the better."

"Possibly," I said, wary. I talked to reporters often enough, but her theatrical flair and her looseness with the truth put her in a separate class.

"I've got your Granny, and your striving, and your verve for earning money," she said. "Mickey gave me all that. I know your rep for being the goodest of the good girls. But now that I'm looking at you, I'm amazed at how wholly wholesome you really are. You're not just playing it. I see that around town, sure, but I see it at the train station, at the calls for extras. By the time those fresh-faced gals have been here for five years, if they last that long, most of 'em have made at least one trip to Tijuana for medical care."

I would spend much of the rest of the evening recalling these words, analyzing them, and in time I would also understand them as entirely representative of Adela, the verbal equivalent of a declaration of intent. The staccato list that hinted at greater knowledge than she possessed, the profligacy of her language, the apparent candor demonstrating that she was someone whom people told secrets to (*medical care* meant abortions, of course)—it was a bravura performance. I resolved to appreciate it without being taken in.

I also wondered if I could play at her game. I knew a few things about her, too. "I was sad to hear of your father's recent passing." Earl Rogers had been a legendary trial lawyer in LA, as skilled a performer as any of us in front of the camera. "I thought of him during Roscoe Arbuckle's trials, of how he might have handled the defense differently. But I've noticed that you've been fairly quiet on the subject of the trials. Am I mistaken?"

"You're not," she said, "and that's very perceptive. I like it when a starlet takes the time to read deeper into the papers than her own notices. The truth is that I haven't been writing about Fatty because Fatty is guilty of nothing besides being fat, and famous, and in the wrong place at the wrong time. That's not an opinion that sells papers, and I'm not going to pretend to have a different one. Not when I have so many other things to write about. You, for instance."

"I'm flattered," I said, "but I fail to see what could possibly interest you about me."

"I'm worried for you, kid. You know about Jack, right?"

That this question caught me off guard strongly suggested that I did not, in fact, know about Jack. If this was a desperate ploy on her part to shake me up, it was an especially graceless one, and she didn't seem the graceless type.

I kept my face placid, void of concern. "I know that he loves me," I said.

"Sure, sure." She placed her cigarette butt into an ashtray with a manicured hand. "But I mean about his drinking."

Sometimes being an actress pays unexpected benefits, and I was quick on my feet that night. "J-Jack *drinks?*" I said, feigning horror. "But isn't that—*against the law?*"

Laughter rocked Adela back on her heels.

Everyone drank a lot. Prohibition had made it chic. The secretaries could get any kind of booze sent anywhere. Gangsters emulated movie stars in their languor and luxury. Our reputation for licentiousness and orgies was burgeoning, partly based on the tales that the Adelas of the press drummed up.

"*Touché*, Doreen," she said. "Which of us sounds like the moralizer now?" She stepped closer, her voice softening. "My dad drank, too, if it makes you feel any better. He was drinking in his bed on the day he died."

"It doesn't make me feel better, and I'm sorry to hear it," I said, "but I really don't think that Jack's in any danger. Though I do appreciate your concern. Sincerely."

Despite my efforts, I had begun to like her. I could see why she had the reputation of being Hearst's favorite reporter—prolific and profitable, every story a dilly—and also why many people in Hollywood considered her a friend, even as she trained the public to slaver for the next luscious rumor. There was a pleasure in being invited to reveal oneself to someone willing to offer confidences about her own life. Maybe this was a trick, too, but I admired tricks.

"I can tell tonight's not the best night for an interview," said Adela, smiling. "You're in a sparring mood, and I'm not, and that's very unusual for at least one of us. But let's make a plan for when your next picture comes out."

"All right," I said, bemused, curious about how an on-the-record conversation might go. "Let's."

"For now, bottom line: I want to help you, kid," she said, tucking her card into my palm. "Call me up if I can give you a boost with anything at all."

"I will," I said, and hoped I would. She reminded me of an on-screen character herself, a brassy woman outplaying her fellows at their own rigged game.

"Meanwhile, watch out for snoops and busybodies!" she said, excluding herself from their company before stalking off to pounce upon another Baby Star.

～

In subsequent weeks, I thought about telling Jack what Adela had said, then thought better of it. Not wanting, I suppose, to consider her implication that Jack was a lit fuse, that I should beware of his going off.

In her reporting on the Frolic, she'd picked me out for particular notice. Of them all, I found the most honest enthusiasm, the most confident praise and prediction behind Doreen O'Dare. Jack encouraged me to befriend her.

Prior to Jack, I had a knack for making everyone fall—to borrow a phrase from the headline writers—a little bit in love. But no one fell fully, not even Victor. That's why Jack came to mean so much. Total love, brisk and consuming, magnetized by fate. "How I hate to leave off. We've only begun!" he'd said at the end of our first solo date, which was funny, because he never left off.

The phrase *hot pursuit* was invented for Jack's courting. His face was a lullaby that kept me awake. Eyes with lashes that a woman would die for.

I was working so hard that summer, starting one picture as another wrapped, that I couldn't get away much. Jack knew that I longed to travel, so he took me to Venice Beach for a ride around the canals, in an actual gondola steered by an Italian gondolier. Within a few years the City of Los Angeles would annex Venice, demolishing the attractions and filling in most of the waterways to make streets, but in 1922 it was still magical, with the Ship Café, the miniature railway, and the amusement piers.

We checked into the St. Mark's Hotel on Windward Avenue for trysts. The afternoon we first went to bed together, I bodily understood the phrase "to have a crush on." The look on his face above me in bed crushed me. I was crushed. I disintegrated. I forgot who I was. It was bliss.

August was making its maneuvers when Jack and I got engaged, clouds of spun sugar and golden shapes of sunset contorting themselves in the sky. He proposed on my birthday, in a voluptuous California dusk, waverings of heat hovering off the hills.

I said yes, and put on the ring. The lampposts practically bowed as we passed.

Too busy to set a date, we said we'd wed by my next birthday: August 19, 1923.

He sent notice of our engagement to all the papers. "They're going to write about it when they find out, no matter what we do," he said. "This way they'll all have it at once. Otherwise, if one reporter gets a scoop out of it, the rest might hold it against us." Any deal he touted got nattered up and down the town; why should our engagement be any different?

The kind of help that Jack gave me happened often in Hollywood, in cases when each half of a couple worked in a different corner of the industry. But the versions of the story that really seemed to fascinate people were those in which—as in the distorted story of my dear Marion Davies and her W. R. Hearst—the man occupied the position of command, the woman the clay in his sculptor's hands.

Jack brought the reviews of my First National pictures over to show the family; they were all raves.

After he left, Granny Shaughnessy reviewed him. "He's what we'd call a man sure of his welcome," she said. "He reminds me of your grandfather. Walking into the room expecting everybody to be happy to see him. It's lucky for him that we are."

∽

The first time when Jack began to wear out his welcome came in the late spring of 1923.

I was wrapping up a stinker of a western with me as a mountain maiden in godawful buckskin who throws herself at a prospector. One drawback to my multipicture contract was that some dreck inevitably slithered in with the gold.

I was back in Hollywood, on break from a shoot at Convict Lake; Jack and I had a date, but he didn't show. I waited all evening, calling everyone who might have a clue as to his whereabouts.

Mickey finally rang me back around midnight. "I can tell you he's safe, but that's all I can say." His voice sounded strained over the line.

"Come on, Mickey," I begged. "Tell me where he's at so I can go to him."

"Listen, Irish, I feel like a heel, but I promised him. He's going to come see you as soon as he's able. I have to leave this between you two, I'm afraid."

Two horrible days later, Jack knocked on the door of the family bungalow, looking undead as a movie ghoul in the afternoon sun: eyes shot with blood, suit torn, cheeks hollow.

"Oh Lord," said Granny, taking one look. "He's been on a spree."

"I need to talk to Eileen," he muttered. His breath reeked of whiskey; I could smell it from inside.

"No doubt you do," she said. "But you go home now. Straighten yourself up. She knows you're not dead, and the rest will wait. Come back when you're presentable."

Hangdog, he slunk off the porch, back to the Athletic Club, where he and many other young men on the rise in the industry kept their lodgings.

When he came back hours later, after dinner, showered and shaved, dressed up and dashing, Agnes didn't want to let him see me. Didn't want us to remain engaged.

As he sat on the sofa in the front parlor waiting, she whispered in the hallway. "Marrying a man means marrying his faults. Being a drunkard is an awfully big fault to have."

"This is the first time this has happened, Mother," I said. "Let me at least speak to him."

"Let the girl go in, Agnes," said Granny. "She's old enough to do this her own way."

I realized, with a jolt of shock that settled into a dull mist of anger, that Agnes was enjoying this. She had waited in Tampa for months, expecting me to humble myself and heed the call of home, and when I wouldn't, she had moved the home to California: an admission of defeat. Now victory flickered into view again, the sour victory of frustrated hopes and diminished expectations that she for some reason relished. My mother never ceased her unspoken demand to be admired for her temperate conduct and milquetoast taste; Granny, on the other hand, had taught me never to give in to the gruesome imperatives of day-to-day life. I did not like the commonplace. When he was sober, Jack was extraordinary. I can see now that I believed I was, too—that like a princess in a fairy tale, my love could transform him.

Agnes said nothing, but shut the door to the parlor behind me. I put on a record to thwart eavesdropping—Bessie Smith's "Baby, Won't You Please Come Home"—before turning to meet Jack's abashed eyes.

"Eileen, I'm so sorry," he began. "I've been the worst cad imaginable. I'd give you flowers by the acre to make it up to you if I could."

"I don't want a bouquet," I said. "I want you to promise you'll never do this again. I was out of my mind with worry. What happened?"

He looked away. Evenings get cooler than you'd think in LA; a fire was crackling in the fireplace, and Jack stabbed at a log with the poker as I tried to keep my frustration off my face.

"I haven't any answer I can give you," he said.

I have tried in vain nevermore to call your name, sang Bessie Smith.

"Surely you can," I said, wanting to understand, and to be reassured.

"I suppose," he said, staring at his hands, no longer trembling, "it's that our marriage being so many months away feels too far off to stand. I suppose it's weakness. Insecurity. Uncertainty that you love me."

I was appalled at that thought, as I was meant to be. I tried to take his hand. "Don't be absurd! Of course I love you."

He drew away, bumping the end table, lurching a scratch from the phonograph.

Then he pulled the poker from the fire, jerked his sleeve up, and seared the skin of his forearm. I strangled a scream. He collapsed to the floor.

My moment of terror settled into a more pervasive dread, and I calmed myself down. Prior to that night I had been able to maintain an instinctive degree of critical distance with Jack, but as the awful smell of his burnt arm dissipated, I realized I would need to modulate my reactions in order to keep him—and maybe myself—safe.

Slowly, but with force, I took the poker from his hand and put it out of reach.

"That," he said, choking, tears in his eyes, "is to remind me, every time I look at this scar, how close I came to losing the only thing that matters in my life."

"Jack, my God," I said, on my feet above him. "That was in no way necessary. I forgive you. I'd never leave you. Just please take care of yourself, and don't do it again."

He stood and embraced me, kissing the top of my head. I told him to go home and get some rest. He apologized again, thanked me, and slipped down the front walk, arm atilt from his body like a bird's broken wing.

I told myself that somehow his betraying me for drink alone was less foreboding than if there'd been other women, too. (Had there been, Adela would have made it known.) Mad though his love for me apparently could be, at least it was exclusive.

In the corner of the yard as he vanished from view, an iridescent flash grasped my eye, and I hoped it might be the Fairy Princess to offer reassurance or counsel, but it was only the green gleam of a humming-bird's tail.

Back inside, I simply told Mother and Granny that we had worked it out. What else could I say? I had a sudden recollection of a time in my life when I told Granny everything; how long ago had that been? Before Victor, I supposed. Jack's behavior tonight seemed to hail from another world; nothing in my prior life had prepared me for it, but I felt strongly that there were precedents in Granny's stories. I just had no way to ask her.

I told them that I was exhausted—true—and stepping out for a stroll to clear my head before bed—a lie.

At a phone booth at the corner of Pico and Alvarado, I did something that I'd been looking forward to doing, though not under these circumstances. I dialed up Adela Rogers St. Johns.

"Doreen!" she said. "To what do I owe this unexpected pleasure?"

Mother Confessor was no empty nickname: I divulged all. "I'm not telling you this for a story, Lord knows," I explained. "But apart from you, I won't share it with any living soul whom I suspect of ever having so much as touched a typewriter. I really believe, I *have* to believe, that this will amount to no more than an unhappy memory that Jack and I will try to laugh off in time. If, God forbid, it turns into something else, then you'll have it all to yourself."

"Well, you're not dumb, it seems. Why me, sister? I know I'm not the only friend you've got."

"Three reasons. One, you knew about Jack and the bottle before I did, so you're already on the scent. Two, sure, I've got plenty of friends, but I've got the phone number of only one troll who camps under the bridge that connects the stars to the public. That's you, by the way."

"Flattery will get you nowhere. Three?"

"Three, because you told me to call if I need a boost, Adela, and I need one. Jack and I are supposed to go to a dinner at Pickfair tomorrow night, and it will be attended by every person in this town who's more famous than me, but he's in no condition to be seen, let alone to be in the presence of that much booze. I don't know what to do."

Pickfair was the portmanteau that the world had adopted for Mary Pickford and Douglas Fairbanks after they each left their spouses for one another. Good sports, they'd also bestowed the name on the lavish lair they'd built on eighteen Beverly Hills acres. It was the Vatican of Hollywood, but heaps more fun.

"Doreen, you're seeing problems where there aren't any," she said. "A woman minus her man isn't zero, she's one. You go to Pickfair alone, and you have yourself a grand time."

"What do I tell them about Jack?"

"Who the hell says you have to tell them anything? If anyone asks, make something up. He's indisposed, whatever. People catch colds. It's fine to let him lift you up, but don't let him hold you back. It's not even a betrayal—it'll be better for him in the long run, too."

The confidence that I'd worked up before dialing was trickling away; my hands were starting to shake. "What if people already know?" I said. "He's been on a bender for three days or more. I don't know where he's been, what he's done, who he's done it with, and he probably doesn't remember himself."

"That's even more of a reason to show up. Make yourself harder to chin-wag about. Listen, if they know, then they know. So what? That bell is rung. What would you have them say? 'Flanagan went on a wild toot, and Doreen's too ashamed to show her face'? Or, 'Doreen was there, all right, and looked like she'd burst into tears at the drop of a hat'? No. Instead, try 'Yes, Doreen was there, and she seemed perfectly poised; I hope she can get that Jack sorted out.' That's weak gossip— which is to say perfect for you. Sleep on it, kid. I'll see you there."

"You're going, too?"

"You bet your multipicture contract I'm going. And if you're not there, I'll never let you hear the end of it."

She rang off before I could protest, or thank her.

I took the walk that I'd lied about taking, and the cool air and Adela's advice finally calmed me down. I went to bed still shaken, but convinced that Jack's mistake would not be repeated and that I'd be fine on my own while he got himself composed.

Although this was years before I had the idea for my Fairy Castle, I was still avidly collecting miniatures whenever my grueling schedule allowed. My costars knew about Eileen's Miscellany, and nary a wrap party passed without a rain of tiny presents. I was mad about anything in Dutch filigree silver: birdcages and candlesticks, helmet-shaped creamers and rat-tail spoons. Little coats of arms and kettles engraved with their makers' initials, their full names unknown. Tongs in a tea set for sugar cubes as small as snowflakes. I also liked tin and pewter, brass and copper. Little cookie cutters in the shapes of birds and flowers, the smallest waffle iron ever made of actual iron. Tankards from which the fairies imbibed their beer.

The opulence of Pickfair reminded me of my collection, except that it was life-size.

I drove myself there in one of Hollywood's first Fords, trying to feel independent. I had allowed a quote in an advertisement that said as much be attributed to me, and in exchange I received the vehicle.

Handing my keys to the valet, I put Jack out of my mind: a necessity if I were to function.

In the foyer, Doug Fairbanks himself was greeting arrivals, showing off with handsprings, reminding me that his famous performance as Zorro barely constituted acting. I still got agog in situations like this— as if I'd broken through the drab horizon to the angels hiding behind.

Adulthood and maturity are not synonymous. I grew up quickly, but plenty of people in Hollywood never did, no matter their age. Though a fun buccaneer, Doug would prove unwilling to be a constant husband. Fortunately, he and Mary were then still in their honeymoon phase.

Mary led me into the dining room. Despite her vivacious gaze, it was hard to maintain eye contact in the bounty of the surroundings: oriental rugs, embossed place cards, silk napkins. She had a soft and buttery speaking voice, not that anyone would know from her pictures.

Adela was there, as promised. Marion Davies, too, in the company of her bulldog, Buddy. She favored wearing slacks and did it before Dietrich; kneeling near the sideboard, she fed Buddy a tidbit.

Longing looks across lavish rooms happen in real life as well as the movies. There, by the floor-to-ceiling windows, brocade curtains closed against any curiosity-seekers lurking in the California night, stood Victor Marquis.

I wanted to go up to him, but I felt suddenly woozy and there were too many people. He winked at me in that old way that I liked and I winked back twice, first with my brown eye, then with the blue, and as he laughed, I turned away.

Lillian Gish stood in a mirrored mock Tudor niche, casting herself as a perfect sphinx, speaking scarcely a word all evening. She often left early for her beauty sleep, and without apology for doing so, no matter how expensive the party. Even when present, she gave the impression of seclusion. If only I could have held myself apart more like her!

But I couldn't. I wanted to be loved. Wanted marriage, and one day, children. I wanted it with Jack.

A servant rang a chime, and we sat, menus atop the plates at each spot. Braised Duck Cumberland, Lobster Americaine, and Scalloped Brussels Sprouts! Cream of Fresh Spinach Florentine! Herb-Buttered Beets! A very arriviste menu, I can now see. Back then we didn't know better, and wouldn't have cared. Most of us had grown up middle-class at best.

All the faces around the table I recognized, save for one under a nimbus of hennaed hair, with cupid's-bow lips and headlamp eyes that you felt like you were still staring into even after you'd looked away.

"Doreen O'Dare, Clara Bow," said Adela. "Clara Bow, Doreen O'Dare."

"I haven't had the pleasure," I said, offering a hand.

"Yeah, I just got out here," she honked in a Brooklyn accent. "Won one ah them beauty contests, and away I went. With nothin' to my name, I had nothin' to lose."

Dinner came out. No one said grace, so I said it in my head. At Pickfair, *lifted palms* meant trees, not hands: exotic plants hoisted by cranes from elsewhere to stud the grounds, their curved trunks putting quotation marks around the beauty already present, emphasizing California's Edenic qualities, the tales it liked to tell itself about itself. Movie magic and reality juxtaposed: the whole estate felt like a set, and those whom you met seemed less like strangers than extras, reel after reel of good-looking people doing good-looking things. Clara

Bow, I decided, was among the best-looking, her radiance comprised of comeliness plus flat-out sex. The neckline of her dress plunged like the deepest arroyo in the hills, and the men at the table had a hard time remembering to look up at her face.

"It's true," Adela said, eyeing her significantly, reading my mind. "Rags to flashier rags, not quite yet to riches."

Clara's accent and her tawdry attire made some of the guests snobbish, but I wanted to like her. I almost pitied her—she was seventeen, and acted younger—so I felt no sense of threat, or rivalry. Not at first.

"I didn't wanna become my ma, cleaning somebody else's house," she said, megaphone-loud. "Or be a typist, getting pawed by my filthy boss."

I felt awkward, sympathizing with what she said but wincing at how she said it. I had come west seeking magic, but the determination to avoid both the demeaning service that Granny had endured and my mother's martyrdom by household drudgery had been a factor, too. "Picture work can have its own monotony, don't you think?" I said. "I mean, it's not being a laundry girl, but—"

"I noticed!" Clara proclaimed. "But laundry girls got better pay." She giggled insinuatingly, though it was impossible to tell what she thought she was insinuating. "Don't listen to me, though. I got no sense when it comes to cents. What do you expect? I'm an actress!"

This got a laugh, mostly from the men, but her flippancy irked me. Most people I'd known—starting with my dad—had been bad with money. Lack of financial savvy was scarcely an exclusively actorly failing, and it didn't seem cute to laugh about. But Clara had grown up even poorer than I, so maybe she had her reasons, and not everyone had a Granny Shaughnessy. Still, one didn't need to be a CPA to see the wisdom in earning more than you spent.

As she shimmied at women and men alike, I wondered—more abstractly than I might have, in retrospect—where her career would end her up. The characters in fairy tales, I thought, often had a cardinal virtue and a cardinal defect. Clara's former was her sex appeal, and her latter was—her sex appeal? I supposed my virtue and defect might also be identical: ceaseless ambition fueled by a desire for security. If only Jack had been there; I would have liked to hear what he made of Clara.

As it was, I settled for Adela.

"How terrific to be that young and ignorant," she said as I was driving her home. "Nothing yet to hold you back."

Adela's demeanor was the product of pleasing oppositions: stylish clothes over a masculine attitude, one she was fully aware of and that she attributed—she later told me—to the fact that she'd been raised entirely by her father after her mother ran off. He'd introduced her to the sporting types she was famed for chronicling, including a boxer she claimed to have received her last spanking for kissing.

"Well," I said, trying to be generous, "I hope for Clara's sake that she steers clear of the reefs in these waters."

"Oh, Clara Bow's career will be a barn burner, you mark my words. She has a trashiness that the boys are going to go gaga over. Even done up, she speaks to the joys of the gutter. A shining twenty-four-karat slut."

"Adela!" I said, shocked, and also ashamed that I'd been thinking the same word. "Where did you learn to talk that way?"

"I've got to get it out of my system now, kid," she said. "Hearst won't let me write it in a family paper."

"The poor girl," I said, confused by the compassion mixed with annoyance that I felt toward Clara. "My dad didn't love me enough either, but good God, it didn't turn me into an alley cat. That statement is off the record, Adela. Off, off, off."

She guffawed like a crow in a treetop. "Oh, when the debutante gloves come off, Doreen! I cannot get enough of it. There's nothing more eviscerating than a proper woman saying out loud what she's secretly been thinking."

A bundle of facts cut and shuffled and tossed in the air for a game of fifty-two pickup: that was how the biographical profiles of up-and-coming stars read. The fan mags reported egotistical sots as "regular fellas," California dudes as authentic cowpunchers. They spun Horatio Alger tales, announcing how some star came from a ramshackle shack in Bumblesburg, Kansas, or some other jerkwater town, when in fact he'd arrived in LA with a yacht and a manservant. There was no point in tearing down new arrivals; better to hoist them upright upon feet of clay, then topple them later. Conceding to convention, Adela did the same when she wrote up Clara.

I enjoyed the evenings at Pickfair because you got to meet the real people. Not that the stories they told about themselves were always true either.

Clara was one of the realest people I had yet met. There was something to learn there.

~

Although my formal education—that phrase makes me picture a diploma in a top hat and tails—stopped after the eighth grade, after Granny and I moved to Hollywood I dutifully did all the lessons that my mother had hired a home tutorial service to mail me. While I was often required to act like a bubblehead on film, I loved to read. Everything I could get my hands on, from Russian realists to recipes—you name it.

My job was selling emotional merchandise, and my product was me: my body, my affect. Work, work, work! I needed to put something in to replace what I was putting out. Books lined my walls like an added layer of bricks buttressing the structure. Fortifications. A fortress.

Scott Fitzgerald's *Flappers and Philosophers* set me to philosophizing. What was the feminine ideal of any given society? America had been mad for virgins, which made stars of my friends Mary and Lillian. Then it transferred its voyeuristic attention to vamps. The former type stood on one side of the dividing line between virtue and vice, the latter stood on the other—but the line never moved.

Now, for a number of reasons—resentment over Prohibition, increased mobility thanks to the automobile, who knows what else—the nation's psychological disposition seemed to be tilting toward permissiveness and qualified acceptance of the so-called *new woman,* known more casually as the flapper: fashionable, independent, with a libertine streak. Even the frequent denunciations one heard of such women amounted to an acknowledgment that they were where the energy was, that they were the team holding the ball.

Hollywood, let's be frank, generally makes a hash of great books, but it can work wonders with weaker material. The book that threw my mind wide open when it came to the potential of the flapper wasn't anything by Fitzgerald but rather some slinky junk. *Flaming Youth* was published in January 1923; it took me until summer to get to it, but once I started I devoured it, certain that it contained the role that could change my life.

The muckraking journalist Samuel Hopkins Adams had written it, but he'd published it under "Warner Fabian," for the book's success was a *succès de scandale*. Sexy-sentimental trash meant for easy inhaling, the plot was packed with red-hot kisses and reckless petting. Most of the women in it were more emancipated than was typically portrayed, none more so than Pat, the youngest daughter of the central Fentriss family. Her seductiveness—and susceptibility to seduction—drove the narrative; on her journey from innocence to experience, she wasn't shy about grabbing the wheel.

I wasn't terribly much like Pat, but I understood her. I was also sure I could play her with more humanity than Fabian had allowed in his portrait of a steamy, debauched creature, rendered with fascinated contempt. Which is not to say that a picture would omit the novel's dizzy titillation: not on your life. The scene of partygoers swimming au naturel, I could tell, would singe the screen.

I had pulled *Flaming Youth* from my nightstand pile during a period of frustration that had been shading toward despair. Despite his superhuman efforts, it was increasingly uncertain that even Jack—back on the wagon, thank the fairies—would be able to loft me to the next tier. Some days I feared I'd never be free of gaga-baby roles, of directors demanding that *Daddy, what is beer?* look. I was also getting fidgety about putting so much of my future in his hands, or anyone's hands but my own. I was ready to throw switches and push buttons.

Granny Shaughnessy told me not to get discouraged, that it was often the last key that opened the lock. Pat Fentriss was that key, I was sure of it. To play her, I'd have to make sure that sex was obviously on my mind, even if we couldn't put the sex on-screen. I'd never given that performance before. I wasn't sure that anyone had—at least not in the way that the story required. There had been plenty of vamps, but vamps wanted power; sex was a means to an end. In *Flaming Youth*, I'd have to show what female desire looked and felt like.

I convinced First National to buy the rights, but they didn't want to give me the part: I was too sweet. I labored to explain that that was the point: Pat wasn't depraved, she was a perfectly normal girl of the modern era, and *Flaming Youth*'s depiction of the desires of perfectly normal girls was exactly what had made it a scandal. I did the screen test, but neither Jack nor I could get a straight answer. One producer suggested that I might be too much of an Old World Irish maiden to play the role. "Why is this town so chock-full of fools?" I wailed to Jack. "Is it just our industry, or is it everyone? Is the water contaminated?"

My impatience reached a hectic pitch. I had to do something real, and drastic.

Makeover as plot device: trite, I know. But that was the only playable card in my deck, so that's what I did. I knew that if I cut my hair, I could become Pat.

I would give myself a bob.

It's hard to explain today what a big deal it was, hacking off hair that had taken years to grow. I had already been rolling mine under to make it look shorter; never again having to twist my hair on rags for curls would be a release. Slashed hair and boyish silhouettes would flatter my un-voluptuous assets, such as they were.

To be clear, other American women had worn the bob before me. Gals from the university up the street, for instance, frisked around in bluntly chopped locks. But the crop had not yet taken over the screen, and the prospect of a leading lady adopting it seemed nearly as radical as the Amazonian severing of one's own breast.

The day that I did it, the air stank, as it often did, with the smell of burning film, as countless rejected takes or unused scenes met their fate in open incinerators on the back lots. Studios could recover the silver from the silver nitrate that way. My hair was more ambiguously the property of a studio—my contract probably had a termination clause regarding my appearance; maybe I should have checked—but it would be unrecoverable, at least for a long time. This had to work.

I couldn't breathe a word of my plan to Agnes. I wasn't sure even Jack would agree with the scheme. Better, as Granny often said, to beg forgiveness than to ask permission, though she was the one person whose permission I asked.

Even she deferred to another authority. We were in my bedroom; she was leaning against the vanity, holding a miniature pair of scissors from Eileen's Miscellany in her cupped palm.

"Good People," she said, her voice quiet, clearly not a performance for my benefit, "this child is making a big decision today. If you've a sense as to whether it's the right one, she and I would be most grateful for a sign."

Within the duration of a breath, we heard a clunk from the other side of the room.

At the premiere of the one film that I did with Sessue Hayakawa, he had given me a Japanese doll, the only one I owned. In the silence of that moment she had fallen, unbroken, from her ledge to the floor.

My hair was as thick and as stick-straight as hers, and the shelf of bangs across her forehead looked exactly as Pat Fentriss's was said to look in the novel.

"Well, here you have it," said Granny. "Time to make the cut."

Granny's hands were no longer steady enough to do the deed, and no arrangement of mirrors would enable me to do it myself. I needed someone who could chop with precision and confidence, and who could also keep a secret—right up until the point when she couldn't.

I rang up Adela, who arrived not twenty minutes later, shears in hand. In a flash I had recruited not only a hairdresser but also a press agent, at least for the project of the day.

In the bathroom, door shut, Granny waiting outside, I sat on the toilet as Adela snipped, ruthlessly at first, then with greater care, red ribbons of hair slithering to the tile like dead things.

"The lengths I'll go to for a story," she said. "Pun intended."

"How's it coming?"

"Off," she said. "It's definitely coming off. I haven't the slightest idea what I'm doing, you know."

She finished, and stood me before the mirror.

I saw the future: sleek and streamlined. My neck curved like a roadway. My eyes looked like searchlights, twice as big but twice as knowing.

"You did it," I said to Adela. "You made me into Pat."

"*You* made you into Pat," she said. "And don't you forget it."

(I'd think of that later, when Jack tried to claim the idea as his.)

"I look like a woman with secrets!" I touched the strands that skimmed my cheek. This, at long last, was it: a way to establish my own brand of S.A., the quaint abbreviation the fan mags used for *sex appeal*.

"The perfect solution," Adela said. "You don't have to be bad, just *play* bad!"

The breeze outside prickled with heat, and we emerged from the upstairs bathroom into my new life.

"Don't you look naughty!" said Granny, hugging me. "You go show that studio that they've got their flapper."

Adela drove me to the First National lot, the wind in my hair, me not caring about it getting messed up. My bob. I had a bob.

My hair wasn't the only factor, but it was *the* factor. Fitzgerald would later call it the most fateful cut since Samson's.

The director cast me on the spot.

Lillian Gish once told me that the key to personal style is to find a look that suits you and ignore the trends. Keep showing up in whatever's flattering until the end of your days, as though it's the height of fashion. I expect my bob and I shall arrive in my casket together.

Chapter 7

The Kitchen

"Now we're up to—the Kitchen?" says Gladys, checking her notepad. "Speaking of which, the museum is treating us to lunch today. I'd say it's about time, unless you object?"

She rises, unlocks a wall panel to reveal a phone, dials and speaks. "Might as well keep on with it while we wait," she says, hanging up.

The recorder clicks on. "The Kitchen is a bustling place when the fairies are on the premises, as you can imagine. The walls are covered in images drawn from fables and nursery rhymes: Jack and Jill, Little Jack Horner, Humpty Dumpty, Puss in Boots, the Lazy Grasshopper, and the Three Little Pigs. And I must point out that purple wineglass on the table: it's the only memento left from my very first dollhouse, one my father made for me from cigar boxes that I found when I was six."

"What's all that above the ceiling?" Gladys asks.

"The castle hosts huge parties, so the Kitchen needs a storage room to store all the items that are only brought out on such occasions. A great dinner party is a kind of theatrical production, you know. No matter how picturesque a finished product seems, there's always a lot of scrambling that no one sees."

A gifted director can practically evoke smells. When we were building it, I aspired for the castle's rooms to appeal to all the senses. If a person looked hard enough here, I wanted them to detect the garlicky scent of the fairies' feast, even if the fairies never revealed themselves to the viewer. I wanted the fascination to feel ineffable and remain in the brain forever after.

~

The romance novelist Elinor Glyn hadn't yet coined the concept of *It*—that would come later, and to the great benefit of my chief rival, Clara Bow—but I could tell that being beautiful was no longer enough and wasn't what the new thing was about: you had to possess a personal magnetism, some kind of aura that made you stick in the memory. Without having the word for it yet, I strove, playing Pat, to convey abundant It.

Emphasizing the awkwardness of her age—neither child nor woman—was easy enough to do, considering that I'd lived my own adolescence on the screen. Flat-chested and boyish—*gamine*, to be French about it—I expressed a covert eroticism, the sense of a girl whose sexuality is hidden just below the surface, a secret more to herself than to onlookers, just waiting for the right man to let it out. Short hair askew, suggestive of the bedroom, galoshes aflap, implying clothes easily removed, Pat was naive but hardly featherbrained.

The plot, of course, was piping hot: Pat's sensation-craving mother dies after a lifetime of booze and men, whereupon Pat, still in high school, seduces and is seduced by her mother's former boyfriend. A pleasure-mad romp amid the gayest company ensues, a spicy society exposé in which Pat smokes and drinks and (implicitly) has sex with more than one man, including a bohemian violinist with whom she has a climactic blowout fight on a yacht. In the final scenes she leaps overboard, only to be rescued by the aforementioned former boyfriend, whom she eventually agrees to marry.

These days the marriage plot might seem like a concession to propriety; I suppose it was then, too, to an extent. Though the Hays Code wasn't yet in effect, and wouldn't be for a decade, a patchwork of censorship boards had sprung up around the country, and every production had to be strategic in deciding which one it was willing to run afoul of. (The strategy could be complicated; getting banned in the right places was fantastic publicity.) But the message of *Flaming Youth* was subversive nonetheless: Pat got to enjoy her wild life and arrive at her happy ending without being punished or presented as a cautionary tale. I liked the notion that a girl could be carnal without being ruined—I hoped very much that I was living that life myself, though no one but I and Victor Marquis knew the details—and I worked hard to win the audience to Pat's side.

It was fun, too, to play a New England girl with an excellent background and a good education, of which I had neither. Hollywood had shrewd people, but it wasn't known for its intellectuals. Most of its denizens consisted of itinerant stage performers who'd never been to school at all, self-taught directors, relentless businessmen, and convent school dropouts like yours truly.

Jack wasted no time beginning his publicity campaign, and even before the picture went into production, it was already so famous—that is, notorious—that society people desired bit parts; we crammed them into the party scenes. Jack came up with the stunt of casting the winners of beauty contests all over the country to plump up the numbers of comely women in the ballroom and around the swimming pool. He was entirely in his element, conducting the chatter about *Flaming Youth* as if it were an orchestra, bursting with ideas, all of them good.

Then, one week before our wedding, he disappeared again.

This time I hid it from both my family and my friends, even—especially—Adela. I told myself that this had to be the nature of best-friendship with a gossip columnist. Although she had sworn that her interest in covering me was on *me*—"Jack's not even among this town's top one hundred dipsomaniacs," she had joked; "there's no story there"—I reasoned that it was actually better for *her* that she not know so she wouldn't be in the position of choosing between me and a scoop.

It's not that I didn't trust her, but I'd seen from my Uncle Walter how ruthless a good reporter could become when catching the scent of a story.

I told everyone that Jack had gone north to San Francisco to visit his parents and told myself to stay busy and stop asking questions: What if he were dead, my true love lost before I'd fully found him? What if he didn't come back? What would I tell the papers if the wedding were canceled?

At the end of that week's shooting days, I didn't want to go home to Granny and my parents, where I'd have to act happy, so I lingered on the lot and began to learn plenty about the technical side of things. I visited the laboratory where they developed and printed the negatives, submersing the reels in a chemical broth, hanging them to dry on long wooden racks. The cutters would read and splice them carefully into a finished print; I convinced one of the technicians to show me how to splice reels myself. The darkroom became a cool, secluded oasis.

I couldn't forget that unpredictability was one of the reasons I loved Jack.

Within a few days he had returned, bearing an almost-ridiculous-enough-to-be-true tale about falling asleep on a yacht in San Pedro, where he'd gone to take publicity stills. "You know how lulling the rocking of the waves can be, don't you?" While he was out, he said, it set sail before anyone realized that he was still aboard. "That's why I've got such a suntan, darling. Bronzed and burnished for my blushing bride." He kissed my forehead. "It took me so long to get back because we ended up in Ensenada. Here, I've brought you a souvenir from that strange port."

"A stuffed frog in an outfit?" I said, holding the desiccated amphibian at arm's length.

"Dressed as a bullfighter!"

"I see," I said, enthusiastically as I could, which wasn't very.

"Listen, dear, I know I'm a goofus," he said, his smile sickly twisting. "You're my luck, Eileen. You're my light. Don't leave me."

The yarn he wove was full of holes, but I let him weave it, then put it on and wore it myself. Wedding jitters, I figured.

So when the day came for me to marry Jack Flanagan—August eighteenth of 1923, two years after our first meeting, the eve of the twenty-first anniversary of my birth—it was, as the cliché goes, the happiest day of my life. But contrary to what the plot of *Flaming Youth* suggested, wedding bells were not the end of the story. Not hardly.

After I had signed on the dotted line to play Pat, Jack had moved up in the organization, too: assistant to First National's production supervisor, earning a princely sum. He'd become one of the best-known motion picture executives on the West Coast.

The *LA Times* called our wedding "the culmination of a film idyll." In the back of the limousine he'd hired to drive us to the ceremony, Jack read aloud: "Devastating, indeed, will be the word of her wedding to Miss O'Dare's many admirers, as she is personally one of the most popular stars in the business, possessing a charming Irish wit, as well as much beauty and tact."

"Enough tact to refrain from yelling at them to knock it off with the Irish stuff," I said, squeezing his knee.

Jack was Episcopalian, so we wed in the sacristy, rather than at the altar, of St. Thomas Catholic Church in Beverly Hills. Immaculately groomed, he stood stunning in his satin lapels and black tie. I wanted to drop my bouquet of sweetheart roses and baby's breath and clutch him with both hands. No one was handsomer.

The ceremony itself was a small affair. Adela and her husband were there, as was my immediate family. The wedding supper was bigger, and when Jack proposed a toast to my parents, his words were gorgeous, everyone in the banquet room lost in his speech. He had that capacity to lose himself, too, and as usual he was the first to get the dance floor fizzing. As someone who labored to feel abandon, I was floored by his capacity for self-abandonment.

Jack and I had moved that day to South Bronson Avenue, about a mile but also a world away from the house I'd shared with my family. I would miss Granny Shaughnessy but relished the privacy: two stories, terra-cotta tiles lining the roof.

At the threshold of the new house, crossing into our life as a married couple, the housekeeper greeted the two of us with a bottle of champagne. I had my share of sips, but Jack made short work of it, then kept going.

To put it in cinematic terms, Jack was no gentle, soft-focus sipper, edges muffled by a glass or two. He was a full-on fade-to-black drunk.

Under the influence, he moved as though rusty, head jerking on his neck like a spigot.

"Darling," I said, trying to grab the bottle. "Don't you think you've had enough?"

Almost a foot taller than me, he held the green vessel out of my reach.

"It's our wedding night, Jack," I tried again.

"Why do you think I'm celebrating?" He finished the dregs and thumped the empty on the table. When people are drunk, certain acerbities of temper become exaggerated. Still, it hurt like a slap when he added, "Don't behave like Agnes."

I sank down onto the sofa and said nothing. The only sound was that of a moth smacking the lampshade until it was joined by Jack rummaging in the liquor cabinet.

"I can see you're determined to become belligerent," I said quietly, and stood. "I have no desire for our wedding night to be a bumbling fiasco, so I'll see you tomorrow."

He pounded, an hour later, on the door of the bedroom I'd locked myself into, the one I had envisioned as a nursery when we toured the place. I didn't respond. My call time the next morning was early as always, so I forced myself to go to bed, stiff as a corpse in my bridal linens. It was many hours before I slept.

I found him in the cold gray dawn, sprawled on the floor between the sofa and an uncorked Scotch bottle. Somehow he'd shucked off his tux, but I wasn't going to ask for the details of his evening. I left.

First National had given me a Spanish bungalow on the studio lot at the corner of Avenue B, and there I donned the pajamas of Pat Fentriss.

We were filming a crucial scene that morning: Pat descends the stairs of her sumptuous New England home after an evening's bacchanalia, picking her path among the rubble of partygoers. Her father, cuckolded and hungover, pathetic and unmanly, plunks a one-fingered melody on the baby grand. For the second time that morning, I had to gaze, stricken, at the feeble remains of human debauchery. We got the shot in one take.

By the time we were done, no one—not my leading man, not the least-known extra, not even the director—had any inkling of what I was going through.

I had kept Jack out of my head all day. Coming home, all I could think about was having the marriage annulled. Cradle Catholic that I was, I knew that marriage was meant to be forever; if I were to get out, this would be my chance.

I walked in the front door of our new home for the second time as a married woman and found helium balloons in gumball colors tied to every table and every chair. Messages inked upon them declared Jack's regrets.

He entered the living room, tidy and sober. Then he spoke.

"I considered shooting myself when I realized how I jeopardized our marriage," he said, his posture erect, like a man before a firing squad. "How I wasted the first night of our new life together."

For a ridiculous instant, his words sounded like title cards in a movie I'd never want to see, let alone appear in. I almost laughed: the exasperated, slightly crazy laughter of someone at wit's end.

He pulled from the pocket of his trousers a handgun. The mother-of-pearl handle glinted with bizarre politesse under the dining room light.

I screamed his name. Then, without quite realizing what I was doing, I seized it from his hand and threw it in the trash as if it were a dead mouse. It didn't go off, thank God.

"I should keep that," he said, "in case I ever need it again."

"You never will," I said, blocking him with my body from retrieving the weapon. I clasped both his hands in mine; he wrested them free, reaching for his pocket again. I was shaking like a china cabinet during an earthquake.

But all he took out was a delicate chain, its heart-shaped pendant gold and dangling.

"I got you this," he said. "To make up for everything. Read it."

"*My Fairytale*," I said, quoting the engraving in winding script.

When he fastened the filigree around my neck, the metal heart weighed a thousand pounds.

~

Flaming Youth wrapped in the middle of September, and though I was already doing preliminary work on my next picture, the days began to drag as I awaited the premiere. Jack was back to his dynamo status, spending ten-hour days ginning up publicity for First National productions generally and *Flaming Youth* in particular. "It's going to be an inferno, Eileen," he said. "Now's the time to feed the flames."

Peeks inside our marriage were a hot commodity in the fan magazines, which staged shots of me in a ruffly peignoir and ivory ballet slippers, as if I had all day to lounge; nobody wanted to see me in my hairnet and cold cream after a day of shooting stills. They asked me for practical tidbits that would appeal to girls and young homemakers: they wanted to hear elaborate recipes that I slaved on for my hubby, not that I'd come home from the set at 10:00 p.m. and shift around the icebox for cold chicken and milk, and maybe some crackers.

The practical tips I might have given them they wouldn't have wanted to hear. Girls who haven't much experience with such behavior—and I was one—marry drinkers thinking *because he loves me, he'll stop*, until their optimism gets washed away like a sandcastle.

Some realities I could share only—off the record—with Adela, tawny and loyal. Because of our respective jobs and temperaments, our friendship was never placid, but the tightrope that we walked gradually became part of the fun. Although I always respected her devotion to her profession and never asked her to lie on my behalf, the items she shared about me in the pages of *Photoplay*, while juicy, were always positive. One day I asked her why.

"Cynicism has had its vogue," she replied. "Also, there's a bevy of doll-babies making daily mistakes to provide salacious copy. I don't need you to be one of them. You're a jazzy angel."

I had dialed her up in late October, in the slow suspension of a Sunday morning, Mass over, Jack hard at work, despite the sabbath. "This is the train you got on, Doreen," Adela said over the line. "It's taking you somewhere, believe me. And, look, if worse comes to worst, it's only a first marriage."

It wasn't to me. *I will love you all the days of my life*, our vows had said, which I took to mean until forever, not whenever I felt like it.

But Adela was more pragmatic than I. Into my silence she said, "I'll see you at Frances's in an hour. You'd better not waste your day off brooding."

Frances Marion was a scenario writer and sometime actor; she had written my picture *The Nth Commandment* from earlier that year. *Please do not empurple the prose* was one of her rules for title card writers. She believed in trusting the performers.

She hosted wonderful hen parties, as she called them, at the hacienda-style home she shared with her husband, Fred Thomson, the star of many a horse opera. There, we actresses could wear simple cotton frocks and not worry about maintaining the illusion that we were encrusted in pearls and peacock feathers twenty-four hours a day.

"Welcome to the Temple of Mammon," Frances said, leading me into the courtyard where the table was set. She was being modest; there was nothing tacky about the house, which, though new, looked as if it had been in place for ages thanks to Frances having hired a tasteful architect. I fantasized about a day when Jack and I could do the same.

Dressed down, downcast, my heart biting its nails over how *Flaming Youth* would do, I sat between two of my favorite hens.

Even dressed casually, Mary was poised: a polished jewel, shiny hair on a head held high. I strove to emulate her unshakable self-possession.

"Why if it isn't that fashionable flapper Pat Fentriss!" she said. "I hope you shan't forget us when you're a white-hot star."

"I could drink three pots of hot black coffee!" Marion said, reaching for her cup. "I was out all night dancing at the Santa Monica Pier."

For all her off-screen hijinks, Marion's work ethic resembled mine: early to arrive on set, late to depart, agonizing over the daily rushes. "You're more like Pat than I am, pal," I said.

"But your *hair*, Doreen!" Marion replied. "It's the living illustration of the spirit of our times!"

"God, I wish I could cut mine," said Mary, a veritable Rapunzel with her ropes of gold. "The public would never forgive me. They want me to be a young ragamuffin forever."

"Mary's hair is one of the few things that holds this crazy country of ours together," Marion said. "Whenever she gets the split ends trimmed they have to be sent to the San Francisco Mint under armed guard."

"I've envied your locks for years, Mary," I said. "I'd so love to have naturally curly hair."

Marion hooted. Mary cackled like a seagull.

"Doreen," Mary said, "these take at least an hour of work the night before. I use three different types of curlers!"

"See?" said Marion. "That's why *Flaming Youth* is going to be the berries. Feminine freedom."

"It's too late for me!" Mary said, her wrist to her forehead. "Save yourselves!"

Dressing in the new style was like being born into a new body. No more corsets, no more stays, no more girdles, no more pain. The ability to move freely—not to mention to dance. To move fast. It was like having a cast removed after a bone has healed.

"I'm glad to do my part to make the pancake look de rigueur," I said, smiling at last. "I never thought I'd see the day."

"Lillian Gish told me," said Mary, "that during the filming of *Intolerance*, Griffith made Constance Talmadge"—a tomboy, flat as a board—"wear padding for her role as Mountain Girl. She was forever removing and losing it. The whole cast would have to go in search of Constance's figure."

"A one-woman wildcat strike!" Marion said, raising her coffee cup. "Here's to Constance!"

"Well, if this new picture doesn't do well," I said, "the whole cast will have to help me go in search of my career."

"God, you're a worrier," said Marion. "Doreen, it's going to be marvelous. Even if it stinks—which it will not—it'll still be a terrific hit, just based on the publicity that Jack's already done. Come on, let's play before Frances serves lunch."

Hen parties meant badminton, lawn bowling, and croquet; we could sweat and shout without eroding our glamour. Marion pulled me from my seat and thrust a racquet in my hand, and I let myself get lost in the volley.

Insects flitted in the languid air. The eucalyptus trees, dry, brushed their leaves together as if shushing themselves. I asked the fairies for a sign that the picture would be a hit.

The sunflowers that Fred, a bird lover, had planted at the property line nodded vigorously their yellow heads.

~

No picture's premiere was complete without searchlights—stroking the heavens if you felt happy, scouring the void if you felt less so.

My happiness the night of *Flaming Youth*'s premiere was total. Jack was at my side, sober as a judge but a thousand times more fun. Jack was a dresser: cool summer suits of linen or gabardine for California, wool worsted serge for trips to New York like this one. We were at the Strand Theatre in Times Square, the most palatial of the venues built for motion pictures and motion pictures alone.

"If you can't sparkle with diamonds, sparkle with wit," Granny Shaughnessy used to tell me. Now I could sparkle with both.

Onlookers thronged. Arrivals of famous attendees were announced over the loudspeaker, breathless declarations of who was swanning in, suited and gowned. I waved. Pickpockets fed upon the distracted crowd. Impassable sidewalks. Banners and buntings. The police swarmed to control the hordes.

It's rare that you can feel your life changing forever. That night I felt it, real as Jack's palm at the small of my back as we made our way to our seats: the hot approach of colossal fame.

This was my first New York premiere since *The Sky Pilot*, since Victor Marquis and I said our goodbyes in Columbus Circle. It was strange to be sitting not as I was accustomed to sitting when a new film of mine was released—next to Granny, anonymous in the dark, spying on people's reactions—but in a box with Jack, watching the elaborate program. The Strand orchestra played as part of the prologue. Once the picture itself was running, the reactions thundered: drowning out the musical accompaniment when there were laughs and raspy with gasps at the piquant scenes.

The culture had been ready to immolate its outmoded norms. Our picture was the match.

Everyone in the audience had grown up in an age when ankles were a treat and knees were an orgy. When a girl who said anything more than *Oh, do go on!* and *Aren't you wonderful!* to her beau was apt to be thought of as impertinent or obnoxious. Men, it was said, wanted a clinging vine, smitten and quiet, frail and delicate, liable to pass out at any moment were they not granted the support of a firm male arm. Into this world erupted Pat Fentriss, smart and capable, a sprite of S.A., illustrating that young women could golf, drive cars, play tennis, buy railroad tickets, and sign checks.

Standing in the wings waiting for Jack to address the audience, I listened to the ovation of the crowd as the film ended. "My life just changed," I said aloud to no one.

I sat with the rest of the cast under the marquee signing autographs for two hours.

~

"The line in front of you was the longest by far," said Jack in the taxi back to our hotel. Upon arrival we tore the clothes from our bodies and had an afterparty for two in a room with enough mirrors to see what we were doing from every angle. Jack's incandescence.

The next morning the papers revealed that the reviewers, too, had singled me out.

Uncle Walter wired, gratified. His telegram upon the breakfast tray quoted snippets from the press that played on the name Doreen, as he'd predicted they would: *adorable Doreen* and *open the door to mischievous Doreen* and *Doreen comes from the Celtic meaning "moody,"* and *Miss O'Dare is an actress of many moods.*

The one that pleased me most was Carl Sandburg in the *Chicago Daily News*: It is evident she and the director cooperated effectively, efficiently, and with belief in what they were doing. They cared.

We did care! I cared so much.

"No more sifting through reviews for crumbs of praise," I said, knocking Jack's cinnamon bun from his hand so I could pounce and kiss him. "We've made it!"

"Girls the world over are longing to be you," he said. "I should have invested in a chain of beauty shops. I could be enjoying a lucrative sideline during the run on bobs!"

"I wonder if there's a market for all that hair," I said. "Maybe we should open a wig factory."

We'd had good reason to expect self-consciously sophisticated New York audiences to be receptive to our message, but Jack wasn't satisfied with that: he wanted us to start arguments at dinner tables coast to coast. Thus we set off on a promotional tour that he convinced the press to play up as a belated honeymoon. Premiere after premiere. I wore gowns stitched with as much crystal as a chandelier, gowns with as many beads as a rosary shop. I was no fashion plate, but Jack chose my wardrobe.

It didn't take long for the moralizers to scribble scarlet invectives: I and the picture were to blame for the death of tradition and of propriety between the sexes. In Wisconsin a theater manager was threatened with an injunction prohibiting a screening, and in Seattle at least one exhibitor was arrested. In Hackensack the Women's Club protested so loudly that they received a private viewing in advance of its local release, only to emerge proclaiming it not a fit picture for young people.

Best of all, it was banned in Boston.

Agnes wired me that news—which I had already heard, of course, since it was my job—with an aggrieved scolding. I tried to laugh it off, but couldn't quite: she was wrong, but she *was* my mother. And she wasn't a hypocrite.

Unlike many who decried us as symptoms of moral decay, her despair was genuine. She couldn't help but take as a personal affront the fact that I was very publicly saying and doing things she had specifically raised me never to say and do. I had never intended my behavior as such. Or had I? I couldn't help but feel guilty for what I was putting her through—partly because I also couldn't help taking a grim sort of satisfaction from it.

Jack tore her telegram up. "Don't listen to her hidebound nonsense, Eileen," he said. "At every stage we've been right, and the public reaction has proven us right. Everyone we wanted praise from is praising us. Even better, everyone condemning us is exactly who we *want* condemning us. They're offended? Well, they're *meant* to be offended." It costs you nothing. As a wistful girl you were a lovely leading lady, like all the rest. But today? You're a sensation."

When we were in Chicago, a letter from Granny arrived under care of Aunt Lib. *Eileen, I know you won't be worrying about Agnes's grousing. Nothing suits and upsets your mother quite like a scandal. Moral shenanigans give her something to feel superior to. Keep doing what you're doing, for you're doing it well.*

I told myself that Agnes and I had both gotten what we wanted. I got the recognition I'd spent seven years in Hollywood seeking, and she got to say I'd done it at the cost of my reputation.

Jack had to go back to Los Angeles after the first handful of stops—honeymoon, schmoneymoon, as the Yiddish-speaking members of our industry had taught us to say—and I continued: Atlanta, Grand Rapids, Minneapolis, and so on.

While I marched from city to city, Jack moved us into a Mediterranean-style home on Rossmore Drive in Windsor Square, a smaller neighborhood tucked into Wilshire, studded with mansions and rife with trees and broad green lawns. We had the money, he explained as he described the new place to me through some hotel's telephone. He wanted a fresh start in a place with no ghosts of our wedding night.

I returned to LA on a balmy Christmas Eve, keen to spend the holiday with him as my husband, my love—not as my business partner or, worse, my boss.

I walked through the front door hollering his name, not caring that I was making such a racket in front of the housekeeper and valet, so zealous was I to be reunited.

But Jack was nowhere to be found. His car was not in the garage, and none of the staff recalled seeing him leave.

"I'm sure he'll return soon," I told them. "You should go home. Be with your families."

After they left, I told myself it didn't matter; I was tired as a worn-out shoe anyway. I couldn't bring myself to stay awake for Midnight Mass. I fell asleep, still in my traveling clothes, on the new sofa in front of the trimmed tree and didn't wake until I heard car wheels rolling up the flagstones. The dial of my wristwatch read 5:00 a.m.

Jack stood in the driveway next to a beautiful car that I didn't recognize. Its front end was smashed. It looked like a fetching boxer with a broken nose.

"Welcome home, darling!" Jack called from behind the windscreen. "This is one of your Christmas gifts. A Nash Roadster Model 42. In emerald green, for my emerald queen."

"And this modification"—I gestured at the damage—"is another, I suppose?"

The look on his face—wide-eyed like a cottontail, certain that if he remained motionless, then he and the dent would both disappear—was equally maddening and comical. I chose to laugh because I'd missed him so much, and I couldn't bear the thought of fighting on Christmas Day. He laughed with me, and we embraced, and the whiskey on his breath was faint enough to mean he was mostly sober. He opened the door of the Nash, and out hopped a dog with a fiery red coat and a bow around his neck.

"This is your second gift!" he said. "Or your third, if you insist. An Irish terrier!"

The creature was only a puppy, but his scraggly goatee made him look serious and wise. He jumped about my knees; I loved him immediately. "We'll name him Fentriss!" I cried as I scooped him up.

Inside, I put a dish of milk and a plate of chopped sausage for the pup near the white marble fireplace.

"I have one more present," Jack said, standing next to the tree, the scent of pine mixing with the coffee I'd put on.

"But you've given me so much already," I said, worried at his extravagance.

"After we spend today with your family," he said, "I've booked us a stay at the Desert Inn in Palm Springs."

I'd been traveling for weeks; the last thing I wanted was to leave again. But I understood what he was getting at. The Desert Inn was a dry establishment. If we went there, he'd stand a better chance at resisting temptation. I threw myself into his arms and exclaimed, "How lovely!"

I had promised to stay with him in sickness and in health, and his drinking was a sickness. Without his help, I wouldn't be the Jazz Age Cinderella that I now found myself. I couldn't very well cast off my prince anytime he got a little froggy.

People would arrive at their own conclusions as to whether my staying was worth it or not. As for me: it was and it wasn't. Anyway, it's what I did.

Chapter 8

The Attic

Our lunch arrives: grilled cheese sandwiches with pickles, french fries, and brownies for dessert. I leave my potatoes untouched; I used to be able to eat like Gladys and remain as gangly as she, but my metabolism is not what it used to be.

"Soda-counter discoveries are just a fairy tale, huh?" says Gladys, sipping an orange pop.

How to explain to Gladys, or to anyone, that as much as the flapper controversy gave me power, it also gave me a fence of sorts to kick against in order not to be trapped. By definition, fame resides in others, so while it may be something you've attained, it always has you more than you have it.

"Largely. You have to have an inclination toward stardom. It also doesn't hurt to have a handle by which the public can grasp you. Rudolph Valentino, the Latin Lover. Charlie Chaplin, the Little Tramp. Clara Bow, the It Girl."

"Doreen O'Dare, the Perfect Flapper."

"Precisely. And once the public grabs that handle, it doesn't let go until it's done with you," I say, unwrapping my brownie. "I wished I could still take the streetcar after I became famous, but it wouldn't have been safe. Rest assured I can take public transportation now, though. I took the bus to get here, in fact."

"You didn't," she says.

"I'm old now, Gladys. To remain a star, you can't lose your novelty. Jack—my husband at the time, a publicist by trade—was a genius at keeping news of me new."

"Only being interested in new things sounds like hell to me," says Gladys. "But I'm a museum person. Pretty boring, I guess."

"I don't think you're boring," I say. We are once again veering toward the topic of preservation, which I'd rather avoid. "You're right, though, that novelty comes at a cost. My real name, as you may have seen on the deed of gift for the Fairy Castle, is Eileen Sullivan. For years, 'Doreen O'Dare' was just the name of the job I did. After *Flaming Youth*, I became Doreen to almost everyone except Jack, even to my family."

She points a french fry at the castle like it's a magic wand, leveling it at the cramped triangular space squeezed above the Princess's Bedroom. "Shall we talk about the Attic next? We can start whenever you're ready."

"The Attic is the most recent addition," I say, "and the only room for which I can claim no credit. Endre Vitez—the museum's former art director—suggested adding it when he began to grow overwhelmed by all the new miniatures I kept sending."

"Suggested? That doesn't sound like Endre."

"Well, he insisted. Clutter gives him a migraine, he said." I picture Endre gesturing with his broad sculptor's fingers, ordering any disarray sorted in his Hungarian accent. "This is where the fairies have agreed to stow things that don't quite fit elsewhere but are too precious to throw away: some Battersea stools, a silver samisen, and Rumpelstiltskin's spinning wheel, whenever it's not in use."

～

The new adoring public of which I was suddenly the favorite plaything could be difficult to please: it wanted novelty, but also clarity. My continued success depended on refining the character of the flapper. I put my whole self into this task, reading pronouncements on the topic in the press, surveying the opinions of everyone I spoke to, carefully observing groups of bob-haired girls I saw from a distance around town. It was a strange sensation, watching them imitating me with the intention of imitating them. I didn't want my performances to become bogus, and independent young women can spot something bogus better than any certified appraiser.

After our return from Palm Springs, Jack became the head of production for all of First National, and I signed a contract at the phenomenal rate of $4,000 a week. My struggles of the recent past—to explain to mentally inferior male superiors how much they said they'd pay me, or to remind them of the need to honor my contract—were no more.

First up was *Swamp Angel*, a comedy-drama in which I did *not* play a flapper but rather a girl from the poor section of a factory town: Jack and I agreed that I ought to keep stretching my wings, and also to see how far I could get my fans to follow me.

Clara Bow was cast in the role of my kid sister, a demure small-town innocent. She showed up with my haircut and demanded more screen time. The dress she proposed to wear was low cut and incongruous for her character; besides, directors were still in the position of second-guessing local officials throughout the country and were not inclined to get a film banned by showing cleavage of any sort, particularly cleavage that made no sense to include. But Clara seemed determined to get us censored.

When the director asked me to take Clara back to her dressing room to help get her sorted out, I tried to befriend her, remembering Mildred Harris's generosity toward me on the *Bad Boy* shoot. The space smelled like she'd taken a morning swim in a river of perfume.

"Let's think about what a girl like Charlotte might wear," I began.

"Okay, Doreen," she said in her Brooklyn accent. "Let's."

"How about this?" I said, holding up a dress that looked wistful and ingenuous.

She was perfectly capable of going from snuggle-bug to tigress in a second-hand's tick. "It's a stinkin' rotten part, and I don't want it," she said, turning her back and listlessly flipping through the clothes on the rack.

Clara didn't yet understand that the public's affection doesn't automatically follow from its attention; plenty of people were already keeping their eyes on her, but that didn't necessarily mean that they loved her or wished her well. She was talented, I could see that, but it was a mistake to think that people would assume brilliance based on her arrogance. I didn't want to fight with her, but she made it close to impossible.

I tried agreeing with her instead. "It *is* a small role," I said, "but you're getting started. Being new almost always means working your way up."

"I ain't a baby," she said, grabbing the frock I suggested. "I won't stand it."

"All right," I said, stepping out. "I'll see you on set."

Watching her work that day, I began to notice tics and quirks that would become her signatures across her considerable oeuvre. How possessed of self-love she was: she couldn't stop hugging herself. I tried to sympathize, knowing how she was sometimes condescended to socially. "I didn't know this place was going to be such a march of the snobs!" she'd said after a particularly awkward encounter at one of Frances's hen parties. And it was true: people did think of her as ill bred. But wasn't it also a kind of snobbishness to ascribe her crassness to her background rather than her character?

On day two, she made a show of inattention.

"Am I boring you?" the director would demand.

In between takes, she reapplied her makeup with sexy vigor while carrying on lively conversations with the electricians and stagehands. It was like the cameras were never not rolling, like she was the star of the movie, or *some* movie, all the time.

Vain people seem full of themselves, but really they're empty. They require those around them to affirm them relentlessly, and even then they can't trust the praise. Trapped in fear of their own lack of worth, they ascribe to you their own worst motives.

"Don't pretend like you're not trying to keep me from getting a close-up!" she accused during our first scene together. "Everyone says you're such a good girl. Such a professional. But I can see right through you."

"Clara," I said, struggling to retain my equipoise, "you're beautiful. I don't mind at all if you get a close-up."

"You're saying that to look like a Goody Two-Shoes. I know you can't stand me."

"All right, now, Clara, that's enough," the director said. "Let's everyone take five."

Clara pouted and looked vindictively innocent. The director explained that she and I could not swap roles as she requested. "Fine," she said. "But if you're not careful, you won't have me to boss around much longer."

On day three she was on set for less than ten minutes. Then she was gone for good.

She arrived that morning with bruises dimming her luminous eyes and her nose wrapped in bandages. The previous afternoon she'd stomped off to her doctor and insisted that he perform a sinus operation, rendering her expressive face defective.

"The surgeon says it'll take me a month to recover."

"You gave no notice to the studio!" the director said, incredulous.

"This *is* me givin' notice." She gestured at her face, then snatched a lipstick from her vanity amid a clattering of hairpins, scrawling a kiss-off across the mirror in ruby matte. "Clear enough for ya? I *quit.*"

The public makes rude noises and cries for red meat when it sniffs a feud, and such was the case when word got out about Clara's departure. But I hadn't any instinct to be an antagonist; I gave no comment, and I vowed to permit no open hostility. If anything, I felt sorry for her.

She went on to have great success with her—which is to say my—bobbed hair. Though I believe, with no sour grapes, that I embodied the concept even before it was coined, it was Clara to whom Elinor Glyn's epochal sobriquet the It Girl stuck when she won the lead role in *It*.

Her triumphs came at a price, and it soon became impossible for her to portray anything but It. She did seem to enjoy her fame, limited and perishable though it was, and could often be spotted driving around in an open Kissel with a pair of chow dogs whose coats she'd dyed the same red as hers. Sometimes Elinor Glyn rode with her, her own hair hennaed to match. With Clara's encouragement, the press made it sound like she got around with every eligible bachelor in town, not to mention a few ineligible ones. It struck me as a little pathetic that she wasn't even the best at being bad. Her antics seemed pale next to those of, say, Pola Negri, who would take her pet tiger for a walk on Sunset Boulevard whenever she needed a splash of attention.

Every sex object is also a death object. A person can only grow so big in such a tiny planter.

When Clara died three years ago, in 1965, I was sadder than I had expected to be. We both could have had longer careers. We both deserve, in my opinion, to be better and more correctly remembered.

To be fair to Clara, at the time I thought I had more control than I did over the way the public perceived me, and I insisted on branching out again. Sweethearts and gamines were well and fine, but I also wanted to be able to play people older than twenty-two, and also historical figures. I was an actress, after all.

Part of my fascination with bygone days manifested in my miniature collection. Tiny looking glasses had become particular desiderata after the director of *Swamp Angel* gave me one. Soon after, I acquired a Chippendale type with a scrolled top, and a cheval glass in a mahogany frame, tiltable from its tapering posts with brass urn finials: oddments crafted by long-ago hands to withstand the blows of time.

I wanted to capture that mysterious aura on-screen. Also, I craved to be cast in a project that even Agnes and my dad would have to admire. When I'd paid them a visit upon my return from the tour for *Flaming Youth*, I noticed that they'd made one notable change to the decor of the house after I'd moved out: they'd put one of the few photographs of my brother Cal squarely in the center of the mantelpiece. Dead children rarely disappoint their parents.

So while Clara was motoring between trysts with a carload of dyed dogs, I was off to the bookshop again. Edna Ferber's new novel *So Big* was just the material I needed: the poignant tale of Selina Peake, a gambler's daughter who struggles to make a life in a farm town outside Chicago at the turn of the century, it was a serious and sophisticated depiction of the challenge of reconciling a love of beauty with the need to survive. The role would require me to age decades over the course of the film. It had to be mine.

I took the book to the studio and stated my case to Thomas Tally and J. D. Williams, First National's founders; the former was thrice my age, and the latter twice. They looked at me in the belittling way that men, particularly powerful men, often did: like I was a bonbon, amusing but insubstantial.

"Doreen O'Dare," Tally said in his Texas accent, thin lips slow in his hickory face, "is youth-oriented and modern."

"Doreen O'Dare," said J. D. Williams, ashing his cigar, "is a flapper."

Doreen O'Dare is sitting right here, I thought. *You may speak to her directly.*

"Who's going to buy tickets to see the *Flaming Youth* girl sittin' in a calico dress atop a vegetable wagon?" Tally asked, flipping the book's pages, returning it to his desk.

"The public wants more than soda-pop romance," I said.

"Cute of you to think so," Williams said, tipping back the straw hat he wore to hide his bald head.

"Miss O'Dare," Tally said, "a painful fact of this business is that very few people, right on up to distinguished executives like the two of us, truly know what the public wants. Otherwise every picture we make would be a smash hit, which I can promise you they're not. Trying new things is brave, and we do brave things sometimes. But *not* doing things that we *know* the public wants is plain stupid, and Mr. Williams and I didn't get to where we're at by being stupid on purpose. I am sure you can understand."

I didn't have a response ready for that. I didn't know that the public wanted to see *So Big* on the screen, with or without me in the lead. I just knew that it could make a great film and that I wanted to do it. As much as I hated to admit it, the public often did seem to favor actors who didn't do much acting. Norma Talmadge, for instance, was always Norma Talmadge: she was like someone you knew, and never vanished into a role. Same for Milton Sills: always delightful, but always himself. Actors who acted were rarely as popular. Gish and Pickford were exceptions: stars whose colors and characters were matched by a certain naturalness. Theirs were the careers I sought to emulate.

I picked my copy of Ferber's novel up from Tally's desk and clutched it to my heart, negotiating through silence.

"We don't want our stars to act too much, Doreen," said Williams, guessing my train of thought. "People stop recognizing them. They lose their value."

"They lose their value when they get stale, too," I said. "Actors need to grow. I don't want to go around at forty pretending to be a kissable little morning glory of just eighteen."

The two of them laughed.

"And I won't," I said, "because by then you'll have found a four-teen-year-old to play those parts. I know, because I've *been* that fourteen-year-old."

All my career I'd been described as childish and naive; why didn't these executives, ostensibly on my side, see that my achievements proved otherwise? True, I had taken to maintaining the persona of Doreen off-screen, because it was easier than continually putting it on and taking it off, less confusing to me and to others. Because people liked it, and I liked to be liked. Because it protected me from predatory men, letting me feign innocent—or, less charitably, ignorant—incomprehension of their darker entreaties. My mother had feared that I'd be despoiled, but for years I had toiled unmolested, thanks largely to refusals that I'd clad not in barbs but in big bursts of wholesomeness, snuggly as a kitten. People want to pet kittens, not have sex with them. (There are exceptions to every rule, I suppose, and I'm glad I never encountered this one.)

I didn't want to put my claws out over *So Big*. I wanted some respect.

"We have a meeting with Jack later this afternoon," Williams said, putting a hand at my elbow. "We'll have to see what your husband says."

"Well, here's what *I* say," I said, standing in the doorway. "I *am* going to play Selina! Now, be good fellows and pass that message along to my husband, won't you?" I gave them a wink that Victor Marquis would have envied.

In the end, it was Jack who persuaded them. "I told 'em the public doesn't want turkey for every meal," he explained when I asked. "The American people demand variety in their motion picture entertainment."

Never underestimate people's desire to be told what to do by a tall man in a suit.

In any event, I was grateful to have got Selina. While we shot, I stipulated that no contemporary music be played on the set; in my previous films I'd had them play jazz. The orchestra leader—yes, we had a small orchestra at our disposal, to help set the emotional tenor—obliged, hunting up tunes from the 1890s.

One piece of advice that Bobby Harron gave me on the *Bad Boy* shoot was to find a real person on whom to base every character. "The littlest quirks you can imitate," he said, "can make the difference between an individual who seems like a fraud and one the audience believes." For Selina, I settled on Granny Shaughnessy: her vibrancy mixed with dignity, her aging a transformation rather than a fading.

By the end of the shoot I saw so entirely with Selina's eyes that for weeks thereafter the world filtered through to me in the perspective of Ferber's indelible heroine.

When the picture came out in December 1924, audiences thronged, and the reviews were largely positive, the verdict being that I, a funny actress, could also pull off drama. Edna Ferber herself told me bluntly at the premiere that she'd doubted a sleek movie minx like me could carry Selina's gravity but that she was pleased to have been wrong.

There were a few bad squibs, too, and I wanted to ball up and use them as kindling, but naturally they stuck in my brain. One critic wrote, breezy and demeaning, O'Dare's acting was splendid, but you just couldn't believe in her wrinkles; so probably she won't be allowed to paint on any more of them for the next twenty-five years, when perhaps (just perhaps) she may have developed two or three of her own.

She was being light, and meant only to praise with faint damnation, but alas!

My success as Selina notwithstanding, Tally and Williams wanted to send me back to playing gamines, because that was the Jazz Age for you. People believed that war and disease had been vanquished, and they wanted to kick up their heels. The public appetite for historical detail and educational spirit was not huge in the twenties.

To make up for it, they did build me a new bungalow on the studio lot—not a dressing-room space like the one I'd had before, but a true house, with a kitchen, a bath, and four other rooms, meant to facilitate the hectic schedule stipulated by my contract. It had space for my maid, my hairdresser, my stand-in; with that many people responsible for the entity known as Doreen O'Dare, it felt a bit like a party in there all the time.

Shortly before Christmas, First National held a proper party for me: an official housewarming to double as a celebration of the release of *So Big*. The magazines aptly described the fete as studded with stars. Norma Talmadge came straight from the set of *Secrets* still in costume, the briefest of outfits from an intimate scene; she brought her sister Constance. Bessie Love and Blanche Sweet—then married to Mickey Neilan—were there, along with a cavalcade of other names, now all but forgotten.

And Florence Marquis. Which meant that Victor, my first love, attended as well.

Everyone has a sad and awful secret or two, I suppose, but I had become all too aware that I was not Clara Bow: the public would not forgive me a disgrace. I couldn't run over and embrace Victor the way I wanted to when I saw him standing near the canapés. His eyes met mine across the room and sparked blue, enough to start a fire, but I greeted him coolly when he approached at last.

"*So Big* is a titanic achievement," he said. "You were always a good performer, but in this you're second to none. My only regret is that I didn't get to direct it. It's one for the ages."

"I pray nightly for the day when you're hired to direct absolutely every film."

"If divine intercession is what it takes to work with you again, then I suppose I ought to get religion."

Victor's praise was second only to Ferber's to me, both because he had been my paramour and because he knew from movies. I had been to see every single one of his pictures since *The Sky Pilot*—pining, sure, but also wowed by his directorial prowess.

"I loved yours this year," I said. "All three of them. *Wild Oranges*, *Happiness*, and *Wine of Youth*."

"They sound like poetry when they come from your lips, Eileen," he said.

I realized how long it had been since anyone but Jack had called me by my real name. I couldn't indulge the frisson, not there. So I brought up something that had struck me—both in the sense of being interested and being wounded—when I watched the last of the three.

"I get the sense that you find Eleanor Boardman most poetic," I said. She was his latest leading lady, and I could tell from the way he lit and shot her that his interest was more than professional. He had done the same to me. "She seems quite talented."

"Four years later, you're still the smartest actress in the business, Eileen," he said, denying nothing. By the turn of the new year he and Florence would be divorced; by 1926 he and Eleanor would be married.

Mickey Neilan stumbled up, and Victor and I parted. When you're on the way up, other people are moving, too, and poor Mickey was moving down.

"Everything about humanity is deranged and sadistic," he began without prelude, "except for you in *So Big*, Doreen."

I demurred, not wanting him to make a scene so early in the evening, but he continued. "Everything the studios do is about the bottom line," he said. "That's all these money-grubbers can understand, Doreen. Wait and see. They're not going to give you another role like that. Not for a long time."

It wasn't the time or the place for such a conversation. I gently took his hand from my shoulder and gave it a pat.

The day after the party I learned that Mickey, in his cynicism, had been correct. I would not be permitted to make another prestige picture (as they'd soon be called) like *So Big* for the foreseeable future.

The public, Tally and Williams explained with what they seemed sure was saintlike patience, preferred me girlish, uncomplicated. They liked my intrigues to be almost unbearably clever, crammed with coquetting. Open palms, big eyes, approachability—that was Doreen O'Dare.

Prescient, too, and impeccable of taste—though I was rarely credited for that. Months later, I took some pride in the fact that Ferber's novel won the Pulitzer.

∽

Stardom, I had been warned by many, could become terrible in its loneliness. I did all I could to combat that feeling: attending parties and events, always being cordial and gracious, but also exercising caution about making new friends, because you could always tell when someone who hadn't the time of day for you when you were obscure was only taking you up because you were acclaimed. No, no thank you.

But the day I met Mervyn LeRoy on the set of *Sally*, I knew we'd be friends for life.

A silent version of a musical comedy obviously couldn't place its fate entirely in the hands of the local orchestras that would accompany its eventual screenings, so the studio had hired Mervyn to buttress its comic ramparts. The word of mouth that preceded him made me think he'd be full of baloney.

"Whatever you do, don't call him a gagman," Jack warned me. "He hates that. Doesn't do anything for him, he says, and his mother wouldn't like it. Makes it sound like he's in charge of choking people." I asked what he preferred, and Jack told me that Mervyn's contract stipulated his title as "Comedy Constructor." He was earning his keep already, for I burst out laughing at the sheer pretentiousness.

But when I met him, we went together like spaghetti and meatballs. A compact man not much taller than I, even including his shock of thick dark hair, I could tell he was zingy even in stillness.

"Mr. Comedy Constructor," I said, extending a hand, "I can't wait to see what we can build for *Sally*. I've got a lot of ideas."

I was testing him to see how seriously he took me, how collaborative he could be. I could do knockabout slapstick, but I preferred comedy-drama: physicality with more of a range. There was a growing stereotype—more common by then than it had been when I was working with Christie—that women weren't as funny as men. I had to pitch my bits twice as hard to directors as they sat there in their canvas chairs with that I'm-from-Missouri-so-show-me expression. (Naturally, explaining a gag kills it almost every time.)

Mervyn's eyes crinkled in a smile. "You can make any actress cry with an onion," he said, "but the vegetable has yet to be grown that can make her funny. You're funny. I've seen all your pictures."

"This might sound stuck-up to say, but so have I," I said, and he laughed. "In theaters all around Hollywood. But not out of vanity."

"I imagine you do it for the same reason I go to see mine: to hear when an audience laughs and when they don't. And I bet you don't only go to see your own. I bet you watch everybody's."

"Have you been following me?"

"Let's get to work," he said. "We'll give you more great gags than there are plums in a Christmas pudding."

The instinct of most people who worked on film adaptations was to dilute; Mervyn condensed. He had a magical touch for *building* laughter—tying gag upon gag, like silk handkerchiefs pulled from a conjuror's sleeve. We concocted character-based comedy as well as pratfalls. The real miracle, we agreed, was when you could get the audience thinking, within five minutes of the start of a picture, *Why, isn't that just like her!* about a person who doesn't really exist.

He was almost scientific in his pursuit of laughs; he liked to haunt the upscale department stores of LA for ideas—"practically factory showrooms of human foolishness," he explained—and once almost got arrested as a shoplifter; the detective let him go after Mervyn explained he was only lifting gags.

Mervyn and I connected over our impoverished childhoods and our senses of humor. While Jack was exuberant, he wasn't funny, exactly; I wasn't attracted to Mervyn romantically, but he had something I'd been lacking since I'd split with Victor: a tennis-player quickness.

He was also my business partner during a brief stint as a Rudolph Valentino peep show impresario.

Today, more than forty years after his untimely death, few people seem to understand the animal magnetism of Valentino. As elegant as

Dracula, Rudy had that little ooze of cruelty about his hooded eyes—a dashing man with lengthy lashes and agile shoulders. A rumor of his having been a gigolo proved untrue, but he was a darn good dancer, not to mention a gymnast and a horseman. And he collected rare books! American men resented him as a foreign lothario, a pretty-boy born for passionate lovemaking. Some petty writer for my uncle's paper in Chicago used the term "pink powder puffs" to slur men who imitated his dress and manner, but that was pure jealousy of his gallantry and grace. Women across the nation fainted at his flickering image.

And he was shooting a picture simultaneous to *Sally* just one set over, closed in with canvas as a prophylactic against swooning.

I can't remember who thought of it first, but Mervyn and I decided to profit by our proximity. We snipped a hole through the fabric on our side to make a window big enough for one hungry eye, and at a nickel a pop, we sold peeks of Rudy in action to all the girls, and to some of the men.

"Do you think anything's painted on the other side of this canvas, Mervyn?" I wondered.

"Something obscene, I hope."

"I'm thinking of what we'll do if Rudy catches us."

"We'll cut him in, I guess. But not for more than ten percent! He can snip his own hole."

On our rare afternoons off, we used our peep show proceeds to treat ourselves to ball games at Washington Park. Even had I not been a fan of the Angels, the field would have a place in my heart: I'd filmed ballpark scenes there for *The Busher*. Back then Charles Ray, my costar, seemed to have a career that was out of my reach: harmlessly handsome, he personified the simple virtues of rural America. Now he couldn't get arrested, and Rudy was ascendant. So was I, but who knew for how long?

The alfalfa patches that used to line the way to the ballpark were almost gone. At night you'd see a plain of lights in their place, as if the king crop had become houses, irrigated by the electricity that kept them bright. The wider world was changing, too: people were plotting to fly the Atlantic and swim the English Channel, battling for heavyweight title after title, gunfighting in Chicago.

But my mind, when it was not on *Sally*, was on Jack and his episodes. When he was up, high-flying and clean, there was no one more seductive. When he was down, and drinking—I felt untellable shame.

By then I trusted Mervyn: with my secrets, my life. I turned to him, a sympathetic listener, increasingly, since I didn't feel comfortable disclosing Jack's darkness to Adela.

Beneath the low wooden awning along Washington Park's left field, holding a hot dog Mervyn had bought me that I was too distraught to eat, I'd pour out my troubles. Jack wasn't as discreet as he used to be, occasionally washing his morning eggs down with Scotch.

"Why do you stay?" Mervyn asked as the teams swapped sides at an inning's midpoint.

"First and foremost, because I love him," I said, then clapped for the Angels to avoid his eyes. "But also—I've never said this out loud. As a star, it's hard to flare, but harder not to fade."

"And Jack is a producer with power," said Mervyn, no judgment in his voice, "so sticking with him helps keep your flame alight."

"It's not only that. I'm stuck, Mervyn. People *know* I've benefitted from my husband's publicity work. And the publicists in this town are a little fraternity. If I ever split with Jack, none of the rest will want to touch me with a ten-foot pole. You must think I'm awful."

"I know you love him," Mervyn said, waving a Cracker Jack vendor away. "He's lovable. Even in his cups, I can't hate the guy. But in the meantime, *you* have to appear perfect. And that means never letting on any problems. There's no margin of error."

"I keep giving him chances. Apologize and try again: that's us."

I felt like a betrayer over such disclosures; Jack wanted to be seen as a sturdy rock of a man. But unburdening myself to Mervyn made it possible for me to keep being funny on-screen.

Without humor, a thing is at best only half-alive: such was the closest I had then to a guiding philosophy. Whenever an endeavor seemed wholly solemn, I'd look to find a smile behind it, and if no smile was evident, I'd keep on moving. I could not let the unsmiling thing become me.

Well, that was half of my guiding philosophy. The other half was *get your own money*, something I did unfailingly: demanding my own credit plates at a time when merchants would issue them to husbands but not to wives, for instance. Good policy, considering the way things ended up.

Chapter 9

The Cave of Ali Baba

A museum staffer enters to clear the leavings of our lunches, and Gladys hits pause. As the doors swing shut again, an aroma drifts into the small, dim space, like a Rubbermaid spatula abandoned in a hot pan.

"Is something burning?" I ask. Gladys sniffs the air and smiles.

"Nah, that's the Mold-A-Rama. Maybe my favorite smell on the planet. You probably saw the machine when you walked in? That one makes replicas of your Dollhouse. I can't get enough of the scent. The chemicals are probably terrible, but I don't care."

I feel that way about the nitrate scent of celluloid. A vinegary odor. Volatile stuff. In chemical terms, I'm told, it might as well be gunpowder. It's the fragrance of my youth to me.

"On the subject of plastic," she continues, "what's that pile of treasure behind the fence on the castle's second floor, above the Small Hall?"

"Oh, that's Ali Baba's Cave," I say. "As any discerning eye can see, the Cave is the only place in the castle where the jewels are fake. I sometimes think the fairies would have preferred that I install a lanai instead."

The sheer quantity of gems required to create the effect of the chests full of loot as described in "The Forty Thieves" was such that we decided it would be fine if we let them be paste. I should have realized that in certain cases, make-believe pales when contrasted with the real thing.

~

The papers engaged in all kinds of fakery about my domestic ecstasy with Jack. The worst, my favorite, the hilarity of which I could share only with Mervyn, was from *Movie Weekly*: "I Love to Ask My Husband for Money," Says Doreen O'Dare. If all the preposterous pieces written about me were placed end to end, they'd reach the very peak of idiocy. All of them promised *an intimate glimpse!* and all of them were fast and loose with the facts. My Uncle Walter had been right years back when he stuck me on the train.

I never asked Jack for money. What I hoped for was a baby. I wanted one. Badly. Ever since I began my miniature collection, I'd especially prized pint-size cradles whenever one of my aunts happened to send one. To envision a fairy baby peeking out of one of those hooded oak containers with rocker feet was divine. I always imagined I'd be somebody's mother.

Abstractly, I believed that if I had a child, she would open for me worlds of undreamt happiness. Concretely, I pictured her with two brown eyes and lashes long as sunset shadows and a mouth like a rose just barely open. But that was not something one said to the press either.

The demands of our work being what they were, the scenes of Jack and me that the photographers staged—us looking cozy, snuggled together in a chair made for one—occurred only when the photographers staged them. "There's no happier married pair in all the world, is there, baby?" he would ask me, to be sure the reporter would quote it.

"No sirree!" I would chirp, gazing at him in a way that I hoped would be written up as *soulfully*, whatever the reporters thought that meant exactly.

As for typical husbandly-wifely routines, Jack might dash into my boudoir at the crack of dawn because the laundry had been delayed and he couldn't find clean socks, and then I might help him hunt some up.

One movie magazine commented, It's Just Too Ridiculous to Think of Doreen as a Married Woman. Too ridiculous indeed. Sometimes too ridiculous for Jack.

"Take a gander at how they made our breakfast table look," I said one morning, pointing at a photo of pancakes and bacon and home-fried potatoes and corned beef hash, as we ourselves sat at our usual repast of toast and a soft-boiled egg. My contract included the typical weight clause, but at the time I was shrinking from stress.

"Maybe I *should* ask the cook to start making this breakfast," he said. "The camera adds pounds, but it can't fix gaunt."

"A little more meat on these bones might entice the stork."

"Maybe it's for the best, Eileen," he said, taking my hand. "After all, you're still just a girl yourself." I waited for him to laugh, but his expression remained earnest.

"I'm a full-grown woman, Jack. It's strange that we haven't had any success yet."

Strange and hurtful. I had recently lost the part of an older character—not as old as Selina, but meatier than a waif—by dint of a producer who looked at my screen test and mused that perhaps to properly portray a mother, an actress must have a child of her own. His dismissal stung less because of the implication that I couldn't act well enough to be convincing—I knew he was wrong—but because it was beginning to look like having the baby I wanted might not be a possibility. I kept thinking of my mother's six childless sisters.

"We can keep trying, of course," he said, and kissed me with passion. "But perhaps it's not the right time in your professional life?"

"I don't know why you pretend to ask," I said. "Whatever you ordain, we do."

I set down my fork and looked into his eyes, tears welling in mine. The promise of our courtship felt lost, in another country. Flirting had been fun because things were gloriously uncertain. Marriage was something else entirely.

"Now, Eileen," he said, wiping his lips on a linen napkin monogrammed DO. "You know that's not true."

"But it is!" I said, giving myself over to the pleasure of airing a grievance. "Ever since you met me you've wanted to pull a Pygmalion, making me over as your own creation. But I was never your statue. I was already incarnate!"

"That's absurd, sweetness. There's nothing to worry about. We'll keep doing our best, and maybe one day you'll have your blessed event."

I pushed my chair from the table and stood to keep from crying. It was normal, I knew, for one's self to be discontinuous; one altered depending on one's social surroundings. But for my husband not to admit the difference between Doreen O'Dare, the perpetual gamine, and Eileen Sullivan, the woman whom he had married, now twenty-three years old, enervated me.

"I'll see you tonight, Jack," I said, and went to find our chauffeur.

These occasional spats would leave me flat. But I couldn't show up on set looking like last year's bird's nest. So I let it go.

Besides, one can be happy and wretched all at once: happy with one's job, wretched over other problems. I had already told Jack that if we had a child, I wouldn't quit acting. I'd be like Gloria Swanson, who'd shown that such a balance was possible. Before Gloria, the children of women stars had been a secret—invisible, nonexistent—and then she trotted her little girl around as natural as anything, making well-dressed movie infants a vogue.

At least I was in good company: Mary Pickford and Lillian Gish and Marion Davies didn't have children either. Mary had tried to have a baby with Doug, but an early botched abortion—one that she didn't regret but that the public would never have forgiven—meant she never could. Lillian, though not quite the virgin she played on-screen, believed actresses had no business marrying: "I love my work too deeply to love anyone else that much." Marion would have had kids, except that her arrangement with Hearst forbade it. She could be his mistress, but illegitimate children would mean the end—of Marion's career, of their relationship.

To the delight of everyone in her orbit, Marion turned her attention to other pursuits, particularly parties thrown in Hearst's castle at

San Simeon. Never finished, "the ranch" (as he called it with deceptive understatement) was ready to be occupied by 1925, the zoo rounded out with forty buffalo he'd ordered to go with the zebras and giraffes, ostriches and orangutans.

She and Hearst were crazy for themes. Kiddie parties were a favorite: guests dressed in short pants and bloomers and played Pin the Tail on the Donkey to win prizes from Tiffany's. Hearst would also throw a costume masquerade at the drop of a wardrobe department hat. At these, actors externally manifested their secret desires. Prudes arrived as ladies of the night. Villains came as heroes. Ingenues showed up as vamps. Frances Marion dressed as a fortune teller, Adela as a cowgirl. Chaplin came as Hamlet. Elinor Glyn attended as Catherine the Great. Once, Hearst came as President James Madison. I dressed as Titania from *A Midsummer Night's Dream*, my favorite Shakespeare play (for the fairies, naturally); I sympathized with her suffering at the hands of Oberon, her husband and king.

The first one I attended is the one I remember best, and not just because we tend to remember firsts. The theme was Christmas in July. The invitation had come to Jack and me, but when the weekend arrived, he was gone on a bender. Had it been anyone but Marion I would have phoned with a last-minute excuse, but she knew how things stood, and I had no reason to feel ashamed.

The floor of San Simeon's vestibule came from Pompeii, covered in ash and bodies in 79 AD. "People died on this floor," Marion whispered as she greeted me.

In keeping with the Christmas theme, we guests arrived bearing a flurry of gifts for our host. Many assumed that Hearst would want the costliest presents, but Marion had told me that he was most touched by the humble and the handmade, so I gave him a pair of slippers that Granny Shaughnessy had crocheted.

From afar, Hearst had seemed a wealthy ogre, frustrated and lonely. Up close, he was less a troll than a Sasquatch, with his rumpled suit, sloped shoulders, and aloof manner.

"Thank you, Doreen," he said in a funny alto that Adela, his employee as a columnist, had warned me that he considered embarrassing. "You're just as homespun as Marion told me. Welcome. I shall have to wear these later."

Somehow his high voice matched his pale eyes.

The Christmas party would not take place until Saturday night. "Our merry little gathering," Marion said, applying the term with perfect sincerity to our crowd of fifty, "will partake of simpler entertainments this evening."

By this she meant that Hearst would make us watch one of her pictures and applaud, a fanfare that she did not always receive from critics, usually due to Hearst and his meddling.

The theater at San Simeon was cold even in summer, and the two of them bundled up in furs, huddling like squirrels. It was cold everywhere there: dank stone and fresh mortar, more monument than home, too huge to be human, its splendor a little woebegone.

The evening's cinematic fare was *Yolanda*, an opulent flop set in Burgundy in the late Middle Ages. The interiors and costumes were stunning, but an hour and forty minutes of chivalric twaddle challenged anyone's ability to remain conscious. I had to elbow the art dealer next to me to wake up and clap.

Poor Marion: a clown by nature, drawn to the ridiculous, living in the now. Hearst mistakenly believed that he needed to manufacture her stardom; as a producer, he poured vast sums into elaborate sets and casts imported from the New York stage. As often as not, these films earned less than no profit—losses useful for tax-deduction purposes at best. Hearst insisted on bespangling Marion, dressing her as a historical personage clogged with cobweb lace. He made her pretentious, when she was the least pretentious person in Los Angeles. That's what kills me to this day: Marion was talented. She wasn't the pathetic aspirant that Orson Welles caricatured her as in *Citizen Kane*.

She and Hearst were mutually devoted, but it could get tense.

"Now," he piped up, rising from his seat, "I thought, if people don't mind, we could watch another of Marion's pictures—"

"That's enough, W. R.," Marion said. "Our guests need to sleep. Otherwise Santa Claus won't visit."

In the morning, beneath the two-story Christmas tree, Santa had indeed left us several ping-pong tables and thousand-piece jigsaw puzzles.

On Saturday afternoon we went out riding. W. R. wore a Stetson and sat astride a golden palomino at the head of the trail. Thanks to Tom Mix and practice on subsequent oaters, I was as fine an equestrian as anyone there, and he kept me beside him. I was glad to be doing it recreationally, not on a set, amid foothills flowered with lupines and poppies. We found upward-sloping trails to climb for a better view, and whenever my dangling fingers snagged the sagebrush it sighed aromatically.

Hearst's eccentricity competed with the scenery. Thousands upon thousands of acres, his estate was snaked with winding paths roamed by antelope and elk. Cresting a ridge, his ranchland stretching to the horizon, he gazed and muttered to no one: "It's mine."

Marion hated riding but came along to please him, and he looked at her the same way he looked at his land: with genuine love that couldn't be disentangled from ownership.

We returned to the castle, and she revived herself and the rest of us with caviar and champagne. Hearst disapproved of alcohol, allowing as a compromise one drink per guest at five o'clock and one more at dinnertime. Those who brought their own booze and got drunk would be escorted back to the San Luis Obispo train depot double time, but people brought liquor anyway, wrapping bottles in shirts and pajamas, telling the staff, "Oh, I'll unpack that one."

What else to call the dining hall except baronial? Silver candlesticks stout enough to joust with. Silk tapestries depicting the defeat of Hannibal. Like many wealthy but insecure American men, Hearst fetishized Europe, hanging the hall—he called it *the refectory*—with heraldic flags and setting the table with blue-and-white Delftware. Every amenable surface was hung with holly garlands. We guests had followed our instructions to dress as Victorians at Christmastide; I'd gone in rags as the Little Match Girl from Andersen's tale.

The menu cards listed an English Christmas feast—mince pies, roast goose, and Yorkshire pudding—but my eyes alighted on the place card next to mine: VICTOR MARQUIS.

"Eileen, my queen of the comedic screen," he said, sitting down by my side, "who, even amid the snows of ersatz Christmastide, possesses a face like a flower on a stem."

"How did an urchin like you sneak past the guards?" I asked. He was attired as Tiny Tim.

"I got my editing done staying up all night, and I caught the afternoon train. Marion said she had some suitable duds and somebody that she knew I'd want to see. So I came."

"Alone?" I asked, more eager than I should have been.

"Alone," he said, and bit his lip.

"Well," I said. "God bless us, every one."

Neither of us touched our English feast, so intent were we on each other's voices. Unprepared for his company, I feared at first it might be awkward but soon simply feared that our unseverable entanglement would be obvious to everyone present. I couldn't remember the last time I had laughed—or made someone else laugh—so hard.

Marion clinked a spoon against a Waterford glass and rose to explain the evening's agenda, her stammer scarcely a blot on her perfection. We'd eat ourselves silly, and then play games. Ready steady confetti: her parties were blurs of fun. She never let anyone remain a wallflower, crossing the room to coax them out, making them bloom with her rain of laughter.

Chaplin proposed a round of hide-and-seek ranging through the rooms of Casa Grande, the largest of all the houses on the hilltop retreat. By no coincidence whatsoever, I ended up hiding in a salon full of suits of armor in an antique chest next to Victor Marquis. Chaplin, who was It—Clara Bow jokes abounded, of course—came in and traipsed around. Victor clasped my hand. I felt guilty, but I didn't resist.

After Chaplin left, we reemerged. "I think he said to go to the billiards room when we get tired of hiding," I said.

"Are you tired of hiding?"

"Very," I said. "I am *very* tired of hiding. But I don't especially want to go meet the others. Do you?"

Victor paused at the threshold of the room and looked up. "Am I mistaken, or is this mistletoe?" he said.

There was no mistletoe.

I wish I could say that I ducked aside when he moved in to kiss me. But I kissed him back with everything I had. Mountains and moonlight and melting snow all over again.

"Victor, I can't," I said eventually, although I could have. "Jack—"

"I know," he said. "I had to try."

We walked to the billiards room in silence. I felt less worried that someone had seen us than over the fact that the kiss had happened at all. Victor joined some other men in a game, and I found Marion, whose dimples could make anyone forget their problems. Tea candles danced like fireflies on the mantel. One guest, sipping immoderately from a hip flask, had become so drunk that he was about to light the wrong end of his cigarette, and Marion dashed to intervene.

I took that as my cue to slip away, too, melancholy in the midst of Christmas in July.

On my way to my guest cottage—one of the larger ones, for I was supposed to have been staying with Jack—I saw Hearst on the path ahead. In his Victorian frippery he seemed sad, slinking away at midnight while his party carried on.

From my window I could see him, solitary in his garden beneath the drooping wisteria, sitting on a bench, head in hand. Money can solve all kinds of problems, materially if not metaphysically. Hearst had a metaphysical sadness, something empty that no prosperity could touch.

My cottage was accented with a Velázquez and a Goya. The carved ceiling had been moved from a castle in Spain. After taking off my makeup and clothes in the bathroom all done up with black and gold, I lay on a bed so large that I looked like a Mervyn LeRoy sight gag. I wished I were not alone.

First, I wished for Victor; then I felt worse and wished for Jack.

My head hurt. I turned out the stupid antique lamp and cried.

The next morning I knew I had to leave before I saw Victor another time. I hauled my luggage to the kitchen, expecting only the house-keeper, finding Hearst.

"An early riser, too?" he said. "I can't laze until noon like the rest of them."

Unlike Marion, he rarely cared to make anyone feel good, and never could he be accused of an easy spontaneity. Marion invited; W. R. summoned. I thought for a moment he might stop me from going.

"I . . . I realized I'd be better off taking an earlier train."

He remained indifferent. I wondered what he cared about besides money and Marion.

On his feet were Granny's slippers.

"Please tell your grandmother her handiwork is superb," he said. "She's from the old country, I take it? I do hope you'll go there—and the better parts of Europe—sooner rather than later. Marion told me about your collection of miniatures. You'll never find finer pieces than on the globe's finest continent."

I couldn't think what to reply, but I didn't have to. He turned on his slippered heel, piece of toast in one imperial hand, and was gone. The cook bustled in with a hard-boiled egg and an apple wrapped in a handkerchief and sent me to the station.

As I was being driven down in the breaking dawn, the landscape around me embodied its name: La Cuesta Encantada. There Hearst and Marion were, living in splendor so sinful it was practically medieval, and I was punishing myself over one faithless kiss.

$\sim$

Later that fall Jack did agree to take me on a European tour, telling me it'd be the honeymoon we'd never had. When we got there, it was work, work, work.

It's not that I didn't have fun; I did. In Ireland they hailed me as "Our Own Doreen." I ate corned beef; I kissed the Blarney Stone. (Slightly sticky.) At Hearst's suggestion, I hunted up miniatures. And at Granny's instruction, I watched for fairies. On the coast I think I saw one: the Fairy of the Waters, riding a conch shell pulled by a dolphin. Thanks to Granny, too, I could sing traditional songs; singing was a pointless skill on-screen, but it was helpful during appearances, when stars were expected to entertain in the flesh.

In Dublin, Jack hired eight pairs of Irishmen—eight tall and eight short—to roam the streets in sandwich boards reading, respectively, I'M SO BIG. THAT'S WHY I WENT TO SEE DOREEN O'DARE IN SO BIG AT THE METROPOLE, and I'M SO SMALL. THAT'S WHY I DID THE SAME.

I didn't want to attend; I wanted to be a private person on a trip with my love. When we arrived at the Metropole, there was a veritable mob, bigger than any I'd seen in Hollywood. The police estimated the crowd at ten thousand or more and suggested that we leave in secret, by the back door.

"No," Jack said. "These are your people, Doreen"—as if I had some political obligation—and insisted that we exit through the front.

We could hardly move. I thought we might be lashed to death by flowers. My armful of red roses all nodded their heads, as if to say *yes, go go go*. A brooch spraying diamonds across my collar got ripped off, the crowd closing around us like quicksand. When we finally made it to the waiting car, the feathered cape I was wearing had been plucked clean.

Chapter 10

The Bedroom of the Prince

When I stop speaking, the basement falls silent. I can hear the ticking of the gold Elgin on my wrist: Gordon's last present before he died. It's hard to tell how time is passing down here in the darkness, the castle so bright it seems alive.

"Shall we move on to the bedrooms?" I say.

"What a bed the Prince gets to have," says Gladys. "I'm not a napper, but it makes me wish that I were. Weren't rest cures something people did in Old Hollywood? I never quite got what that meant."

"They were indeed a fad, and we were indeed exhausted, but it was understood by all that these rest cures cured nothing: not exhaustion, not addiction, not infidelity, or pregnancy, or whatever other malady might require someone to vanish for a while. Announcing a rest cure became code that you were in distress. I never took one."

In my sixties, I'm now on an enforced rest cure of sorts. Far fewer people care where I am. If only I could have banked some of my busyness back then, the way I saved my salaries.

She clicks the recorder on as if to say we won't be resting down here for long either. "The Bedroom of the Prince," I say. "Done in Russian blue, in an Eastern style."

I haven't thought in years about why I picked that style for this room. I told my craftsmen that it was based on a Slavic fairy tale I liked, Pushkin's "The Tale of Tsar Saltan," which was half-true; the unstated other half was that I was thinking of my own Prince Only Partly Charming. I built the room partly as a tribute to his dream of making us Hollywood royalty and partly as a means of shrinking him to a manageable size.

"I thought the Fairy Prince would want a polar bear rug," I continue, "but good luck finding a miniature polar bear. I took an ermine skin to the taxidermist, and he made one for me, with a mouse's teeth standing in for the bear's."

~

I charmed the bosses at First National with my quick return to the States—or maybe they just recognized that they'd snared a world-class sucker whom they shouldn't allow to slip away—and they awarded me a brilliant new contract and a production unit all my own.

The press played it up as a special gift from Jack. First National had put him in charge of all my pictures.

He decided that my first project of 1926 would be *Irene*, a shop-girl comedy in which I'd play yet another ethnically inflected waif, a working-class Irish lassie from an overlarge Catholic family whose da is a drinker and whose ma is a rock.

"What a challenging departure from my previous roles," I told Jack.

"The departure," he said, "is that it's going to make us twice as rich as anything prior."

Early in the film, Irene gets kicked out of a party at a lothario's love nest for refusing to cede her virtue; I was afraid that this would play as an insipid signifier of her pureheartedness, so I brought in Mervyn to make it a gag. We had Irene meet another party evacuee walking home alone on the dark road; Irene pulls out a pair of roller skates, each woman puts one on, and leaning on each other, they zip down the street.

The bit doubled up everyone on set with laughter when we shot it, it doubled me up when I saw it in rushes, and it doubled me up again months later at the premiere. And in that dark theater I began to notice, amid the ruckus of hilarity, voices that I recognized—my friend Mary, my friend Marion, my friend Lillian, my friend Adela, all laughing at these two women, skating together, supporting each other—and then I was quite surprised to find myself in tears.

The Doreen O'Dare Unit gave me a personal cameraman, too: Henry Freulich, who made me look like a princess, even when I felt like a gal who'd slept on the hearth.

In my next film I'd essentially be playing both. *Ella Cinders* was a modern-day retelling of the millennia-old fairy tale, this time about a small-town girl who seeks to see her name in lights. The idea of Hollywood as a contemporary equivalent of a handsome prince was very much not original to the film's scenario: the words *Cinderella story* appeared in the profile of every actress in town who wasn't the heiress to a railroad fortune, and even a couple who were.

It made sense that the fairy tale was as relevant as ever. I was making millions, but in what profession but mine could women do the same? At a time of booming prosperity, they were still pushing mops, jabbing typewriters, feeding sewing machines, serving food. Saleswomen, I learned while researching my shopgirl part in *Irene*, made less than half of what salesmen did. Little wonder then that Cinderella tapped into a national fantasy of finding both love and wealth.

In fact I had thought of some of my earlier parts, *Flaming Youth* included, as Cinderella tales of a sort. Not everyone agreed with my interpretation; more cynical critics held that my signature characters were everyday gold diggers with a dash of winsomeness. Nuts to that, I say. Anyone uncomfortable with the notion of a young working woman accepting a gentleman's generosity ought to be demanding that shops and factories pay them more, and more fairly. If these girls went on "dates" and accepted the new custom of "treating," who could blame them? How else were they to afford their ice cream cones, let alone their nights on the town? Who didn't want someone with dazzling eyes and big shoulders to whisper in her ear, *Kid, you're too good for this dump*, and whisk her off to someplace graceful?

In a sense, that's what Jack had done for me. Sure, somebody else might have come along and done the same. But somebody else didn't. Jack did.

∾

One afternoon when I was in between pictures—reclining by our swimming pool, lost in the play of bright surfaces and shadows, as real and unreal as the movies themselves—Jack came home reeking of booze.

"What are you doing here?" he asked, suit rumpled, black hair askew, towering over my chaise.

"I live here. I have a one-day break before we start shooting *It Must Be Love*, remember? Happy to see you, too."

He murmured something unintelligible and began to slouch off.

"Wait," I said, rising. "I have questions. First, wasn't today the publicity meeting over *Irene*? Second, why do you smell like a pirate galleon?"

"That's bay rum, darling. I had my hair cut."

"It hurts my face when you lie to it like that," I replied, clutching my towel. "You look like a bum, and you're behaving like one."

"How'd you like a detailed critique of *your* personal appearance?" He grasped my arm.

In past scenes such as this, copious weeping would have been my way out, but the cycle had hardened me. "I'd prefer it from someone who's not seeing pink elephants."

"Dammit, Eileen." His wit, evidently, had drowned at the bottom of a bottle.

This wasn't the first time he'd grabbed me, but it was the first that his fingers tightened hard enough to cause real pain. The snip-snip of the gardener clipping the hedges on the other side of our fence sounded loud to my ears—a promise of someone to help if things got out of hand, but also someone to be embarrassed about should he catch us in this attitude. I tried to wrench away.

"You're hurting me, Jack," I said, and he finally let go. "Looks like I'll have to wear long sleeves tomorrow."

"Darling, I'm sorry, I'm so sorry," he said, horrified at the marks. "I don't know what got into me."

I wanted to say I knew exactly what it was that had gotten into him, and in approximately what quantity, but that was no way to tamp down the fight. Instead I said, "Let's go inside and have you lie down."

He could barely get his shoes off as he lay atop his unturned-down bed. In the mirror over his dressing table my face shone pale despite my abortive attempt at a suntan. His conduct was turning me into a sad cliché—the classic clown with an aching heart—when really he was the self-made buffoon. Our marriage seemed like a room with black walls and no door.

The telephone rang; I raced to answer before it woke Jack. Adela's voice crackled across the wire. "Come to dinner with me at the Ambassador this evening, won't you, Doreen?"

The last thing I wanted was to leave, lest Jack wake up and go out again. I felt sure that the abysmal charade that our marriage had become would be apparent to anyone who saw me no matter what length sleeves I had on. I tried to laugh it off. "My dear," I said, "I fear I cannot, for today I am simply too *tragique!*"

"I bet," she said, "given how Jack decided to play hooky on the First National meeting." She paused, then, "Word about his troubles is getting out. That's what I want to warn you about. I've never spilled the beans on him, and I never will without your say-so, but other reporters are starting to sniff around. Once it's out, I'll have to do my job, Doreen."

"Why," I cried, "this unholy joy in the spreading of shame?"

"It pays the bills," Adela said.

"I'm sorry, Adela, I'm not talking about *you*. I just mean—well, your public, I suppose."

"The morality of Hollywood always constitutes a grave national crisis, Doreen. You know that. Disrepute sells magazines. Sure, these little scandals don't matter much. But that line of argument won't take you far, because that's exactly why people love them: they *don't* matter much. Other people's wrecked lives are damned entertaining, and a chance to show the other ladies at the country club how superior one is, how sharp the scalpel of one's disapproval. It's a rotten situation, I know. On the other hand, they *do* pay you an awful lot."

"I know you're right," I said. "But I hate it."

"I'm sorry to put you on the spot, chum. I'll accept your excuse for not coming out this evening. But one of these days, you're going to run out of excuses for Jack. I hope you have a plan for what happens then."

I hung up. Jack's snore echoed down the hall. It sounded like someone rearranging furniture: a cosmetic fix, when the beams were rotting.

Ambition might consist, more than anything else, of the willingness to work oneself to death. How else to explain my trip to New York, with almost no rest between pictures, with a man I still loved but increasingly didn't trust?

When I woke up next to Jack in our room at the Ambassador Hotel on Park Avenue, the off-gray daylight of Manhattan did nothing to elevate my mood. It was late September, and I sensed that he was due to disappear again. I'd learned to recognize a certain queasy shift in his chord, an added tone that signaled a good time about to degrade. On the train he'd ordered ginger ale like a general ordering a tactical strike, a sign that he'd soon give in to the harder beverages.

The director called New York the best city in the galaxy, though I begged to disagree. I had never liked it there, with its congestion of buildings and humanity. Too much hurry and not enough air. I missed the West. Rain began almost the second we arrived and persisted for days.

I tried to refocus my attention on the things that did please me about shooting our new film, *Orchids and Ermine*. Per Jack's strategy, I was back to flappers, playing Pink Watson, who moves up from her job as a receptionist at a cement factory to a switchboard girl at the De Luxe Hotel. A rollicking comedy of mistaken identity, it meant that I got to work with Mervyn again. I came up with a joke for the title cards at the expense of rich older men who, when their wives turn forty, want to trade them in for two twenties.

Jack decided that we'd simply incorporate the inclement weather, which proved to make some of the scenes even funnier than planned. On Fifth Avenue—where, as a title card put it, "all good little minks go when they die"—we filmed a water-soaked chase sequence between a taxi and a double-decker bus that was a veritable ballet of light physical comedy, following Jack's instructions to the letter, even though by then he was nowhere to be found.

I got caught up in the vivacity of the scene, but after we wrapped for the afternoon, I was saddened by the sight of all the real-world people on the real-world streets, their faces pale as bird excrement beneath the mouse-gray sky. Automobiles honked and splashed stormwater from the gutters.

While I was growing up, I was fascinated by miniatures of praiseworthy workmanship: a fountain pen that held one drop of ink, a teapot hammered from a single copper penny, a camera that took pictures one-fourth by five-eighths of an inch. In Manhattan, I had access to these items; as a successful film star I had the money to buy them. I stayed out as long as I could that evening, adding to Eileen's Miscellany: visiting shops, buying little editions with Etruscan bindings and gold leaf, plus enough miniature furniture for a whole town of fairy mansions.

I was using tiny things to hide from the gigantic problem of Jack.

I trudged back to Midtown. Men hunched by in Chesterfield over-coats and mackintoshes; women struggled in the wind, their umbrellas like bat wings. Were any of them putting off going home, too? Did everyone walk around self-deceived, chess pieces that believed themselves to move of their own volition?

Anxious, I returned to our hotel and stopped at the Ambassador's front desk. A dozen messages were waiting: the First National New York office calling to see where he'd been.

I stood and listened outside our suite on the sixteenth floor: stumbling footsteps, unintelligible muttering. I squared my shoulders and went in.

Jack liked to dress well, drunk or sober; lately he'd been wearing the soft, striped shirts of English broadcloth that we'd gotten on our trip, as well as a classy topcoat against the weather. Gazing around the suite, I saw his elegant clothes strewn across the floor, and there was Jack pacing from wall to wall wearing only a terry-cloth robe. It was a sign that I should have walked out. But it was night, and it was my room, too; where was I to go? I wanted to help him, to put him to bed.

But I didn't do that either. I set the messages on the dresser and looked him in the eye. "Didn't you realize they're looking for you?"

"Oh, hi, hello, how are you, I missed you," he mocked. "God, you're a different person in public. The Doreen O'Dare of the screen is an angel, but as a wife? What a shrew."

I refused to take the bait, stooping to pick up a discarded sock.

"Don't pull that routine," he said, yanking a pair of his underwear from under a chair. "Tidying up. As if I can't take care of myself."

He could reach a point where reason eluded him, and he came to find his own anger delectable. It usually took him a while to work up to that state, but I had apparently walked in when he was already well past it.

"You really go out there and turn it on, don't you?" he snapped, grabbing my wrist.

"Yes. I do. Because that's my job."

His eyes were glassy and suspicious. He seemed lost for a response. The silence puckered. I tried to pry his fingers off. "On the subject of jobs," I said, "I can't save yours for you forever if you keep doing this."

"Save my *job?*" he said, grabbing my other wrist. "Save *my* job? How about *your* job? You'd be nowhere if it weren't for me."

"Jack, please," I said, inwardly furious—at him for never being satisfied, at myself for trying to have this conversation with him at all. "You're not fit company for man or beast."

My feet left the rug. He was picking me up—easy enough, given his height.

"Jack, please. I'll leave you in peace, just put me down."

So much of life is sorting what you do from what gets done to you. Was this my fault? It felt like it could be my fault. I knew what he was; I'd known when I married him. On his forearm, inches from my face, the white mark where the poker burned him.

"Put you down?" He laughed: an ugly, wet sound. "I lifted you up. I made you a star. You're goddamn right I can put you down."

He carried me to the window. Now he was the one trying to pry my fingers from him. My engagement ring had never looked so hard and glittering.

He freed an arm, tore the curtains from their rod, and flung the window wide. I watched the scene as if it were one of my own movies, with a degree of eerie remove. The hero—the villain?—was about to drop the heroine sixteen stories from the window of the Ambassador Hotel. The heroine began to weep and plead, but softly, so as not to cause a scene. As if a scene were not exactly what she needed at that moment. Didn't she understand that her life was in danger?

The breeze shifted; for an instant the air took on the dry crack of autumn. I came back to myself.

"Don't cry," Jack was saying. "Don't bother. You're an actress. Do you think I believe you feel anything for me?"

I did as he said—stopped crying—and looked into his eyes, haunted and void, the empty blue of swimming pools. He had my entire body out the window, and now I felt the wind, stronger up there than it had been on the ground. I kicked my legs to reach the sill. I didn't want to move too quickly and break his grip or kick too hard and pull him out, too. What a way to end a marriage that'd be. *At least it's stopped raining,* I thought. *That's nice.*

"Jack, you're going to regret this," I begged to a face I could scarcely recognize. "Jack, think about what you're doing. Please."

I prayed for intervention: a rap on the door, a jangling telephone, a bellboy delivering a telegram on a tray. Anything. I stared at the garish garlands of electric lights lining the streets below. Beset by spasms of my own mortality, I struggled not to struggle, tried to treat it like a stunt, my hands clasping Jack's arms inside his robe.

Through the night air a butterfly swooped—black wings with yellow edges and iridescent blue spots, the type known as a mourning cloak—and landed on the white limestone above Jack's head. Granny said that if you saw a butterfly fluttering near a corpse, then that was the soul; it ought to be taken as a sign that the person had entered upon immortal life. Jack and I were both still alive. What were any of us doing here, two hundred feet above Park Avenue?

We hung in a tense and vital moment. I forced my legs to relax. One of my step-in pumps slipped off. I hoped it didn't hit anybody below.

Then by merest chance—was it?—someone knocked lightly, then entered.

It was Mervyn LeRoy.

He was holding a tiny cut-glass punch bowl that I had bought at a shop that afternoon. "I found this in the hallway," he was saying, "and I knew there was only one person it could—"

He froze, looking at Jack, me, the torn curtain billowing in the wind. "What the hell?" he said. "Flanagan?"

Jack became crisp and automatic, chill as a receptionist. He withdrew me from the window and set me down.

I fell to my knees, thanking God silently for the dropped fairy bowl.

"Hello, Mervyn," Jack said. I crept away from him, uncontrollably shaking.

"Doreen," Mervyn said, trying to reach me.

Jack switched back.

"How *dare* you walk in without waiting to be asked?" he screamed. "You're sleeping with him, aren't you? You two disgust me. But you're a *Catholic*, Eileen. You're tied to me for life. Don't think it'll be that easy!"

Jack had apparently ordered from room service earlier; now he picked up whatever was at hand and threw it—at Mervyn's head, at the mirror, at me. The Seafood Salad and the Fruit Cocktail, the Roquefort Cheese with Toasted Crackers and the Baked Stuffed Tomato. The Banana Blanc Mange whipped through the air, losing its cream and half maraschino cherry. It would have been like a Sennett comedy had I not feared for our lives.

I knew Mervyn was brave, but he was nearly a foot shorter than Jack. I had seen Mervyn mad before, and Mervyn was getting mad.

"No," I told Mervyn. "Run."

And that's what we did, Jack too unsteady to catch us.

No time to wait for the elevator, we made for the stairs. We didn't speak until we were out on the sidewalk. Panting, we stood on the pavement beyond the awning, about where my body could have landed if Jack had dropped me.

"My shoe!" I said. There it was. I put it back on. The absurdity hit me. "This is just like a bit that you and I would come up with, Mervyn!"

"This isn't a bit," Mervyn said. "We ought to call the cops."

"The *police?*" My hysterical laughter at my hapless shoe stopped. "Mervyn, they won't care. I've talked it over with Adela. They treat wife-beating as a private family matter, not a crime. It won't go anywhere."

"He was about to kill you, Doreen."

"I don't think we can say that," I said. "It was the liquor. Besides, the newspapers would go nuts over it. The gossip would be terrible. For the film. How many people are working on this film, Mervyn? And for me. It would be the end for me."

The papers always referred to Mervyn as a youthful funster, but he looked about ten thousand years old. He opened his mouth, thought better of it.

We started to walk, falling in step, huddled under Mervyn's umbrella. It had begun to rain again. I had no idea of where to go in New York. Neither did Mervyn. My head throbbed. The city sobbed. The water over everything looked like crumpled silver.

Mervyn and I wandered the streets of Manhattan, too frightened to go back, the chill goose-pimpling our skin. In Little Italy we stopped at Lombardi's; I wasn't hungry, but Mervyn made me eat. We were able to sit at a table in back, undisturbed. At least in New York nobody cared who you were. Then again, shaken and bedraggled, I probably wouldn't have recognized my own face in a crowd.

"I want to go home," I said, picking at my pizza. "To LA."

"We have to finish the picture," Mervyn said. "You're a pro, Doreen. Maybe too much of a pro."

We pounded our shoe leather into the pavement as taxis hooted around us all through the long night, dim and cold and dripping.

We returned to the Ambassador at dawn. Jack was gone.

Chapter 11

THE BATHROOM OF THE PRINCE

Parched, I take a sip of my water. These new Styrofoam cups: I dislike them. The way their surface scratches your lips. The way you leave a tacky lipstick kiss on the rim. But the Museum of Science and Industry has embraced them as blithely as everywhere else has these days.

I set the cup down and meet Gladys's eyes.

"I have a somewhat sensitive question," she says. "Not for the tape."

"Uh-oh," I say. "You may fire when ready."

"Okay," she says. "Don't laugh, but do you really believe in fairies?"

"Gladys, when you lost your milk teeth, what did you do to dispose of them?" I ask. "Left them for the Tooth Fairy?"

"Sure. But that's kid stuff. You built the castle as an adult. But you stick to the premise that the castle is for the fairies. I'm curious: Is that the final piece of decoration? Or do you believe it?"

If you glance at the right moment, you can sometimes catch the castle's occupants. The majordomo, large and fat. The attendants, like dancers with all their curtsies. The fairy child in the turned-up chair who likes to read with his feet in the air. Noblemen whose every gesture obliges the court. Chamberlains. A retinue. A princess who's true blue, and whose prince is, too. A cloaked figure, narrow as a candle flame, whom the others seem to avoid.

But I don't tell Gladys that. "When you watch a movie," I ask, "do you believe it?"

"No," Gladys says. "I mean, well, yes. I don't believe that it's true. But if it's good, then I'll buy into it."

"Over the years," I say, "I've helped tell a lot of made-up stories. What I've figured out is that the minute you start trying to *convince* anybody of anything, you're a dead duck. What you do instead is create an *occasion* for them to pretend, to feel joy at what seems enchanted. We make that enchantment real."

She nods, gesturing now to the Prince's Bathroom. "More real, maybe, than any full-sized bathroom I've ever seen."

"There was a mania in Hollywood for fancy bathrooms." I shrug. "I couldn't tell you why. The walls of the Prince's Bathroom are made of translucent alabaster, as is the tub, which is shaped like a Chinese lily. I'm fond of the turquoise frogs, and of the gold mermaids—or merrow, as they say in Ireland. Over the scallop-shell sink is one of my favorite tiny looking glasses. The frame is gold and has a sapphire at the center surrounded by diamonds."

∼

I tipped the Ambassador staff to high heaven to clean up the room and keep quiet about it. Then I changed clothes and went right back to work as I waited for Jack to show up.

He did at last, bearing hangdog assurances—he was sorry, he hadn't meant it, it'd never happen again—and a pair of tickets to game 2 of the World Series. How he got them, never mind in his condition, I'll never know, but that was Jack.

When Victor Marquis and I were working on *The Sky Pilot*, he would often say, in the face of delays and setbacks, "We have to deal with conditions as we find them." I tried to apply the same attitude to subsequent productions, and to almost everything else in my life, including Jack. I convinced myself, as I always did, that it would work:

that he wouldn't harm my happiness and safety again, that he'd be careful in the future of his career and pride. Or, if he did act up, I'd handle it better next time.

People who have the ability to keep going *unscathed* through scathing ordeals are believed by outsiders not to feel those things. But the depth of our feeling is the very reason we have to keep moving. Back in Tampa, while the other kids were frightened of the bay, I would push away from shore and slip across the waves. But underneath I was kicking and kicking, a smile on my face, my face on my head, my head above water, where I needed it to stay.

That was before I ever saw the Pacific, of course.

We wrapped the location shoots for *Orchids* and returned to Hollywood with relief. I was pleased to be back in a bewitching landscape, prettier than New York, which seemed a city of cold tombs after what had happened. Rumors of mountain lions prowling the Santa Monica foothills stalked the local gossip. Marion Davies told me that the cats had been seen on Mount Lee and Cahuenga Peak—a wilderness not completely erased.

Young hopefuls kept arriving in California by the busload. The boys could join studio crews or snag positions as chauffeurs, or become scouts or agents, managing their fellow aspirants. The girls had the harder go of it, subject as sparrows to hawkish men.

I called Adela, in her professional capacity, and gave her, not for attribution, a few details of what had transpired in New York. I wanted word to get out to certain people in the industry; I wanted Jack to know that a few people knew. A little insurance policy.

∽

Thanks largely to Jack's never-ending publicity, First National had chosen me to be their leading light from the end of 1926 and into 1927, and this meant more work, nearly nonstop. We finished the interior scenes for *Orchids* in early December, at which point I needed a pause. The speed was exhausting.

When Lillian stopped by for a Sunday visit, she found me thin and careworn. "Doreen, we've got to plump you up!" she said. "I'm going to get you some cream puffs and fry you up some bacon sandwiches."

She glided out for the supplies to do so, wearing her customary drab disguise.

"As usual, nobody recognized me," she reported gleefully upon her return, taking off her hat and plain cloth coat, revealing a rayon frock you could find on any LA housewife. With Lillian it wasn't only the costume but her entire demeanor that allowed her that freedom. When she sought to be incognito, her posture and attitude dwindled; she erased all traces of her gravity and refinement.

"You didn't have to walk," I said. "I'd've lent you the car."

"You know I enjoy my exercise," she said, delving into a cabinet.

I tried to help, but she pushed me back into my chair with one little hand.

I had no appetite, but it was good to see her.

"Lord knows I know the value of hard work," she said, standing at the stove, wielding a frying pan that looked twice her size. "But would it be the end of the world if you took a break for a bit?"

That night I told Jack that she was right. A life well spent is the greatest success, and I was no longer delighted with how I was spending mine. I still loved making pictures, but I needed to rest.

On my behalf, in his capacity as production manager, Jack wrote to Richard Rowland, the head of First National. I had met Rowland several times: a balding man whose round face, round cheeks, and round wire-rimmed glasses belied his almost mineral hardness, which I suppose one had to have to head a studio.

In his letter, Jack made the quality-not-quantity argument: better to have me make a slightly smaller number of top-shelf pictures than to grind out more for the sake of grinding. Rowland was a quantity man, a real why-have-one-pearl-when-you-could-have-a-necklace kind of guy.

I'm afraid that's a shade unconvincing, he replied, *considering what we're paying Miss O'Dare, not to mention you.* But Jack persisted, and Rowland acceded. He had been after Jack to rein in his drinking, and he couldn't resist getting a dig in when he wired his consent not to Jack, but to me: *Take two months' break & tell little Irishman not to worry.*

"He said yes!" I cried, and flung my arms around Jack, after tossing the crumpled telegram into the fire.

~

Pure idleness not being in my nature, I used the time to do research. *Naughty But Nice,* slated to start shooting in early February 1927, was a finishing-school comedy. Jack had decided it was best for me to play an entirely new type, a nouveau-riche country gal whose family sends her off to the haughty East Coast after striking oil on their Texas ranch.

Mervyn was then working his way toward being a director in his own right, but I managed to recruit him as my comedy constructor. We devised a bit in which my character camps out on a roof, then hurtles earthward after moving in her sleep. I did it dozens of times. The quilt I was wrapped in broke my fall, mostly, but I still ended up covered with bruises. The pain was such that leaving the set, I asked for and got the next day off.

The following morning—as I was sleeping in, or trying to, after a terrible night—the telephone rang. It was Jack's secretary, announcing that he had been drinking in his office.

He'd been pulling long hours with his sales manager and the head of the story department to review the upcoming schedule, making sure that all was shipshape for Rowland's annual visit to the First National facilities in Burbank. Jack knew Rowland had concerns about his reliability, and the pressure had finally gotten the best of him. Now Jack was drunk, intractable, on his way to incapacitated. "This is a very bad time for this to be happening," she said.

The chauffeur sped me to Burbank, winding through the mountains on Ventura Boulevard, a white glare in the air. It was going to be hot. Pink berries from the pepper trees at the studio gate drifted along the pavement.

Mervyn had already been on the lot, and he and Adela met me there. Writers, studio heads—they'd all have a bottle of something in the desk's bottom drawer, and they'd bring it out to have a snort: to celebrate, to console, to dull boredom, you name it. But to be sloppy on studio property, as Jack was? Unacceptable.

Mervyn entered first, and Adela gently closed the heavy wooden door. Jack's desk looked like an earthquake had struck. Swaying a little, as though in the aftershocks, he sat behind it in his swivel chair, squinting at us through a haze of cigarette smoke. During the rainless seasons in Hollywood men could wear a shirt, a sweater, and white flannel trousers and in that lax manner look casually sharp. Jack was in the outfit but looked dumb as could be.

"Come on, Flanagan," Mervyn said, "we'll run you on back to Beverly Hills." Jack, thank God, let himself be led. As we worked our weaving way out of the building, I could feel all the eyes of First National tracking our progress.

After we got him home and tucked into bed, Adela delivered a cool diagnosis. "You need a steady man, Doreen," she said, perched like a cat on the living room sofa. "Not a gibbering infant."

An instant before she said it, I'd have agreed completely. But something about hearing him attacked—even by a friend, even in a gesture of loyalty—set me off.

"I won't have my husband spoken of that way. I need to make a phone call."

In the hallway, I dialed the studio.

"Mr. Richard Rowland, please," I said. Mervyn raised his eyebrows. "No, I don't want to leave a message. I need to speak to him immediately."

Rowland was a dapper man, ever fresh from the tailor; even his voice over the line sounded groomed. "Rowland here. How can I help you?"

If anything could save Jack's job—and I wasn't sure that anything could—then this would be it. I steadied myself. "This is Mrs. Jack Flanagan speaking. I just called to say hello."

"I see," said Rowland. I could practically hear him assembling the puzzle pieces: if he fired Jack now, he'd also lose me. "I hope you're able to spend the rest of your day off in ease, Mrs. Flanagan. I personally wouldn't dream of doing anything to disturb your peace."

"That's very reassuring to hear," I said. "In that case, I'll see you back on the lot tomorrow."

I hung up and flopped into a chair.

Adela had been jotting. She flipped her reporter's notebook closed, then saw me watching her and correctly identified the expression on my face as dread. "Not to worry, kid," she said. "This isn't for *Photoplay*. They don't deserve it. It's notes for me, for future reference. That was a hell of a maneuver."

"Thank you," I said. "When you say 'future,' I hope you mean quite distant."

"I can't say," she said. "It'll be up to the muse, and she's a fickle bitch, if you'll pardon my French. But it won't be soon, I promise you."

∼

For what remained of March, and on into April, Jack attacked sobriety like an offensive lineman. Dry as the Sahara, he worked as hard at First National as a whole team of men. But I remained perpetually on edge. Each time he entered a room, I never knew which Jack it was going to be.

Sober, he was as sweet as an angel, but I couldn't take him to parties any longer; he never came with me to see Marion at Hearst's. The story we all agreed upon was that Jack had to work, but in truth he wasn't wanted—not by me, and not by the judgmental and abstemious W. R. either.

I had to use all my powers to remain fit for work, but I did it: we finished *Naughty But Nice*. Casting around for a new starring vehicle, First National decided it was time for Mervyn to direct me, which was such great news for both of us that we waited for the other shoe to drop. (Once again I could look back with fondness on a time when that phrase was merely metaphorical.) And drop it did: the property they wanted to attach us to was a stinker—*When Irish Eyes Are Smiling*, a sappy piece of stereotypical claptrap.

I thought maybe I could wait out the clock. My contract expired at the end of May, and Jack and I talked about using that lapse as a chance to renegotiate, to insist on being directed by Mervyn, but with a different script.

Before we could advance unto the breach calmly, however, Jack dove in headlong. The rumors that soon they'd fire him had gotten more dire; instead of waiting, he quit as production manager of First National, alleging mistreatment and disrespect. There may have been more to it, too; I suspect that word of my call to Rowland had made its way back to him, and he felt emasculated by it. He knew he could never do the same for me. But he could do the opposite; he could do it in reverse.

That afternoon he came home early.

Sitting in the bath, hot water up to my ears, trying to ease the pain of a day's work, I heard the front door slam and his feet taking the stairs two at a time. The door swung open in a swirl of steam.

"I told them I was leaving," he said, "and that you were coming with me."

"Jack," I said, "tell me you're bluffing."

The water in the tub felt instantly cold. Outside, honeysuckle continued to climb perversely around the open windows, and the sunshine beat naively in.

"I'm unhappy with how I'm being treated, Eileen." He sat on the edge of the tub, scooped up some bubbles, flung them back down. "You should be, too. Think about it."

According to him, my expiring contract said that at the end of this twenty-four-month period, I was to have completed eight pictures—but I hadn't, due to the delays on the script for *Irish Eyes*. This was absolutely fair and reasonable, given that they couldn't expect my approval for a terrible story. When I pointed out that some of the delays were mine, taking the occasional pause from a breakneck pace, he became outraged.

"Eileen, listen to yourself!" He gave the water a little slap. "Where in the contract does it state they have the right to work you to death?"

The following morning I did what he asked: I sent First National a wire saying that they owed me $1 million for the unfinished eighth film and that we'd have to undergo arbitration to resolve it.

Adela came by at the beginning of June to say that First National planned to turn around and sue me for a million dollars, claiming the delays were my responsibility, and that I had to complete *Irish Eyes* or else.

And that's how Jack and I ended up aboard the Santa Fe *Chief*, speeding for Chicago and on to New York: me to avoid service of process, him to try to crash the First National board of directors meeting and plead our case.

The press clamored for details, and we did our best to avoid them. We holed up miserably in the Ritz-Carlton on Madison Avenue. Since returning from our previous New York stint, neither of us had spoken the name of the Ambassador Hotel, and during this one we never set foot within a block of it.

I had come to hate New York even on its best day, but these circumstances made it extra odious. All I did was play hide-and-seek with process servers and watch Jack drink. Gazing out the window at the sheen of gasoline on the asphalt, I longed for the earth to reassert itself as it did out West. I missed our courtyard with its fig and apricot trees. Jack would order me a silver dish of Neapolitan ice cream and I, appetiteless, would watch it melt. I tortured myself by reading the papers. The way they covered the dispute made me want to puke.

Given Jack's profound investment in our shared Irish roots—even my engagement ring was cut in the shape of a shamrock—I shouldn't have been surprised that the press played up the ethnic angle. Jack's temper had become renowned by then. Doreen, as readers will remember, walked off the First National lot following her husband's resignation as production manager, one article declared. Jack Flanagan is Irish, and, therefore, hot-headed. But even now with the battle at its height, Richard Rowland and the rest of the F.N. execs admit a sneaking liking for young Flanagan, and believe that soon he'll get over his spell.

These stereotypes of Irish manhood—rash, mercurial, ultimately charming enough to win over his enemies—were maddening. I found their portrayal of me as a long-suffering Irish wife even more hurtful, as if Roman Catholicism and a diet of root vegetables had reduced me to some kind of innocent presexual child, too dumb to make her own decisions.

For someone who had always done her best without complaint, it was disorienting—not at all restful—to sit around in plush luxury doing nothing, not to mention doing it while the target of such animosity. Granny had raised me to understand that courtesy should not be a bonus; it should be automatic. These proceedings felt excruciatingly rude. I'd expected anger from Rowland and his business partners, but most of my friends also suddenly developed shoulders colder than polar bears. I'd never felt so alone in my life.

Aunt Lib, in town with Walter for a meeting of newspapermen, came to the Ritz to see us in our exile. I had lost so much weight, falling below a hundred pounds, that she called a doctor.

The physician, who'd been keeping up with the coverage, prescribed a less distressing lifestyle. I laughed in his face; he laughed back, knowing his advice was unfollowable at this juncture. "I also prescribe milkshakes," he added.

Aunt Lib offered to take me out to get one. A malted, actually: butterscotch, my favorite.

Fashionable as ever, she'd kept up with the times, wearing a brown canton crepe dress with a bolero blouse and gilt buttons. "If you look better, you'll feel better," she said, helping me don a flower-print chiffon with fluttery pleated fans and jabots. I added a cloche hat to deflect attention from my famous hairstyle, and we were ready to go.

Elm seeds fluttered down like we were in a parade as we strolled past Bryant Park, and the scent of linden tinged the air. I breathed the relief of letting someone care for me, really care.

"Far be it from me to presume to tell any other woman what to do in her marriage," she began—exactly the kind of overture she'd include when she was in one of her advice-giving moods—"but I'd be remiss if I didn't testify that getting divorced is far from the worst thing that can happen to a girl. If I had insisted on remaining with my initial mistake, I'd never have had the chance to be as happy as I am with your Uncle Walter."

I bit my tongue, choosing not to remind her of their own tempestuous cycle of quarrel-and-kiss. "Noted, Aunt Lib," I said. "Thank you."

I really did note it. I wasn't ready yet, but I lost myself in thought, scripting out the pros and cons and practicalities of splitting from Jack.

And that's when they got me.

An ancient lady in black widow's weeds, her hair cobwebbed beneath her ebony hat, wandered up to us.

"Why, Doreen O'Dare?" she exclaimed in a warbling voice. "Is that really you?"

Happy to see a friendly face—a stranger, a fan—I said yes, and went to shake her hand. "May I please have your autograph?" she said.

As soon as I took the sheet, I saw that I'd been served.

"Oh no!" I said. "What a disgusting ruse!"

At that, the old lady slumped against Aunt Lib and began to weep disconsolately. "I really am a fan, Miss O'Dare," she keened into a hankie. "It's only that I need the money! I'm so ashamed."

I comforted her on a bus bench for a full ten minutes and ended up giving her an autograph anyway before marching back up to our room at the Ritz.

After that incident, Jack changed his tack. Having been served, I'd have to appear in court; if I failed to do so, First National could get a default judgment that would grant them access to any of my assets: our joint bank account, our and my family's homes, my miniature collection. He backed down from his latest threat—that we'd sail for Europe and make pictures there if the board of directors failed to grant him what he asked—and they agreed to see him.

In the end, we resolved it. Under my new contract, my weekly rate would be higher than when I'd left; they also released me from the missing eighth film on the expiring contract and extended my new one for another four. For his part, Jack would return to First National at an increased salary but would no longer run the studio. He'd be an independent producer, in charge exclusively of Doreen O'Dare projects. It was an impressive piece of lawyering, all in all: it resolved the conflict, put me back to work, gave Jack some victories to salve his pride, and indicated to me—decorously, but unmistakably—that Jack was now my problem, not theirs.

I was relieved, for the most part. During those weeks in limbo I'd been letting myself visualize worst-case scenarios, and when I pictured them I was surprised to find that they didn't seem so dreadful. In the loveliest, I made one more glorious picture and retired at the height of my popularity. I extended the fantasy: if I couldn't have kids of my own, fine, I'd adopt. I wanted to be a mother badly. I didn't care whether their faces resembled mine or not.

The hatchet between us and First National was not so much buried as sunk to the bottom of the ocean, such that Jack and I were able to return to Los Angeles in a leisurely fashion: by sea. Jack, in the grip of one of his manias, had bought us a yacht while we were in New York; his idea was that we and Richard Rowland would sail to New Orleans on a no-hard-feelings cruise, then return the rest of the way by rail. I figured there was a chance—perhaps one in twelve—that at some point Jack would murder Rowland, wrap his corpse in chains, and dump him overboard. As it happened, the journey was perfectly pleasant.

Aboard, we began planning the details of my next four pictures. *Irish Eyes* was shelved, thank God. We decided instead that it was time for me to do a war picture. I had adored Victor Marquis's *The Big Parade*—a great film even adjusting for my secret bias—and I lobbied hard that our subject be the Great War. Thus was it decreed that I'd star in *Lilac Time*, based on the Broadway play. Since Rowland was in a generous mood, I got him to agree to bring in Adela for the adaptation.

Jack had the ability to purge bad blood instantaneously, and that August and September, he redoubled the elbow grease. I did, too, but nothing felt the same. My bad feelings lingered as the days shortened and the weather cooled, then gradually got replaced by worse ones.

October 6, 1927. Al Jolson thrilled the ears of the theatergoing public with his zippy rendition of "Toot, Toot, Tootsie (Goo' Bye!)"; to me it felt like the onset of a migraine.

The Jazz Singer was the first feature-length film that had both a synchronized recorded musical score and lip-synchronous singing and speech. In harmony with its theme of Jewish assimilation and inter-generational conflict, Warner Brothers premiered the picture in their flagship theater in New York after sunset on the eve of Yom Kippur. The papers declared that when Jolson, in close-up, uttered the line, "Wait a minute, wait a minute, you ain't heard nothing yet!" the audience became hysterical.

Reading about the pandemonium the next morning, I was terrified at what the innovation might mean: for the industry, for me. It had taken us so long to get past gimmicks—locomotives running straight into the camera lens—and figure out how to make art, to use our techniques in ways that caused them to vanish and the characters and stories to emerge. Now, in a flash, we were back to gimmickry.

But Jack's head stayed level. "I love a challenge, darling," he said, helping himself to a fig from a dish of them. "This gives me ideas."

"What kind of ideas?" I asked, putting my coffee cup down atop the photograph of Jolson in blackface, mouth open so wide you could practically see his uvula.

"We could put some sound in *Lilac Time*," Jack said. He abandoned his breakfast, rang for the chauffeur.

"But it says that this Vitaphone technology doesn't lend itself well to all productions."

"True. We'll figure it out. I'm going to dash down to the studio and talk to some folks."

This was one of Jack's most attractive qualities: problems that other people—including me—saw as insurmountable obstacles, he took on as riddles to be solved. He was more the man I'd fallen in love with that morning than he'd been in months, maybe years. He seemed to recognize that in himself, too. I said a quiet, conflicted prayer: for him to succeed, for synchronized sound to fail.

I took the unfinished piece of cinnamon toast from his forsaken plate. No matter how masterfully they pontificated, the future was as unguessable to studio executives as it was to anyone else. A director was only as good as his most recent picture. Same for a star: an actress's fame was as fragile as a soap bubble. You'd need a crystal ball to prophesy which pictures would succeed, and nobody owned one.

But Jack had a better sense of such things than most. Sinking my teeth into a corner with his bite marks, I figured that if he thought he had a good idea, then he probably did.

These days, if they think of it at all, people have the mistaken notion that sound rushed in with *The Jazz Singer*, and with that, a soundproof door slammed on the silent era. But there were scarcely two minutes of talking in *The Jazz Singer*, and the sound sequences were isolated, somewhat awkward. It wasn't quite new either: as far back as 1921, Griffith and others had experimented with synchronized dialogue, but it hadn't caught on. The shift to sound was halting and chaotic, like entering a hallway whose length you couldn't determine.

∾

Lilac Time centered on the romance between French farm girl Jeannine—*c'est moi*—and a British pilot. It was difficult to shoot and in the end cost over a million dollars to produce, a significant gamble, especially coming off our well-publicized spat with First National. But it was so fun to work on, because it felt like old times: Jack and I collaborating in concert, unstoppable. Harmonious on set, amorous at home.

With all the war scenes, not to mention the full-size French village, we had a cast and crew of about three hundred who lived in a tent city out in El Toro. With a full complement of extras, our ranks grew to seventeen hundred. Our armies fought upon—and our planes fought above—a fifty-acre stretch wherein we recruited distant eucalyptus to stand in for French yews. Most of our pilots were Great War veterans. Committed to contributing to this authenticity, I learned my lines in French, right down to the curses.

Not long after our picture about heroic Great War aviators went into production, *Wings*, Clara Bow's picture about Great War aviators, also went into production. They were shooting on an airbase in Texas, with an even bigger budget and the cooperation of the US military at their disposal, and it soon became clear that their film would make it to theaters sooner. This irritated me—I hadn't quite forgiven Clara for her repugnant behavior—but Jack figured we could use their quick progress to our own advantage. He hired away the chief stunt pilot for *Wings* to oversee our aerial dogfights, and with him came all the experience he'd gained working on that film, as well as his insider's knowledge of all their stunts. Instead of being in danger of seeming like a pale imitation, we were now likely to cash in on their film's success.

Since we were going to anger her anyway, I snatched something else from Clara. To play the British pilot we needed a little-known male actor with idol potential, and Jack took my suggestion that we try Gary Cooper.

Cooper, I'd gathered from the gossip mill, had caught Clara's eye—among other portions of her anatomy—when he'd had a bit part in *It*. He became one of her regular paramours, and she'd gotten him cast in increasingly prominent roles in her pictures, including *Wings*; now, rumor had it, they were on the outs. Men were slow to see his appeal, but women felt it instantly: a guileless smile and a rawboned physique, six feet two in stocking feet. His sincere love of horses, football, and prizefights shone out from his sun-bronzed face beneath his wavy hair. A breath of fresh air from Helena, Montana, he was perfect for the part. Jack liked him for the publicity angle, too, because each new star tossed some spice into an already boiling pot.

In postproduction we added airplane engines and machine guns and other sound effects, along with the pièce de résistance, the song "Jeannine, I Dream of Lilac Time." I can't tell you how many parents I met in subsequent years who'd named their daughters Jeannine in honor.

We sent the finished print to New York, where a hundred-piece orchestra recorded the accompaniment.

On the morning of the premiere, the film on which the score was recorded broke three times. I'd die of embarrassment if it didn't work that night. "Leave it to me, darling," Jack said, and hired another hundred-piece orchestra to be there in person that evening should it break again—the kind of safety net only the most devoted producers can weave.

The premiere was at the Carthay Circle Theatre in Beverly Hills. It was the kind of desert-by-the-sea evening that made people who were just visiting Southern California start looking at real estate listings. The palm trees—developers were really planting them in earnest by then—waved their fronds in applause. I arrived in a cloud of peach chiffon that Marion Davies had helped me pick. Jack and I were mobbed—a throng the likes of which I hadn't experienced since my feathered cape got plucked in Dublin—as we entered beneath the Spanish bell tower and the neon CARTHAY CIRCLE sign that you could see for miles.

The soundtrack played without a hitch—I appreciated Jack's safeguard but had also put a little extra honey in the fairies' milk dish the night before just in case—and it was clear by the time we left for the afterparty at Café Montmartre that we had a hit on our hands.

There amid the luminaries—Jack Dempsey, Joseph Kennedy, and Al Jolson, God bless him—was a lovely girl I didn't recognize, with eyes the size of Clara Bow's and a haircut identical to mine. I'd never seen her before, but beneath the chandeliers at the edge of the dance floor she was regaling anybody in her proximity about box office and production schedules.

"Are you in pictures?" I asked.

"Why yes," she said, extending a hand. "I'm Doreen O'Dare."

"Oh," I said, perplexed. "Glad to make my acquaintance. How am I this evening?"

And the girl ran away, trailing a cloud of Shalimar.

Chapter 12

The Bedroom of the Princess

Into the silence that follows the recorder's click, the kids' voices from the corridor continue, with a slight shift in timbre: the nearly imperceptible difference of children who have been fed. Most of them will carry no particular memory from this day; one or two, perhaps, will have seen something that steers the course of their lives.

I stretch in my chair; my neck has begun to tighten. "If you'll permit me, Gladys, all this talk of the Prince's Bathroom reminds me that I could use one myself."

"Follow me." Gladys hangs her burnt-sienna sweater over the back of her chair.

Departing the controlled air of the Dollhouse's chamber to enter the broader space of the museum is reminiscent of exiting a darkened theater into the brightness of day.

Amid the flushes, rushing faucets, and mingled admonishments of mothers to their children to wash their hands, I think about how Gordon adored this place, built in 1893 for the World's Columbian Exposition. A buff of Chicago history, Gordon told me about the White City, and how Daniel Burnham planned it. The scheme intrigued me, as a fellow maker and planner. Burnham's White City was like Chicago, and also like my Fairy Castle. These things settle on some kind of continuum. Or maybe they slide? Gordon's devotion to Chicago helped me fall in love with the city even as I fell in love with him. He was so proud when we installed the Dollhouse here. Almost twenty years ago now.

I dry my hands and return to the dim room where Gladys awaits. I see her looking closely at the Bedroom of the Princess.

"The princess is the star of everyone's favorite tales, isn't she?" says Gladys, clicking the recorder on.

Putting this room together, even more than with the others, I understood how film can enchant. Like in "Sleeping Beauty," when the last good fairy bestows the sleep of one hundred years, touching the members of the court so they become unconscious until it's safe to wake. Looking back, I suppose Hollywood did that to me. While it was happening it felt like my whole life, but it was eighteen years, and then it was over, with little trace remaining: a weak and idle theme, as Shakespeare wrote. A dream I keep remembering.

"In miniature rooms you have to exaggerate space to create a sense of reality. Accurate scale looks wrong. We debated endlessly about the floor: what material could be suitable for the Princess's feet. Gold was too ostentatious. Silver was too chilly, wood too pedestrian, pun intended. The only good option was this mosaic of mother-of-pearl. The Bristol glass pieces were mostly bestowed by strangers. A lady in Philadelphia brought me a cream jug and a sugar bowl, and when I tried to pay her for them, she said, 'It's treasure enough that you should treasure them.' A lady in Kansas City did the same with the two Staffordshire lambs."

"People offer items to the museum all the time," says Gladys. "Mostly we say no. Except to people like you, who've really got something."

"It's rather fun, I think: a little museum inside a big museum. The toilette set on the ivory dressing table was made by a Boston jewelry designer. 'My gift to the Princess,' he said. And I'm quite fond of that wood-and-ivory harp as well. Have you ever heard it play?"

"No," she says. "How do you play it?"

"I don't play it. The Fairy Princess plays it."

Gladys laughs.

I wish I'd thought to ask the museum to allow me to host a slumber party here for my grandchildren when they were a bit younger. On the right night, in the right mood, I could hear the fairies' music. Dancing is their chief amusement: hand in hand in circles. Sometimes to the tunes of their own fiddlers, others to the rhythms of crickets and frogs. I think the grandkids would have been able to hear it, too. The youngest once told me she heard it while playing in the woods—an echoing, she said, like from the bottom of a cauldron, or the hollow of a tree. Very matter of fact. Although they share not a drop of blood in common, she'd sounded very much like Granny Shaughnessy when she said it.

I swim back to the present. "Above the door leading to the bathroom," I say, "is a very fine mural of Peter Pan."

∼

In those glowing months while *Lilac Time* raked in the public's dollars and my personal appearance caused a national mania, First National was sending out a thousand signed photographs of me weekly in reply to letters from fans. Exhibitors voted me the top box office draw of 1928. Jack was as happy as I'd seen him in years, and I told myself that the heights of fame could substitute for the lift of alcohol.

In the meantime, we assisted another old friend too attached to the bottle. By mid-1928, Mickey Neilan's hot temper had cost him, too: he'd blown through his early fortune from the Pickford pictures, alienated MGM and Louis B. Mayer with noxious anti-Semitic grumbling, lost his production company to bankruptcy, and was eking out a living as a director for hire. "A gulp of booze makes a bitter life go down easier," he liked to say, but it was indisputably harder in the long run.

A carouser and a spendthrift, he remained a charmer, though it's easier to work with someone like that than to be married to them: he and Blanche Sweet were headed for divorce, and I couldn't blame her.

Given his reputation for being difficult and past his prime, First National did not entirely trust him, so Jack and I hired him at a fraction of what he was worth to direct me in *Her Wild Oat*. When we convened on the set, Mickey's face was beefier than when we'd met, but he still had all his hair and a spark of fun in his eyes that ignited the fun in other people.

"The so-called human beings of Hollywood are barbarous," he said, sipping a coffee that was half whiskey. "All except for you, Doreen." He had largely abandoned his dislike of Jews by adopting a dislike of everyone, which I supposed I should welcome as a defeat for bigotry.

"You know that's not true, Mickey," I replied. "But lately it's been a struggle for me to disagree. When I'm at my worst, I see my career—all my struggles to build it up—as a stupid game. You work yourself silly in order to be allowed to do even more work. It's like a pie-eating contest where the prize is more pie."

He did a spit take, barely missing the script on the table before us. "I've never heard you that pessimistic, Doreen. I like it."

"That makes one of us."

"I know, Irish, I know. You still look as fresh as when we worked on *Dinty*, if that helps."

I found that hard to believe, though I wanted to nevertheless. America obsessed over its girls but deplored its women. Nobody wanted you if you couldn't stay young and eternally unthreatening: the feisty waif, the zany coed, the radiant dancer, the scrappy shopgirl. "That was eight years ago, wasn't it?" I said.

"Son of a gun. Eight years." He shook his head. "Now you've seen that it's not all chewing gum and cream sodas. I wish it could be for you, but it's not."

"It's still good fun, though, from time to time."

"Damn right," he said. "Go get in costume and let's run this race."

We got the picture done in under two weeks, when normally even a feature as simple as ours would take six to eight. Speed was of the essence, as the lawyers say, because I needed to knock off the next four films in my new contract pronto. We were able to shoot all of it using existing sets in Burbank and at the Hotel del Coronado in San Diego Bay; Mickey picked the wooden Victorian beach resort for its court-yards, verandas, and promenades, its colonnades echoed by the masts in the harbor, its unimpeded pathways leading to the beach. So what if there were sometimes palm trees in the background of a story set in New York? Who cared if the hotel detective's badge displayed the Great Seal of the State of California? The audience could suspend its disbelief.

Mickey had done a fine job, but Jack and I had hired him mostly as a means of helping him financially. After his directing career was finally over, he ended up a cab driver for twenty years. "I had a great time spending my money," he'd say. "Don't feel sorry for me."

Jack fell off the wagon again, hard, but insisted on doing the edit-ing as always. In that state he chopped the tops off all the gags, turning what should have been a laugh-a-minute romp into a head-scratching potpourri of reaction takes, nearly ruining the picture. Mickey, a more functional alcoholic, caught it. We sent Jack to a sanitarium and reed-ited it ourselves.

Then, while Jack was away, theoretically drying out, I discovered another betrayal.

Adela called me to ask why I was dragging my feet on joining the newly formed Academy of Motion Picture Arts and Sciences. I stood at the phone in the hallway, a post-wrap bouquet of lilies from Mickey perfuming the August day.

"*Photoplay* wants to know if you think you're too big for those particular britches, or what," she said.

"I didn't realize I'd been invited."

"Well, people know that you and Jack are friends of Mickey's," she said, "and Mickey's been free with his opinions over the years. And the Academy is Louis Mayer's project. So—"

"Adela, you know that's not it at all!" I said. "Of course I want to join!"

"If I were a detective," said Adela, "which at times I very nearly am, I'd see whether any clues associated with this mysterious missing invitation led me to Jack."

I had been thinking the same thing. "I can't call him now, Adela."

"Fine," she said. "But drop a line to Mayer and get the scoop."

Mayer's secretary told me that yes, they'd sent an invitation to attend the first meeting, but they'd never heard back. Yes, Louis still wanted me as part of the board; would I like to come to the organizational banquet later that week? They'd be discussing a slate of internally bestowed Awards of Merit; they were planning to do it annually.

I would, and did, arriving in the dining room of the Biltmore not as Doreen O'Dare Flanagan but as Doreen O'Dare.

When he came home that afternoon and I asked him about it, Jack began to cry—to actually cry, though *he* had sabotaged *me!*—admitting that he had thrown the invitation in the trash because he couldn't bear the notion of me alone among the potentates, everyone thinking that I was the powerful one and he was the drunk.

"You *are* the drunk," I cried. "You just got back from the sanitarium and I can see you've already been drinking."

Jack clung to the legend of himself in his mind. "Is it wrong, Doreen, for a man to crave credit for his discovery?"

Doreen. My heart fell to the carpet. A slap, a wet smack.

"I'm sick of you seeing me as your invention!" I said. "And I'm *Eileen*. To you of all people. Not Doreen."

"Eileen. That's what I said: Eileen. Anyway, can't a man be side by side with the girl he loves?"

I couldn't stand to look at him. I didn't want to explain to the chauffeur, so I walked all the way from Beverly Hills to the house where my parents lived and there collapsed, an anxious wreck, in the arms of Granny Shaughnessy.

"You need some time away from that man, Doreen," she said. It still felt like a victory that she and my parents called me by my screen name, the name that Uncle Walter gave me; I wasn't quite sure why. "You should come stay with your family awhile."

The idea was appealing, but I couldn't. "You know what the press will do if I move back under my parents' roof, don't you?"

"Then let's all go somewhere else, child. The magazines will love that, won't they? A wholesome family trip."

This sounded better; this could work. Jack could stay behind on his own for a change. I sat up, wiping my eyes with the backs of my hands. "What about Rome? I've never been to Rome."

"Isn't Rome where your old friend Victor Marquis just started shooting his new picture? Seems like a bit of a distraction from our family vacation."

I hadn't realized that Granny had been following Hollywood production schedules so closely, but that was, in fact, exactly what I'd been thinking. She was right: not a good time. "Then where should we go?"

"Oh, I've always rather wondered what fairies are like on tropical islands," Granny said. "Haven't you?"

～

We sailed from San Francisco, bound for the Territory of Hawaii. As we pulled away from the Matson Terminal, a calm settled in: a quieting of the roar of my deafening popularity. White as a starlet's teeth, the ship was the fastest in the Pacific. "Twenty-two knots," the captain, elated to have a celebrity on board, informed me.

I took pleasure in the fact that this trip was verification to my parents of the success I'd become: I was able to whisk them away upon cerulean waves. But in the mirror in my cabin, I appeared tired, my face quite gray. You can receive a hundred pounds of candy from strangers weekly and still feel lonely. I had to refine my nervous system—which certainly was nervous—and to find some way to stop feeling putrid.

Before I left I'd spoken with Adela. Divorce was a serious scandal for a gal-next-door movie star like me: "Not just another game that you'd play before breakfast," as Adela said. The public's forgiveness was an open question. If I were seen as throwing over the man who'd made me, there could be an uproar. Even if there wasn't, simply giving the sense that I'm not the girl they thought they knew might impact my take at the box office. Yet little did the public know that I was inching ever closer to the maudlin sob-sister stories that were Adela's stock-in-trade. You can't have roses without a little manure, I knew, but nevertheless, this stunk.

At dinner on the first night of the cruise, over Santa Barbara Artichokes with Sauce Mousseline, I raised the subject.

"Well, there's no use watering dead flowers," Granny said contemplatively. "The only question is whether they're dead."

My father nodded, looking down at his almost comically sumptuous plate: Leg of Lamb Chipolata, Squab Chicken Souvaroff. All this food, so little desire to eat.

"You're a Catholic, Doreen," my mother declaimed. "A good Catholic."

As if that were reason enough to remain with Jack—a producer who took his title literally, who seemed to believe that he produced not only my pictures but me.

When we got to Honolulu, I couldn't comprehend why anyone on the globe lived anywhere but Hawaii. We were staying at the Royal Hawaiian—the Pink Palace of the Pacific—on Waikiki, a tranquil strip surrounded by bungalows and palm trees, bathed in breezes. When I walked on the pier, dolphins swam close and smiled at me in that way they seem to.

Enthusiasm, I supposed, was endemic to my nature, and I needed a new enthusiasm to ensure my survival. I learned to surf on Oahu. A member of the hotel staff taught me how to play the ukulele. These were fun diversions, but felt a little desperate. I needed something else.

One day Granny mercifully persuaded my mother to take her out shopping—Agnes gave me claustrophobia—leaving me to lie on the white sand of the cordoned-off guest beach. As I stared into the azure

Polynesian sky, and as the sky looked back with quizzical blankness, my father walked up and sat down next to me.

All my life I had wanted my dad to like me, to recognize my value. With rare exceptions, such as our excursion to see *Cinderella*, my memories of him mostly consisted of being hit: only, he always claimed, to prevent a daughter with wayward propensities from going astray, though I could always feel anger at his own humiliations fueling the blows. While my squabbles with Agnes were more constant, the chill between him and me was more profound.

My father cleared his throat softly. "Doreen," he said, "if I may, I believe you've been suffering what's commonly known as the blues."

This took me by surprise; he had never been much for emotional analysis or inquiry. I turned over on my towel and looked at him above my sunglasses, appreciating his overture.

"I have," I admitted. "It's a hue through which I'm not used to seeing the world."

He nodded, looking out to sea. "Do you remember," he said, "that dollhouse we built when you were small? You'd found some cigar boxes, and—"

"Of course I remember," I said, sitting up. "I loved that house. I played with it till it fell apart."

"Well, that's a real testimonial to my craftsmanship, isn't it?"

"It's a credit to how much I loved it," I say. "That's all."

He smiled. "I was saying to your mother last night," he said, "that when we get back to Los Angeles, it might be a good time to build you the best dollhouse of your life."

Even before I had quite registered what he was saying, my breath caught in my throat.

"You've been talking forever about building one," he continued. "A huge one, once you have kids." He grimaced over the tender subject, then quickly moved on. "And it *would* be tremendous for children someday. But in the meantime, it would be a bang-up place to house your Miscellany. Don't you think?"

My collection of miniatures had grown big enough that I could no longer look at them all at once, and indeed I wasn't sure exactly how much I had. "I could furnish quite a large number of rooms," I said.

"Ever since you met that fellow in London, he was a knight of some kind, Sir Nevile—"

"Wilkinson," I said. "And Lady Beatrix." The Wilkinsons had built a miniature mansion, Titania's Palace, which had become quite famous. They had undertaken the project after their daughter reported that she had seen fairies in the garden and expressed the opinion that they deserved to live in a fine house, as opposed to muddy holes in the ground.

"Right. You came home saying you wanted to do something similar. All your pieces are made at the same scale, aren't they? Standard 1:12?"

To this day I don't know much about fashion, but at that moment I became a strong proponent of the then burgeoning sunglasses trend: they hid your eyes so no one could see you were crying.

All that time, my dad had been listening. He'd paid attention, at least, to this particular thing that mattered to me. He cared enough to lend a hand.

"We'll need Granny's knowledge of fairies, too," I said. "If she'll help, then I'm in."

That afternoon in the hotel's Surf Room Restaurant, with the gentle scent of coconut oil wafting in through the wide-flung windows, over tea for Granny and pineapple juice for me, we had what I assume was the strangest of the subdued and dignified conversations taking place.

"Oh, it's a grand idea, Doreen," she said, eyes as green as the whisk ferns in the courtyard. "Before we left Tampa I told you the fairies would reveal a way to repay your debt to them. This might be just the thing."

"I'll tell Dad we can set about planning."

"Wise girl," she said, setting a chunk of macadamia sticky bun on my plate. "Money means nothing to the Good People, as you'd imagine.

Neither does fame. But I do suggest you give them the lion's share of your jewels."

Almost all of my jewelry came by way of apologies from Jack and therefore served mostly to memorialize his misbehavior. "Out of curiosity, why?"

"Well, remember the stories. Fairy gold is unreliable. How often does it become something other than precious after it falls into human hands? Leaves, gingerbread, gorse blossoms. Fairies don't much value anything that changes its shape, even precious metals. That's why they'll want your gemstones."

"Fine by me," I said. Purposeless wealth made me uncomfortable.

"That said, nothing lasts forever. Not for the fairies, not for human beings. You're going to have to start keeping that in mind."

∼

My father—deliberate, playful when he wanted to be, a bit of a philosopher—would help boss the job. "I want the water to run and the lights to burn," he said. "This will be a real house. We have to think of function."

He savored the challenge to his underutilized engineer's mind almost as much as the chance to divert me from my marital sadness. His burst of energy helped me realize how low he'd been, and for how long. How burdensome he must have felt, living for years off his daughter's earnings. For the first time in my adult life I saw him as a fuller person, partly because he was finally seeing me as one. We weren't equals—not any more than we'd been in my youth—but now I was the more powerful: his boss, in a sense. I found it dizzying to square the new sweetness of the man before me with the person I remembered from before, and eventually I quit trying.

As for me, the Dollhouse felt as though it harbored some additional purpose as yet unspecified. I trusted that if Granny thought the project was the right thing to do, then its subtler objective would reveal itself when the time was right.

∽

Our planning proceeded apace as the *Malolo*'s ivory hull steamed us back home to LA. It seemed fitting that the genesis of the Dollhouse was linked so closely to being borne about the ocean by a legendary vessel: Noah's ark must have been one of the world's first miscellanies.

Right away we hired Horace Jackson, a set designer for First National, to make the blueprints. I could tell when we met that he truly understood the spirit of the project. "The architecture must have logic, but no sense of reality," he said. "We must invent a structure that is everybody's conception of an enchanted castle."

We hired Harold Grieve, a future member of the American Institute of Interior Designers, to propose the interiors. (Harold would shortly redesign Jack's and my Bel Air mansion, but the Dollhouse came first.) The fairies, he said, "will shop all the auction galleries in Fairyland. There'll be a mixture of periods and places. Aladdin's Lamp will have an oriental connotation. But how will that go with pre-Tudor English? We'll come up with a new theory of interior design."

Both men's immediate enthusiasm was a welcome surprise, but I suppose it shouldn't have been. Harold relished the chance to work with reduced encumbrances of practicality and physics, and diminished size meant expanded scope: he rarely got a chance to do a whole house, never mind a castle. Horace, for his part, recognized a rare opportunity for a set designer: to create a world that wasn't tied to a particular story.

We couldn't, we decided, use my entire collection: some would have to be left out. I spent my rare free time making ruthless decisions. And many new pieces would have to be acquired. I did my best to educate myself.

My bible for the project would eventually be a copy of Emily Post's *Personality of a House* that Harold gave me. Ugliness seemed to her a source of physical agony. I underlined practically every other sentence.

By the time I got home from Hawaii I was so immersed in the Dollhouse that I'd nearly forgotten the original aim of the cruise, which had been to give me a break from Jack, but also to give Jack a break from me—the hypothesis being that if having me around was stressful, then maybe he'd get help while he was on his own. Not so. He'd been drunk for the entire three weeks.

If I hadn't returned with the Dollhouse plan to animate my non-working life, then the state in which I found him would have nearly destroyed me. As it was, I was able to say, "Okay, I'll see you at the lot on Monday," and retreat to my study.

By the end of that weekend, I had established that Jack wasn't the only one in our household with a knack for publicity. People in Hollywood had known for years that I was a collector of miniatures; now I had the studio press agents put the word out beyond Hollywood. A photographer shot me with some of my most impressive objects and furnished the prints to newspaper editors. Within weeks, letters poured in from dealers far and wide with offers of pieces for sale—and in some cases to give away, just for the reflected glory.

Exhilarating to seize so much control! To be director and producer of the Dollhouse combined. To be not out in front but behind, constructing a magic world of make-believe that reflected me but didn't *feature* me. This was that old feeling again, the sense of fun and possibility that I'd had while borrowing makeup from Mildred Harris, showing up on the Triangle lot to perform in my own clothes. The Dollhouse seemed as fresh as the pictures did when they began, there in that land over which D. W. Griffith cried *Let there be light.*

The light was mine this time, mine and my team's.

As difficult as it was to tear myself away from the Dollhouse, the chance to collaborate with Mervyn—as director this time, at long, long last—made it easier to go back to work. The picture we were doing was *Oh, Kay!*, a frothy comedy in which I'd play an English aristocrat, a runaway bride who slips away on her sloop and gets captured by a band of bootleggers.

I didn't even mind how the former fishing boat that played the role of the rumrunners' ship stank like a cannery. We shot on and around Catalina Island, its silver-sand beaches agleam with quartz, its chaparral aromatic of sage. The climate, Mervyn said, was positively Aegean.

"I'll have to trust you on that," I said. "I've never been."

"Neither have I," admitted Mervyn.

For authenticity's sake, he had me learn how to sail; Jack's and my cruise with Richard Rowland had involved no seawomanship on my part. The experience of tacking and gibing and beating into the wind around the Gulf of Santa Catalina—achieving mastery by accommodating a fickle invisible force—was a pleasure similar to being in charge of my Dollhouse. I felt excited, fully awake.

Back on the mainland we were forced to realize how drastically technology was changing the industry. The movie palaces, with their acres of seats, were being wired for sound—not to come from the orchestra or the organ, but from the pictures themselves.

While all of us waited to see what toll talking pictures would exact, the royalty of Hollywood went on an investing spree. In spite, or maybe because, of the tumult in the industry, the luminaries of Hollywood wanted to put their newfound wealth to work, to take part in the national optimism they'd helped gin up. Speculation in securities became common and fashionable; we could move piles of dollars as easily as the wind moved leaves. "You and your friends would do well to remember that the law of gravity applies to the stock market, too," cautioned Granny. Everywhere I went, I overheard women in furs and Parisian gowns debating how many shares of Richfield petroleum to buy.

When there's a sickness going around, you can only do so much to avoid catching it. *Oh, Kay!* had given me the sailing bug, so I indulged myself by acquiring my own yacht. *Better not to share Jack's,* I thought spitefully; *he'd pilot it drunk.* The real reason, I now understand, was to feel in control as Hollywood skidded.

I named the vessel *World's End*, which speaks to my frame of mind at the time.

I took Marion for a spin one afternoon in late September. The air was cool and smelled like kelp.

"W. R. is determined that I've got to learn elocution," she said. Wearing a sailor's blouse, toying with a winch, she could have been awaiting my direction in a picture. "The whole country's talking talkies, he says." She spoke these words in her Brooklyn-Irish accent, staccato with its stammer.

"Oh my," I said. "How's it going?"

"It's going terribly. This stutter may be endearing in person, but it'll kill my career in the cradle if I don't ditch it."

"What's W. R. having you do?" I was concerned for Marion's sake, but also looking for tips myself. It didn't seem like anyone was safe.

"He imported the Shakespeare coach who trained John Barrymore. I spend every afternoon locked away in the library, struggling to recite the words of the immortal Bard."

"Oh, Marion," I said. "Shakespeare's good company, at least."

"I'd like it more without a gun to my head. Even if the training takes, how much good will it do me? Will people really want to hear us bellowing our lines into the balconies? We're going to need new voices, just like we needed new faces when this business first started. We're right back where we were in 1915."

I hoped she was wrong but had been thinking much the same thing. "Whatever happens to us," I said, "I hope it happens soon. Hollywood's never been the pure heaven the developers say it is, but I hate this hanging around in purgatory."

The sun still shone, but a cloud passed over our moods. We made our way listlessly back to San Pedro through the West Channel and gave up for the day on trying to have fun.

~

Because our contracts gave us total authority over my pictures, Jack and I hadn't felt the unsteadiness as readily, but First National had been on shaky financial ground for some time, and in early October Warner Brothers bought a controlling interest. Warner was the main pioneer of Vitaphone technology, and upon the announcement of the deal, the *LA Times* reported that in the course of a few weeks, the voices of such stars as Doreen O'Dare will be heard.

"News to me," I said, showing Jack the morning paper.

"You're the biggest box office draw for two years running," he said, shuffling it aside with barely a glance. "If anything they're going to have to pay you more to talk."

His bravado buoyed me out the door and to the lot, but it dissipated the moment I arrived. Waiting for me was Roy Pomeroy.

Short and balding, with only a lank tonsure of hair around his crown, Roy had been an undistinguished technician prior to the coming of sound, when some executives sent him to the Western Electric labs to study the intricacies of Vitaphone; upon his return they greeted him as if he were Thomas Edison. That fall, when the Lasky studio made him their director of sound and he began to slouch around making tests of all the stars, he became as instantly recognizable as the Grim Reaper, and about as welcome.

"Doreen!" said Roy. "Just the little lady I was looking for." He had the tendency to spit when he spoke; I resisted the urge to wipe my face. "You heard about the Warner Brothers deal, I gather? Well, their higher-ups need to know what they're buying before the deal closes, and you're First National's biggest star, so they've decided that today's the day we do your test."

"Oh, have they?" I said, suddenly conscious of my pronunciation and tone.

"I'm sure that for an accomplished actress like you, everything will be fine," he said with an insincere smile.

This was an ambush. Roy had pounced on Mary Pickford the previous week: "The microphone might as well have been a firing squad," she said. She had passed, but how ludicrous that a career like hers might have been killed at the whim of a new set of instruments.

Sound as a science was poorly apprehended, the technology finicky. The idiosyncrasies of Pomeroy's recording tools might render anyone's speaking voice unsuitable. It reminded me of my first screen test at Essanay—how we weren't sure how my mismatched eyes would look in moving pictures—except that at Essanay only my dreams were at stake, not my livelihood.

Roy escorted me into a sound studio, surrounded by executives from First National and Warner Brothers: a pack of indistinguishable men in darkish suits. Richard Rowland was apparently in New York—cleaning out his office, for all I knew.

I entered the studio alone. They jammed into the sound booth to listen to my fate.

"Now speak into the microphone like a good girl, Doreen," said Roy.

"What do I say?" I asked, stalling.

"Say a nursery rhyme," he said lazily. "Say anything." This test meant less than nothing to him, apart from being a chance to burnish his new reputation as a sonic wizard. He was the butcher; my voice was just the meat.

I leaned toward the vented surface of the microphone. It looked like some insectoid eye.

"Little Bo Peep has lost her sheep and can't tell where to find them," I said. I turned the wattage on; I did my job. I'd die before I'd let a patronizing muckety-muck throw me. "Leave them alone and they'll come home, wagging their tails behind them."

Chapter 13

The Bathroom of the Princess

"I guess most of what I know about that time comes from *Singin' in the Rain*," says Gladys.

On the rare occasions when I reunite with my surviving friends from those days—usually Mary or Lillian, usually at a revival screening at a film festival at a moldering theater in some hard-to-get-to university town—we often make bets about how far we'll get into the Q&A before someone brings up *Singin' in the Rain*. "Never seen it," I say.

"You're kidding."

"Nope. Had I ever been a prisoner on a chain gang or overindulged on hard-boiled eggs, I probably would have skipped *Cool Hand Luke*, too."

"Ah," she says. "It must have been stressful. Is that why you stopped? I mean, clearly there's nothing wrong with your voice."

"Why, thank you," I say. "And no, I kept going and did make some talkies. Some good ones, too, if I may say so. The question for me was less whether I could, more whether I wanted to. By then I'd been in Hollywood for over twelve years. I was twenty-six, but I'd been working since I was fourteen, and it wasn't as fun as it had been."

"I see your point."

"Among the most beautiful of voices," I say, "were those belonging to the undines, water nymphs associated with the rolling waves. You'll find the story of one etched on the crystal walls of the Bathroom of the Princess."

Gladys fumbles for the recorder. "Wait! Take it from 'among the most beautiful,' please. That's how movie directors do it, right?"

I smile, and do as she asks.

"Like all water spirits, this undine lacked a soul, and her only way to get one was to marry a human man. Any marriage has its risks, and if the man is unfaithful, he's fated to die. The undine's tragedy was to choose a man who betrayed her."

∾

A constant procession of big names arrived on the First National lot for their own sound tests, and from their expressions they may as well have been waiting for the guillotine.

Roy Pomeroy wrote notes beside the names: *weak voice, strident, southern drawl, guttural, hesitant speech, affected mannerisms.* Ramon Novarro got *south of the border* but was deemed okay, because that meant he could continue to play exotic types. Vilma Bánky got *impenetrable Hungarian accent* and opted to bow out for marriage and wifedom. The Talmadge sisters also knew when to go. *Leave 'em while you're looking good,* Constance advised Norma by wire, *and thank God for the trust funds Momma set up.*

Sometimes mental faculties became an issue, even when voices weren't: stars now had to memorize lines. Alma Rubens, a living ghost, addicted to heroin and cocaine for years but still hanging on, was given the boot because she hadn't any memory.

As Marion had predicted, passing all the tests with flying colors still wasn't enough. *Nobody wants a bunch of mimes anymore,* grumbled the executives. First National and Warner Brothers sent the stars for voice lessons, and never let you forget who was picking up the tab.

My teacher was Constance Collier, the English stage actress and coach, who had gained acclaim in the Edwardian era by playing

Cleopatra at His Majesty's Theatre in the West End; at a statuesque fifty years of age, her carriage remained queenly. Even on a Burbank studio lot it wasn't hard to imagine her—haughty, imperious—crowned in silver, carrying a scepter.

"Is it true," she asked bluntly, before we began, "that you make $10,000 per week?"

"No, ma'am," I said. "I make $12,500."

It took her all day to teach me the proper elocution of "mother," a second day for "father." The directors obsessed over pear-shaped tones and correct stage diction—no room for variation, Constance explained.

As I was leaving, a studio boss from Germany inquired about my progress.

"Does two words in two days count as progress?" I asked.

"Cheer up, dollink," he said, deliberately exaggerating his own accent. "Tomorrow maybe you vill loin a sentence." I forced myself to laugh.

"Happily," said Constance, "she has no discernible regional accent."

I wasn't quite ready to go home, so I took a walk around the studio property. It reminded me of an early-summer day in 1916, the year I left Tampa, when the whole city busied itself with frantic preparations for a tropical storm: boarding up windows, stocking up on supplies. That's what the First National lot felt like, only the storm was the coming of sound. I watched a group of cowhands wrangling their steeds, retraining them to respond to gestures since verbal commands would no longer do. One piebald mare resolutely refused to cooperate; she wouldn't even look at the trainer, kept turning her head. The Constance Talmadge of horses.

I couldn't help but resent that our impending doom was just another boom year for the studios. New arrivals came in droves, as they'd done for over a decade, only now they brought singing voices and brains geared for memorization.

Ours was a lingering demise. My existing contract was to make silents—now we had to start calling them that—and that's what I planned to do. Almost everyone who had been making silents kept doing so during that closing window; we'd been getting steadily better at it and didn't intend to stop until we had to.

My own last silent film was called *Why Be Good?*—as in *why be good at this old-fashioned craft anymore?* I couldn't help thinking after it was in the can. I paused in January 1929 to see how the winds were blowing. It had become pretty clear that Warner was planning to expand its controlling interest in First National into a full merger of the companies. Jack and I had gotten the message that we'd only be secure for as long as I was popular; I got the sense that their executives resented the control First National had allowed me. They didn't like a woman calling the shots.

They sent over a round of stories that they thought I should develop with an eye toward synchronized sound. I sent my usual feedback, rejecting many for slim premises and heroines who were unbearably dumb.

Instead of responding to me directly, Richard Rowland wrote a letter as the voice of First National depicting me as spoiled and big-headed. He sent copies to the newspapers and fan magazines, many of whom had portrayed me as high-hatted during the contract dispute a couple years back.

"How could they do this to me?" I asked Adela, who had come over to do a piece for *Photoplay* about *Why Be Good?*

"Look around, Doreen," she said, waving her cigarette at the gardens surrounding the pool, as if studio executives might be hiding in the bushes. "They're doing it to everyone. Every woman, anyhow. Look at Louise Brooks."

"What happened to Louise Brooks?"

"Well, she passed her sound test. Then Paramount told her she could either stay, but without the raise her contract called for, or she could quit. So she quit. She left for Germany. Rumor has it that Paramount plans to claim her voice is unstable if she ever comes back. They didn't expect Brooksie to tell them to go to hell, and it rattled them."

"In the last meeting I had with him before he sent his defamatory letter, Rowland told me, quote, 'Women are fine for looking at. But now we're talking.'"

"Sounds like our Richie."

I closed my eyes against the sun and watched the colors behind my lids. This coming of talkies felt like the turn of a kaleidoscope. A great dislodging of idols. "They're using sound as an occasion to knock the powerful stars down, aren't they?" I said. "If somebody had come up with a way to let audiences smell what's in the picture, then Rowland would be writing letters saying I rejected their soap powder suggestions."

"Did you come up with that just now?"

"No, I've been waiting for an occasion."

We sat in silence for a while. Adela's notebook lay closed on her lap. She could probably write the *Why Be Good?* piece in the car on the way back to her desk, just in the time she spent idling at traffic signals.

Better a slow fade, or a rapid collapse? A suffocating sink into quicksand, or a seismic shift? I thought of La Brea Woman, found in the tar pits; I didn't want to get stuck like that.

"Lillian told you what they're doing to her, didn't she?" said Adela.

"She did." For decades to come, the consensus opinion would be that Lillian Gish's fragile virginity simply went out of style, but that wasn't so. MGM had given her an $800,000-a-year contract but then used the chaos of sound to push her into lesser roles until she quit, her contract unfulfilled. In their statements about the break, the studio pilloried Lillian, the greatest actor of our generation, as a sexless relic. She didn't respond; it was beneath her dignity. She had taught me that a woman in our business had to present the face of an angel but clad herself in the hide of a rhino.

"Luckily," said Adela, snuffing out her Lucky Strike and riffling through her handbag, "I've got your international figures for *Lilac Time* here. As well as the domestic ones for *Synthetic Sin*. And they're stellar."

"I used to think that would mean I'm safe, since money's all that matters in Hollywood."

"Not just Hollywood, chum. Wait till I tell you about banks."

"But," I continued, "now I'm afraid that counts against me, too. It makes their point that the business is too dependent on stars, when it could be dependent on gadgets. Don't put any of this in the story, Adela. I'm no good at being cynical."

"It's sweet that you think they'd let me use any of this," she said, "but don't worry. You know I won't. I *would* like to chat on the record, though, about how you're doing so damn well that you and Jack are building a mansion."

As ever, Adela's instincts about putting forth a persona were unerring. To show that my star wasn't waning, Jack and I had decided to make a splash in Hollywood—or rather, since we had already made splashes in Hollywood, and Hollywood was by then not mere geography but a state of mind, we decided to make a splash in Bel Air, specifically a mansion-size splash. After years of renting our house on Rossmore, we'd bought three acres of land and a half-built estate.

Driving through Bel Air one Saturday, we had seen the incomplete Spanish Revival, evoking the hacienda of a bygone don. With the help of a quarter-million rectangular green friends, we persuaded the owner to turn it over.

At thirteen thousand square feet, the house had so many rooms that I'm not sure I ever set foot in all of them. Its partially complete state presented an opportunity to have it done up—like my Dollhouse—exactly to my taste. I fired the architect and brought on Harold Grieve. At first I only asked him to do the bathroom, but he insisted he'd do the whole shebang or nothing at all.

He tore down walls, enclosed the breezeway. Inside the house's horseshoe shape—lucky, I hoped—he built a flagstone patio. At his direction, we bought an adjacent property to erect a tennis court and Olympic-size swimming pool, complete with cabana and reflecting pond in between. At one end of the horseshoe, he whipped up a guest-house, at the other a cinema.

"Wired for talking pictures?" Adela asked. Her lips puckered, as they often did—as if she could kiss you for your gift of an anecdote.

"You're darn right it is! Be sure you put that in."

"'Doreen O'Dare is all optimism for talkies,'" she said. "You got it."

"It's going to be done by late July. If you need a hook for your ending, say something like, 'And with that, the elfin Miss O'Dare had to flit down to Grauman's Chinese, where she'd be meeting Grieve to discuss the interiors.'"

"Hey now," she said. "Do I tell you how to do *your* job?"

"Quite frequently, yes."

"True, true. But I'm always right."

∼

Grauman's Chinese Theatre. Harold had chosen it as the location for our rendezvous so we could stroll among its temple bells, pagodas, and guardian lions for inspiration. It had opened barely two years prior yet hadn't been wired for sound—a condition more indicative of the swiftness of the change than Sid Grauman's lack of foresight. In the early-spring sunshine, the concrete blocks of handprints and signatures in the Forecourt of the Stars seemed like a cemetery for those on their way to being forgotten.

I'd done my footprint ceremony on December 19, 1927: the sixth star to be thusly immortalized. MAY THE CHINESE THEATRE HAVE GREATER SUCCESS EVERY YEAR IS THE WISH OF, I'd written. *Doreen O'Dare*, I'd signed.

I jumped ten feet when Harold tapped me on the shoulder.

"Doreen?" he said, a question in his voice. I was hatted and sunglassed, as I had to be now in public to avoid being recognized.

We studied the forty-foot-tall curved walls, with their copper turrets and the lotus blossom fountains.

"I'm looking to evoke some of this majesty in your master bedroom suite," he said, pointing at the coral columns. "We'll do a fireplace, and a balcony overlooking the grounds."

I had something that I'd been putting off telling Harold, but it could wait no longer. "I adore the idea of the master suite," I said. "The press will play it up as the epitome of luxury. But I need to ask that you make the bedrooms on either side of it into separate his-and-hers boudoirs."

Harold stopped walking and turned to face me, his high, egg-like forehead crinkling in concern. "I see," he said. "It's because of Jack, isn't it."

"His drinking's worse than his chintzy taste in furnishings, I'm afraid." I laughed to keep from crying. Besides insisting that his home office be done up in a light-sucking dark blue, Jack had demanded that Harold appoint it with Grand-Rapids-department-store-style furniture; Harold had found a way to harmonize the mass-produced items with various antiques, but the balance I sought would be more elusive.

"All right," said Harold, ever discreet. "We can do that."

"I told him that this way he could have the steam room he's been talking about ever since he got back from the sanitarium. He jokes that it'll keep him from getting fat, but it's a lunkheaded shortcut he thinks will sober him up."

Jack had gotten flabby—baggy-eyed and slow. The doctor said his liver was almost destroyed.

"Personal sauna for Jack." Harold jotted. "Got it."

"What I didn't tell him," I said, "but what I need you to keep in mind is that I don't ever want to see him by accident. I must control the flow of my coming and going."

"I'm sorry, Doreen," said Harold, shaking his dome of a head. I'd always thought he looked like Shakespeare. "Not that I can't do it; I can, and I will. I'm just sorry for your sake that it's necessary."

Back at our house on Rossmore that evening, Fentriss barked joyously as I walked in, sharp nails clicking on the tiles of the portico. Jack called to me from the kitchen.

"Darling, you'll never believe the bull the studio tried to make us eat today," he said, rooting in the fridge for the fixings of a sandwich.

"Try me," I said.

"Based—they claimed—on the strength of *Lilac Time*, they offered you a new contract of fifteen thousand a week."

"Jack, that's a raise. Where's the bull in that?"

"Doreen, you're not listening." He sighed like a schoolmaster at a slow-witted child. "They offered it to *you*. The catch is that they didn't want *me*. I refused on your behalf."

"Refused?" I steadied myself against the counter. "Jack, the contract extension has been up in the air for weeks. My future, despite your assurances, is anything but secure. You should have told me so *I* could decide."

"You'd have done the same thing," he said, trying to put his arm around me. "We're a team, darling. Both or nothing."

I wriggled from his grasp. "Are we, Jack?" I said. "If we were a team, then you'd have brought their offer home so we could talk it over, at least explore the possibility that I might stay on with them while you find your own job for a change."

His face went slack, and I stalked upstairs to our bedroom. He followed and found me standing there, indecisive. It was a hot night even for June, the darkness choked with creeping flowers, wisteria weaving nets around our house.

"I'm the best at what I do," he said, sinking like a rag doll onto an ottoman.

"Sure, you surpass yourself every day," I said. "In awfulness. All you do is sit and guzzle. I do all the real work!"

His mood shifted. "I despise myself for being a weakling, you know that. I've been a beast, dearest. I'll get better."

"You say that every time!"

"I say it because I wish I had the power within me to make it true."
I knew from his expression that there was something he wasn't telling me. "What, dare I ask, did you agree to on my behalf instead?"

"That you'll take a smaller raise to thirteen thousand per week provided I come with you. And that you'll do *Smiling Irish Eyes*, but as an all-singing, all-talking picture."

When Irish Eyes Are Smiling, the script that First National had wanted me to agree to during our contract dispute, had hung around the studio like a rancid stench, like an animal that had died in the wall somewhere.

"I won't do that picture, Jack."

"It's better. They've rewritten it for sound. Lots of people have worked on it."

Removing the words *when* and *are* from the title wouldn't transform that script into something other than a stereotypical pile of Irish clichés. "It's insulting to Granny. It's insulting to our ancestors. Besides, don't you remember what happened to Frances?"

Two years earlier, Frances Marion's cartoonish picture *The Callahans and the Murphys* had been protested so aggressively by the Irish American leagues that MGM withdrew it from distribution.

"Ah," Jack said. Then he stopped speaking, lips smacking wordlessly like a dying fish.

"I cannot keep doing this!" I screamed, blindly running into my vanity, knocking over a bottle of perfume: Toujours Moi by Dana turned the carpet yellow and suffused the air with orange blossom and spice. As I ran down the stairs, the name seemed a joke. Would I always have to be the me that Jack thought he'd made me?

From the phone in the foyer I dialed Mervyn LeRoy. "I need to get out of here."

"I'll come right by," he said. "We'll go somewhere fun. Don't forget to wear the rug."

After the success of *Lilac Time*, the First National costume department had loaned me a flouncy blonde wig to wear around town;

otherwise I'd get mobbed when people spotted my telltale bob. That's how I ended up sitting across from Mervyn, like some platinum lamb, in a booth at the Brown Derby.

Mervyn knew Hollywood like he knew his own pocket, and he thought, correctly, that the hat-shaped restaurant might cheer me up. Built by Herbert Somborn, one of Gloria Swanson's earliest husbands, they were open all night. This was an adventure.

"A ginger ale for the lady," Mervyn said to the waitress. "And a coffee for me, please."

"Why the Brown Derby?" I asked.

"Given all the time you spend thinking about tiny objects, I also thought it was funny to put you inside a gigantic hat."

Mervyn wanted me to order something hearty and foisted upon me the famed Spaghetti Derby, while he feasted on the shirred eggs and poultry livers. EAT IN THE HAT blinked in neon outside.

A passing couple was talking about a new picture they'd seen and paused by our table to let a waitress by. "I thought Doreen O'Dare was as good in *Synthetic Sin* as she's ever been in anything!" the woman said to the man, who nodded.

"I hope she can hack it in the talkies," he replied.

Mervyn raised an eyebrow, as if he were directing a reaction take.

"It's like one of Granny's fairy tales," I said when they were out of earshot. "The king goes amongst the commoners in disguise and finds out what they really think."

I could hardly manage more than a few bites of spaghetti but fared better when Mervyn ordered me the lemon chiffon pie. He tucked into his own slice of coconut chocolate cake.

"I'm not a king," I mused, taking a bite of whipped cream, "but I do have some power that maybe I should be using."

"To get out of *Smiling Irish Eyes*, you mean?"

"If only," I said. "Maybe I'd be less upset about my own life if I tried to do something for other people."

The free-for-all of Hollywood was a thrill, but over the years it had come to wear on me. I wouldn't trade the memories for all the world, but perhaps if anything went, then nothing counted.

"Talk to your pal Marion," he said. "She knows all about that."

I imagined visiting Marion at her beach house in Santa Monica. *Beach house* doesn't do it justice: a white Georgian structure with a dining room to seat twenty-five, Tiffany chandeliers, thirty-seven fireplaces, an art gallery, and a library with a movie screen that rose from the floor at the push of a button. I never would have guessed that she possessed a dedication to charity that seemed completely at odds with her lavish extravagance. She paid for the education of her cook's daughter, she footed the bill for an operation to correct the crossed eye of one of the studio electricians, and she supported innumerable relief funds for sick children and abandoned animals. Her generosity was legendary. And tax deductions weren't the reason she was doing it; that's not how income taxes worked at the time.

"You're right," I said, finishing my pie and feeling more resolved. "I will."

Mervyn paid. I wasn't ready yet to go home, so he drove us up to the mountains to gaze at the glittering grid of the city, the valley a web of dancing lights. Staggeringly grand. So gorgeous as to make you almost panic with ecstasy.

When Mervyn dropped me off, it was after midnight. The house on Rossmore sat dark and still. Jack was gone but had left me a note, schoolboy-esque: *B-L-U-E spells blue and that's what I am without U.* Somehow he'd scrounged up a new bottle of Toujours Moi, wrapped in blue paper, but now the smell could only be noxious.

～

I had hoped, after I'd evaded it for so long, that *Smiling Irish Eyes* would prove to not be as excruciating as I'd feared. Careful what you wish for: it was worse.

I was to play an Irish lass in love with a poor musician who toils in a peat bog. He and I compose a tune; it becomes our song. He moves to America, plays the violin on Broadway, and forgets about me in favor of the fast women he meets in the footlights. I follow him to New York, find him onstage singing our song and smooching some dame, and—Irish temper high, too much of a dummy to understand the fourth wall—flee back to Ireland. He follows and explains how theater works; I forgive him; we all immigrate to the States with our massive Irish families.

I had done stupid material before, God knows, and I resolved to be a professional. But though I had plenty of ideas about how to achieve the correct balance of smarts and laughs, my pleas were given no wing.

First National launches Doreen O'Dare's first dialogue picture, declared the press release, with the appropriate accompaniment of Erin's tunes, jigs, and brogues.

The new sound stage was a charmless box of concrete meant to keep out birds and wind and traffic. Before, a call for *quiet on the set* just meant that John Barrymore needed to focus; on *Smiling Irish Eyes*, the hush that followed the director's cue was such that I could hear my costars' hair growing.

Even with precautions, a lot could go wrong, and did.

Tempo was an imperceptible quality that a picture had to possess—imperceptible, that is, unless it was bad; then everyone perceived it. In the early days, sound made almost every tempo poor. There was no overdubbing; if you made a mistake, you couldn't correct it. Worst of all, since the film was matched to the recording disc, and there was no way to cut the record, we couldn't cut the film. We had to follow the script exactly, and if anything failed, we couldn't remove it before the final product was shown.

When we watched the final version, I saw *Smiling Irish Eyes* for what it was: a seemingly never-ending bore.

∾

Kathleen Rooney

Following insult and injury with yet more insult, the studio let me know that Clara Bow had surpassed me in popularity. "You toy around and she puts out," Richard Rowland said with his customary delicacy. Fine by me: every flapper role she got was one I didn't have to turn down. Besides, Clara had a terrible accent that had relegated her to the dreaded Pomeroy category of *bad voice*: her days were numbered. *Make that money and invest it wisely*, I thought as she cranked out the last of her silent films. *As I know you won't.*

⁓

With the summer having been consumed by the shoot, I took August to settle into our new estate in Bel Air.

One afternoon Harold was over finishing up Jack's boudoir. "I like a map for a man's study, don't you?" he said, hanging a Gothic *mappa mundi* opposite the bed, one that taunted me with its expanse of places I longed to go.

Harold knew all sorts of things that I did not, but I felt excited to learn, like the categorical subtleties that differentiated a piece of earthenware from a piece of faience, or vermeil from sterling, or a peridot from a tourmaline.

Our conversation turned to the Dollhouse. We set about establishing a scheme for the organization of my further collecting: historical objects, objects of use and beauty, objects of curiosity. Such discussions remain my happiest memories from those days.

The telephone rang. The maid called for me.

"Not now," I said. "Take a message, please."

"It's your mother, Miss O'Dare. She says it's an emergency."

It was far worse than an emergency. There was no word for the severity of what it was. Granny Shaughnessy was dead.

I walked down the stairs and stood outside, Harold behind me. The California sun beamed down as always, but grief hung over me like a black parasol. Or, I thought, the blackness had always been there, pouring down on me unnoticed like the sunlight's malevolent twin. And it was Granny who'd been the parasol.

She had seemed as though she would live eternally. At my age now, I can see my ignorance.

At the funeral, Granny's face was masklike. Shrunk and sunken, she lay in her casket, five thousand miles and eighty-seven years from her place of birth, and it was I who'd brought her here. How I longed to see her green eyes open.

I said one last Hail Mary on the kneeler in front of her catafalque. As I mouthed *amen*, Agnes knelt beside me, placing a black-gloved hand upon my shoulder—a shock, for she was not demonstrative.

"She was so proud of you," my mother said quietly. "From the day you were born. She and I, as you well know, didn't always see eye to eye. But I'm proud of you, Doreen O'Dare. Your father and I are proud of you."

She was the picture of distant composure. But in her eyes behind their net veil, I finally saw the sorrow beneath her brittle domestic propriety. How often had I wished that my mother could feel freer to emote—like the actress I'd become. But she and I were more alike in our self-possession than I had wanted to believe.

"Thank you, Agnes," I said. "Mother. Thank you."

I leaned on Jack as he led me from the coffin.

Granny had continued to attend the Immaculate Heart of Mary, the house of worship that she and I found on our first day in LA, near our little bungalow on Fountain. Crammed with her church friends, every pew in the narrow Gothic nave was filled.

As I waited for the cortege to the cemetery to proceed, Victor Marquis moved through the crush and sat next to me. I hugged him for long time. "I'm too sad even to cry," I said.

"I've never thought it wise to tell anybody bereaved that their loved one is in a better place. So I won't say that. The best place for her was here on Earth with you."

"I don't know," I said, trying to adhere to my Catholic beliefs. "She's with God. I suppose that's better."

"What's our motto, Eileen?" Victor asked, gentle smile lines around his eyes.

"Love Never Dies." The herringbone weave of his trousers brushed my leg. I longed to hold his hand.

"Wherever she is now, her love for you remains. She believed in you before anyone else did. Your career is a testament to her. Be sad, of course. But her love for you is immutable."

"I try to think of her as not gone, but changed," I said, recalling the catechism. "Thank you, Victor. I can't tell you how much it means."

"LND, Eileen," he said, and kissed my hand. I smelled his cologne for a second above the incense, and I wondered—then scolded myself for wondering—whether he'd picked it out himself or his wife Eleanor had.

For all her talk of fairies, Granny never had much to say about ghosts. For weeks after her death, I lay before sleep straining to hear a chair creak or a dresser slide across the floor in the hope that it might be her, coming to say goodbye. I never heard a peep.

Smiling Irish Eyes came out the first week of September, and the reviews hit like so many punches to the gut. I'd been bracing for as much, but this was the first time I couldn't discuss the reception with Granny. Maybe it was for the best that she never saw it; the stereotypes were atrocious to such an extent that they banned it in Ireland.

With Adela's help, I made it clear that I had finished *Smiling Irish Eyes* only due to contractual obligations and that I was very satisfied to have those obligations fulfilled. Adela provided a drumbeat of coverage about Granny's death, which garnered my fans' sympathy; they understood why I might be ready to take a small break. "I shall finally travel the world with my husband," I told them, thinking less of Jack than of the map on his boudoir wall.

"As long as you're still curious about tomorrow, you'll be okay," Granny Shaughnessy used to say. I was still curious.

Chapter 14

THE GREAT HALL

"I can't believe I didn't think of this sooner," says Gladys, eyes like light bulbs behind her glasses. "Now, I don't want to get ahead of myself—I don't have a lot of curatorial pull—but have you seen our *Yesterday's Main Street* exhibit?"

I have: full-scale mock-ups of storefronts from 1910 bearing advertisements for hair tonic and sarsaparilla, alongside a nickelodeon for silent pictures. I was eight years old in 1910; Gladys was a quarter century from being born.

"I could talk to my supervisor about rotating your films into the nickelodeon," she says. "People who come here will want to see the films, and people who see the films will want to have a look at your castle."

"That would be difficult to do," I say.

"It'll probably depend on the budget. And we wouldn't show feature-length films in the nickelodeon, of course. We'd have to use clips."

"Well, good news!" It comes out sounding more brittle than I had hoped. "You couldn't show my films at full length even if you wanted to. Almost none of them exist anymore. *Flaming Youth*—the one that made stars of me and my bob—is almost entirely lost. The Library of Congress has one reel. Eleven minutes. All that remains."

Gladys looks as if she's inhaled a frog. "Doreen, that's awful. Is it because of the film? The instability of the nitrate?"

"For early films in general, yes, instability was a big problem," I say. "For my films specifically, it was because the Museum of Modern Art in New York failed to guard against that instability."

"Oh my God," Gladys says. "I have nightmares about this."

Fairy gold is unreliable, Granny cautioned. *How often does it become something other than precious? Leaves, gingerbread, gorse blossoms.*

"When I first came to Hollywood," I say, "there was scarcely time to think of the future, and hardly anyone did. After film prints finished their theatrical runs, the studios would recycle them for the silver. I can't overstate how dangerous it was to store this stuff. A reel of nitrate film can combust spontaneously. It'll keep burning even underwater, spitting poison gases the whole time."

"*Flaming Youth* but literally," says Gladys.

"After we made *So Big,* I began to realize that the pictures we were making weren't just cultural artifacts; they were works of art. In 1944, upon invitation by MoMA—*they* contacted *me,* let me be clear—I was honored to make a gift of fifteen of my films."

"What happened to them?"

"They got shunted to the side of some storeroom and forgotten about. No temperature control, no ventilation. A few years ago, before my husband Gordon died, I got a request from a film festival, so I inquired with the museum. When they'd told me over the phone what had happened, I insisted on going to New York—I've always hated New York—to see for myself. The reels smelled like camphor, or mothballs. The film had turned rusty and crumbly. A syrupy goo was bubbling from it. It was almost comical, like something in a horror flick."

"They're lucky they didn't blow up their damn museum."

Over the years I've scoured the world for surviving prints, with some small success. Motion pictures were the artistic event of the century. Not just my pictures, mind you, but the entire medium.

The Fairy Castle taught me to love hunting for things. And trying to help.

This, I suppose, is one reason why I haven't started work on the autobiography that Adela has urged me to write: the story's still in process and I haven't figured out the ending.

"It makes me sick to my stomach," Gladys says. "The origin of a whole new art form, just gone."

"Gladys, if you keep being so compassionate, I'm going to cry. Anyhow, who's got time to mourn the past?" I compose myself, dismissing the subject with a wave of my hand, still adorned with the diamond my dead Gordon gave me. "It's one more reason I'm glad to have built this castle. At least I've achieved one durable thing."

"And it's in safe hands here, I give my word on that," Gladys says.

"Time to move ahead," I say.

"Right." She scans her clipboard with her felt-tip pen. "Two rooms left. The Great Hall?"

Click. "The largest room in the castle. The vaulted Gothic ceiling towers over a floating staircase. The fairies, being winged, have no need for handrails. The statue of Pluto and Proserpina is an eighteenth-century French copy in ivory of Bernini's original."

"What language is that inscription in?" Gladys asks, pointing at an emerald four-leaf clover that sits in a gold box.

"Oh, that's Gaelic," I reply. "It means 'Love Never Dies.'"

"Is that message meant for anyone in particular?"

"For me," I say, "and whoever else needs to be reminded."

In a direct contradiction of my statements to the press, I did not travel the world with my husband. By then Jack could scarcely travel from his bed to the toilet, let alone from the front door to work. I had wanted a child for so long, and now it seemed that I had one—a bad one: cross, contrary, and prone to tantrums.

By the early fall of 1929, his spells of heavy drinking were arriving so often and lasting so long that it made little sense to call them spells.

At the dinner after Granny's burial, he became loud and nasty, which prompted him to go on the wagon again and to give me a bracelet as one of his many peace offerings. I had it chopped up to make a chandelier for the Dollhouse.

One cloudless morning in late September, the scent of pancakes wafting on the air, I tripped over an empty bottle on my way to make sure he'd get up and ready to face the day. Once I started looking, I found liquor hidden all over the house.

In the fight that followed, he first accused me of trying to keep him from his bootlegger, then promised up and down that he'd never call the man again.

"You bring out my finer nature," he said, clasping my hand.

"I'd hate to see your baser one," I said, and pulled away.

Outside it was a breezy day of honeyed perfection, and Jim, our chauffeur, was scheduled to collect us. Jack and I were to attend a small luncheon in honor of Winston Churchill, who'd been recently ousted as chancellor of the exchequer; he was in Los Angeles to meet with W. R. Hearst and shake some Hollywood hands. Yet here we were in Jack's boudoir, him drunk as a skunk, still in his underwear.

Bloated and red, he stunk of whiskey and sat in an easy chair clutching the morning paper; the headline was about Churchill. It looked like an establishing shot in a melodrama. The civility of our estate—monogrammed silver, linens, and heirlooms—was utterly out of keeping with the wild state in which he sprawled.

"This can't continue," I told him.

"My state of undress?" he tried to joke, rising. "I'll fix that."

"Our marriage."

The drunkenness drained from his face.

"I don't believe you mean that," he said. "Because that'd be an end to you. The last anyone hears of Doreen O'Dare."

"If you expect me to cry, I haven't any tears left."

"Worse than that," he continued with growing vehemence, "the only parts of your life anyone *will* still care about are the ones you spent with me. Actresses don't get second acts."

"I'll think of a way to be all right," I said, with a bravery I did not yet feel.

"Ha," he said. "You'll figure it out with your fabulous eighth-grade education."

"At least I'm smart enough not to miss lunch with Churchill."

"Everyone thinks Doreen O'Dare is such a sweet girl," he hissed. "But in actuality she's a prissy bitch."

"I should have thrown your love letters into the trash bin long ago," I said, quite calm. "But better late than never. I want a divorce."

"The hell you do," he said.

He lurched toward me. No longer tall and upright, he'd become a drooping man, yet his grip on my shoulder was surprisingly strong, as the drowning are said to possess extraordinary, destructive strength. With my free hand, I reached for the only weapon I could think of, my high-heeled shoe, and whacked him in the chest with it, over and over, trying to make him let me go. The heel marked his pallid flesh with half a dozen pink semicircles.

He glanced at his reflection in the looking glass above the fireplace and laughed.

In an instant he'd grabbed the shoe from my hand and thrown it through the mirror. His hands were around my neck. "I will keep you," he screamed, "as long as I want you. And you will stay till I throw you away. But you will never divorce me, Doreen! Never."

Such hammy dialogue, I thought. Then I saw spots.

The next thing I remember is the chauffeur, Jim, waking me, inside my own bedroom.

"Miss O'Dare," he said, touching my cheek with a white-gloved hand. "Are you all right? Do you want me to call the police? Shall I take you to your parents?"

I experimented with a couple of breaths, then a hum or two. Everything seemed to be in working order. "No," I said, sitting up, still dizzy. "Neither, please."

"But Miss O'Dare—"

"Thank you for saving my life. I'd like you to drive me to the Biltmore Hotel as planned. I've been looking forward to this lunch, and I'm done letting my husband spoil things for me. Give me a moment, please."

While Jim waited outside, I adjusted my wardrobe to hide my bruising. We made good time on the drive downtown. On the way to the hotel dining room, I paused for a few convulsive sobs in the ladies' room, popped a couple of aspirin, and steeled my resolve. No amount of publicity stuntman hijinks or passionate apologies could make me forgive him this time.

Jack's assault had aggravated my neck, and I felt such tingling in both hands throughout lunch that I could barely manipulate the silverware. I don't remember a word that the future prime minister said, but I'd had my goddamn lunch with Winston Churchill.

On the way home we picked up Adela, who helped me find an attorney. Her father had been a lawyer, and she knew all the best. Jim was happy to provide a statement, and when we called him up, Mervyn was at the ready with one of his own. "I wrote it all down the morning after it happened," he said. "I found a notary public at the Ambassador Hotel and signed it. I figured you might need it someday."

Jim delivered me, Adela, and my new attorney to my parents' home, where I'd be spending the night. I wanted them—Agnes in particular—to hear the attorney's explanation of what was happening and why.

Within twenty-four hours, I had filed for divorce in Los Angeles County.

∿

If you're interested in something, then you are in control; if you're *fascinated* by something, then it is. I was fascinated by my Dollhouse.

My dad had told me that I could move in with him and my mother—into Granny's old room if I wanted to, which she would have liked—but I said thank you, no, the Bel Air mansion was mine. Let Jack find someplace else.

Besides, the guesthouse off the loggia was the perfect workshop for the Dollhouse, and fairies are the most unimposing guests.

Over the seven years it took to build—from when we drew up the sketches to when we finished the landscaping in 1935—over a hundred people worked on the job. Most were from the motion picture industry: men who specialized in scaled-down scenes of natural disasters and other catastrophes too costly to film at full size. Henry Freulich, my personal cameraman, planned the display lighting.

Harold Grieve continued his unstinting dedication as the designer. "I pledge myself to the last drop of blood," he declared, "that this will be more gorgeous than any full-sized mansion."

Harold had both enthusiasm and restraint, unlike so many of us in Hollywood, with our cotton-candy-pink stuccos and not too overly disciplined gardens, our furniture upholstered in Italian silks, our Venetian glass mirrors, travertine benches, and iron torchères. Chinoiserie monkeys and bone-china flowers. Textures and colors, fabrics and finishes.

He was almost sadistically candid, as I needed him to be, but he would never just say no imperiously. "Doreen, my dear, to put that piece there would antagonize the cohesion," he'd explain. Or, "We are attempting to induce aesthetic delirium." His perfectionism was infectious: correct design and accurate representation, not to mention proper perspective and harmony of detail, soon became my bugbears, too.

Making movies was no place for perfectionists; a picture could go from scenario to filming to editing to warehouses to theaters and then vanish forever in a matter of weeks. With the Dollhouse we could slow down. I became patience personified.

But something was missing.

I had been moving for years from victory to victory; my divorce, I realized, was the last battle to win. I had faced all the challenges of Hollywood, and I had met them. So what?

I found myself thinking of Agnes and her original opposition to my Hollywood dream: deploring vanity, she never understood why I thought I belonged on the screen instead of in the audience. She never seemed to doubt that I *could* do it; she just thought I shouldn't, because it was unchristian, unfeminine. Another battle that I had won: she was wrong, and now we were both proud of what I'd achieved. But she'd guessed the limits of it better than anyone else.

Stardust is still dust. After a while you want to brush it off.

The Santa Anas blew one hot October afternoon, turning the city grimy, the air dry and wrathful. My dad came over so I could show him my ideas for the library. He looked at the plans; I looked at my face in the wall mirror, pale as a ghost. "I am not on the path to a virtuous life," I said.

"You've never hurt a fly, sweetie. You're just upset."

True. But what was I really doing? "I've not helped many people either," I said.

My flappers and shopgirls had instilled new confidence in young women—maybe, unless they'd just reflected and profited from new confidence that was already there—but that was over now: Clara Bow and her cohort had turned it into something drearier and more lubricious. All my wholesome conduct on-screen didn't amount to much if it weren't backed with tangible action. "I only know how to satisfy my own microscopic soul!" I moaned, reverting to my overdramatic childhood habits.

He sat me down in front of the drafting table. "When we had close to nothing, your mother and I always gave to those who had less. That made me feel richer than payday, in a funny way."

I remembered that feeling, though I hadn't thought of it in years; it came back to me like a scent. "You would always hand me the family coin to put in the collection plate at Mass."

"That was your favorite part. You loved to imagine who the money would help."

It had confused me back then, my parents' ability to be kinder to unseen strangers than to me, their flesh-and-blood child. But some seeds are long-germinating, and as he said it, it came to me: the castle could be a massive collection plate.

"That's it. The Dollhouse. It's what Sir Nevile did with Titania's Palace: he toured it around England, charging a small fee to see it, then donated the money to child welfare."

I could picture it: the finished Dollhouse, resplendent and incandescent. Contented souls lined up, tossing in their few cents, staring happily. "The States are much vaster than the UK," I said. "A million dollars for children's charities doesn't seem out of reach, does it? How do you even estimate something like that?"

Watching my face, he smiled for real—all the way to his eyes, for the first time in a long time.

"Maybe you should call Adela and tell her your plan? Put out a press release? Drum up some interest like—" He stopped; he'd been about to say *like Jack would do*.

"Not yet. We're still a long way from being finished, and I don't want anyone thinking it's a ploy to distract from the divorce. We can tell the crew, of course. I'll let vendors and craftsmen know. We can make a big splash when we're closer to touring. And I *will* call Marion Davies; I've been meaning to bend her ear about charity work."

The press had already been covering the castle since we'd made the announcement that we were building it—and infinite fan magazines had mentioned my miniature collection even before that—but they seemed to have a hard time figuring out how to frame the story.

Some reporters had decided that I was goofy for building the Dollhouse, and that was fine: I'd rather be taken for a cockeyed fool than a stonehearted cynic. They depicted me as a nutty little woman-child, but I knew what I was doing.

Men with tomfool schemes—obsessive innovator D. W. Griffith, undisputed visionary Cecil B. DeMille—were routinely hailed as geniuses, and breathless coverage turned some of their screwiest indulgences into landmarks of film history. A gal like me, on the other hand, was an eccentric dame with a babyish dream and too much money on her hands. That was fine. They'd see.

∽

When you love what you're doing, the work does itself. As with pictures, as with my marriage, I never wanted to be able to say, *I guess I could have tried harder.*

It turned out I had an aptitude for managing projects. There were any number of things associated with the construction of the Dollhouse and its furnishings that I had no business doing, but I was happy to track down the people who could, and to convince them to do the tasks well and on time. Had I been a bit older and arrived in Hollywood earlier, I might have become a director when that profession was still fairly open to women; it's probably best that I didn't, since it didn't stay that way for long.

Whenever an artisan told me no over the phone, I wanted to snap the receiver in two, but I kept my tone as sweet as peaches and kept wheedling: one more try. Working in pictures had given me a limitless capacity for rejection, and I was able to persist; their refusals were like gasoline sprayed on a bonfire. Some of the artists protested that they weren't miniaturists. "Oh, I know," I'd say. "I'm inviting you to *become* a miniaturist." I reminded them it was for children's charity. I pointed out that it was a chance to demonstrate their superior craftsmanship. I suggested that their most despised rivals might also be interested in the job. And I persuaded most of them.

One night the fairies came to me in a dream. We stood beneath a sycamore tree amid the reds of sunrise. I asked them whether my purpose in building the Dollhouse was good. *We don't care,* the Fairy

Princess said. *Use the castle however you please. We only want it built.* I asked whether my purpose would succeed. *For what do you desire to be legendary?* When I was fourteen, I would have answered: for acting. That night, my answer was: for generosity. The Fairy Princess fluttered forward. *Your day is still to come,* she said, *and is coming.*

I woke up with a new state of peace. For twenty-seven years I had been living at top speed. In the pastels of morning, the dream dispersing, I remembered the tale "Three Heads in a Well," as Granny used to tell it: *Once upon a time,* it began, *and a very good time it was, though it was neither your time nor my time, nor nobody else's time . . .*

That would be the castle's time: splendid and unhurried. Fairy time.

I dressed and went to meet Marion and Mary at the I. Magnin department store on Hollywood Boulevard, where Ivar Avenue came down from the Hollywood Hills. Being chic did not come easily to me, but shopping was a fun pretext for us to discuss my plans.

The sales associate whisked us inside and led us to a plump sofa.

"I love W. R.," said Marion, flopping beside me, "but it's nice to leave him at the castle sometimes." Her stutter, I noticed, was barely in evidence; all that coaching to prepare for the talkies. "He's probably roaming the parapets alone like a Gothic monk, or headed off for the hills with his shotgun or a fishing rod. But enough about his castle. How's yours?"

"Well, as you know, I've realized that it's for kids," I said. "Not mine, but for the children of America, if that's not too grandiose to say."

"It's not," said Mary, and that gave me more confidence. She was almost as famous for her open-handedness as for her pictures, putting out a bucket on all of her sets requesting donations for those in the industry who hadn't any work. In 1921 she had helped found the Motion Picture Relief Fund.

"My advice to you is the advice that W. R. gave me," said Marion. "To get by, Jill has to know her business quite as well, and perhaps a little better, than Jack. Be prepared to be underestimated. And don't be afraid to make a stink if you aren't being taken seriously."

"That's the going line in this town," agreed Mary. "Women are silly, working to save their little dogs, while the men figure out this titanic art form."

"I've noticed," I said.

"Here," she said, pulling a card from her bag. "My accountant. The best of the best."

"Will both of you geniuses promise to be at the kickoff when the time comes?"

"Wouldn't miss it!" they said in unison, and in the pear-shaped tone prescribed by Constance Collier. They exchanged a look and dissolved into laughter.

The sales associate laughed, too, a bit uncertainly, and announced, "The girls are ready to begin the show."

Lest Magnin's customers muss their coiffures or rumple the garments in which they arrived, the store provided models of each customer's own size to try the clothes on. The associate began her running narration as three young women, looking like our stand-ins on a set, strutted in the newest fashions, trying to convince us of the merits of summer furs: leopard coney, red fox, gray squirrel. She was mad about underthings: rayon slips and nainsook pajamas, seco silk and French val lace. Robes, kimonos, and negligees. Chiffon-weight hose.

"Sometimes the simpler styles are the most becoming," I said, a touch overwhelmed.

The monologue continued: gloves of French lambskin and Milanese silk. Hats with azure accents and silk rosettes. Grosgrain bows on crocheted straw.

Marion loved to sew and made many of her own dresses; she knew quality when she saw it. She helped me settle on a smart suit—something for divorce court—and we each walked out with one new outfit.

On the street, an old man with a Pekingese walked by, and Marion crouched to pet it. Nobody loved animals more than she did, especially miniature dogs. The man seemed not to recognize any of us, which afforded her the chance to make a sweet to-do. "They have faces like terrible pansies!"

"Where are you off to next?" I asked her.

"I'm off to see to a few things at the beach house," she answered.

"To the studio," said Mary, "for a meeting over a talking picture. I still think sound is like putting lipstick on the *Venus de Milo*, but since *Coquette* did well, I'm expected to talk again."

"I'm off to call your accountant, Mary." I hugged them both goodbye.

Mary's mention of sound—the topic was unavoidable—evoked the infernal clop of history. The talkies had gotten us. Everyone in town seemed to regard their approach like that of some strange creature, loose in the streets. A killer beast, or a domesticable pet?

If I'd listened a bit harder, I might have discerned that the dread of something other than sound in motion pictures was sifting through the streets, and doing so far more broadly than Hollywood alone.

When I got home, before I could call Mary's accountant, I had to return a call to my attorney. Jack, via his lawyer, wanted to apologize and was begging me—begging me!—to keep his drinking out of the papers. I said I'd consider it, then called up Adela.

"For once in my life," she said, "and let's pray it's the only time, I agree with Jack. I think it's good for both of you to keep liquor out of your complaint. For one thing, you don't need it; you have no shortage of other grounds to cite. For another, it'd make him even less employable, and you don't want to reduce his ability to support himself. For a third, half the judges in LA County are dipsomaniacs themselves. You don't want the judge to excuse Jack's behavior because he's a sympathetic fellow drunk."

Adela's advice seemed smart: better to keep things quieter. I agreed to charge Jack with only—only!—abuse and cruel treatment, leaving the booze out.

That fall, as I worked on the Dollhouse and waited for the wheels of justice to grind, I continued to keep up in a halfhearted way with all aspects of motion picture production; it still wasn't clear what the divorce would cost me, and if I needed work that's where I'd be able to find it. I'd always enjoyed writing with Mervyn and figured I'd learn more about the craft. A line in a booklet called *How to Write for the Talking Pictures* struck me: *Everyone knows that the biggest scene of a picture or play, cut out from the same and viewed of itself, holds no force whatsoever and is very often ludicrous,* it said.

The author's point was that it was necessary to accrete scenes leading up to the climax. Was the divorce to be my climax? Was my story still building? Would it end up a tragedy? A farce? I had plenty of pathos, and the courage required for an unequal struggle, but what result would arise?

Tuesday, October 29. I was halfway through the book when the stock market crashed and the whole world changed.

Chapter 15

The Chapel

Gladys cracks her knuckles.

"I was born during the Depression," she says. "Mother almost never talks about it." She pauses. "Don't take this the wrong way, but if you wanted to help, why not drop a big check straight into the hat of some agency and be done with it?"

"My resources weren't commensurate to the scale of the need. My role, as I saw it, was to give, but also to inspire others to give—not from obligation alone, but from a sense of fun. There's nothing more disempowering than despair. As much as the money, I wanted to bring people hope. The problem during the Depression—and there are economists a few blocks from here who'd object to this oversimplification, but who cares—was that people got scared and stopped spending money. A collapse in aggregate demand led to a deflationary spiral, as they say in the trade. Some wealth evaporated, but most of it just hid."

"You seem to know a lot about this," Gladys says.

"I worked for twenty years as an investment advisor."

"What?" Gladys says. "Where? When?"

"Here in Chicago. I retired last year. I did that job longer than I made movies."

"Huh." I see she's taking it in. "Sorry. You were saying?"

"The Fairy Castle," I continue, "was meant to be an occasion for people who thought they had nothing to help those even less fortunate—to 'lend it, spend it, send it rolling along,' as the old movie song goes—and to get a bit of magic for themselves, too. My friend Mervyn LeRoy directed that movie, by the way."

"You were asking people to have a little faith," Gladys says. "Which brings us at last—"

"To the Chapel. The final room."

Gladys restarts the recorder.

"I gather it's not fashionable to believe in God nowadays, but I can't help myself. The design of the Chapel pays homage to the Book of Kells. My grandmother saw it as a little girl when her family traveled to Dublin, and she never forgot it: the blend of Christian and Celtic symbols, humans mingling with mythical beasts. When Jack and I were in Ireland, Trinity College arranged a private showing for us. They keep the book under glass and display one page a day. It was in the middle of a chapter, so I didn't get to see any pictures.

"Nearby is a gift my parents bought me on a trip to Italy, a crucifix over three hundred years old. Under a magnifying glass, Jesus's face has an expression of infinite sadness. I think he looks a bit like Lillian Gish."

Gladys snorts. "Sorry," she says. "We'll edit any extra noise out of the finished version."

I smile; I never tire of performing, it seems. "The most precious object in the Chapel," I say, "is the sliver of wood framed in that gold monstrance, given to me by my dear friend Clare Boothe Luce. She received it at her first audience with Pope Pius XII after she became the ambassador to Italy. It's thought to be a fragment of the one true cross."

Gladys looks up from her clipboard. "The cross," she says, "that Jesus died on?"

"That's the one, yes."

"Do you believe that?"

"Clare Boothe Luce believed it."

"Sure," Gladys says. "But, I mean, do *you* believe it?"

I reach into my coat pocket and find my gloves; soon it'll be time to go outside. "Do I believe that there's a piece of the one true cross in the castle that I built to house a group of six-inch-tall invisible fairies?" I say. "That's the question that the Chapel is meant to prompt, isn't it? And I think the answer it suggests is that every object, like every moment, is brimming with hidden miracles awaiting those who would find them. So yes, Gladys, for the record, I do believe it."

The panic of 1929 brought a fat decade to a close, and the tightening of resources triggered a contraction of compassion. Prior to the crash, and even afterward, those who won in the stock market were respected as investors, but those who suffered losses were derided as gamblers. Who had any sympathy for a gambler, really? The consensus was that anybody suffering had brought it on themselves.

That didn't last. It soon became clear that no one was immune: farmers, factory workers, and movie extras all saw the future shrinking. The anguish seemed even more perverse in LA's perpetual sunshine: shabby men and weeping women, parched and hopeless, winding around the block for soup.

Marion would sometimes swoop in and take over all the cafeterias on Hollywood Boulevard to feed the hungry at her expense. Most of us just gritted our teeth and tried to get our bearings.

Everyone dies eventually, and one could argue that whether they end up in Forest Lawn amid ponds and statuary or in some potter's field doesn't make much difference. People whose fame rose hot like bread in an oven and those whose renown collapsed like a failed soufflé all passed from the earth like those who'd never been famous in the first place. But the Depression made fate's fickleness feel especially oppressive. It was hard not to suspect some deep-rooted malice, some limitless punishment being meted out for innumerable transgressions.

Because I'd heeded Granny's advice to steer mostly clear of stocks in favor of savings accounts and real property, my wealth was mostly spared. My more acute nervousness at the time was over the outcome of my divorce, but I needn't have worried. In May of 1930, the judge granted me my divorce "due to the many humiliations you suffered from Jack Flanagan."

In court, Jack wore a morning suit and a blue cornflower boutonniere: the same bloom his eyes had put me in mind of the night we'd met, the fateful eve of my nineteenth birthday. He'd lost all the weight he'd gained and then some. He was so skinny that his jacket looked held up by dowel rods.

All through the proceedings I'd felt his hateful stare, and I hadn't been able to bring myself to meet it. In the wake of the judge's pronouncement, as my lawyer was trying to shake my hand, I finally turned to look. Jack studied the marble floor. Everything I'd loved about him had drained away. I'd made the right decision, but his averted face made me exhausted and sad.

I ran the gauntlet of photographers outside the courthouse. How they relished in the crumbling of my fairy-tale marriage! You work so hard to win the crown, and then everyone lines up to behead you.

By then I was dating a stockbroker, happy to be involved with someone outside the industry. Albert Parker Scott awaited me in his rattletrap automobile. His battered old car was a bit of an affectation; he'd been one of the few in his profession who'd intuited that something was wrong in the summer of '29—an instability that others weren't seeing—and he'd sold short, hoping to earn a little money on a downturn. He was thrilled at first, then faintly horrified, to see the bet he placed against the market pay off beyond his wildest expectations.

Albert insisted that everyone who could afford to get back into the market absolutely should, both for altruistic reasons—to help slow the avalanche—and self-interested ones; he suggested some stocks I could scoop up for cheap. When I protested that that felt predatory, he laughed. "Better not call the fire department if you see a house burning. Somebody might give you a reward!"

He and I married in 1932; our life together was bright and easy, as clear and as shallow as a mountain brook. Albert was quite an outdoorsman, in fact: tan and hale, with twinkling eyes. He wore plus fours to play golf, a sartorial choice that showed off his muscular calves. We both loved sailing and got involved with the keelboat events of the 1932 Olympics, which were held in LA. Whenever I was anxious about an impasse with some aspect of the Dollhouse or upset with some distracting dustup—usually involving Jack—Albert would tease, "You don't have to smile, baby. Let's go to the beach. You can swim and listen to the sad sea waves."

That always made me laugh. But he and I suffered from a hundred tiny incompatibilities. He liked to own books, whereas I liked to read them. He didn't understand or appreciate my friends, nor I his, particularly.

But it was good not to be alone.

Jack continued his public decline. While our divorce was in process, he'd announced doomed engagements to a series of actresses; once it was final, he wed one. That marriage collapsed within months, with her claiming mental cruelty: Jack couldn't look at a photograph of me, she said, without breaking down in tears.

Fortunately for him, I suppose, my photo hadn't been appearing all that often. Because I'd been lucky with money, I could afford to extend my break, and the experience with *Smiling Irish Eyes* still stung. Every time I sat down with my address book to call studio executives, I'd end up on the phone with goldsmiths and engravers and antique dealers instead.

Not long after his second divorce, Jack tried to kill himself by walking into the sea at Malibu. Almost certainly by coincidence, the spot he picked to do it was a hundred yards from Adela's beachfront home; once he got past the breakers, she phoned her neighbor John Gilbert—known as the Great Lover prior to the talkies, now himself washed up, skulking around—to row out and save him. Both men were drunk, so this process took a long time, and its successful outcome was by no means foregone.

Adela—she told me this later, with a hint of apology—stood on the beach and watched Gilbert haul Jack in like a prize halibut. And when the keel of Gilbert's dinghy finally touched the sand again, she dug out some old notebooks and sat down at her typewriter.

In Adela's film treatment, which she titled "The Truth about Hollywood," the washed-up alcoholic succeeds in taking his own life. ("I'm not saying it's what should have happened," she told me, "only that it was a better ending.") She sold the story to RKO, and they adapted it in 1932 as a film called *What Price Hollywood?*

"You ought to be furious," Albert said after we'd seen the picture. "Adela sold you out."

"Oh, sweetheart. The support Adela's given me through the years is worth a dozen *What Price Hollywoods*. Besides, you don't get mad at a shark that eats you. It's what sharks do."

As it happened, there weren't a dozen: there were three. In 1937, Selznick made a picture called *A Star Is Born*, starring Janet Gaynor and Fredric March. Adela wasn't credited—given her close acquaintance with many lawyers, I assume she made some kind of side arrangement—but it contained aspects of her original story that the first film hadn't used, including the line, "This is Mrs. Norman Maine," an unmistakable echo of the call she once heard me place to Richard Rowland in order to save Jack's job.

They remade *A Star Is Born* in 1954 with Judy Garland and James Mason; I prefer the 1937 version. I can understand the impulse to return to the story, and I won't be surprised if it happens again. There's a lot there to chew on.

~

My marriage to Albert lasted a couple of years. The fact that our professions were headquartered on opposite coasts pulled us in opposite directions. We parted in the world's most amicable divorce and remained friends until his dying day.

After a divorce, to hear the papers tell it, men are bachelors once more, but women are practically defunct. With Albert gone, I could see myself rattling around the Bel Air house like a pea in a barrel, and I didn't like what I saw. It's hard enough for any divorcée anywhere to go out on the town alone and not be thought lonely; being a movie star doesn't make it easier.

I didn't succumb to that thinking; I was too busy plotting. It was time to put myself on the screen again. I had to stay relevant. For the Dollhouse tour to work according to plan, I would need the cachet of a star.

As bad as *Smiling Irish Eyes* had been, it proved that I could handle myself in talkies, and after my three-year absence, the studios perceived enough pent-up demand among my tried-and-true fans that they didn't require much convincing. I did four more sound films, of which the first was the best: *The Power and the Glory*, which costarred Spencer Tracy. The critics adored it, particularly my new grown-up persona—*a sophisticate with dash*, one wrote—but audiences did not, apparently unenthusiastic about me in that kind of part.

The last was the worst: a turgid adaptation of Nathaniel Hawthorne's *The Scarlet Letter* seemingly hell-bent—so to speak—on proving the opposite point we'd made with *Flaming Youth*: great books often make weak movies. It was the only project I ever did for purely mercenary reasons—to earn the dough to finish the Dollhouse—and if it didn't exactly shore up my legacy as an artist, it burnished my reputation as a professional. "Anybody can give a good performance in a *good* movie," Lillian Gish once murmured to me over coffee.

It was as good a place to stop as any. With great relief and zero regrets, I quit.

∾

Adela approved of my decision to step away—"Sometimes the juice isn't worth the squeeze"—and helped spread the news that I'd now be focusing exclusively on my charity tour.

We were almost ready to embark. I and the Dollhouse would depart Hollywood in the coming spring of 1935.

The publicity for the tour suggested—not in so many words—that after I finished my charity initiative, I'd be back to resume my Hollywood career. I had no such plan. Dry palm fronds rattled in the Santa Ana winds, and I longed to leave. No more gazing at the edge of the continent into the Pacific void. For the first time since I'd arrived in LA, I'd begun to weary of its makeshift quality: all the sham fronts and gimcrack houses, the agglomeration. Sweet at first, the desperate pleading to attract and beguile had grown pathetic. After double divorces, my own home had a mortuary air. Where before I'd smelled flowers, I now smelled cobwebs and dry rot. I never wanted to become a pitiable eccentric, wearing the same expensive gown until it tattered. The country was ravenous with spiritual hunger, as was I, and I wanted to feed it.

I didn't dare admit to Adela or any other journalist that I was trying to figure out—as the cliché goes—who I was. Acting made peculiar demands on one's spirit; I had done it for so long, and with such single-minded dedication, that I wasn't entirely sure of what effect it had had on me. There were actors who could commit to this routine emptying of selfhood in service to their art; I was learning that I was not among them. Once I was talking to Dorothy Gish—whom I never got to know well—about how the public had it all wrong when they imagined Lillian to be as fragile as her on-screen personae. "Then again," Dorothy told me, "I have no idea what my sister is really like."

You might think that organizing a national tour for a one-ton dollhouse would be hell's own job, but you'd be wrong: I loved it.

I hired a publicity man named Maurice Fitzgerald to help me razzmatazz the tour stops. When he first set foot in my office and saw the array of calendars and invoices and bills of lading all over my workspace, he declared, "A cluttered desk is the sign of a cluttered mind," then began sorting paper with a smile. "Allow me."

"*Allow* you?" I said. "That's why you're here. I *demand* you!"

Always with an unlit cigar in his hand and a derby on his head, he was a prince of efficiency. It was a pleasure to work with a publicity man who wasn't my husband.

We'd kick off in New York—my least-loved city, but America's financial and philanthropic heart—then go by rail from Philadelphia to DC, from Pittsburgh to LA, and of course to Chicago. In subsequent months, then subsequent years, we'd crisscross the country: Toledo, St. Louis, Boston, Detroit, Peoria, Omaha, Cincinnati, Birmingham, Newark, on and on. In every city we'd display the Dollhouse at a department store, and visitors would pay a small fee to see it: one dime for children, two for adults. The department stores would collect matching funds from local benefactors and dispense the proceeds to kids' charities in the community.

"What the public needs to know," I said, "is that we'll turn their dimes into thousands of dollars."

Maury and I came up with a press release:

On Its Triumphant World Tour of Mercy

The Dollhouse That Helps Handicapped Children Smile Again

In addition to seeing the Dollhouse you will have the warm satisfaction and certain knowledge that you are contributing your share to the bet= terment of the city's destitute children.

I had gotten my wish to be Cinderella; now I wanted to transform into the Fairy Godmother. Granny had always loved the fairies for their childlike natures, for always making festivals; Hollywood was my fairy-land until it wasn't, and now I'd make my magic elsewhere.

"The entire country seems to be suffering from dreamer's block," I told Maury as we watched the Railway Express crew load the disassembled Dollhouse for its trip to the East Coast. "I want to wow both kids and businessmen!"

He shook my hand as I boarded the train. "If anybody can, it's you and this castle," he said. "It'll make the lion lie down with the lamb."

I settled into my compartment, noting the worn faces among my fellow travelers, all as ignorant of the purpose of my journey as I was of theirs. *Remember to look up!* I wanted to beseech a nation fixated on its stumbling feet. *Remember to look.*

~

How courtly department stores were back in those days! Enormous mirrors and polished oak, beveled glass and marble stairs. We held the dedication ceremony for the Dollhouse on an April evening in 1935, on the fifth floor of R. H. Macy's in Herald Square, where it would be on display for a fortnight.

President Roosevelt himself was not able to attend, but he sent his mother Sara, a stately matron of eighty with marcelled white hair, who laid the golden cornerstone. Former governor Al Smith was there, too, happy to join the cause of a fellow Irish Catholic.

"I am glad to be present at the opening of Doreen O'Dare's Fairyland Dollhouse," Smith said into the microphone, his words broadcast live across the city. "I am always glad to be of service to the hospitals of New York, which do so much for the people, regardless of race, color, creed, or condition of pocketbook."

I gave my own speech, to great applause. "Tonight there is a reward for all of those who have labored so lovingly to make the Dollhouse perfect—a reward which may be measured only in spiritual delight—of joy in a job well done."

Looking at the faces of the citizens assembled and ready to help, I could no longer blame people for wanting happy endings in my movies;

I wanted one in real life. It might take forever, but we wanted to build a better and more charming world, one block at a time.

"That is one pretty pile of bricks," Governor Smith said to me as we were leaving. "You'd have to have a bowl of ice water for a soul to be unmoved."

Over 115,000 visitors came to see it on opening day. Construction workers and stevedores came alongside the schoolkids. People made pilgrimages from all five boroughs, from the suburbs, from Connecticut and New Jersey. I watched them stream in and take comfort at the appearance of such bounty. People came back again and again, for its marvels couldn't be apprehended at a glance, and could never be fully plumbed. There was more than enough for everyone. Eyeful after eyeful: you'd never run out.

Some critics scolded me, of course, for building something fanciful at a time of real hardship, a dollhouse when we needed public works. Come on, I responded; a great nation ought to have both. A piece of art was a door to somewhere else: somewhere beyond the Depression, beyond the smallness of our terrified selves. The Dollhouse was no less a bridge than any constructed under the WPA; it was one that anyone could cross, and it led somewhere that no other bridge could go.

After New York, I was even more eager to go on to the smaller stops, places where I'd meet the sorts of poor and striving people I hadn't seen since my childhood. Departing from Grand Central, I felt myself at the gateway to a continent: all the lines radiating across the nation.

I rode the newly debuted streamlined train, the *Zephyr*, named for the god of the west wind, stainless steel and sleekly streaking like a sea serpent on wheels. When I walked through the vestibules between cars, I braced myself for the wind.

I kept a little red morocco diary in which I jotted my daily adventures.

The porter taught me the difference between hoboes, tramps, and bums. Hoboes traveled and worked; tramps traveled and begged. Bums might or might not ride the rails but drank and took dope. All of them often got injured or killed jumping on and off. The safest times were when the steam trains had to stop for water; since diesels didn't have to, the hazards increased.

Some of the riders who rode without paying sought seasonal employment: picking fruit in the Pacific Northwest, cutting sugarcane in the South, or harvesting wheat on the Great Plains. They hopped both freight and passenger trains, hiding in the blocked doorways of baggage or mail cars. I understood why the porter spoke of them with annoyance, but I wished better times on all of them.

Each place we stopped, we saw men, women, and kids tramping the streets looking for work that didn't exist.

"It has been my observation," Victor once told me during one of our winter walks in the mountains, "that a talented actor is first, last, and at all times an actor. I'm not suggesting that you go through your days playing various parts, but only that every new contact you make with life is one you can use. Store them up on a shelf in your brain. People of all classes—you should know 'em. Constantly widen the old horizon."

I didn't think I was an actor any longer, but I was doing it for its own sake.

Dreams seemed to unfurl faster on a sleeping berth speeding through a peaceful night: a silver needle stitching through a scenic vista.

In Washington, DC, we had senators, society leaders, and foreign ambassadors. In Los Angeles, two thousand people came to glimpse not only the castle but also the movie stars glimpsing the castle.

But the stops we made in the nation's inexhaustible middle were the ones that remain most vividly with me.

In Omaha we held the usual reception in the Brandeis department store, with the reassembly of the castle attended by the mayor and representatives of the fifty local charities that our proceeds would benefit. I went on the radio with the governor, broadcasting live from inside the limestone structure.

That weekend, we opened the castle first and exclusively to eight hundred children from hospitals and orphanages. Tubercular urchins with tangled hair who'd worn blasé faces as they arrived came suddenly alight at the sight of the Dollhouse. Everyone has an aesthetic sense that seeks to be satisfied. All the movie premieres I had ever attended paled to nothing in comparison to meeting those kids. I stayed all day, both days.

When children were unable to shake my hand due to weakness, or paralysis, or because their hand was missing, I would touch their cheeks, or knees. I tried to have individual conversations with each of them so they didn't feel reduced to bodies in a brigade.

Wonder usually enters through the eyes but takes place chiefly in the mind. Although the Dollhouse's miniatures could not be removed or handled, I'd had extras made for the blind: replicas they could touch.

Sometimes their conditions made them hard to understand, but I tried. The questions they asked! It was as though they thought Hollywood might as well be on Saturn.

I gave them gifts. Teddy bears for the littlest ones. Silver compacts for the older girls, who seemed to me the saddest; no one wanted them, but everyone wanted something from them. Autographed photographs. Postcards of the Dollhouse. Crates of goodies. A room without books is a very dead space, so I piled them on.

At the end of the visits on Sunday, the children sang and handed me poems they'd written. One tiny blonde girl with cornsilk hair, feet in braces, read one that ended, "Thanks for not making us wrassle to visit your pretty castle."

I still have it in my scrapbook. I wish I knew what happened to her.

~

It was glorious, but not at all what I had expected or prepared for. Throughout the time spent and the effort exerted in building it, throughout all the hours of discussion with Harold and Horace and my father, I had been animated by a vision of what the Dollhouse would look like through the eyes of its visitors. Now that the tour was underway, I barely thought of the structure and its furnishings. I thought only of the people.

The nation was vaster in every way than I had anticipated, teeming with language and custom and culture that I had never imagined existing, much less ever seen captured by any motion picture, accurately or poorly. It was a land of appalling inequality and injustice, more dire than I thought possible, as well as instances of dignity and courage and kindness that constituted heroism on an epic scale.

When I was alone aboard the train in the idle times between cities, I mostly thought of debts. For years I had considered the debt that Granny Shaughnessy suggested I'd owe to the Good People, and the means by which they'd collect it. With the Dollhouse now built, I'd hoped it to be discharged. But once I began to meet the hundreds of thousands of struggling Americans who came to see my creation, the debt I found myself recalling was the one that Uncle Walter collected for getting *The Birth of a Nation* past the Chicago censors, the one that opened the doorway that led me to my career and fame.

Through all my frustrations and difficulties, with every triumph that seemed just barely won, I had rarely paused to consider the magnitude of my initial good fortune, or its nature. As I sped across the continent with a ton of aluminum and a trove of miniatures, as the only evidence of the fulfillment of my one childhood dream began to blister and dissolve in its reels, this debt began to seem more and more like the one in urgent need of settling. It still seems so today.

The tour continued joyfully, in both endless repetition and infinite variety—not unlike making a motion picture. If only the nuns who had educated me could have seen me on my knees at the cathedrals in each city, what might they have thought? I was praying for love, but now for the first time my prayer was for everyone, for every frightened person in the world.

In Chicago, some spirit at Holy Name heard my plea and chose to send an extra measure of that love my way.

We set up at the Fair Store at State and Adams. Uncle Walter covered the story himself, complaining that none of the young whelps in the city room knew how to do real reporting. A museum in itself awaits you, he wrote, in the Eighth Floor Toyland.

Aunt Lib couldn't stop beaming at what we'd made. "It's a masterpiece, Doreen!" she exclaimed. "The closer I look, the stranger it gets."

As in other cities, I did not decline to attend the champagne receptions that preceded the public opening. Part of the magic was this chance at inebriated elegance, which is where large philanthropic commitments often get made.

I had always prided myself on the practicality of my bob, but never had I been more grateful for its forgiving nature than in Chicago, where the wind truly did blow night and day. High above State Street, I expected the reception to amount to meeting many women greeting each other with "Darling, that hat is *divine*," and who frolicked around in fine French frocks. That's what I'd come to expect on the East Coast.

But in Chicago they were a down-to-earthier sort. Chicago had a virile civic pride that I hadn't noticed during the summers when I was young, and I was reminded of why I loved the winding lakefront: sandy beaches and broad old trees, filthy river crisscrossing the grid like some industrial Venice, skyscrapers so tall they were swathed in clouds.

Marion had helped me pack for this leg of the trip; I wanted to keep my suits simple, so she suggested they all be Chanel. "Do take your mink," she said. "And for the reception, this seafoam-green taffeta with silver kid slippers."

I was glad to be wearing it that night, the night I first caught sight of Gordon Graves, and he of me.

I spotted him across the top of a tall centerpiece of white marguerite daisies, mixed freesia, pink tulips, and blue bachelor buttons. I pushed it aside to see him better.

He caught me looking, and all I could think to say was, "You have beautiful table manners!"

He laughed. "I see you don't keep all of your magic in your castle," he said, and it went to my head. At thirty-four, I had been feeling faded; now I will always associate the scent of freesia with unexpected aphrodisiac properties.

The sun had set. The sky sapphired and spangled itself with silver. Gordon's eyes were not sky but rather delphinium blue. When he asked if he could take me to dinner the following evening, I agreed immediately.

The average businessman has no imagination, but Gordon was not an average businessman. Vice president and director of the Chicago office of Merrill Lynch, he was a little gray about the temples at forty. Over dinner at Café Brauer in Lincoln Park, he made it clear that he understood what I was doing.

"Your Dollhouse is a symbol of national activism," he said, cutting into his steak. "You performed the magic trick this country needed: taking the conspicuous spending of a fun-loving flapper's private pleasures and transforming them into a model of civic consumption. It's not frivolous. Well, it *is* frivolous, which is what makes it *not* frivolous. Pretty neat, if you ask me."

He brought up his family before I asked. His son Gordon Graves Jr.—who went by Buzz—was twelve, and his daughter Edith—Edie—was five. His wife had died in 1933, and he missed her. He knew something about my struggles with Jack, but who didn't?

It had been raining unpoetically all day long, but as we emerged it shifted to snow—like a spell being cast, like fairy dust. The snowflakes started to do that maneuver where they float upward like bubbles under the sea, and it was so terribly pretty that I almost couldn't stand it.

There, on the corner, we kissed. The air turned liquid blue. I knew I'd found my love.

But I didn't stop touring with the Dollhouse, and he didn't ask me to.

I rode the *Super Chief* often between Los Angeles and Chicago to visit Gordon and his children. I learned how to dress for the Chicago cold: astrakhan and fur-lined hats. I fell in love with the children, too—quiet and serious with creamy skin, blue eyes for Edie, brown for Buzz. Shy at first, like small adults, they welcomed me, too.

I remember the first time I sang to Edie at bedtime. Strange is the performance whose aim is to put its audience to sleep.

Our wedding—his second, my third—was a small affair. We held it at Riverview Amusement Park, with the kids at our side, and had a supper of hot dogs. Jack and Albert had both been extravagant, but from Gordon I learned that modest expressions of love can be the most profound.

"To new beginnings," he said, "but more importantly to true beginnings." His wedding toast, with Coca-Cola.

The greatest relief is laughter, and Gordon made me laugh again. He was not just a gentleman but a gentle man. He'd never raise a hand to me or to his kids. I loved him so much that I missed him when he was in the other room. He loved me without illusion, with an ardent regard.

The morning after our wedding I awoke to the scuffling of a pigeon's feet on the windowsill and felt completely where I belonged. The sight of his shaving cream, his pipe, his toothbrush next to mine! The sound of Buzz and Edie in the kitchen making us breakfast—french toast with strawberries! Very hot coffee!

They say you can't miss what you've never had, but I've found that not to be true; I missed never having been a mom. When we finally moved in together as a family, Buzz and Edie gave me the chance to design children's rooms inside my own house, made to withstand the kicks of shoes and the whacks of toys.

I loved his kids. Our kids. They tracked Lake Michigan beach sand in and out, but I didn't mind. I put too much holly around the eggnog bowl at Christmastime. I fed them as much ice cream as they wanted when they got the measles. I had always had a violent dislike for when actresses told the magazines that their most important role was *mother*. It wasn't my most important one, but it was important. Acting was acting, and parenting was parenting, and I valued both.

I managed to raise $650,000 by the time Pearl Harbor was attacked; then I had to stop. It had become unpatriotic to travel too frequently: civilians were asked to stay off trains since they were needed for troops and equipment.

Gordon thought it gauche to let one's personal wealth pile too high. He believed in tithing, and then some—not to the church, but to the community—so we gave huge sums away each year. He didn't like paying barbers, so I cut his hair. He wore a terry-cloth robe and leather slippers around the house. The unstrained ease we shared was like nothing I'd ever felt with Jack. Gordon was never moody, and always forgiving of others and himself, though he did very little that would require forgiveness.

Happy endings are corny, but I figured I might deserve one. From 1941 on I rarely left Chicago except to travel, as I'd always longed to, with Gordon and the kids, or later to visit them at college.

It was thanks to Gordon that I ended up becoming a financial advisor myself.

Over breakfast one morning I asked him to help me invest my savings. Squeezing a lemon over a tall glass of tomato juice, he said, "I think that you ought to figure out how to do it yourself."

"But, Gordie," I replied, "I can't even balance my own checkbook!" An absolute lie.

"You ought to be ashamed to admit it," he said.

"That was exaggeration for effect. I was trying to make a point."

"So was I. Anyone who can do sixth-grade mathematics can learn to invest."

"I suppose I ought to remind you that I *did* only finish eighth grade."

"You're way ahead, then," he said. "Actuarially speaking, women live longer than men, so it behooves a woman to hold her own. If I can't convince you of that, then rest assured that time will."

Armed with addition, subtraction, a basic grasp of fractions, and an ability to multiply to get percentages, I crash-coursed through our little household college of finance and became a star pupil.

I invested in a cosmetic company after finding a nail polish shade of theirs that I admired so much that I took it with me around the world, leaving it scattered like rubies from a potentate among manicurists of many cities. Next, I bought a face cream from them and didn't care for it at all, and sold my stock accordingly, and was filled with regret when they continued to rise.

"I learned from my mistake, at least," I told Gordon.

"Only fools don't," he replied.

In the future, I would not be quite so localized.

I came to enjoy investing so much that I joined Merrill Lynch as a specialist in helping other women invest. *The stock market will take its spills,* I told my clients. *You can't have a nervous collapse every time your stock goes down a point or two. And you don't need a pile of money to get started—a small amount will do.*

I threw myself into my new job, but from afar: to be on the floor would be too disruptive. Tyrone Power once stopped to visit us after finishing a picture in Europe, and Gordon took him one morning to the floor of the Board of Trade. The price of wheat fell by an eighth of a point globally because the brokers stopped trading and crowded Ty for his autograph.

From time to time over the years, I'd get a letter from Jack. He rarely said much except that he'd gotten sober; he'd become a leader in a new movement, Alcoholics Anonymous, and it had kept him on the wagon. Plenty of good gets done by troubled people, so I was happy for him and happy he helped others, but I never responded. I hope he found some peace.

As he was about many things, Gordon was right about vital statistics indeed. He died in 1964 while we were on vacation in Phoenix, Arizona; he was sixty-eight. I was sixty-two then, and left quite well provided for, but all the money in the world couldn't recompense my loss.

Victor couldn't make it to the funeral, but he sent a note of sympathy and a bunch of violets.

And Clare Boothe Luce sent a note that made me feel better:

> Frankly, all women deserve to love and to be loved, for existence without love is inhibited at best, and meaningless at worst. It's abominable that women are asked so often to sacrifice their personhood to maintain their womanhood. Only the rare man who is spiritually generous and truly secure, perhaps, has the capacity to love a woman enough to permit her to be altogether a person. My Henry is a man like that and so was your Gordon. I'm so sorry, Doreen.

I had Buzz and Edie. I had my boards and my charities and my women's investing workshops. By then I was a grandmother, too, and I saw the children often. But in the gloomiest nights after Gordon's death, I could not help feeling that I was right back where I was when I broke things off with Jack: alone again, but much less happy about it.

Epilogue

The Castle in Moonlight

I hike up my glove to check my watch. I have an engagement this evening for which I can't be late, but it looks like I have plenty of time.

I feel fortunate, watching my friends age, that I can still remember everything. They can recall their youths without flaw, but later events disintegrate. I'm not sure which I'm more sad about, them or the ones who died too soon. When stomach cancer took Marion Davies in '61, a few months after Jack, she was funny till the end. *What's your dying wish?* I asked her. *Anything you want.* She wished not to die, then gloated over the loophole she'd found.

These days I serve on boards, I organize quiet philanthropy. Eighteen years of flashing across screens was plenty for me, thanks. Now being behind various scenes is pleasing.

When my parents and I were in Hawaii, as the Fairy Castle was beginning to take shape, my surfing instructor showed me a common day octopus he'd found, a mottled beast on the shallow reefs that shot a cloud of mystifying ink whenever threatened. With its predator discombobulated by the shimmering blur, the octopus escaped: safe, secret, no longer seen. That was, at the time, what the castle was for me: a chance to stop saying *Look at me!* and instead say *Look over here!* while I disappeared.

But I'm sadder than I've admitted—to Gladys, to myself—at being erased. I want people to remember my films and my dollhouse, and to remember that I made them. I'm glad I got to make this recording: to arrange each room with my mind and my voice while I still can.

"Gladys," I say, "I'd like to thank you for sailing back across all these voyaging years with me today. And for looking with attention at what I put together. It's a great honor."

"Doreen, the honor has been mine. I just wish I'd done a little more homework."

"I wouldn't worry about that. There's an advantage to not over-preparing for this. It puts you closer to the perspective of the visitor."

"I'm not talking about the Fairy Castle. I'm talking about you. Like that you worked as an investment advisor!"

"I'm retired from Merrill Lynch. I still advise friends, generally in exchange for dinner. May I give you my card?"

She takes it, a bit sheepishly, saying, "If you need anything, or just want to show friends the castle, give me a call."

"Is the museum working on acquiring anything exciting now? If you're at liberty to say?"

"I'm hoping we'll get more materials from the space program. Apollo 8's going up this month. I wish the museum could get the cap-sule. It's got to go somewhere."

I'm struck by the thought of it.

"You know," Gladys continues, "I wouldn't have thought of it before today, but the role your Fairy Castle played during the Depression is kind of comparable to what the moon shot does today. They both create a kind of public wonder at an anxious time."

She doesn't need to say more. In April there was terrible unrest in Chicago, and in many other cities, after Martin Luther King Jr. was murdered, then more violence at the Democratic National Convention. Between the two—a horrible bridge of sorts between them—fell Robert F. Kennedy's assassination. It happened at the Ambassador Hotel in Los Angeles, the site of the first WAMPAS Baby Stars Frolic in 1922: my coming-out party in Hollywood, a memory that I forgot I treasured until it was soiled.

"It has always been easy to see the castle as pointless," I say. "It's surplus, like going to the moon. You hear arguments now similar to those I heard then. 'Why don't we worry about the problems here on Earth?' Well, we *should* worry about those problems. But also taking the time to care about something superfluous can end up being crucial. Liberation in the form of fun."

Gladys rises to her feet, stretching like a house cat. I stand up, too. "*This* has been fun, but God," she says, "that chair you were sitting in is awful. Sorry these are so threadbare. Looking at the castle all day has made me unforgiving of crummy furniture."

"Threadbare but comfortable," I say.

"Before you go," prompts Gladys, "one last thing."

I nod. I adore this part. "Ready?" I ask, finger poised.

"Ready," says Gladys.

I flip a switch, and little fillips of light spring to life on the ten-inch-tall tree standing in the Castle's Great Hall. It's installed each December, part of the annual *Christmas Around the World* exhibit. Whenever I'm in town over the holidays, I have the joy of lighting it. The tree, like the castle, is meant for children everywhere, which includes all of us.

I glance at Gladys, a modest grace to her face. She looks at the castle, it looks back, and they pause in a state of reciprocal absorption.

We walk through the doors into the hum and noise of the rest of the museum, rife with the bustle of closing time, and pause before the Mold-A-Rama, huge as a jukebox. I pay, and it pings like a pinball machine through a moment of gadgetry until it spits out a three-inch-high replica of the Fairy Castle in bone-white plastic.

"A memento of a day well spent, I hope." I hand it to Gladys.

"Absolutely," she says, holding the castle to her nose and sniffing. "Would you like me to call you a taxi?"

"Thanks, but no need," I say.

"Merry Christmas, Doreen." She shakes my hand. "I'll be in touch."

"You'd better be," I say.

I step outside. Unlike the Christmas tree in the castle, the bare branches are like pencil scratches. It's the blue hour, twilight, when daylight drains from the bowl of the sky and darkness pools in the lake. I walk to the bus stop.

Hollywood always portrays Chicago as a gangland paradise, but I knew better when I moved in with Gordon and the children. I fell under the spell of the seasons then: the subtle melancholy of September, the February ennui. Buildings vast as icebergs soaring above the frozen December snowscape. My impressions of Chicago, still, are mostly about how real it seems, not staged—how it's simply itself, not standing in for somewhere else.

The northbound bus arrives, and I take a seat on the right side so I can look east, to the lake. Ahead of me sits a young woman in a red cap. I think of Granny Shaughnessy and her tales of the merrow—common, so they say, on the wilder coasts. Sometimes they wander the shore, and they wear a red cap called a *cohuleen druith*; if it gets stolen, they can't return beneath the waves. Granny said that the webbing between a merrow's fingers—thin as the membrane of an egg—was the giveaway. This girl is wearing gloves, so I'll never know.

I get off at my stop and stroll beneath the streetlights. I wanted to withdraw from the limelight before the limelight withdrew from me, and I did. The secret I've discovered is that you can remain in obscurity for so long that people will think you're dead. Then you're free.

This time of night, every lit window is a version of the Dollhouse, a diorama staged for looking wonderingly in. A game I used to play growing up in Tampa: I'd saunter the street toward my family's house in the evening, pretending I didn't know who lived there, trying to imagine what a stranger might think. Curious whether nice people resided inside.

Upstairs, in my apartment, I change for dinner. I put on a gown I got in Paris when I was there with Clare Boothe Luce: an attempt on her part to cheer me up after Gordon. Peach silk—it still fits, and four years later is still in style.

One afternoon there, while Clare was off on a separate adventure and I was strolling the Champs-Élysées, I felt a tap on my shoulder, and a voice came from behind.

"What, Madame Zaza, have I got in my hand?"

I didn't have to turn around.

"Why, Professor LaTour, it can only be a dime."

"Clairvoyant, as always," said Victor Marquis, "and as always correct." I whirled to embrace him.

He was still married to someone else. I wasn't ready yet to be over Gordon. But we had a sweet visit, unexpected amid the shrugging finesse of France.

I'm ready now.

I take the elevator down and walk to the Pump Room, the restaurant next door to my building. Chandeliers and wall sconces and cream-leather booths. The maître d' leads me to my usual spot.

A bottle of champagne in a melting bucket of ice rests tableside. Seated next to it is Victor Marquis, holding a bunch of violets.

He stands and we kiss, once on each cheek, then sit and stare at each other, smiling.

"Punctual as ever, Eileen," he says. "Though I'd wait for you as long as it took, you know, frustrating as that can be."

For the first time since we met, neither Victor nor I is married to somebody else.

"Let's not call it frustration," I say. "Let's call it delayed contentment."

Behind spectacles now, his eyes have lost none of their intensity. The attention he pays remains undivided.

We are here to talk about a new idea of mine, the founding of a television production company. I still spend half the year in LA, and I enjoy the medium of the smaller screen. I figure why not get behind the kinds of programs we'd like to see? Victor, as in his younger days, is game.

Our interest in reuniting is not merely professional.

"What do you say," he says, after we decline to peruse the dessert menu, "that you and I go and take in a movie?"

"Are you asking me on a date?"

"I believe I am," he says, standing.

"Well, I accept. Sitting in a theater is still a bit like sitting on a train to me. You feel you're going somewhere."

"I just want to hold hands with you in the dark," he says, helping me on with my coat.

We emerge onto State Parkway, the night wind in the trees and a few flurries of snow drifting quietly down.

"May I?" he asks, and I accept his arm in mine.

In the cold, speech has the delicate white bloom of a dialogue balloon.

We walk up the street in companionable silence, like a pair of lovers at the end of a picture.

I try to envision the title card that would flash before these two aging people fade from the screen, but nothing seems to fit. *And they all died happily ever after? But not for a while?* Granny always knew how to wrap up a story. I'm terrible at endings.

But I do know how to begin.

AUTHOR'S NOTE AND SOURCES

The story of Doreen O'Dare is inspired by the life and work of the actor, collector, investor, and philanthropist Colleen Moore. She made approximately sixty-four films in the span of eighteen years, and in 1927, at the height of her Hollywood earnings and acclaim, the *Los Angeles Times* called her "Peter Pan with a collegiate figure and a Wall Street brain."

An effervescent comedian whose bobbed hair and insouciant physicality came to define her age's idea of modern young womanhood, by 1929 she was riding a three-year streak in which she led the world in box office receipts. Yet by the time I'd first heard of her when I was a little girl, almost nobody in the world had seen her films or remembered her name.

Through a quirk of fate, my family had moved from Louisiana to Illinois in 1988. That summer, my parents took my sisters and me to Chicago's beloved Museum of Science and Industry. There, though it's not especially scientific or industrial, I fell under the spell of Colleen Moore's Fairy Castle: the one-ton dollhouse that she donated in 1949 and that resides in the basement of that palatial monument to human achievement.

Formerly the Palace of Fine Arts at the 1893 World's Columbian Exposition, this setting was, to my elementary-school self, the ideal atmosphere in which to encounter the dollhouse: some of the finest art I'd ever seen. Bedecked with diamonds and pearls, emeralds and alabaster, this astonishing structure had been constructed by an obvious genius. And she'd done it in the service of providing a home for the fairies from the tales I adored for their unvarnished perils and elemental strangeness: Sleeping Beauty, Cinderella, Jack and the Beanstalk, Hansel and Gretel, Prince Charming, the Seven Swans, and on and on.

My family had to tear me away. I could have stayed there all day, listening to the audio tour on repeat and feasting my eyes on the library of bound books, not quite one inch high, written by the likes of F. Scott Fitzgerald and Daphne du Maurier, or the platinum chairs in the Princess's Bedroom with green cloisonné seats.

In a way, I did stay. I never stopped thinking about the woman who the placards explained had one brown eye and one blue, who had grown up Irish Catholic, and who never swayed from her belief that being a movie star was what she was born to achieve. The wall texts and photographs made clear her vivacity, her sense of humor, her ambition, and her work ethic.

The idea of a grown-up—a professional at the peak of her talent and skill—spending seven years and hundreds of thousands of hard-earned dollars building this fantasy edifice, then taking it on the road in 1935 in the heart of the Great Depression to raise the country's spirits along with funds for children's charities, blew my mind with the possibilities of what the right kind of adult could do.

That day, I felt an unbreakable connection to Colleen Moore, one I've felt whenever I've returned to gaze at her masterpiece—often taking other people with me to do so. Thus, it's an honor and a delight now, in some sense, to take innumerable other people with me by way of this novel, not merely to see her castle but also to see her life and achievements anew.

Writing of her role in *Flaming Youth* and other flapper films, Colleen explained that "a flapper is just a little girl trying to grow up—in the process of growing up." I am grateful to her for growing up just enough but never too much to lose touch with the child she was.

To be clear, this is a work of fiction and not a biography. The attitudes and opinions expressed by Doreen O'Dare are imagined. That said, I encourage everyone to read Colleen's books, because her energy and exuberance, her elegance and grace, shine like fairy wings on every page:

Silent Star: Colleen Moore Talks about Her Hollywood. Doubleday & Company, Inc., Garden City, New York, 1968.

How Women Can Make Money in the Stock Market. Doubleday & Company, Inc., Garden City, New York, 1969.

Colleen Moore's Doll House (photographed by Will Rousseau). Doubleday & Company, Inc., Garden City, New York, 1979.

I also recommend watching as many of her films as are currently available. Though many of them are tragically lost, some of the best that remain include *Little Orphant Annie*, 1918; *The Sky Pilot*, 1921; *Irene*, 1926; *Ella Cinders*, 1926; *Orchids and Ermine*, 1927; *Naughty But Nice*, 1927; *Her Wild Oat*, 1927; *Lilac Time*, 1928; and *Why Be Good?*, 1929.

Additionally, I recommend reading as much as you can by Moore's real-life friend, the journalist and gossip extraordinaire Adela Rogers St. Johns—including her autobiography, *The Honeycomb* (Doubleday & Company, Inc., Garden City, New York, 1969)—and watching *What Price Hollywood?*, the 1932 film she wrote based on Colleen Moore's and John McCormick's troubled marriage and work life, which would subsequently be remade over and over (without credit to St. Johns) as *A Star Is Born.*

Film historian Kevin Brownlow's *The Parade's Gone By . . .* (University of California Press, 1968) was indispensable as I worked to capture the long-vanished milieu of Colleen and her colleagues, as was the 1980 British TV series *Hollywood: A Celebration of the American Silent Film*, narrated indelibly by James Mason.

Last but not least, I could not have written this book without Jeff Codori's *Colleen Moore: A Biography of the Silent Film Star* (McFarland & Company, Inc., Jefferson, North Carolina, 2012).

ACKNOWLEDGMENTS

Thanks from Chicago to Hollywood and back again to:

Lisa Bankoff, Abby Beckel, Logan Berry, Kim Brooks, James Charlesworth, Alicia Clancy, Christen Enos, Julia Fine, Elisa Gabbert, Fern Josephs, Alice Hargrave, Virginia Konchan, Caro Macon Fleischer, Dale Panger, Eric Plattner, Robert Puccinelli, Mitchell Rathberger, Rachel Robbins, Beth Rooney, Martin Seay, Deborah Shapiro, Christine Sneed, and Kimberly Southwick.

To my family, especially my mom and dad for taking me to the Museum of Science and Industry in the first place, and Rose and Luka Rooney Super for letting me share my love of Colleen Moore's dollhouse with the two of you.

To all the poets who do Poems While You Wait, all of the authors from Rose Metal Press, my students and colleagues at DePaul University.

To anyone who has ever talked with me about silent movies, miniatures, or fairies—or any of the other innumerable small things that re-enchant the disenchanting world.

And above all to Colleen Moore for your life and work—the magic you performed while you were alive and the magic that continues in the art and legacy that you left behind.

DISCUSSION QUESTIONS FOR
FROM DUST TO STARDUST

1. Without Granny Shaughnessy, Doreen's childhood would have been a sadder and more frustrating one. Did you have a support figure in your life apart from your parents? Who were they, and what did they do to believe in and encourage you? Are you that figure now for someone else?

2. How do Doreen's feelings regarding her parents compare to her feelings regarding her Aunt Lib and Uncle Walter? How do these relationships shape Doreen's ambitions and sense of who she is?

3. What initially attracts Doreen to Granny's fairy tales and to the fairies themselves, and how does this affinity remain significant throughout her life and career, in acting and otherwise?

4. Have you ever been so drawn to a job or vocation that you'd do almost anything to get the chance to pursue it? Describe that pursuit, saying what it is and why—or why not.

5. Why are magic and wonder so important to Doreen? How does a sense of enchantment relate to empathy, community, and even to democracy?

6. How do Doreen's achievements and struggles in Hollywood—with male directors, with coworkers, with

getting paid on time, with being allowed to do projects that stretch her talents—relate to the workplace as we know it today?

7. Why is Doreen so dedicated to her husband Jack Flanagan, even after it becomes clear that he's not the ideal spouse, or even the ideal producer?

8. How do the friendships in Doreen's Hollywood circle help her endure and succeed? What do Mary Pickford, Marion Davies, and Lillian Gish do to buoy one another in a challenging field? And how do these friendships contrast with Doreen's rivalry with Clara Bow?

9. Doreen's friendship with the reporter and gossip columnist Adela Rogers St. Johns seems unlikely at first but quickly becomes vital. What's the dynamic between movie stars and the press, and how do Doreen and Adela illustrate this symbiosis?

10. From the moment her uncle gives her her stage name, Doreen's Irish American heritage becomes a fundamental part of her brand. How does this aspect of her identity get celebrated and exploited as her career unfolds, and what does it illustrate about representation and stereotypes?

11. Doreen throws herself into the construction of her Fairy Castle at a time when both her marriage to Jack and her career as an actor seem highly uncertain. Do you have hobbies or activities that you immerse yourself in when you need relief or distraction? How do they help you?

12. Doreen realizes that her life, though satisfying and full of achievement, is missing a component of service to other people and connection to the wider world, which leads her to take her castle on tour to raise funds for charity. Do you have a volunteer activity or philanthropic cause that you feel similarly dedicated to, and how does helping other people end up helping you?

ABOUT THE AUTHOR

Photo © 2022 Beth Rooney

Kathleen Rooney is a founding editor of Rose Metal Press, a nonprofit publisher of literary work in hybrid genres, as well as a founding member of Poems While You Wait, a collective of poets and their vintage typewriters who compose poetry on demand. Her most recent books include the novels *Lillian Boxfish Takes a Walk* and *Cher Ami and Major Whittlesey*. Her poetry collection *Where Are the Snows* won the 2021 X. J. Kennedy Prize and was published by Texas Review Press in fall of 2022. She is a winner of the Ruth Lilly Prize from *Poetry* magazine and the Adam Morgan Literary Citizen Award from the *Chicago Review of Books*, and her criticism appears in the *New York Times, the Minneapolis Star Tribune*, the *Brooklyn Rail, Chicago* magazine, the *Los Angeles Review of Books*, and elsewhere. She lives in Chicago with her spouse, the writer Martin Seay, and teaches English and creative writing at DePaul University.